YOU CAN TEACH AN OLD
DRAGON NEW TRICKS.

Praise for the Novels
of Katie MacAlister

Love in the Time of Dragons
The First Novel of the Light Dragons

"Ms. MacAlister has once again taken a crazy plot and fascinating characters and tossed them with a lot of fun and a dash of mystery to create a darned good reading adventure. Who would have thought dragons could be so sexy?! Katie MacAlister, that's who. Hail to the powers of the creative author." —Fresh Fiction

"An extraordinary paranormal romance. Ms. MacAlister has created a wonderful world of dragons, demons, and other assorted characters. . . . The dragon men are hot and their mates know just how to stand up to these aggressive alpha males. *Love in the Time of Dragons* is a funny, romantic, and sexy novel. Once I started to read it, I couldn't put it down. Katie MacAlister has another winner on her hands!" —The Romance Readers Connection

"Katie MacAlister's books are funny to the core and this book doesn't disappoint in that regard. The world she's created is rich and interesting, and her plots never fail to suck the reader in . . . clever." —Examiner.com

"If I had to describe one consistent emotion I had throughout this entire book, it would be amusement. MacAlister has long held sway over my paranormal romance leanings because of her humorous they-don't-take-themselves-seriously novels." —Romance Reader at Heart

"An amusing, lighthearted frolic held together by a female who has no memory of ever being a dragon in her past lives. Tully the terrific makes the tale fresh and exciting." —*Midwest Book Review*

"An intense, twisted love story." —*The Romance Reader*

"There are plot twists and turns that kept me riveted . . . awesome story and a definite recommend from me." —The Long and the Short of It

continued . . .

Steamed
A Steampunk Romance

"MacAlister hits it out of the park with this highly entertaining steampunk fantasy. There's danger, adventure, romance, and lots of humorous moments as Jack and Octavia discover that the laws of love always trump the laws of physics."
—*Booklist* (starred review)

"*Steamed* is the first book of the Steampunk series and introduces readers to an interesting alternate reality.... A unique story, *Steamed* is both funny and captivating."
—Romance Reviews Today

"*Steamed* is at first blush an adventure, with the requisite hot, sweaty sex scenes. But MacAlister hasn't skimped on the plot, characters, or world building.... *Steamed* is a fun book set in a world that has just begun to be explored and I wouldn't mind seeing what happens next."
—SFRevu

"An entertaining, wacky steampunk romantic fantasy filled with humor ... fast-paced."
—*Midwest Book Review*

"If you like alternative reality stories, an imaginative mixture of Victorian-like society with everything steam powered, and the juxtaposition of a modern man from our world trying to fit in and win the woman, then you will like this book!"
—The Romance Studio

"Katie MacAlister ... is charting new territory with her foray into a new perspective on steampunk."
—Fresh Fiction

"MacAlister's past record for writing awesome romance will make her fans want to indulge in her latest book, *Steamed*."
—MyShelf.com

Me and My Shadow
A Novel of the Silver Dragons

"Just like always, MacAlister delivers the fun, even in the drama. The characters are engaging, quick, and inhabit a universe that only a genius can imagine."
—Romance Reader at Heart

"A fabulous urban fantasy.... Fans will enjoy visiting the chaotic, charming world of Ms. MacAlister, where the unbelievable becomes believable." —*Midwest Book Review*

"This clever, hilarious, adventurous, and, at times, surprisingly poignant addition to the Silver Dragon series is sure to please MacAlister's many fans." —*Booklist*

Crouching Vampire, Hidden Fang
A Dark Ones Novel

"Ms. MacAlister entertains readers with a captivating romance, supernatural politics, and her always present touch of humor." —Darque Reviews

"The story line is fast-paced, filled with humor and action as Katie MacAlister balances the two nicely." —*Midwest Book Review*

"Witty, with a splash of romance and a dark puzzle to unravel, *Crouching Vampire, Hidden Fang* is a surefire hit!" —Romance Junkies

Holy Smokes
An Aisling Grey, Guardian, Novel

"[A] comedic, hot paranormal caper." —*Booklist*

"A wonderfully amusing relationship drama...a laugh-out-loud tale." —*Midwest Book Review*

"Hysterical....MacAlister hits the humor button dead-on.... This cast of wacky—if somewhat dangerous—characters makes for giggles galore, while also producing some hair-raising adventures. MacAlister has written a cure for the common blues!" —*Romantic Times*

Katie MacAlister

The Unbearable Lightness of Dragons

A Novel of the Light Dragons

A SIGNET BOOK

SIGNET
Published by New American Library, a division of
Penguin Group (USA) Inc., 375 Hudson Street,
New York, New York 10014, USA
Penguin Group (Canada), 90 Eglinton Avenue East, Suite 700, Toronto,
Ontario M4P 2Y3, Canada (a division of Pearson Penguin Canada Inc.)
Penguin Books Ltd., 80 Strand, London WC2R 0RL, England
Penguin Ireland, 25 St. Stephen's Green, Dublin 2,
Ireland (a division of Penguin Books Ltd.)
Penguin Group (Australia), 250 Camberwell Road, Camberwell, Victoria 3124,
Australia (a division of Pearson Australia Group Pty. Ltd.)
Penguin Books India Pvt. Ltd., 11 Community Centre, Panchsheel Park,
New Delhi - 110 017, India
Penguin Group (NZ), 67 Apollo Drive, Rosedale, North Shore 0632,
New Zealand (a division of Pearson New Zealand Ltd.)
Penguin Books (South Africa) (Pty.) Ltd., 24 Sturdee Avenue,
Rosebank, Johannesburg 2196, South Africa

Penguin Books Ltd., Registered Offices:
80 Strand, London WC2R 0RL, England

First published by Signet, an imprint of New American Library,
a division of Penguin Group (USA) Inc.

First Printing, May 2011
10 9 8 7 6 5 4 3 2 1

I have always loved the ladies who hang out with me on my message forum, but this book is dedicated to one member who went above and beyond the call of duty to make me giggle, squeal, and send her many text messages demanding to know if she was there yet— Vinette DiCarlo-Pérez. Thanks for everything, Vin! You're the best.

Chapter One

"Lady."

Blinking at the sudden sound of a male voice, I turned to see who was speaking, at the same time taking in the noxious smells that wafted around me. I appeared to be in some sort of a dark, rough alleyway that lay between two rows of tall, narrow houses, the overhangs of which blocked out any streams of sunlight that might try to make it down to the ground. Not that there was any sun to be seen now, since it was nighttime, but I was willing to bet that even on the hottest day of the year, the alley would remain dank and unwelcoming.

A crude wooden door next to me bore an almost illegible plaque informing unwary visitors that one Master Bertram would mix pigments for a small fee.

"Painter's shop," I murmured to myself, my nose wrinkling at the smell. I was used to the scent of items commonly used to make paint—plants, ore, and such—but the odors that assailed me had their origins with hu-

mans and animals. I eyed an open barrel next to me that
made my eyes burn. Urine, no doubt, collected for the
purposes of making paint. "Just my luck—I haven't had
a vision for a month, and when I get one, it has a great
big barrel of pee in it."

"Dragon."

The woman's voice called my attention back from
where I was trying to avoid stepping in any of the refuse
that clogged the close alley. Skirting the urine barrel, I
took a few steps toward the dark figures that stood almost invisible in the deep shadows cast by the buildings,
faint light from a couple of sputtering torches the only
means of illumination.

The distant sound of voices raised in song reached
my ears as in front of me two figures approached each
other.

"Why have you summoned me to Rothenburg?" the
man demanded to know in an arrogant, somehow familiar voice.

I took a couple of steps closer until I could see the
face of the speaker, dimly lit by a torch that leaned
drunkenly from a nearby iron sconce.

The woman's form moved, blocking my view for a
moment before she shifted to the side. "You ignored the
warnings. You were told what would happen if you continued. Now you must pay."

I moved to the left, my eyes widening as I watched
Constantine Norka, once a black dragon and heir to the
wyvern of that sept, laugh first at the woman, then at the
two men who emerged from the darkness behind him.
"Do you think to frighten me? I am afraid of no dragon
alive, and certainly not of you and your friends."

The woman's jaw tightened. The two guys behind

Constantine closed in, although they kept a respectable distance from him.

"It will be our pleasure to teach you how wrong you've been," she said with a wholly unpleasant smile. "You thought I did not mean what I said? Then you are foolish as well as wrong."

Constantine laughed again, shaking his head as if in dismay when the woman's hands started moving in an intricate pattern that I knew would cast a harmful spell. "You are here to chastise me, I suppose? I'm not the one who is foolish, then. You have not heard that your precious Baltic is no longer in the sept of the black dragons?"

What the hell? Was Constantine insane, or was I? Sometimes it was hard to know the truth, since my memory of the last five hundred years had been more or less wiped out. But some of that had returned since I'd found Baltic two months past, and I didn't remember a thing about this little bombshell.

The woman checked, a frown between her brows as she said quickly, "What nonsense is this?"

"It is the truth." Constantine leaned casually against a battered wooden door. "He was declared ouroboros at the command of the First Dragon for crimes committed against dragonkin. So not even you, who have Baltic in your pocket, can change the fact that I will be named wyvern."

The woman looked stunned for a few seconds, blinking rapidly as she digested this information. I knew exactly how she felt—if what Constantine said was true, when had it happened? And why on earth hadn't Baltic or someone told me about it?

"I do not believe you," she said in a somewhat faltering voice. "Baltic would not . . . What crime did he commit?"

Constantine shrugged. "It is of no matter to me whether you believe me. I do not discuss sept business with those outside the weyr, so if you wish to know more, you will need to ask your pet himself." A little sneer crept over his face. "I've long said Baltic was a weakling; that he hides behind a woman's skirts proves the fact that he is the basest of cowards, as well. How much did he pay you to threaten me?"

Her hands fisted. "He did not send me, if that is what you mean. I came of my own accord, as a friend to Baltic, because I know well that you have done your best to usurp his rightful position."

Constantine snorted. "*I* am the heir to the wyvern of the black dragons, mage, not Baltic. He did his best to undermine that fact with Alexei, but it is I who am victorious, while he is no longer even recognized as a dragon."

Alexei? That name rang a bell in the dim recesses of my memory. He was the wyvern before Baltic. Which meant that the time this vision was presenting must also be before Baltic was wyvern—but that couldn't be.

The woman swore under her breath. "This is some trickery of yours, I am bound to believe. You said the dragon ancestor was involved. How did you manage that?"

Her words came out with the velocity of bullets. I stepped back, not wanting to get within range of eye contact with her.

"I am well-known to the First Dragon," Constantine bragged with an easy smile. The two men behind him, evidently hearing the confidence in his voice, moved back as well. "But you are mistaken in thinking I had anything to do with Baltic's fall from grace. He managed that himself."

The woman took a deep breath, her hands still fisted. "I will investigate your claims, dragon. If they prove as false as you are, then your suffering at my hands will treble."

Something wasn't right. How could I be having a vision of this time? I shook my head at the thought. I couldn't. It just wasn't possible.

"Yet more threats. How I will live in fear," Constantine answered with obvious amusement.

"This doesn't make any sense," I said as I moved forward until I was next to him. "I wasn't even born until Baltic had been wyvern for almost a hundred years. Constantine, what is happening?"

The woman smiled again, and it was just as unpleasant as the previous time. "I look forward to proving to you that I am not to be taken lightly."

"Hello? Can anyone hear me?" I waved my hand in front of the woman's face, but obviously neither she nor Constantine registered my presence, which made sense, seeing as I hadn't been alive at this time. But why was I seeing this moment in the past? And who on earth was this woman that she felt comfortable speaking in such a threatening manner to a powerful dragon?

"This conversation is putting me to sleep. If you are done with your empty threats, I will leave you to practice your vainglorious speeches."

A little corona of blue-white light crackled around her at Constantine's words. I frowned at it, trying to remember where I'd seen something similar, shaking my head when my brain refused to cooperate.

"The day will come when you will regret those words," she warned.

"I regret only the amount of time I've wasted on you. You lured me into your grasp by telling me you could aid me, when all along it was Baltic you championed. I knew that, of course, for despite your opinion, I am no fool. But it amused me nonetheless to watch you cavort in your attempts to promote his cause while hindering mine. Your antics are no longer entertaining, however. Quite simply, Lady Antonia, you bore me."

The woman reached right through me to slap Constantine. Both of us jumped. I stared at her in stark surprise, examining her face. Lady Antonia. She had to be Antonia von Endres, the famous archimage, and once Baltic's lover.

I narrowed my eyes at her, wondering if that was why I had been given the vision—to engage my jealousy? En*rage* was more like it. . . .

"All right, I'm willing to admit that I'm lost," I told the pair. "The only other visions I've had have been memories of my past that the dragon inside me used to try to get me to remember who I am. I've never once seen one where I wasn't there in person. But assuming this is a really pathetic attempt to incite jealousy, I have to tell you guys that it's failed. I'm not jealous of Baltic's relationships before he met me. Not in the least. They don't matter at all. Not even the fact that you would give him your infamous light sword just because he was so incredible between the sheets matters to me." A little belch of fire erupted around Antonia's feet. I pretended I didn't see it.

Without another word, Antonia—not seeing the fire any more than she had seen me—executed a one-eighty turn and marched off into the darkness, her two bully boys following with only brief smoldering glances at Constantine as they passed him.

I watched until they all disappeared into the shadows, then turned my gaze to Constantine. "You're not going to take that, are you?"

He ignored me, just as I assumed he would, instead rubbing his face as he muttered something rude under his breath before turning to walk away in the opposite direction.

"I guess you are going to take that. Well." I looked around the unkempt area, stared for a minute at the nearest shuttered windows of the tall, narrow houses, and made a frustrated gesture. A dog barked in the distance. A rat sat on the edge of the urine barrel and considered me. A duck wandered past, quacking softly to itself. "Now what the hell am I supposed to do?" I asked no one in particular.

My voice echoed against the building, growing louder and louder until it seemed to fill my head with pounding, nonstop noise.

"Stop!" I yelled, my hands over my ears as I doubled up in pain.

"OK, but I thought you'd like them."

My eyes shot open at the matter-of-fact voice. I looked into the eyes of a nine-year-old boy, one who held a portable music device in one hand, a black cord trailing from it to my head. "Brom?"

"You don't like Rampaging Wildebeests?" He looked at the music player, then at me, his serious brown eyes considering me with a perception that belied his nine years. "OK, but you were dancing around like crazy to 'Take Me by the Horns' the other day. I thought you'd like their new CD."

With a shaky hand I pulled off the headphones my son had put on me while I was off in vision-land. "They're very nice. Loud, but nice. Are you done settling in? And ... er ... how long have you been standing there?"

Brom sat down beside me on the warm stone bench that clung to the side of the house. "Yeah, I've unpacked, although I hope this is the last time we move. And a couple of minutes. You had a funny look on your face. Were you thinking about something a long time ago?"

I hadn't told Brom much about the visions I'd had a couple of months before. They ceased after that fateful day when we had been ostracized from the weyr by the rest of the dragons, and I assumed the part of me that had once been a dragon in centuries past had given up trying to get me to acknowledge it. "Something like that. I told your stepfather that three houses in two months was enough, so hopefully he'll stop insisting we move every few weeks."

"Jim says Baltic isn't my stepfather, not unless you marry him, and you're still married to Gareth, except maybe he's married to Ruth. Jim says that's illegal, and that Baltic is going to string him up by his balls if he ever finds him again. Jim says you might do the same."

I eyed my child. "Trust that demon to become your go-to source of information. Honey, when I said you could talk to Jim despite the fact that we are at war with the other dragons, I didn't expect you to discuss our personal issues."

Brom squinted at me. "Is it true?"

"That Baltic is going to string up your father by his testicles? No, of course not."

"No, is it true that Baltic isn't my stepdad until you guys get married?"

I slumped back against the rough stone of the old farmhouse that Baltic had taken as our latest refuge against possible attacks by other dragons. Explaining the intricacies of my relationship with Baltic hadn't been high on the list of things I wanted to do. "No, it's not true. You know that I was born many hundreds of years ago, right?"

"Yeah. You're a dragon."

"I was born a dragon. I'm not one now. Now I'm just a wyvern's mate with a dragon inside. . . . well, that's kind of complicated. Let's stick to the easy stuff. I was born several hundred years ago, and met Baltic, who was the wyvern of his sept."

"The black dragons. The one that Kostya runs now," Brom said, nodding.

"Exactly." I wondered briefly how Baltic had ended up back in the sept, and with enough standing to take control when the previous wyvern left, but figured that was something speculation wasn't going to answer.

"And Kostya used to be his homey, but now they beat each other up. And Kostya keeps breaking Baltic's nose."

"Just twice," I said, irritation rising at the memory of events a week past, when we had run into the black wyvern in London. "And only because Baltic was behaving properly and Kostya was being a rat fink. But that's neither here nor there. When I met Baltic all those hundreds of years ago, I became his . . . er . . . wife. Then some things happened, and Kostya killed Baltic, and I lost my memory, and then about fifteen years ago, I married your father. Or I thought I did—I didn't realize that Baltic had been resurrected, which meant I wasn't really married to Gareth. So because I married Baltic first, I don't need to marry him again in order for him to be your stepdad."

Brom looked somewhat skeptical, but he didn't dispute my somewhat convoluted explanation of the complex relationship I had with Baltic. "Jim was wrong, then?"

"Yes. Even demons as old as Jim can be wrong. You don't have anything to worry about—Baltic is your father in all ways but actually having a blood relationship. You know he loves you, don't you?"

"Well . . . he claimed me as his son. That's the same thing, isn't it?"

I sighed and gave Brom a swift hug and kiss on the top of his head. "For Baltic, that's the very same thing. Remember what I told you about some men?"

"They have problems expressing their emotions, and you have to read between the lines," Brom parroted from a previous discussion.

"Exactly. Baltic isn't the sort of person who marches about telling everyone he loves them. Kind of like someone else I know," I said with a little nudge of my elbow into his side. Brom had lately developed a horror of demonstrating affection whenever anyone else was around, feeling it was beneath his dignity. "His actions speak louder than his words, remember. And if he didn't love you, he wouldn't have gone out of his way to find houses that had space for you to set up your horrible mummy lab, now would he?"

He rolled his eyes. "Maybe. He does hug me."

"There you go. You know, sometimes people need to know that you love them, too, and Baltic hasn't really had anyone to love him for a very long time, so he needs all the affection we can show him."

"Is that why he's always making you kiss him?"

"He's not exactly making me kiss him," I said with a little laugh. "I like doing it. But yes, because he spent so much time alone, he gets a little bit insecure, so I go out of my way to let him know I love him."

"By kissing him." The look on his face was priceless.

"Yes, but you don't have to kiss him if you don't want to. A hug does just as well."

A little frown pulled his brows together. "Gareth says guys who do that are gay."

"Gareth is a twerp, and you shouldn't listen to him." I looked up, noting the love of my two lives heading toward us, a familiar scowl on his handsome face. "Just remember that both Baltic and I love you, and nothing else is as important as that. Are you packed for your visit?"

"Naw." He pursed his lips and watched as Baltic marched toward us. "Maybe I'll go do that now."

"If you want to visit May and Gabriel, yes, you should. Hello, handsome." The last sentence was addressed to the dark-eyed, dark-haired man who stopped in front of me, his hands on his hips as he frowned down the long length of his torso to where I sat.

"Mate." He shifted his glare to Brom. "Are you still intent on spurning your fine home and returning to the silver wyvern's house?"

I bit back a little snort of laughter. When the dragons had exiled us from the weyr and declared war, I had worried for Brom's safety, but was assured by all that while the dragons took their wars very seriously, they did not extend warlike acts to children. That Gabriel allowed May to invite Brom for a weekend stay at their house in London—so he could visit the mummies at the

British Museum—was, I felt sure, a sign that the determination of the weyr to remain at war with Baltic and me was waning.

Baltic interpreted it differently, feeling it was Gabriel's intention to undermine his relationship with Brom. It took three weeks of negotiation between Gabriel and Baltic before he agreed to the event, and then only after making some fairly obnoxious statements to Gabriel about what he would do should Gabriel not take care of Brom in a manner that Baltic felt reasonable.

Brom looked thoughtful for a moment, slid me a quick glance, then leaned forward and hugged Baltic. The latter looked so surprised that I did laugh, although I covered it up with a little cough.

"I'll be back Sunday night," Brom told Baltic, releasing him. "I promise I won't like Gabriel more than you."

Baltic blinked at him for a moment or two, then clapped his hand on Brom's shoulder and said, "You are my son. Of course you will not honor anyone more than your mother or me. It will be good for Gabriel to see that, however, so you are right to wish to demonstrate such. Pavel will be ready to drive us there shortly. Do you need money?"

Brom wasn't at all a mercenary sort of child, but he did have eclectic—and very expensive—tastes, and despite the fact that he received a generous allowance, his eyes lit up with hope.

"I've already given him money to see the museum and buy a few mementos." I shooed Brom toward the house. "He doesn't need any more."

"Aw, Sullivan!"

"Your mother has spoken," Baltic told him, then pulled out a money clip.

"Baltic!" I protested when Brom quite happily took the bills he offered. I took the money from Brom and gave it back to Baltic. "He'll just spend that on things he doesn't need."

Baltic handed it back to Brom. "He is a boy. Boys need spending money."

Brom nodded rapidly.

"And you're trying to raise funds to restore Dauva," I pointed out, retrieving the money and stuffing it into Baltic's pocket. "That's not going to happen if you don't stop slipping him money every time he leaves the house."

Brom's face fell.

"No pouting, buster," I told him. "Go get your things packed."

"My son does not pout," Baltic said with a stern look bent on Brom, interrupting him as he was about to protest. "Ysolde does not wish for me to give you cash. I will not go against her desires. We will both do as she bids."

"Thank you. I know you just want Brom to be happy, but I appreciate your upholding my authority despite that."

"You are my mate and his mother. I could not do anything else," Baltic answered, watching as Brom, with dragging steps, slowly made his way to the house before yelling after him, "Tell Pavel to give you one of my credit cards."

Brom cheered and raced off.

I put my hands on my hips and glared.

"You did not wish for me to give him cash. A credit card is not cash," he pointed out, blithely ignoring the obvious.

"You are incorrigible. You're just lucky that you're so

incredibly handsome, I'm willing to overlook that fact now and again."

"I know what it's like to not have money," Baltic said with a half shrug.

That stopped me in my tracks. "You do? I thought all dragons were rich as sin. When were you poor?"

"When I was resurrected. There was only a handful of black dragons, most of whom were in hiding, so none of them could help me. Then I located Pavel, but he had taken to robbery to survive." Baltic made a face. "He wasn't very good at it. He was in a mortal prison when I found him."

I wrapped my arms around his waist and kissed the corner of his mouth. "I had no idea. So you and he got together and started raising money?"

"Yes. Our first concern was our safety, then Dauva. Now that has changed."

"Changed how? You still want Dauva back."

"Yes, but now my first concern is you and Brom. Dauva will wait until I know you are safe and content."

I looked up at him, this man who for centuries was reviled by other dragons as a murderous madman, my heart full to overflowing with admiration and love. "Without a doubt, that is the loveliest thing anyone has ever said to me. Kiss me."

"Gladly, but I will point out first that you said the very same thing last week when I told you that the sight of you makes my stones tighten."

"Putting aside your own desires so that Brom and I will be happy definitely trumps your testicles," I answered, licking his lower lip. "Fire?"

"You have your own fire," he murmured, interest lighting the dark depths of his black eyes as I wiggled against him, reveling in the way my body fit against all of his hard planes. "You should give me your fire, mate."

"All right, but it's your turn next time." I bit his lip gently, my fingers working free the leather thong that held back his shoulder-length brown hair, concentrating as I did so on rousing the dragon that lived deep within my psyche. I had yet to master the skill that came so naturally to all dragons—harnessing their fire—but Baltic insisted that I practice it every day in hopes that one day I would return to being the dragon I once was.

I focused on the moment, allowing the scent of him to sink into me. The feel of his body moving restlessly against mine did much to stir the embers, but it wasn't until he took charge of the kiss, possessing my mouth in a way that left my toenails steaming, that I felt able to pull on my dragon fire.

Baltic gently bit my neck, knowing how much I loved that, and, sure enough, the dragon fire rose within me until it erupted from me in a belch of flame, splatting against Baltic's chest, then dissipating immediately.

I eyed his chest with a critical gaze. He stopped nuzzling my neck and sighed. "You have not been practicing as you ought."

"I haven't had time, what with moving every couple of weeks. Speaking of which, I hope you don't find anything wrong with the security of this house, because I don't plan on moving again for a long time."

"You are changing the subject," he said, his sleek ebony eyebrows pulling together. "You swore to me that you would practice taming your fire. You have not done so."

"I've been busy, as I just said." I pinched his arm, just to let him know I didn't appreciate either the frown or the arrogant, bossy tone of his voice. "Besides, we have your fire. That's enough for me."

"The fact remains that you promised me you would do something, but have not."

I glanced up at him, suddenly curious about an unfamiliar note in his voice. "Why are you making such a big deal about this?"

His face was hard and closed, but there was a devilish light of enjoyment in his eyes that he couldn't disguise, much though he tried. "You must be punished, mate."

"Punished! Are you out of your ever-livin' . . . wa-a-a-ait a minute. What sort of punished? Punished as in you're going to go all Drake on me and tell me what to do all the time, which will only serve to piss me off, or punished as in something naughty we used to do three hundred years ago, but which I've forgotten?"

One corner of his mouth twitched, his eyes downright wicked now. "Perhaps a little of both."

I squirmed against him, the unspoken intent in his eyes making me shiver with anticipation. "Well . . . Brom *is* going to be gone for three days. I suppose I could put up with a little dominance in order to explore our past relationship. Who knows? It might help me find the dragon inside me. Hmm?"

"There's going to be a dragon inside you—that I promise," he answered, flames licking up my body as he leaned forward, about to kiss me again.

A voice interrupted us. "Phone for you, Ysolde."

I sighed into Baltic's mouth and turned to accept the phone that Pavel, Baltic's guard and oldest friend, held out to me. His face was unreadable, but amusement danced in his dark eyes. "I wouldn't have interrupted you, but it is the silver shaman. She says it is important."

"Kaawa?" I asked, taking the phone. "I wonder what she wants. Hello, Kaawa? How are you? Is everything all right?"

"Mate!" Baltic demanded.

"One moment please. Baltic has to vent his spleen, and I've found if I don't let him do it, he gets more unreasonable than usual," I told her before she could answer my questions.

"I am not unreasonable. I am never unreasonable, as can be seen by the fact that I am allowing my son to leave my protection. Must I remind you that you agreed, when you begged me to permit Brom's visit, that you would have no other interaction with the silver sept?" Baltic asked, frowning fiercely.

"Yes, but this is just Kaawa. She's not really a dragon."

"She is the mother to the silver wyvern. What I do not understand is why you would be happy to have Brom visit Gabriel, when it was he, along with the other wyverns, who accused me of killing blue dragons and named you ouroboros."

A little pang spiked into my heart. Even though I didn't remember anything about my past as a dragon other than what the visions had shown me, the moment when both Gabriel and Kostya formally severed my ties with their respective septs was painfully strong in my memory.

"I'm going to talk to her, Baltic. She's a nice woman, she's learned in dragon lore, and she wants to help me resolve the issue with my inner dragon. And before you say it, I know you're learned in dragon lore, too, but you haven't been able to help me deal with this whole 'I used to be a dragon' thing, and Kaawa has. Kind of. Oh, and speaking of that, I have something I want to ask you about the past, but that can wait until I'm done with this call."

He looked for a minute like he was going to argue the point, but a quick glance at my forehead had him muttering under his breath instead as he turned and stomped off, Pavel following in his wake.

"I'm so sorry about that, Kaawa. You know how Baltic is."

She chuckled in my ear, her voice, thick with an Australian accent, warming me even though we were continents apart. "Not really, but from what Gabriel has told me, you have your hands full. How are you, child?"

"We're fine. Brom is about to visit Gabriel and May for the weekend, as a matter of fact. It's very kind of them to invite him for a stay, considering the war and all."

"Pfft. That is more of a formality than anything, don't you think?"

"Well, that's what Aisling and May say, but Baltic takes it very seriously. He's busy with plans to free his friend Thala from wherever it is Drake has her stashed. I probably shouldn't have told you that, but I figured not only would you *not* carry tales to Gabriel, but the wyverns probably already know that Baltic wants Thala back."

She was silent for a moment. "I would not carry tales, no, but I will tell Gabriel anything that I feel endangers him or his wintiki."

"I would expect that. I can assure you that despite the animosities all around, I wouldn't condone a plan to harm any dragon, let alone people I like."

The smile came back into her voice. "You did not tell me how you were feeling."

I thought about the strange vision. "I'm fine as well."

"One of my dreamings spoke of you. You have a great confusion inside you, child, and it is growing if it can reach to my dreaming."

"It's growing?" A little shiver skittered down my back. "I don't know what to say to that other than it makes me feel more than a little freaked out. What confusion? The dragon, you mean?"

"That is part of it, yes." Her voice, normally so warm and soothing, went a little rough. "I do not know. . . . I am not sure, but I believe that something has changed. What would that be?"

If anyone else had been so nosy, I would have had a thing or two to say to them, but Kaawa had tried for the last few months to help me discover why the dragon I used to be was buried so deep inside me that it manifested itself only with visions of my past.

"As a matter of fact, something did happen a short while ago. I had another vision."

"That is significant, but not such that it should affect my dreaming," she said slowly.

"This wasn't a vision of things that happened in the past, Kaawa. Or rather, it probably was, but it didn't concern me. It happened before I was even born."

"Tell me," she urged, and I sat back down on the stone bench made warm by the sun and leaned against the side of the house, the drone of bees as they bustled about a nearby hydrangea bush providing a lazy, sonorous background as I described what I had witnessed.

"I don't know why my inner dragon would want me to see that—what does it care about Constantine before he had anything to do with me?—but I assume the significance must have something to do with the First Dragon having Baltic kicked out of the sept. Or do you think it was Antonia? She used to be his girlfriend, you know. Or maybe it was Constantine himself? It's so confusing! It's enough to drive me insane."

"You're not insane," she said slowly, obviously thinking it over. "But I do not think it was the dragon within you who gave you that vision, child. The events that happened were beyond its scope."

"No? What did, then?"

"You are marked by the First Dragon. He is the only one who could have the ability to allow you to see things beyond your knowledge, and I can well believe that such an act would disturb my dreaming."

I rubbed the spot on my forehead where the First Dragon, the father of all dragonkin who ever were, or ever would be, had touched me. It had left a mark that was identical to the sept emblem that Baltic and I bore, that of an etched sun, but over the last few months, the mark on my forehead had faded until it disappeared entirely. "I'm sorry to be so ignorant about this, but I thought your dreaming was a representation of your faith, tied in to the land and animals. How could the First Dragon have an impact on that?"

"I have two dreamings—the wintiki, or night bird, and light. It is the latter that was disturbed. I have long suspected that the First Dragon's songline was located in Australia, although I have yet to prove it."

"A songline is . . . ?"

She laughed. "I did not call to give you a lecture in Aboriginal history, Ysolde. It would take much time to explain it all, but for now I will simply say that a songline is the dreaming and trail created by spirit beings such as the First Dragon."

"All right. So because he left behind some sort of an ancient trail, that's affected your dreaming?"

"Yes. Only his touch upon you would result in such a thing. Tell me again what vision he gave you."

I described once more the scene between Constantine and the female mage.

"I have heard nothing about the event Constantine described," she said thoughtfully. "There is no record of Baltic being expelled from his sept. And it is unheard of for the First Dragon to interfere with the weyr. I wonder if Constantine . . ." Her voice trailed off.

"Could he be lying?" I asked, and thought about that for a minute. "I don't know. I don't think so. I'm just going to have to ask Baltic about it."

She laughed. "It is always a challenge to get information from a dragon, and doubly so when it concerns something they do not wish to discuss."

"And well I know it. But this is too big for him to hide—at least I think it is. I certainly feel like being declared ouroboros is a life-altering event. If it's true, what could he have done to piss off the First Dragon to that extent?"

"That I do not know, and I suspect you will find it difficult to get Baltic to tell you. But I admit I would give much to know the answer."

"Let's look at the facts: the First Dragon resurrects me when Constantine kills me."

"Yes," Kaawa said.

"Then he tells me, five hundred years later, mind you, which is a bit annoying, that I am supposed to do something for him."

"And you somehow let him down before—didn't he

say that?" Laughter was in her voice, taking the sting from the comment.

"Yes." I sighed. "There's just nothing like knowing you've let down the one dragon ancestor you've failed in the past, and he's told you to do something for him without telling you what it is, and oh, yes, don't blow it. Again. You know, it's a wonder I'm still sane, having that hanging over me."

"I don't think it's a bad thing, Ysolde," Kaawa said slowly, her voice now meditative. "You have warranted his trust for some task. That is an honor, no matter how you look at it."

"With the bottom line that if the First Dragon sent the vision about Constantine to me, then it must be related to whatever it is I'm supposed to do."

"Perhaps. Perhaps not. It is definitely odd."

"I agree, but what am I supposed to do about it other than try to worm the information out of Baltic?"

"I am afraid I do not know, but I suspect you will find that answer for yourself."

"I wish I knew how I was supposed to do that," I said, weary of constantly being in the dark concerning whatever task the First Dragon expected me to perform.

"If I could answer that, I would be able to tell you what it is the First Dragon desires of you," she said with a little laugh. "Talk to your mate. Encourage him to tell you about his past. The answer may well lie there."

"It might," I said, a sudden insight coming to me. "But you know, Kaawa, if it was something Baltic did that is connected with my task, then it seems to me that the First Dragon would have given me a vision of that event, not of a discussion by two unrelated people casually mentioning it. No, I think this is a very big—if obscure—

hint about something the First Dragon wants me to do about Constantine. He was the focus of the vision. But what is it I'm supposed to do? He's dead, after all. He *is* dead, isn't he?"

"I believe so, yes. I have not heard otherwise."

"No, but you didn't know Baltic was alive for almost forty years, either."

"Gabriel knew something was amiss in the weyr. He could feel a disturbance," she pointed out.

"True." I vaguely remembered May telling me something about that, although Gabriel had been hard put to believe that it really was Baltic who had returned to the land of the living.

"It could be something to do with the female," Kaawa pointed out before continuing. "I must hang up now, child, but I am relieved to know that it was the First Dragon who touched you, and thus my dreaming, and not a malevolent force. Be well."

I thanked her for troubling herself, still trying to figure out something about the vision that would clue me in to what the First Dragon wanted me to do. "It may be an obscure hint, but it's surely better than no hint at all," I said to myself before glancing at my watch. I headed for Brom's room at a fast trot, since Baltic hated to be late for appointments. "Another vision or two, and I bet it'll all be clear to me."

My words echoed hollowly off the empty hall as I took the stairs two at a time, leaving me with a sense of ill-fated foreboding.

Chapter Two

"Ysolde. Brom." Five seconds passed. *"Baltic."*

"Hi, Gabriel." I smiled at the small group of people standing outside a house in an elite section of London. "May, is that a leather catsuit? I've always wanted to wear one, but I just don't have the figure for it. It looks fabulous on you. Hi, Maata. I hope you're not going to regret offering to take Brom to the British Museum again. I thought he wore you out the last time he dragged you through it. Good afternoon, Tipene, it's nice to see you again. Oh, Gabriel, I spoke with your mother a little bit ago—it seems one of my visions disturbed her dreaming and she was checking up on me— she sends her love to both of you. She is so sweet. I can't tell you how much I appreciate her concern for me. For us. Is she coming back to visit you soon? I'd love to see her again if she does. Maybe we could get together for a clandestine dinner or something, one that no one in the weyr would have to know about. I have a new recipe for the most divine stuffed mushrooms that I'm dying to try out."

Beside me, Baltic heaved a silent sigh. "Mate—" he started to say in protest.

"It's called polite chat, Baltic. May and I are going to do it, so you can just stop seething." I smiled again at May and Gabriel, both of whom were now looking amused. Gabriel's elite guards, Maata and Tipene, stood directly behind them. Maata's lips twitched, but she kept her face as stony as Tipene's.

We made quite a group on the sidewalk.

Baltic, Brom, and I stood with Pavel, all facing the silver dragons. Although May had invited us inside the house, Baltic and Gabriel insisted that the terms of the arrangement called for the handing over of Brom to be conducted outside the confines of their home.

"You had another vision?" May asked, her eyebrows raised.

"Yes, a very interesting one." I slid a glance toward Baltic, who was staring moodily at Gabriel. There hadn't been enough time for me to broach the subject of the vision with him, but I fully intended to do so at an appropriate time. "I think it had something to do with what the First Dragon wants me to accomplish for him."

"Really?" Interest lit up her blue eyes, and much to her wyvern's dismay, she moved out of formation, took me by the arm, and tugged me toward the gate that led to the minute garden at the back of the house. "Tell me about it."

"May!" Gabriel demanded, incredulity rife in his voice.

"Ysolde, this is a breach of protocol," Baltic snapped. "You are violating the terms that the silver wyvern and

I set down. You will come back here immediately and stand by my side, as is your duty."

"Boy, they get cranky if you mess with their plans," I told May.

"I wouldn't go so far as to say that Gabriel gets cranky, but he can be a teeny bit inflexible when it comes to Baltic," she agreed.

"Mayling!" her mate said, clearly aghast.

She grinned and blew him a kiss.

"I'll be back in a couple of minutes. Go get a latte or something," I told Baltic as I followed May around the side of the house.

"I do not want a latte! Mate! Return to my side!"

"Oooh, you know how I love it when you get all domineering and pushy," I told him over my shoulder. "Would you like me to call you Drake now or later?"

May snickered.

The word Baltic said in response wasn't polite, but considering it was in Zilant, the centuries-old language used by dragons before English became the standard means of communication, I let it slide with a little giggle and a wave at Brom, who was in the process of disappearing into Gabriel's house with Maata.

"I figure we have about five minutes before Baltic insults Gabriel to the point where they start duking it out," I told May as I took the seat she pointed me to. "We're going to have to make this fast."

"I'm all ears." She sat opposite me, saying not a word while I recounted the experience I'd had earlier in the day. Neither one of us thought anything about the fact that I would tell her something so intimate as the vision I had—through the dragon shard we had both once borne, there was a connection between us, a tie with the

First Dragon that made it perfectly reasonable that she should hear about the vision he had given me. Her expression never wavered as I described the scene, but I knew she was as taken aback as I had been upon hearing Constantine's statement regarding Baltic.

"So what do you think?" I asked when I had finished.

She was silent a moment. "I think we need Aisling."

"Oh? Why? There was no demon or anything like that where we'd need a Guardian."

"No, but three heads are better than two, and she has a way of getting information out of Drake that just might be useful. If Baltic isn't forthcoming about what Constantine said, I bet Aisling can worm it out of Drake."

"Good point."

She pulled out a cell phone and punched in a number, holding it up to her ear as she spoke. "Plus, she's kind of tied in with all of this. Kostya is Drake's brother, and since Baltic and Kostya were friends—before Kostya killed him, naturally—that gives her a sort of an in, if you will. Hi, Aisling? It's May. Do you have time in the next few days to meet with Ysolde and me? She's had another vision, and I think you're going to want to hear about it. Hang on, let me put you on speaker so Ysolde can hear, too."

She pressed a button and held the phone out between us.

"I'd be happy to see you both, but you are aware that the boys aren't going to like it."

"Quite aware," I told the phone.

"OK. Just wanted to make that point. In fact, Drake has forbidden me to see you, Ysolde. He seemed to think May and I might have something up our sleeves to end this stupid war. Honestly, dragons. So suspicious."

The laughter in her voice had both May and me smiling, since we had intended to get together in the near future for just that purpose. "Let me look at my schedule to see when I can get away without Drake knowing. . . ."

After exactly five minutes to the second, we heard a commotion from the street and hurried around the house to find the two wyverns nose-to-nose, shouting in Zilant.

"Do you understand what they're saying?" May asked me as we watched.

I listened for a minute. "Not a whole lot, but I think Gabriel just told Baltic his mother was an ass. Or possibly a porcupine. And that, I believe, was an invitation for Gabriel to conduct an act that is anatomically impossible."

Baltic stopped in mid-insult to glare at me. Gabriel didn't follow suit, although his dimples were nowhere in evidence when he held out his hand for May.

"You are finished?" Baltic asked sourly. He didn't hold out his hand for me, but I went to his side regardless, knowing that his feathers had been severely ruffled.

"Yes, we are finished. Thank you for being so patient." I leaned into him and smiled at Gabriel. "Please let us know if Brom goes over the line with his demands for trips to the British Museum. And thank you both for offering to have him despite the state of things. We'll be back to get him on Sunday night. It was nice to see you all again."

Baltic felt enough pleasantries had been exchanged and hustled me into the back of the car, which was illegally parked a few yards away. "That is enough, Ysolde. When we were planning this, you did not say you wished to conduct a social visit with the silver dragons."

"Would you have agreed to one if I had?" I asked, curious.

"No." He got in beside me, telling Pavel to drive on. "They declared war upon us. It is for them to ask us, not the other way around."

"When did you say Thala resurrected you?"

He shot me a curious glance at the abrupt change of subject. "In 1971. Why?"

"Because for a man who's forty years old, you sure do act like you were raised in the Dark Ages."

"I *was* raised in the Dark Ages."

"That was supposed to be sarcasm, Baltic."

"I know what it was. I simply chose to ignore it," he answered, taking my hand in his. I couldn't help but smile. He was so bristly when it came to other dragons, and yet I knew how much he had suffered over the years. I figured he was due a few bristles now and again.

"Speaking of Thala, what's the latest on your epic plan to spring her?"

Pavel gave a short bark of laughter as Baltic, with great relish, answered. "We have located her whereabouts at a house in West Sussex. Pavel will reconnoiter there this weekend, and then we will attack."

I sighed. "I don't suppose you would like to try to release her without violence?"

"That did not work, which you know since you insisted on holding talks with Drake Vireo regarding the subject."

I paid little heed to the acid in his voice. "It's worth trying to reason with Drake and the others again. After all, Gabriel did make an effort to be civil by inviting Brom to stay. Perhaps the wyverns are trying to offer an olive branch."

"I doubt it." The look he gave me said much. "I know you do not wish for this war, but it is not of our making. We have taken no actions against any member of the weyr."

"Nor have they done so against us. Well, except for Kostya breaking your nose again last week, but that had more to do with the fact that you called him a 'house-stealing, backstabbing, traitorous whoreson pain in the ass' than with the war against us."

Baltic rubbed his nose. "The fact remains that it is for them to call off the war and make the first move."

I was silent, but my heart wept for the state of things between us and the weyr.

Baltic, ever sensitive to my moods, put his hand on my leg and gave it a reassuring squeeze. "If I were to tell you that we will kill as few dragons as is necessary to free Thala, would that make you happy again?"

"Oh, I know full well that despite your reputation as an unbridled maniac, you're not a fan of killing just for the heck of it, but that isn't my point. I don't want *anyone* else to die, Baltic. That includes whatever guards Drake has put into place around your friend."

"What would you have me do?" he asked, clearly exasperated.

"Well . . ." A thought occurred to me, one that would ease my conscience at the idea of sneaking around behind Baltic's back and yet might well serve to achieve a much-desired end. "If you aren't willing to talk with Drake and the other wyverns again about them releasing Thala, then perhaps I can. Or rather, perhaps I can talk to May and Aisling. And Cyrene, of course, although . . . did it seem to you that something was a little off in Kostya and Cyrene's relationship when we ran into them last week?"

"Something is most definitely off with Kostya," he growled.

I patted his knee. "Personal judgments aside, I got a feeling that we had interrupted an argument. I wonder ... no, that doesn't really matter. What was I saying? Oh, if I talk to Aisling and May about Thala, I'm sure I could get them to see reason. They don't want a war any more than we do—wars are dangerous things, and they don't want their respective loved ones in any danger. I'm willing to bet you that they can go a lot further in convincing their wyverns to release Thala than you can. After all, it was you the weyr was after, and now they've met you and seen you're not the madman they thought you were, so they really have no reason to hold Thala prisoner."

"I will not have you put in any danger," he said stiffly.

"May and Aisling?" I asked, not bothering to finish the question.

He harrumphed. "I concede that neither of the mates is likely to harm you, but I do not trust the wyverns."

"You trust Gabriel with Brom," I pointed out.

"That is because no wyvern would attack a child. My son will be safe with the silver wyvern. My mate is a different matter."

"I'm not proposing to stay with Gabriel, just have a little talk with May and Aisling. And I think I'll call them when we get home and set up a lunch tomorrow to meet with them." I tried to sound as nonchalant as possible, but I'm no actress. My voice sounded stilted and filled with the knowledge that we'd already set the meeting time. Luckily, Baltic was still considering the subject of his second guard, Thala.

"I do not like it, but if you insist on trying, I will not prevent you," was all he said before he and Pavel turned the discussion to the best ways to infiltrate the house where Thala was being kept.

It wasn't until that night that I had time alone with him.

"Where's Pavel?" I asked as I set a deliciously scented beef bourguignon down in front of him.

"He will not be here for supper. He has gone to see a friend," Baltic answered, holding out a chair for me.

I started to sit, but looked up quickly. "A friend? A romantic friend, you mean? A guy romantic friend?"

Baltic frowned at me as he took his seat. "No, female. I told you he did not have a preference as to gender."

"Oh, a girlfriend. Drat. And you can stop giving me that look. I've told you for two months now that I don't have bizarre sexual desires, and have absolutely no wish to participate in a threesome with Pavel or anyone else."

"That is good, because I have changed my mind about allowing you to watch when Pavel is with a male partner. I have discussed the matter with him, and although he was willing, I have decided it is not seemly in my mate to be aroused by the thought of males with other males."

"I've told you and told you that it's just mildly interesting!" I slammed down the spoon I was about to use to serve him. "By the rood, Baltic, I'm not a sex-crazed pervert!"

"I never said you were."

"No, but you're implying that because a girl likes

a little spice now and again, she's a whack job. And I'm not. You know I am more than happy with our sex life."

The irritated look on his face slid away to one of smug satisfaction. "Yes, I know. Last night you shouted your pleasure so loudly it almost deafened me."

"Oh, I did not. Don't exaggerate," I said briskly, serving us both. I paused in the act of passing a bowl of salad, remembering the events of the night before, and a little flush warmed my chest. "Although I have to say that I highly approve of your use of the feathers. That was very inventive."

He allowed a small smile to curl the corners of his mouth. "It was something I read in a book. I had wished to try it with you before that bastard Constantine killed you, but was unable to find suitable feathers."

"Speaking of Constantine," I said slowly, pausing to savor a mouthful of the bourguignon.

"We weren't."

"Yes, we were. You just mentioned him."

"Mentioning someone is not the same as speaking of him. I do not wish to ruin my digestion by speaking of that murderous traitor."

"Well, we're going to have to risk that, because I want to talk to you about him."

Baltic set down his fork and shot me a penetrating glance. "Why do you wish to do so? Are you fascinated by him the way you are with thoughts of Pavel and males? Do you regret me taking you from Constantine's side? Do you wish I were he?"

"For the love of the saints, Baltic! Get over the thing with Pavel already! As for Constantine, no, I don't regret

anything. Well, that's not true. I regret hurting him when
you claimed me as your mate, but that was much of his
own doing. And even if I did regret you de-mating me
from Constantine, which I absolutely don't, it wouldn't
matter because he's dead." I paused a moment. "He *is*
dead, isn't he?"

Baltic's eyes narrowed. "I did not kill him, if that's
what you are asking."

"It's not, and stop giving me dragon answers."

"I am a dragon. I answer. Thus I give—"

"Argh!" I yelled, slamming both hands down on the
table. "You're doing this deliberately, aren't you? You're
trying to piss me off so I won't go back to the subject
you don't want to talk about, but it's not going to work,
Baltic. You may be able to distract me other times, but
not now. Not when it's something this important."

He looked completely outraged. "Why is Constantine
so important to you? I should be the only one who is
of that much importance in your life! Excepting Brom,
and I allow that he is of primary importance as well. But
other than him—"

"I cannot wait for you to stop being so damned insecure!" I yelled.

"I am not insecure! I simply wish to know why my
mate is lusting after other wyverns!" he yelled back.

For a moment an image came to my mind's eye: a
man so overwhelmed with grief, he had dropped to his
knees at the memory of his love, his anguish swamping
everything around him. Instantly, I was on his lap, holding him tight to me, tears wetting my lashes as I kissed
his face. "My love, my only true love, never have I lusted
after anyone but you. Not in the past, not in my dreams,
not even in those fantasies you consider so outrageous.

I chose you in my other life, and I chose you in this one, as well."

He allowed me to comfort him, not saying anything, but his grip on me was as hard as steel. Although I had treated the subject with some lightness when speaking to Brom, the truth was that Baltic's emotional scars ran so deep, I began to wonder if they would ever heal.

Dinner was forgotten as I did what I could to provide a balm to his aching heart. It wasn't until after he had allowed me to love him—dragons, I had found, are dominant even so far as intimate relations are concerned—that I felt comfortable again broaching the subject.

"Baltic, stop sleeping. I want to talk to you," I told him, prying myself up from where I had collapsed against his chest.

He cracked one eye open and considered me with some annoyance. "I have just pleasured you within an inch of your life, or so you claim, and now you wish to talk? *My* Ysolde—"

"Yes, I know, your precious old Ysolde would have never bothered you at such a time, but since I am not as perfect as she was, you're just going to have to deal with it."

He surprised me with a chuckle as he pinched my behind and shifted me so that I was draped more comfortably across him. Idly, I stroked my hand across the heavy pectoral muscles over his heart, tracing out the sept symbol that he bore there.

"You were hardly perfect, my love. You always wanted to talk after lovemaking then, as well, although usually you did not require much response from me."

"Probably I knew I wasn't going to get one. I seem

to recall you going right to sleep after such acts," I said, kissing his collarbone.

He grunted and closed his eyes.

"I want to talk about Constantine and you," I said, propping my chin on my folded hands.

His eyes popped open to glare at me, and he probably would have come up with some outraged declaration or other if I hadn't stopped him by continuing. "I want to know why Constantine was meeting with Antonia von Endres and, more important, why the First Dragon had you kicked out of your sept."

He went absolutely still under me, not even breathing for the count of ten. Then he blinked. "How do you know about Constantine and Antonia?"

"You want to tackle that subject first? OK. I had a vision today. Not a vision like before, but one where I wasn't even born when the action happened." I gave him a quick outline of the events I had witnessed.

His face adopted a shuttered expression. "Why did you have that vision? It does not make sense. Neither that bastard Constantine nor Antonia has anything to do with you."

"They do if the First Dragon wants me to perform some task related to one or both of them."

He was silent again, then finally said, "I did not know they had met, although I suspected it. Antonia was very ambitious, and she expected me to be the same."

"Ambitious how? Becoming the heir, you mean?"

"No, I was already fighting for that," he said, lazily stroking my back. "She wanted more for me than to just be the wyvern of the black dragons. She wished for me to control the entire weyr, so that we could join our power and rule the Otherworld."

"Good god. So she thought she could do that by offing the competition?"

His shoulders twitched. "I told her it was folly, that I would challenge Constantine for the position of heir and win it rightfully, but she was not known for her patience."

"So what happened that you were booted out of the sept?"

"A complicated circumstance that has no bearing on your vision" was his answer after a long pause.

"I don't want to pry into something you'd rather not talk about," I said slowly, moving a little so I could trace the lovely thick muscles of his chest. "But knowing what happened might give me some insight into what exactly I'm supposed to do about Constantine."

"I assure you that the situation had nothing to do with the traitor."

I looked at the face that I loved so dearly, reading in the set of his jaw and the obstinate glint to his eye that I would not get further information. That didn't stop me from asking one last question, however. "That's how the First Dragon knew you, isn't it? You did something he didn't like and he asked your wyvern to boot you out. Why has no one ever mentioned that? At the *sárkány* two months ago, Drake and the others seemed surprised to find out that the First Dragon knew you."

"No one outside of Alexei, Constantine, and a few others knew of the circumstance," he said reluctantly. "All but one are dead."

I pounced on a name I recognized. "I thought you said that whatever you did had no impact on Constantine."

"I said it was not his concern. That is not the same thing," he said with usual dragon caginess.

"Will you tell me someday what happened?" I asked as his body relaxed once again, his eyes closed, and his arm wrapped securely around me.

He pinched my behind again; then one side of his mouth went up and he pulled me up to kiss me. "When the time is right, yes."

I couldn't help but wonder just how many hundreds of years from now that would be.

Chapter Three

"I hereby declare this inaugural meeting of the Mates Union in session. Jim, must you chew with your mouth open? It's ruining everyone's appetite. Thank you. Where were we? Oh, yes, we're officially all present and accounted for, except Cyrene, who is in Greece for a water elementals retreat. On the agenda today is Ysolde's situation with the First Dragon's demand that she do something for him, the problem of the weyr war against the light dragons, and, Jim, so help me god, if you blow any more spitwads through that straw, I'm going to take away your milk shake."

"I was just making a decorative spitwad mosaic of Cecile on the wall," Jim protested, opening its eyes very big in an attempt to look innocent. "Bastian said for us to make ourselves at home, and that's what I'm doing."

Aisling glared first at the demon, then at the wall across from where we sat in a corner booth. The pub, May had informed me, was owned by the blue dragon wyvern and was a favorite spot for May and Aisling to meet for lunch.

"Wipe it off, or you can't have a hamburger for your lunch," Aisling told the demon, handing it a napkin. "Yes, that's an order."

"Geesh, ever since you had the spawn, you've gotten über-bossy," Jim complained as it took the napkin in its mouth, speaking somewhat indistinctly around it.

"I hope someday to see your babies," I said, a little sadly, since I loved babies.

Aisling made a face. "I'm dying to show them off, but Drake is being downright obnoxious about the subject of you and Baltic visiting them. I know all moms think so, but they really are the most adorable babies, although no one can pronounce their names."

"What are their names?" I asked.

"Ilona and Iarlaith."

"How do you spell that?"

She told me.

May laughed as I ran the names through my mind a few times.

"They're lovely names, Aisling. I can see why no one can pronounce them, though. I do expect that someday Brom will announce he hates his name, even though it's a perfectly ordinary name."

"Er . . ." Aisling and May exchanged glances. "Yes. I'm sure the twins will give Drake and me endless grief about their names as well someday, but for now they're just two little bundles of utter cuteness. I have some pictures on my phone. . . . Oh, sorry. We're kind of getting away from the meeting, aren't we? Business first, baby pictures later."

I looked around a bit nervously. "Are you sure it's

OK for me to be here? With the war and all, I wouldn't think the dragons would like my being here. Especially the blue dragons."

"I cleared it with Bastian ahead of time. He said we could have the pub for an hour before it opened, and that no one would make any sort of an attack on you. And despite the fact that he broke Baltic's nose, he really is a nice guy."

"But he still thinks that Baltic killed his dragons," I protested.

"Maybe he does, and maybe he doesn't," Aisling said, shrugging. "I kind of think he doesn't. I mean, Fiat is nuts enough for two, and he knows that Fiat was involved, but with you saying Baltic isn't ... well, that's part of our agenda, so we'll come to that in good time. For now, don't worry—you're safe enough here."

May looked musingly at me. "How did you get Baltic to agree to let you come today? I assumed that letting Brom visit us pushed him to the limits of his patience."

"Oh, it did, but when I pointed out that we might put our heads together concerning a few things, he decided the risk of someone swooping down to kill me was not going to be very high with you two present."

"Drake would never attack you," Aisling said, looking mildly offended.

"Nor would Gabriel."

"I know that, and you both know that, but Baltic ... well, you have to remember what he's been through. My death, his death, his resurrection ... it's taken a toll on his emotions, and I suspect it's going to be some time before he realizes I'm not going to be snatched from him again."

"You know," Aisling said, dabbing at her eye with a

tissue, "when I first saw Baltic, I figured he was a madman. But I can't imagine what it would be like to survive when your mate was dead. The pain he must have suffered for all those years . . . it doesn't excuse his actions, but it does make me understand his motivation behind them."

"There's no excuse for him shooting at you all at a *sárkány*, certainly," I answered, sniffling back a couple of tears of my own. "But I'm glad that you guys have come to realize that he didn't kill all those blue dragons."

"Someone did," May pointed out. "Fiat won't talk, but pretty much everyone agrees that it would have been physically impossible for him to have killed *all* of them. He must have had help, but who helped him?"

"I don't know, but I'm determined to find out. I want this stupid war to end. I want us to be part of the weyr. I want to be able to invite you over for dinner."

"Dinner? Ooooh, I'm so there," Jim said, plopping itself back into its seat. "Can I come for a visit?"

"Jim!" Aisling scolded. "You don't ask people to visit them, you wait for them to offer it first. Besides, I'm not going anywhere that you need to stay with Ysolde, and if I was, I'm sure May would be delighted to have you."

"Of course," May said, although she looked anything but thrilled at the thought.

"May knows I love her, don't ya, May? But the eats are better at Soldy's place, and it's always fun to watch Baltic come unglued."

"Regardless, you're not going to invite yourself to Ysolde's house when she has so much on her plate right now. And speaking of that, you were going to tell me about this new vision you had. May said it was something different."

"Oooh, gossip," Jim said, looking interested. "Spill!"

By the time I was finished explaining about the vision, our lunch had come.

"Well," Aisling said, her fork poised over a plate of seared pork loin and caramelized onion. "That certainly is different, all right."

"Obviously the First Dragon wants me to do something about Constantine, but I'm at a loss as to what," I said, admiring the oak-roasted salmon and new potato salad that sat before me.

"No fries?" Jim asked, looking up from its mammoth hamburger. "How can I eat a burger without fries?"

"Too much fat," Aisling replied with a meaningful look at its midsection.

"I'm not the one who was just telling Drake she's still got to lose her baby fat," it answered.

"Do you want to eat that hamburger or wear it?" she asked sweetly.

"Sheesh! You guys are witnesses. Cranky demon lord alert." Jim went back to its hamburger with only a few mutters.

"As for your situation, Ysolde," Aisling continued, "I'm at a loss as well. Unless you think that the vision meant Antonia von Endres killed Constantine and that you're supposed to avenge his death."

"But *did* Antonia kill Constantine?" May asked. "All Gabriel's said is that Constantine disappeared right at the time that Kostya killed Baltic. Which we now know is when Ysolde died."

We were silent for a moment. I knew that they were seeing the same remembered image as I was—that of my body lying in the snow, still and unmoving, while a man stood over me with a blood-drenched sword.

"He killed me, but I'm supposed to avenge his death?" I asked the table at large.

"It does seem rather odd," May agreed, munching on a grilled tuna, chickpea, and coriander salad. "But like Aisling, that's the only thing I can think of."

"It's just so vague," I said, feeling a bit overwhelmed. "I wish I knew for certain what it was I should be doing."

"You could always ask the First Dragon," Jim said around a mouthful of hamburger.

We all stared at the demon dog.

"What?" it asked, a piece of onion dangling from its lips.

"Just when I think you were only sent to me to torment me, you pipe up with a bit of genius like that," Aisling said, giving it a hug.

"Does that mean I can have some fries?" it asked hopefully.

"No."

"Of course," May said slowly, a smile forming on her lips. "Ysolde can summon him. We can just ask him what he wants her to do."

"We could . . ." I considered this idea. For some reason, I was hesitant to go to the trouble of summoning the ancestor of all dragonkin, but really, did I have a choice?

"She can't summon him if her magic is still wonky. I don't supposed Dr. Kostich has lifted that interdiction on you, Ysolde?"

"No. I sent him a letter telling him that since he managed to blackmail that mage sword away from Baltic, the least he could do was lift the interdict and let me rejoin the Magister's Guild, but he sent back a bill for the thirty-seven years of training I had while I was his apprentice, so I figured I'd better let it drop."

"He's such a pain," Aisling said.

"A huge pain," May agreed.

"Just like a sharp stick shoved up the—" Jim's eyes opened wide when Aisling removed its plate from in front of it. "Hey! Demon starver!"

"Hardly." Aisling gave it back its hamburger and we all resumed eating our lunches.

"I don't like summoning him without a very good cause, and I'm not entirely sure I can do it again, since I wasn't trying to summon him before, but I don't see any other way to determine just what I'm supposed to be doing." I took a thoughtful sip of lemon water, then added, "I'll do it tonight. Baltic is supposed to go down to Burleigh House to eyeball the rough plan Pavel made, so he won't be in my way when I summon the First Dragon."

May and Aisling looked at me in surprise. "You know about Burleigh?" Aisling asked.

"Drake's house in the Sussex countryside? Of course I do."

"Well, hell. That was supposed to be a secret from you guys. I guess I'll have to tell Drake that Baltic knows where Thala is being held."

"As we're on the subject of Thala . . ." I bit my lip. "I don't suppose you two would like to help me get her out of there?"

"Ahem!" Jim said loudly.

"Sorry—you three. And Cyrene, of course, assuming she's back from her water thing by then."

"You want us to help you break out the weyr's prisoner?" Aisling was clearly astonished by the idea.

"Yes, I do."

May and Aisling exchanged a glance. "Let me make

sure we're all on the same page, here. You want us to set free the woman who helped Baltic attack our house the day I had the twins?"

"I realize that she's no one's favorite, but yes, I would like your help. In fact, I *need* your help."

"Why?" May asked.

"Why do I need your help?"

"No, why do you want her out?"

"Oh, well, a number of reasons," I said, putting down my fork and leaning back against the curved settle. "For one, Baltic wants her out, and if we don't get her out peaceably, he's going to attack. I don't think anyone wants more dragon deaths—certainly I don't."

"But she's Baltic's lieutenant," May protested. "They worked together to try to destroy us."

"Yes, but that's all changed." I waved away the pesky events of the past. "Things are different now. And besides, she's Antonia von Endres' daughter. That might have some significance to the First Dragon's task."

"There is that," Aisling said thoughtfully.

May gnawed on her lower lip for a moment. "Gabriel would be very angry if he knew I was working to free the weyr's prisoner."

"Drake wouldn't be angry," Aisling said with a wry smile. "He'd go ballistic. It was our house that Antonia helped Baltic destroy. Drake's still a little cranky about that day."

"Well, I was kind of hoping you guys wouldn't tell."

May and Aisling exchanged another glance.

"We couldn't do that," May said slowly, a light of amusement in her blue eyes. "But I think there's a way we could work out a deal."

"What sort of a deal?" I asked, suddenly wary.

"Dragons love deals," Aisling told me. "You wouldn't believe the things I can get Drake to do if I present it in the light of negotiations."

"Yeah, like the time you *negotiated* him into chasing you around the house while you wore nothing but a gold chastity belt?" Jim asked, snickering.

"It was a medieval girdle, not a chastity belt, and from here on out I'm going to lock your door at night."

"Meanie. Bet Soldy would never lock me in my room just so she and Baltic could have a kinky three-way orgy with Pavel."

"I have never had an orgy, three-way or otherwise," I told the demon, setting fire to its napkin with a flick of Baltic's dragon fire.

"OK, OK! No need to go overboard! You almost burned my garnish!"

Jim went back to munching on its frilly lettuce as I considered the two women sitting across from me. "What deal is it you want to make?"

"You want Thala free," May said simply.

"Yes."

"And you're mated to Baltic."

"Yeees," I said again, slower. "I don't see where this is going."

"You want our help to free her."

"Am I supposed to be seeing something?" I asked, confused.

"I'm a silver dragon," May pointed out. "And what do the silver dragons have to do with Baltic?"

I shook my head. "I still don't— Oh! The curse!"

"Yup." Aisling nodded. "We were going to ask your help with that anyway, but this is the perfect opportunity to get both things done at once. May and I will help you break out Thala, and in return Baltic lifts the curse that he put on the silver dragons when you died." She paused for a few seconds. "You'd think he'd let the silver dragons find mates now that you're alive."

"You'd think," I said, sighing. "He does like his grudges, though. He still feels that since a silver dragon killed me, it's only right that none of them should have any mates born to them."

"Dragons can be so stubborn sometimes," Aisling agreed. "Where were we? If you get Baltic to take off the curse, then when Drake and Gabriel find out what we've done, they won't be able to be all pissy, because the curse will be lifted. Kind of a 'you scratch our back and we scratch yours' situation, only with dragon claws and stubborn wyverns."

"I've asked him a couple of times about lifting it, and he seems pretty adamant that it's not going to happen," I said with deliberation. "So I can't promise you he will lift the curse, but I can swear to do everything in my power to make that so."

"We need that curse removed," May said warningly.

"I know you do, and I promise I'll move heaven and earth to make it happen, but it might take a bit of time, more time than we have right now. Baltic is going to Riga for a few days to start the reclamation work on Dauva, which means it's the perfect moment to deal with the situation concerning Thala. I can't guarantee he will lift the curse in the next day or so, but I know that if I have some time to work on it, eventually I can make him see reason."

May looked skeptical, but after exchanging yet another pregnant glance with Aisling, she acquiesced. "I don't like it, but I guess that's the best we're going to get. We'll consider your word as your bond on it, though."

"Thank you. And I will start working on Baltic right away. I'll talk to him before he leaves for Latvia, and after he's gone, I'll summon the First Dragon."

"I wish I could be there," May said with a sigh. "But Gabriel would never allow it."

"This might help with the weyr situation as well," I pointed out. "If we get Thala out, she's likely to talk about what happened during the time Baltic was in France when all those dragons were killed."

"Then again, she might have been the one to kill them," Aisling said.

"I don't think it's likely she'd do something against Baltic's wishes, and he had no reason to want the deaths of those dragons. His involvement with Fiat was simply an arrangement dating back to Baltic's resurrection."

"There will have to be some terms, you know," May said, sipping a glass of white wine. "Such as prohibitions against attack by Thala."

"Oh, don't worry, I think we can get her to agree to anything in order to get out of her prison," I said, filled with confidence.

"You don't know that for sure," May said. "We *are* at war, after all."

"Yes, but she takes orders from Baltic, and he doesn't have any desire to attack anyone now that he and I are together. The war was declared against us, remember. Unless you guys can get them to call it off?"

"I wish it was that easy." May shook her head. "Every time I talk to Gabriel about it, he tells me it's weyr law, and no matter how he may feel personally, he is duty bound to uphold weyr law."

"Drake more or less said the same thing. Honestly, if they weren't sexy to the tips of their toes, I'd be completely fed up with dragon stubbornness," Aisling said, moving her plate away from Jim's covetous stare.

"What we need is to get everyone together in a nice quiet place—the wyverns, and Thala, and even Fiat. I just know if we could get them all together, we could clear Baltic's name."

"I don't think Drake would go for that," Aisling said, chewing thoughtfully on her lunch.

"Gabriel might, if the curse was lifted." May's expression showed there wasn't much hope otherwise.

"Baltic is going to be a bit sticky," I said hesitantly. "He's bending over backward now to make me happy because . . . well, to be honest, because he's so grateful we found each other again. But he's still rather hard to persuade about some things, and the weyr is definitely one of them. But . . . hmm . . . if we add meeting the wyverns to the conditions for freeing Thala, in addition to lifting the curse, it might be possible to get him there."

"Are you sure?" May asked somewhat skeptically. "That seems like a lot of concessions for him to make, and even since you showed up, he doesn't strike me as the sort of man who makes concessions easily."

"No, he isn't, but really, does he have a choice?" I set down my fork and ticked off items on my fingers. "You won't help free Thala unless he lifts the curse on the silver dragons. I won't rally you both into helping with Thala unless he agrees to meet with the weyr. And Gabriel won't agree to a weyr meeting to end all this ridiculousness unless the curse is lifted. Therefore, in order to free Thala, he's going to have to agree to meet with the weyr and to lift the curse. It's just that simple."

Aisling laughed. "I doubt he's going to see it that way."

I had my doubts as well, but I kept them to myself.

"So how are we going to get Thala out, assuming all goes according to plan?" May asked. "There's no way you're going to convince the weyr to release her just because he lifts the silver curse. No one really cares about that but us."

"I care," Aisling pointed out. "Ysolde cares."

"That's because you're two sane women, and not stubborn wyverns." May gave a little grimace. "Drake would probably agree to her release because he and Gabriel are friends, but Bastian and Jian have no reason to want Thala loose, and I doubt if even Kostya would sanction letting her go."

"We're simply going to have to get her out ourselves," Aisling said with a cheerful smile.

"Oh, man, not another one of your plans from Abaddon?" Jim grumbled, perusing the menu again. "We gettin' dessert? I could go for some tiramisu right about now."

"Hush, demonic annoyance. I'm not a professional Guardian for nothing, you know. I got Drake and Kostya out of that aerie prison, so there'll be no trouble getting Thala out."

May looked as doubtful as I felt.

"Yeah, you and your professional Guardian skills did . . . and Gabriel and Maata and Tipene and me, but we're just little bits of squashed egg beneath your august toes, huh?"

Aisling shot it a narrow-eyed look.

I considered the matter for a moment, then said, "I'm simply going to have to use some magic. With my magic, and Aisling's Guardian skills, and May's . . . er . . ."

"She's a master thief," Aisling said with a smile at May. "She's even better than Drake."

"You can imagine how thrilled I am with that praise," May answered with a grimace. "But Aisling's right—I can get into places unseen, and given the agreement we have been discussing, I would be happy to do whatever I can to free Thala."

"But your magic is kind of odd because of the interdict," Aisling pointed out.

I sighed. "Yes, it is, which means I'm going to have to go see Dr. Kostich and insist that he lift the interdict. I haven't really pushed him about it before, but I think it's time to strip off the kid gloves and make him do it."

"Oooh," Jim said, its lips an O. "Can I watch when he melts you into a puddle of goo?"

"Ignore it," Aisling said, throwing her napkin at the demon. "I have faith in you, Ysolde."

Silence fell for a few minutes as we all considered what had to be done.

"There's no sense in delaying," Aisling said abruptly. "The sooner we get this done, the better for everyone. I'll talk to Drake tonight about a big *sárkány* with Fiat and Thala, and you and Baltic."

"And I'll explain it all to Gabriel," May agreed.

"I'll tackle Baltic tonight as well."

"Yeah, but are you going to talk to him, too?" Jim asked with a lascivious wink. "Or will you have time to talk with all that *tackling* going on?"

"Honest to Pete, I can't take you anywhere. Stop

being such a rude demon." Aisling smiled at us both. "So, we're agreed?"

"Agreed," I said, nodding.

"Me, too," May said.

"Excellent. Mmm, this roast pork is really outstanding. Would anyone like a bite?"

Jim lifted up its head hopefully. "Yeah, I—"

"Anyone *human* want a bite?" she corrected with a meaningful look at it.

May pursed her lips.

"Oh, sorry. I forgot you're not . . . never mind. Ysolde, would you . . . no, you're not, either. Er . . . moving on. I believe that's taken care of all the business at hand, so if there are no other issues to deal with, I move we call this meeting officially over."

I smiled and lifted my wine. "To the successful completion of whatever it is the First Dragon wants of me."

"To no curse on the silver dragons," May said, lifting her glass.

"To peace amongst the dragons," Aisling said, clinking our glasses with hers.

"To sexy little Corgis with the fuzziest butts imaginable," Jim added, slurping loudly out of its water bowl.

Chapter Four

"You are being ridiculously obstinate."

"And you are being unrealistic." Baltic jammed a few articles of clothing into a small bag. "I am the wyvern, Ysolde. You are the mate. I have yielded to you on more occasions than I like, but about this I will not."

It came as no surprise that he outright refused to lift the silver dragon curse. What did take me aback was his flat refusal to even consider the idea of meeting with the other wyverns.

"If you don't agree to meet with the weyr, then the whole thing is off." I couldn't help the note of pleading in my voice as I followed him when he went from the closet to the bed with a few more items of clothing. "Thala will remain a prisoner, and we'll remain at war."

"The war doesn't matter to me, and Pavel and I will effect Thala's release when we return."

"At the cost of how many dragons?" I asked, slapping my hands on my legs as he zipped up the bag. "You said yourself that there was far more protection around her than you imagined. You can't just waltz in and get her—you would have to fight, just the two of you against Drake's huge army of men intent on keeping her prisoner. And much as you annoy me at times, I don't want you killed!"

"*I* will not be the one to die," he said with brash arrogance.

"By the rood, man! I don't want *anyone* to die!"

He dropped the bag onto a chair next to the bedroom door. "I have decided, mate."

Tears of frustration sprang to my eyes. My throat worked for a moment as I watched him gather up his keys, wallet, and cell phone. "Please," was all I could get out, but the word was imbued with emotion.

He turned slowly toward me, his face dark. "You ask too much, Ysolde."

"I know. But I have to. Don't you see? I want you safe, but I also want to have a future. You keep saying I'm a dragon, but you're denying me the chance to have roots. I want to explore my dragon self, but I can't so long as we're outside of the weyr."

"The two things are not mutually exclusive," he said, taking my hands in his and gently pulling me against him.

"They are for me. We did a war once, Baltic, and it ended in unthinkable misery. I will not go through that again."

His eyes closed for a moment, his face twisted with the same pain I felt so deep inside me.

"Please," I whispered against his mouth, allowing myself to melt against him. "Talk to the weyr again. With Thala and Fiat cooperating, we can get all of the issues straightened out, and then we can be happy."

"I have you. I *am* happy."

I melted a little more, reveling in the taste and scent and feel of him, my hands drawing intricate patterns on his back. "Meet with the wyverns, give serious thought about lifting the silver dragon's curse, and I swear that Aisling, May, and I will have Thala free by the time you return from Dauva."

He was still and silent for so long that I was about to give in to despair, but at last he swore under his breath, and kissed me swiftly. "I will do this one last thing for you, mate, but this is it! There will be no more boons! It is the absolute last one—do you understand?"

"I understand," I said, smiling up at him.

His gaze slid toward the bed, but before I could do so much as kiss him, he sighed and gently put me away from him. "I will miss my flight if I allow you to thank me properly. I do not like this plan you have to free Thala, but I am aware that it is not you the wyverns want dead, so you may proceed with it despite my misgivings. You will not put yourself in any danger, however."

"So bossy," I said, giving in to my desire and kissing him. "Fire. Please."

He bathed me in his dragon fire as he took charge of the kiss, allowing me to feel both his passion and his love.

"Farewell, my heart," I said as he picked up his bag. "Come back to me safe."

He paused for a minute at the door, a curious look on his face. "You said the exact same thing to me three hundred years ago."

"But then you were going out to battle Constantine. You won't be doing that this time," I said, smiling a little at the bittersweet memory.

"Perhaps. Perhaps not," was all he said before leaving.

I stared at the door for a few minutes wondering what the hell that meant, but chalked it up to Baltic's indulging in a little mystery. He liked to do that, claiming it was his way to bring back all the many missing gaps in my memory. To be honest, I thought it was more his way of teasing me, but since I enjoyed puzzling out a good mystery, I didn't quibble.

Two hours later I watched the sun begin its descent into the gentle hills to the west before considering the chair that sat before me. I stood in a back corner of the velvety green lawn, well away from the house and anything that might accidentally get in the path of my sometimes wonky magic.

The frog that sat on the chair in a glass jar looked back at me with shiny black eyes.

"Just in case something goes wrong and I turn you into a banana, I want to apologize now. I don't think it will, but I feel obligated to warn you that with the interdict on me, my magic doesn't quite do what I intend it to do. Also, in case the banishing does work, please note that I have fixed in mind a location two miles from here next to a stream, so you should be able to find a new home there. I hope you won't mind relocating. Are you ready? Good. So am I." I closed my eyes for a moment to gather my thoughts, and remember exactly what I had said two months ago when I inadvertently summoned the First Dragon by means of a banishing spell.

"Taken with sorrow, all I cast from me," I said, taking strength from Baltic's dragon fire, which still mingled with my own deep inside me. "Devoured with rage, banished so you will be."

I opened my eyes, but nothing happened. The air didn't shimmer; no dragon formed out of nothing; the frog wasn't even gone. He belched at me and ran his tongue over his left eyeball, clearly not the least bit impressed.

"Maybe I didn't concentrate hard enough. Let's try it again." I took another deep breath, focused my attention on thoughts of the First Dragon, and repeated the spell.

All was silent around me except for the chatter of birds in the distance and the subdued hum of a couple of bumblebees as they flitted amongst three scraggly wild rosebushes.

"Right," I told the frog. "I see what the problem is. The first time I did this, I wasn't trying to summon the First Dragon—I was trying to banish everyone else. So I'll focus on that instead. You ready for a little journey? Here we go."

I recited the spell a third time. The frog fell asleep.

"Stars and stripes forever," I snapped, storming around the chair. I tried it four more times, but I didn't banish so much as a blade of grass. "And I didn't even get a banana." The now-freed frog made an unsympathetic noise as it hopped away into the garden.

I was about to return to the house when a sort of fog swept over me . . . a cold, biting, familiar sort of fog.

"I will let you live only because you are my godson and namesake." The man's voice, deep and rich with sorrow, pierced the blinding whiteness.

I shivered and wrapped my arms around myself as

I tried to peer through the wind and snow that were storming around me.

"I ought to kill you where you stand," another man's voice answered, and like the first, it was familiar. I moved toward them until two figures were visible in the nearly blinding storm. "You drove Baltic to this, drove him mad, and now he is dead. I may have killed him, but the blood is on your hands, Constantine Norka."

"Flee while you can, Kostya," Constantine answered, his shoulders slumped in weariness. "Go far away and hide until the remaining black dragons are no longer sought."

"I am not afraid of you! I am not afraid of battle!"

"It would not be a battle; it would be a slaughter. Flee, I tell you. You are Toldi's son, and I can do no less, but do not try me further. Go now, before we bring down the castle."

"You don't have to destroy Dauva," Kostya said, his face dark with anger. "For god's sake, I know you hate us, but there are innocent women and children who have sought protection inside its walls!"

Constantine shook his head, the flakes of white snow standing stark against the rich honey blond of his hair. "Ysolde sent them away. She herself told me that there was no reason to attack, since only Baltic and she remained with a handful of men."

"Where is she? You will return her to me. I am wyvern now, and I will protect her."

Constantine lifted his head, his expression stark. "She is dead."

Kostya stared at him in disbelief. "How?" he finally choked out.

"You can see for yourself," Constantine said, turning slowly and moving deeper into the storm. "I have not touched her body."

Kostya staggered after him, both men disappearing into the whiteness that seemed to cut right through me, stripping away my breath and leaving me reeling.

It took me a while to recover from that vision, but it did tell me one thing. "This *has* to be about Constantine. But what am I supposed to do about a dead man?" I asked a little while later.

"That is the question, isn't it?" May said, the cell phone connection cutting in and out a bit as we passed through a short tunnel. "Tell me again what you did to summon the First Dragon."

I slouched into my seat on the train that was at that moment whisking me to London and an appointment with my former employer, who just happened to be the powerful head of the Otherworld, ruling a good percentage of the immortal world. Quickly I went over what had happened—or rather, not happened—ending with, "Do you think that time at the *sárkány* was just a fluke? Have I really lost all my mage powers? What am I going to do if I can't summon the First Dragon?"

"I don't think it was a fluke, and I don't think you've lost your powers. There's one thing missing from your attempt today."

"Oh? What's that?"

"Dragons," she said succinctly. "I'm willing to bet that you pulled on Baltic's fire to help you summon, and it seems very likely to me that the collective presence of all those dragons helped the summoning along."

"Great." I leaned my head against the window. "Now

I have to wait until the next *sárkány* to summon the First Dragon."

"Not necessarily. We'll try it again tomorrow, when Aisling and I arrive for our assault on Burleigh House."

"But you two are only mates," I pointed out.

"Yes, but I have a connection to the First Dragon. Perhaps that will be enough to let your summoning work."

"Possibly." I sighed and gathered up my things as the train pulled into the station. "Time for me to go beard the magey lion in his den. Wish me luck."

"You don't think that maybe you should hold off petitioning Dr. Kostich until after you try summoning the First Dragon again? Perhaps it's the interdict that is helping the summoning."

"It could be, but I don't really have a choice—I promised Baltic we'd have Thala out by the time he returned from Dauva, and that means my magic has to be in working order. I don't think Drake's guards are going to be too awed if I threaten them with bananas."

May laughed. "No, I suppose not. Good luck, then. I'd have you pass along my good wishes to him, but frankly, I'd rather see Dr. Kostich in Abaddon."

It didn't take long to get from the train station to the hotel that Dr. Kostich favored when he stayed in London. I consulted the reception desk, gave them the false name I had used to book the appointment with the archimage, and was duly informed to proceed to the third floor suite where Dr. Kostich was waiting for me.

"Good evening," I told the unfamiliar young man who opened the door.

"Evening. You must be Uma Thurman." He stood

looking at me for a second while I damned my inability to think of a good pseudonym. At last he stepped back and waved a gracious hand. "Please come this way."

I was escorted to a living room I knew well from my previous time in Dr. Kostich's employment.

"Your appointment is here, master. A Miss Uma Thurman."

Dr. Kostich was looking out the window, his profile to me. He frowned for a moment, then looked toward the door, saying, "The actress? What does she—*you!*"

"Hello, Dr. Kostich. I hope you don't mind me using a fake name, but I knew you would never see me if I used my own. You don't mind if I sit down, do you?"

"Of course he doesn't mind," a woman's voice said from the doorway that led to one of the bedrooms. I spun around, surprised, a smile forming when I saw the woman walking toward me with outstretched hands.

"Violet!"

"Tully, how lovely to see you again." She took my hands and kissed me on either cheek, her faint French accent just as elegant as she was. Petite and dark-haired, she had a graceful air that I always coveted, since she never allowed herself to be ruffled by any circumstance life threw at her. It might have had something to do with the fact that she was over a hundred years old, but I suspected her placid personality was the underlying force. "It's been . . . what, five or six years? Father, you didn't tell me that Tully was visiting you. Sit down, my dear, and tell me how you are. Is that delightful boy of yours here? And what's this about you really being a dragon? Father refuses to talk about it, so it must be something quite shocking."

"She is not sitting down. She is not staying. Tully Sullivan, you are shameless and without any sense of moral rectitude, using my open-door policy in this manner," Dr. Kostich said, storming over to us. "Adam, remove this person from my presence."

The young man at the door hesitated, looking at me warily.

"Oh, Father, no. It's been forever since I've seen Tully, and she's just the person we need with our problem," Violet begged. "Let her stay, please. We have lots of news to catch up on."

Dr. Kostich's frown deepened, and I could see he really did want to boot me out, but Violet had always been the favorite of all his children, and it was well-known amongst the mage apprentices that she could wheedle just about anything out of him. "She is not welcome here."

"Of course she is. Sit, Tully. Oh, I suppose I should call you Ysolde now, since Father tells me that's your true name. And such a pretty name it is. What brings you to see us?"

"Er . . ." I slid a glance at Dr. Kostich. He stood glaring at me, but finally, with a disgusted noise, dismissed the young man at the door with a gesture and sat down in a chair opposite us. "Well . . . it's kind of a long story."

"The best kind. I can't wait to— What's this?" Violet leaned forward, squinting slightly at my chest. She gaped openmouthed at it for a moment, then turned an outraged look upon her father. "An interdict, Father?"

He looked down his long, narrow nose at her. "Yes, an interdict. She betrayed my trust, allowed her behemoth of a wyvern to try to kill me, and threw conjured bananas at me. Any one of those acts would be sufficient grounds for an interdict—with all three, she's lucky I didn't have her banished to the Akasha."

"For the love of the saints . . ." Violet shook her head. "Tully wouldn't betray you. She was the best of all your apprentices."

"You're just saying that because the pair of you used to get up to all sorts of mischief when I wasn't looking."

Violet grinned, her face coming alive with delight. "Do you remember that time in Prague, Tully, thirty or so years ago, at the GOTDAM conference when Father's other apprentice—what was her name? I've completely forgotten it, but she was the most annoying person. Quite the backstabber, too, which is why, when she was flaunting in front of us the fact that she was dating the head of the Oracles Union, we set it up so she thought he was betraying her with a Guardian, and she kicked him out of her room while he was naked, and he went to Father to demand justice, and of course, right at that moment a group of Diviners came down the hall, and they thought Father was having a wild orgy—"

"That is quite enough," Dr. Kostich interrupted with a stern glance at his daughter.

"I'm afraid I don't remember that," I told Violet sadly. "My husband—the man I thought was my husband— wiped my memory. But it sounds like we had fun."

"Oh, we did. You weren't a real apprentice yet, still just a student, but we had some lovely times together."

Dr. Kostich snorted and made a gainful attempt to take charge of the conversation. "Why are you here, Tully Sullivan?"

I flinched at the zing of pain that shot through me when he spoke my full name. Although my history with

Dr. Kostich was somewhat unusual, he was the most powerful mage in existence, a fact he didn't let anyone, least of all me, forget.

"I've come to ask you to lift the interdict," I said quietly, knowing he hated histrionics.

"No."

"Father!"

"No!" he said louder, his glare shifting to Violet. "You don't know what she's done, Violet."

"No, but I know Tully, and she wouldn't do any of the things you mentioned a few minutes ago."

"Well . . ." I gave her a weak smile. "I did actually shoot a few balls of energy at him, and they happened to turn into bananas, but that was only because he was trying to kill Baltic, in the process of which he ruined a couple of chairs and a tray full of antique crystal. And for the last time," I said, turning back to Dr. Kostich, "Baltic is not fat! He's a dragon! Their dragon form is bigger than their human form!"

Violet blinked a couple of times.

"Not to mention the fact that Baltic willingly gave up the light blade to you when he didn't have to. I think it's only right and fair that since he did that"—I wasn't going to mention that retrieving the famous von Endres sword was third on Baltic's list of things to be done, right after freeing Thala and rebuilding Dauvà—"then you should take the interdict off me."

"That does seem only fair." Violet nodded, looking thoughtfully at her father.

"No. She must be punished for the way she betrayed me. She—what is it now, Adam?"

The young man I assumed was the apprentice who replaced me stood in the doorway, holding a phone. "It's from the head of the watch, master. He says he must speak to you about an urgent matter in Paris."

Dr. Kostich sighed and got up, bending a prohibitive look upon both Violet and me. "I forbid you to discuss any more of this, Violet."

She rolled her eyes and waited for him to leave the room before asking, "Just how did you betray Father?"

I grimaced. "I didn't, not knowingly. I couldn't help it if there's a dragon buried deep inside me and I didn't know it. I thought I was mortal."

"Even I could see you weren't mortal, but you do appear to be human," she mused, examining me closely. "Clearly Father is going to have to lift the interdict."

"If you can convince him of that, I would be eternally grateful."

"Grateful enough to help me?" she asked quickly.

"You need my help? With what? My magic isn't very good, if you remember."

"No, no, it's not your magic we need."

"What exactly do you need help with?"

"A dragon. No, more than one, a group of dragons."

"Which sept?"

"I don't know. That's part of the problem, you see. Do you remember Maura? No, come to think of it, that was before I met you."

"I'm afraid I don't recognize the name, no, but I do recall that you had a daughter."

"Did I ever tell you that, oh, about ninety-five years ago, I was madly in love with a red dragon named Lao?"

I shook my head, even though I was startled by what she said. "As I said, my memory was pretty much destroyed."

"No matter. There isn't much to tell. We lasted for a

few years, then parted ways. But he left me with a little present in the form of a baby daughter."

I stared at her with growing amusement. "Dr. Kostich has a half-dragon granddaughter?" I couldn't wait to tell Baltic!

"Yes, but he doesn't discuss her much with people. He doesn't like to dwell on what he refers to as 'my little indiscretion.'" Violet laughed. "He dotes on Maura, of course, because she is a dear girl, if a bit headstrong, but that she gets from Father, as well."

I bit back a little giggle at the thought of Dr. Kostich and his headstrong granddaughter.

"Maura is very smart, just like Father. Being part dragon, of course, she didn't inherit any of his mage skills—well, to be fair, none of us did, although my brother Mark is able to do some simple polymorphs on rocks and other inanimate objects—but Maura did turn out to be the most gifted Summoner."

"Summoner?" I asked, the word ringing faint chimes in my brain. "That's something to do with ghosts?"

"Yes, she's very talented. She raised an entire village of Turks two summers ago, when she was spending some time at an archaeological dig. Not only can she raise ghosts, she can also raise shades, and you know how difficult that can be."

"Shades? I don't think . . ." I searched the black mass that was my memory. "Aren't they ghosts, too?"

"Well, technically, yes. Evidently there are all sorts of flavors of spirits, but where a typical ungrounded ghost is bound to the Summoner until Released, shades have more autonomy. They can become corporeal for periods of time, and usually aren't bound to anyone. Maura is one of the few Summoners who can successfully raise shades, although she is very careful about misusing her gift. And that's another bone Father has to pick, since he'd much prefer her to be under the purview of the L'au-dela rather than that of the Akashic League. Still, she's happy with her job . . . or she was until she fell in with some bad dragons."

"And you don't know what sept they belong to?" I wondered if they had something to do with the blue dragons.

"No, that's just it—they don't belong to any sept. They're a tribe of—what do you call them?—outcasts."

"Ouroboros dragons?" I blinked a couple of times, thinking briefly of telling her that both Baltic and I were ouroboros in the eyes of the weyr.

"That's the word. Evidently when you're an outlaw, you form a tribe rather than a sept, or some such nonsense." She made a dismissive gesture. "And Maura is in up to her neck with those outlaws, Tully. She's caught up in some horrible tangle and is too stubborn to ask for help."

"What sort of a tangle?" I asked, still a little bemused by the whole idea of the dragon-hating Dr. Kostich having a half-dragon granddaughter.

"I don't know," she said simply. "She won't tell me. But I know she's in trouble, and dragons being what they are, it's impossible for me to get an outsider to help her. But you are a dragon now, aren't you?"

"Well . . . kind of. My dragon is essentially dormant, but I am a wyvern's mate, and evidently that's quite a big deal in the weyr."

"Yes, exactly." She nodded. "You're important, and have powers, and these dragons who've waylaid Maura will be in awe of you. You are the ideal person to help us."

"I don't quite see how, but of course I'll be happy to be of any use I can."

"And you will be rewarded, naturally. Father will lift the interdiction, and you will help keep poor Maura from doing something she would spend the rest of her life regretting."

Dr. Kostich reentered the room, his eyes snapping with irritation as he glared at his daughter. "I specifically forbade you to mention that subject to strangers, Violet."

"Tully isn't a stranger, Father," she said with a stubborn look that matched his own.

"She is no longer one of us. I do not recognize her as a mage," he argued.

I sighed. Why was nothing in my life ever easy?

"I don't care if she's a demon lord!" Violet said, getting up and marching over to her father, her hands on her hips. "She's said she would help us with Maura, and that's all that matters. But she won't do that if you don't lift the interdict!"

"I have no intention of doing anything of the kind, and we do not need her help!" he snarled back at her.

The argument went on for another twenty minutes before Dr. Kostich, saying extremely rude things about his daughter in Latin, snapped a very testy "I will not lift the interdict. To do so now would be the sheerest folly. But I will agree that if she can help with Maura, I will remove the interdict then. And I do this only because Maura is foolish enough to get involved with dragons! I hope that will serve as a lesson to you both!"

"I need to be able to perform magic if I'm supposed to put the fear of god into a bunch of outlaw dragons," I pointed out.

"Yes, she does. As entertaining as it sounds to turn things to bananas, I don't see that the bad dragons are going to have a whole lot of respect for that."

He ground his teeth for a moment. "I will *not* lift the interdict."

My hopes were dashed on the rocks of despair.

"However, I will temporarily bestow upon her the Grace of the Magi. That should allow her to perform such magic as is necessary to free Maura from the hold of the ouroboros tribe."

He made an intricate gesture over my head, bathing me in a blue light that skimmed along the surface of my skin until it disappeared with a residual tingle. I took a deep breath, aware of a warm sensation that seemed to wrap around me. "Without intending to sound ungrateful, I'd rather have the interdict lifted."

His eyebrows bristled at me. I had the feeling I was just seconds away from total annihilation.

"Er . . . that is to say, thank you. I'm sure your blessing will help. Violet, if you would please give me all the information you have about Maura and these unknown dragons, I'll add her to the list of things I must take care of."

Dr. Kostich, still muttering, shot me a look that for ten seconds held me frozen in time, my heart stopped, the air locked into my unmoving lungs, my blood slowing until it lay limply in my veins. He released me just as he left the room.

I sank into a chair, raising a shaky hand to my throat. "I really hate it when he does that."

"Stop your heart? He does it just for effect, but I've told him many times that he doesn't have to be quite so extreme to get his point across." Violet sat down at an elegant antique writing desk and made a few quick notes. "Last I heard, Maura was in Germany. Here's the address I have for her, but I will warn you that she's fairly resistant to being helped. She claims she can handle the situation, but things have gone from bad to worse, and I think it's long past the time when she can hope to escape without the direst of repercussions."

I took the sheet she handed me, wondering if Baltic would know about this group of dragons. "What are they doing that puts your daughter in such dangerous circumstances?"

Violet stood, clearly ending the conversation. "They attacked Suffrage House, and stole several items of immeasurable value from the L'au-dela vaults."

"They stole from the headquarters of the Otherworld?" I shook my head. "How is that possible? I thought the security there was impossible to break."

"That's exactly what Father wants to know." She looked down at her hands for a second before leveling a steadfast gaze at me. "He's had to put out a price on all their heads, Maura's included. But that's not the worst."

"I'm fairly certain I don't want to know what could be worse, but go ahead—I'm braced." I got slowly to my feet.

"The artifacts they stole are theurgical in nature." She waited a moment for that to sink in before nodding. "Yes. Clearly they intend on challenging the powers of the L'au-dela itself, and we both know how that's likely to turn out. Save my daughter, Tully. Save Maura from what will surely be her destruction, and Father will lift the interdiction. I will see to it that you can name your reward, as well."

A vision of the light sword danced in my mind. I straightened my shoulders and gathered up my things. "I'll call you when I have some news."

"Tully..." She bit her lip. "Maura believes she is stronger than she really is."

I gave her hand a squeeze. "Don't lose heart. I may not be much of a mage, but dragons are very hard to kill, and with your father's blessing, I'm confident that I'll be able to get Maura back to you without too much trouble."

Don't you hate it when your words have a way of haunting you?

Chapter Five

"This is so *Mission: Impossible*! It's just like the old days when I helped you out, Mayling!"

The expression on May's face was completely missed by her oblivious twin. "Er ... yes. Aisling, what do you see?"

"Two guards along the south side, just as Drake said there would be." Aisling lowered the night vision goggles and lifted her wrist to press a button on her watch. "The new shift should be coming in another fifteen minutes."

"Are you sure this is the time to be doing this?" I frowned into the darkness. The house loomed up as an inky shape against an only slightly lighter sky. Fantastically shaped blobs of darkness lay scattered between us and the house, giving the eerie sensation that the house was guarded by more than just a handful of dragons. I eyed one of the shapes, convinced I had seen it move, but I knew it must just be a trick of the dim moonlight. *They are only yew hedges*, I told myself. *They just happen to look like mangled, unspeakably frightening beings.* "The new guards will be wide-awake, won't they? They'll have a better chance of seeing us than tired guards."

"True, but the shift change gives us a couple of minutes when the guards' attention is on each other, rather than the house," Aisling pointed out. "That's the best time to make our move."

"Don't worry, babe, we've done this before," Jim said, snuffling my leg. "When Ash and May broke into the vault at Suffrage House, they did it right at a shift change, too. Worked like a charm."

"I don't mean to make trouble, but I'm a bit worried about my magic. It was never very reliable, and I haven't had a chance to try it out since Dr. Kostich gave me the Grace of the Magi. I used to suppose things went wrong because I lacked the skills to control the magic, but now I gather that's because I'm not supposed to be able to use magic at all due to the dragon inside me. Did that shrub just move?"

The three women turned to look where I pointed.

"I don't think so. Do shrubs move on their own?" Cyrene asked doubtfully.

"No, of course they don't," May said calmly.

"Not normally, but what if those aren't ordinary shrubs?" I asked, watching one of the dark blobs with suspicion. "What if Drake did something to them?"

"Man, someone's going to give me the heebie-jeebies if she doesn't stop with all the inanimate-objects-moving-on-their-own bit," Jim muttered.

Aisling snorted. "I assure you he hasn't done anything other than make sure there's round-the-clock security on the house, and let me just add that it wasn't easy getting details on exactly who is here on guard duty, and when the shift change happens. I had to pretend I wanted to stay at this house in order to get the details, and even that wasn't easy. We're just lucky he had to go to Budapest for a couple of days to take care of some business concerns, because there is no way in Abaddon I could have slipped out without him knowing I was gone. Jim, stop leaning so hard on me. The bushes aren't evil. Ysolde is just seeing things."

"I'm sure it's just the moon going behind the clouds," May said after giving the shrub in question a considering look.

"Hmm." I looked at my own watch. Twelve minutes to go. "Is Gabriel away from home, as well, May?"

She smiled. "Home as in his house in Australia? No, we're still here in London until a few things are taken care of." She gave her twin an odd look, but Cyrene, sitting on the ground with her back to a tree, was too busy sending a text message to notice.

"Actually, I meant is he gone from your London house, so that you could help me out with this project."

"Oh, no. He's in England."

I raised my eyebrows. "Did you have to go into the shadow world to sneak out?"

"I didn't sneak out." Her smile widened. "Gabriel's here. Well, in Reevesbury, not out here with us, obviously."

Both Aisling and I gawked at her.

"He's right here?" Aisling asked.

"That Gabe's a deep one," Jim said as it wandered over to Cyrene, where it peered across her shoulder to read what she was texting. "Whoa, you're saying *that* to Neptune?"

"Jim!" Cyrene shoved it aside, hastily tucking her

phone into her pocket. "It's illegal to read someone's text messages!"

"In town here, yes," May repeated, dragging her gaze off her twin.

"Is Brom with him?" I asked, worried that Brom might somehow get involved with my plans.

"No, he's still in London with Maata and Tipene. I believe they were going to have a mummy movie marathon tonight. We thought it was best he stay there until you pick him up tomorrow. You didn't want Gabriel to bring him, did you?"

"No. Not that I think there's going to be any trouble, but I'm much more comfortable knowing he's out of the blast zone, so to speak."

May took in our worried expressions. "Don't worry that Gabriel's going to do anything to interfere with our plans. He realizes that this is probably our best shot of getting Baltic to lift the curse. Plus he never really saw the reasoning in keeping Thala prisoner any longer."

"A sane voice in a crowd of maniacs," I murmured.

To my surprise, Aisling laughed. "If you knew how often I've thought that about dragons . . . But you gotta love them despite their archaic rules."

Aisling, May, and I smiled. I thought of Baltic, so infuriating at times that he made me want to pull out my hair, and yet so filled with love that just thinking about what he'd been through had the power to bring tears to my eyes.

"Why don't you try your magic now?" May suggested as Cyrene rejoined us, Jim following her. "We've still got nine minutes. It would be a good opportunity to see if this Grace Dr. Kostich gave you will help."

"Good idea." I looked around for something upon which I could cast a spell.

"Oooh, magic!" Cyrene said. "I love magic. Can you change Jim into something? Like a toad?"

"Hey!" Jim protested, backing away from her.

"Tempting, but I think I should start smaller." I narrowed my attention on a small rock that was partially visible in the soil at the base of a nearby willow tree. "I'll do a simple spell to turn that rock into a tongue stone."

"What on earth is a tongue stone?" Aisling asked, moving next to me to watch as I picked up the rock and dusted off the bits of grass and dirt that clung to it.

"It's something that was taught to me by a member of a Serbian Romany tribe. They are traditionally made from small meteorites or, alternately, lightning-struck stones, and are highly charged with power that is used for divination purposes. Anyone can make a tongue stone, but since it's made by burying it and urinating on it"—I gave Jim a sharp look as its ears perked up—"I'll use the magical equivalent."

"Mage pee? Ew," Jim said, snuffling my hand as I passed my hand over the stone, drawing a pattern in the air.

"I've never actually seen a mage work," Aisling whispered to May. "I thought they did spoken spells, not wards."

"There are elements of both in mage work," I said, trying to find the place in my mind from which the magic flowed. I knew if I could just find it, I'd be able to cast the spell, but it seemed to be obscured by Baltic's dragon fire. I'd just have to use that instead.

"From the farthest star, to the deepest earth, stone

borne of lightning, to me you will speak." I held the stone over my head, drawing on the fire to imbue the stone with the power of divination. "Lightning-borne, wrought in fire, plunged in water, buried in earth. The elements combine in thee; reveal your true nature now!"

There was an instantaneous flash of blue-white light, thankfully silent. I lowered my hand, aware almost immediately that something had gone wrong.

"Er . . ." Aisling pursed her lips.

"That doesn't look right," May agreed.

I stared in surprise at the small brown and white rabbit that sat equally astonished on the palm of my hand. "Well, crap."

"A bunny!" Cyrene said happily, taking it from me.

Jim shouldered me aside to get to her. "You mean dinner! Yum."

"You even *think* about it and you're going to the Akasha," Aisling warned.

"It's not real," Jim objected. "It's really a rock. Right, Soldy?"

I went over the spell again, trying to figure out what I'd done wrong. "No, it was all correct. That should have done it," I said, shaking my head. "The tongue stone spell isn't anything at all like a polymorph spell. It should have worked. Why aren't you a stone?" I asked the rabbit.

It twitched its nose at me, then leaped from Cyrene's arms to scurry off into the night.

"You guys are no fun at all," Jim grumbled, watching it leave with much sadness.

"I think it's probably safe to say that your magic is still affected," May said, hesitating before she continued. "Perhaps we should do this another time, when it's been restored?"

"I don't know when I'm going to have another opportunity," Aisling said. "Drake doesn't like leaving the babies for long, and with all due respect to Gabriel, he won't entertain the subject of letting Thala go. I'm afraid that for Jim and me at least, it's going to have to be tonight."

"It'll be all right," I said after some thought. "I think the problem is that I had to use Baltic's fire, and not my happy place. That no doubt caused the spell to go a bit wonky."

"Your happy place? Is that anything like a door in your head that you open to see things differently?" Aisling asked.

"Not really. It's the place in my mind where my magic comes from. It's calm there, and filled with light, and I use that light to make things happen. The problem is that I haven't been able to find it since I came out of that last fugue, but I'm sure that's because of everything that's happened. Dr. Kostich used to tell us apprentices that we might occasionally lose track of our happy place, but we never lost it for long."

"I don't know about anyone else, but I would give good money to see Dr. Kostich say the words 'find your happy place' to someone," Jim said.

May laughed. "Me, too."

"You're sure your magic is up to this?" Aisling asked me. "If not, we can sacrifice Jim or something in order to get the same effect."

"Hey! Ixnay on the acrificesay!"

"It'll be fine," I reassured her, not feeling quite as confident. A lot was riding on my ability to break down the various protective spells that were no doubt covering all entrances to the house.

"Right." She consulted her watch. "We're almost at the zero hour. Everyone ready?"

There was a murmur of assent.

"I hope I get to use my Taser," Cyrene whispered to me as we followed May, who as the official shadow walker, took the lead to watch for any stray guards we hadn't pinpointed earlier. "I've been dying to try it out, but Kostya is just completely unreasonable and won't let me use it on one of his people."

I slid her a quick look, but said nothing other than that if everything went as we planned, we wouldn't need the Taser.

May waved us forward. We skulked along the edges of the eerie hedges, my unease not at all lessened by proximity with the hulking black shapes, but the thought of Cyrene at my back with a primed Taser gave me enough peace of mind to get past them to the side of the huge stone house. At the far corner of the house, the shadow of a man could be seen, no doubt one of the guards waiting to be relieved.

"This is interesting," Aisling said softly as she paused next to a window.

"What is?" I asked.

"That's a bane." She pointed at the window, sketching out a shape. "I assumed Drake wouldn't use them since the dragons need to get in and out of the house daily. But if he ordered up banes on all the entrances . . ."

"We're up excrement creek without a flotation device, not to mention a paddle," Jim finished. "You aren't thinking of using me for that bane, are you, Ash? Sweetie? Honey? Baby? You wouldn't do that, would you? 'Cause I just got my coat looking the way I like, and if you go and make me break that bane, it'll destroy my fabulous form, and—"

"And you won't stop bitching about that for months. Yes, we know," Aisling interrupted, patting the demon dog on its head. "Don't worry, I'm not going to try to break the bane. Those are three-demon jobbies, and we just don't have the time. Whoops. Incoming!"

We ran for the creepy hedge as the staticky sound of a walkie-talkie moved toward the dragon at the corner of the house.

"We should have about three minutes while they chitchat," Aisling whispered.

"This way." May melted into the darkness, with us following in a line. We went around the side to the back of the house, thick with shadows since the moon was behind clouds.

"No bane on this one," Aisling said softly. "This is it, ladies."

May and Cyrene held penlights as Aisling, muttering to herself, rolled up her sleeves and wrestled with the ward that had been drawn on the window to keep people from using it. After some words I felt were best ignored, she finally stood back, panting. "OK. Your turn, Ysolde. I can't do anything with the malediction, so it's all yours."

"What's a malediction?" Cyrene asked her twin as I reached out with both hands to touch the powerful spell woven into the surface of the window.

"It's like a bane, but uses dark magic as its source of power," May answered.

"But Ysolde doesn't have dark powers, does she? Why can she break it?"

"I can't," I said, trying to calm my mind and focus my attention on the feel of the malediction. "But arcane magic has much power against dark magic, and it can be used to break down dark spells. I think I have it, but just for safety's sake, everyone should probably stand back."

"Two minutes, thirty seconds," May said, glancing at her watch.

All three women moved backward into the deep shadows, leaving Jim standing next to me.

I glanced down at it.

"Never seen a malediction broken," it answered my unasked question. "Besides, it's not like you can turn me into a rabbit. I'm a demon. We don't polymorph easily."

It had a point. I closed my eyes, the feel of the malediction making my fingertips numb as I searched for the spot in my mind that would let me draw power from everything around me.

It wasn't there.

"One minute, forty seconds," May's voice reached me from the blackness. "You should probably hurry, Ysolde."

I shook out my hands, refocusing my attention. I could do this. I tried to hold a picture in my mind of the arcane magic, glowing bluish white, of the sensation of joy that manipulating it gave me. I tried to remember what it felt like to cast a spell and watch it succeed, but none of that helped me find the place in my mind that I so desperately sought.

"Dammit."

"One minute."

"Problems, Soldy?" Jim asked, nudging my hands.

"No." I bit my lip as I hesitated, but the feeling of the dragons around me decided me. "Here we go."

I placed my fingers back on the malediction, pulling hard on Baltic's fire, which always seemed to slumber within me. It roared to life, filling me with its power, racing down my veins until it sparked along my skin. I held the malediction for a second, then unleashed the full force of my magic upon it.

Golden light flashed before me, then reflected off the window and bounced away, dazzling my eyes in the process.

"Um . . . Ysolde?" Aisling's voice sounded strained as I blinked rapidly, trying to clear the stars from my vision. "I think we have a problem."

"What? Not another rabbit?" I squinted at the window, expecting to see it changed into a furry little rodent.

"Gloriosky!" Cyrene gasped. "Is that . . . is that . . ."

"Yes, it's me," Jim said, its voice filled with resignation.

I spun around and felt my jaw sag as I beheld a brawny dark-haired, dark-eyed man. A *naked* brawny man. "Jim?"

The man put his hands on his hips, his lips twisting sourly. "I can't tell you how much I hate human form!"

Chapter Six

"I've never been so mortified in all my life, and that includes the first time I was kicked out of the Court of Divine Blood for trying to get busy with the Sovereign's favorite collie, and that little misunderstanding with a male boggart who thought I was into bondage. Change me back!"

Aisling whapped the demon on its butt as May and I peered from the darkened room we'd climbed into, through the slightly opened door, to a lit hallway. "Hush, Jim! We'll deal with your situation once we have Thala out of here."

"Order me to change again! Maybe the first time didn't take because you weren't bossy enough, not that I believed I'd ever have a reason to say that, but still, Abaddon might have frozen over or something equally unbelievable."

"I think you look quite handsome, Jim," Cyrene told him. "And you have a really nice butt."

"Man, I just knew this was going to happen! Last time I got forced into human form, there were chicks all over me," Jim grumbled as it adjusted the sweater I'd given it, and Aisling's jacket, both of which it had tied around its waist as sort of a makeshift loincloth. "How am I going to suck Cecile's ears when I'm in this form, huh? Huh?"

"Jim, I know you're upset—" Aisling started to say, but fell silent at a gesture from May, who hurriedly closed the door, counting under her breath.

"Guards?" Cyrene asked almost inaudibly.

"Two of them," May answered, her ear pressed to the door. "You're sure Drake said Thala was on the third floor?"

"Positive," Aisling answered, jerking when a sudden buzzing started about her person. "Sorry! I thought I turned my phone off. Thank god I left it on vibrate. . . . Oh, no. It's Drake. I'm going to have to take this, ladies. Jim, go with them and be helpful. Yes, that's an order. Drake? Hi. What's up?" Aisling moved off to stand near the window.

"Let's go," May said after peeking through the door. "We have less than a minute before the shift change is over."

We left Aisling speaking softly to her dragon and hurried up thickly carpeted stairs until we reached the third floor. We hovered uncomfortably on the landing while May slipped into the shadow world to reconnoiter, returning almost immediately to urge us forward. "We're out of time. We've got to make this quick."

"I'm setting my Taser to stun," Cyrene said, fussing with her gadget as she followed behind us. We hustled down a vacant hallway, stopping in front of a door that bore obvious wards.

"We need Aisling," May said, eyeing them. "Unless you can do something with them, Ysolde?"

I glanced at Jim, who glared back at me, its arms crossed over its bare chest. "Er . . . I think that might not be as helpful as we'd all hope. I can go back and get . . . Never mind, here she comes."

Aisling all but ran down the hallway to us, her face pale. "Did you find her?"

"She's here, but there are wards, and Ysolde is understandably hesitant to try to undo them," May answered. "What's wrong?"

"Everything. We've got to get her out of here, right now. Drake found out I was gone, and it was a short hop from that to what we're doing. He had his jet turn around while they were over the Channel. He's furious, and no doubt calling up all the dragons in the area to rout us out and safeguard Thala." While she spoke, she worked on the wards, finally giving up to simply force her arm through them to open the door. In the dimly lit room sat a woman in an armchair, holding a book and looking up as Aisling, grunting and swearing, pushed herself through the wards into the room.

"Hi. You're Thala, right? I'm Aisling Grey. We're here to get you out, but we need to be quick because Drake knows what's going down."

The woman, of medium height with coppery brown hair, stood up slowly, confusion fading from her face at Drake's name. "Did Baltic send you?" she asked.

"Er . . . not really. I'm afraid we don't have time for you to collect your things. I'm also afraid I'm going to have to shove you through the wards, and it may pinch a little. I wish I could make this easier for you, but needs must and all that."

"Understatement of the year," Jim said with yet another pointed look at me.

"I said I was sorry," I told it quietly. "I don't know what happened to change you, but I'm really, really sorry, all right?"

While I was apologizing, Aisling pushed Thala through the wards, the latter's face distorting wildly as the ward fought to keep her from passing. But Aisling isn't a Guardian savant for nothing, and after only a few painful moments, she and Thala emerged from the grip of the ward, both of them panting as they collected themselves.

"Thank—" As Thala turned to thank Aisling, her gaze fell on me. Her eyes widened in shock for a few seconds, before filling with a fury unlike anything I'd ever seen. "Ysolde!" she hissed.

I took a step back at such blatant hostility. "Hello. I'm afraid I don't remember if we've met before."

"You live? How? You were beheaded! How did you survive that?" She grabbed my arm in a painful grip, shaking it as she spoke.

I jerked my arm back, rubbing the bruises she left. "I didn't. I was resurrected."

Her anger seemed to grow. "Who resurrected you!" she almost screamed.

Immediately both Aisling and May hushed her, glancing nervously down the hallway.

"This can wait. We have to get out of here. *Now*," May said authoritatively. "We'll go out the way we came."

"I'm not going anywhere with her," Thala said, her face suffused with color. I thought for a moment she was going to spit at me.

"She's the one who arranged for your release," Aisling pointed out.

"Why are you so angry with me? Did we know each other?" I asked, confused and hurt by her reaction to me. "Is it something to do with Baltic?"

"We really don't have time for this," May said, her head cocked to catch noises from the stairwell. "I hear more voices than I should. We need to move now."

"This way," Aisling said, pointing toward the hall behind Thala.

She crossed her arms and sent me a look that said in no uncertain terms that she'd have liked to see me beheaded again. "No. I will not leave with her."

"I don't understand why—" I started to say when Cyrene, with a roll of her eyes, reached out and shoved her Taser on the back of Thala's neck, causing the woman to jerk a few times before dropping to the ground, her eyes rolled back in her head.

"I love this thing," Cyrene commented with great satisfaction as she examined the results of her handiwork. "I'm going to carry it with me everywhere!"

"Thanks, Cy," May said, hurrying back to us. "Let's get her out of here."

"Why is she so pissed at me?" I asked, moving to her legs. "What did I do to her?"

"No clue, but we don't have time to work it out now." Aisling started to help me with her legs, then stood up. "It would take too long for us to carry her that way. Jim, so long as you're in human form, you can carry her."

"Me!" Jim squawked. "I'm a Newfie, not a pack mule!"

"You're also stronger than any of us, and we'll move faster if you sling Thala over your shoulder and carry her. Now get cracking! We have to get out of here before Drake lands at the nearest airport."

"I've said it before and I'll say it again—nothing good ever comes of human form," Jim complained as it bent over to pick up the unconscious woman.

"Goddess!" Cyrene squeaked, flinching and covering her eyes.

May shuddered and slipped into the shadow world.

I spun around so that my back was to the gruesome sight. "Aisling, much as I appreciate you helping, next time, can you make sure Jim is wearing at least a pair of underpants before it does that?"

"Sorry," she said, grimacing in sympathy.

"Hey! Not havin' fun here, either!" Jim grunted as it stood up, Thala flopping on its shoulder. "I think I just ruptured a spleen or two."

"I'll see how many of them there are," May said, her voice muffled and distant from the shadow world.

"Let's just hope that not too many of them have had time to arrive," Aisling said as we moved down the hallway.

"And that my spinal cord doesn't snap," Jim grumbled, awkwardly following us. I winced as it moved too close to a half-moon table, whacking Thala's head with a painful-sounding *thunk*.

"I can zap people," Cyrene offered, waving her Taser happily. "I bet I could get a good dozen dragons with it before the battery runs out."

"Too many," came a disembodied voice, followed shortly by May as she emerged from nothing. "There's at least a dozen outside, looking for signs of entry. Thank god we reset the window alarm once we got inside. They're focusing their search out there, not in the house itself."

"How are we going to get out?" I asked.

Jim groaned and leaned against the wall, partially

squashing Thala in the process. "You better decide quick, 'cause I think a kidney just imploded."

"I'll have to distract them," May said. "I'll slip out through a back window and lure them in the direction opposite of the car."

"These are Drake's men. . . . They might not recognize you, May, and Gabriel would have a hissy if any of them tried to harm you. They know me, though, so I'll go be the bait," Aisling said.

"How about we both go?" May suggested.

"I can go, too," Cyrene offered. "I can zap any of them that get too close."

"You stay with Jim and Ysolde," May answered, adding quickly when she saw Cyrene start to frown, "You'll be responsible for keeping them safe."

"Oh! Good idea! I'll zap the ones that come after us."

Jim groaned again. "Can we just go before my back compresses until I'm only four feet tall? I'd hate to see what that does to my fabulous Newfie form."

"Ysolde de Bouchier," Aisling said, taking my hand to draw a ward on my palm. "Unto you I bestow the power over my minions. Jim, stay with Ysolde until I can get you back, and stop complaining. We all know you'd rather be in dog form, and I'm sure we'll figure out how to make that happen, but until then, just do what Ysolde says and put some pants on as soon as you can."

We parted at the top of the stairs, Aisling and May promising to make a huge ruckus and draw attention away from the north side of the house.

"I'll call you tomorrow," Aisling said, then stopped herself and glanced at her watch. "Later today, actually, to make arrangements for Jim. Good luck, everyone!"

It took some time to get down to the ground floor,

since Jim insisted its shoulder was caving in, forcing it to reposition Thala. Unfortunately for her, it dropped her while trying to shift her to its other shoulder, but luckily no one seemed to hear the loud crash as she bounced down the last couple of stairs.

"She's going to be black and blue by the time you're done with her," I pointed out as Jim stuffed her through the window through which we'd entered the house.

"And your point is . . . ?" Jim said as it released Thala's legs, letting her slide through the window to the ground outside. "In case you missed the news flash, she's not the nicest person in the world. She tried to kill Kostya and Savian, not that the former is anything to worry about, but I like Savian. Whenever I stay with May and he comes over to visit, he slips me pastries."

"Sorry." Cyrene's voice drifted in through the window. "Was I supposed to catch Thala? I thought I heard a voice, and I wanted to see if he was Taserable. Are you guys coming?"

The ten minutes that followed had more in common with a Monty Python skit than a *Mission: Impossible* episode, but May and Aisling turned out to be the perfect decoys. As Jim staggered away from the house with Thala, I could hear the crackle of radios and shouts of alarm coming from the distance, to my great relief growing more and more distant as each minute passed. To Cyrene's intense disappointment, we didn't encounter a single dragon on our way out of the house's grounds, nor did she approve of my insisting that we hide should a stray dragon run past.

"What's the use of having a Taser if I can't zap dragons with it?" she complained.

"You'll just have to use it another time," I told her,

pausing to peer down the lane where we'd parked the car before waving everyone forward.

"Maybe Kostya will get out of line and I'll be able to nail him," she mused.

I shot her a curious glance. "Things not going well with the relationship?"

"Oh, it's not that," she said with a half shrug. "It's just that . . . well . . . this wyvern's mate business isn't all it's cracked up to be. Kostya insists that I put the welfare of the black dragons ahead of everything else, and I just can't. I'm a naiad! Ned says that's why mixed relationships don't work."

"Ned?" I dug out my car keys and unlocked the car.

"He's just a friend of mine," she answered coyly.

"Man, you're dating Neptune on the side? Kostya's going to blow a gasket when he finds out." Jim dropped Thala into the backseat. "Can I be there when you tell him?"

I gave Cyrene a long look before getting into the car. She slid into the front passenger seat, shooting Jim an irate glance as it shoved Thala's legs off the seat and climbed in next to our sleeping beauty.

"I am not dating Ned. I just happened to run into him a few times. We may have gone to dinner a couple of times when Kostya was off doing whatever it is that is so much more important than spending time with me, but that's it. There's nothing wrong with me seeing the head of the order of water elementals, you know. It's not like I'm madly in love with him or anything like that, even though he is really sensitive and understanding about everything to do with my spring, and he appreciates all the trouble I take over making sure that my lakes and rivers are all in tiptop shape, whereas Kostya just tells me it's a waste of time. A waste of time! Ha!"

So that was the way the wind was blowing. It was interesting, but really none of my business. I made a mental note to tell Baltic, though. I knew he would be interested in finding out that Kostya's quasi mate had evidently lost her rose-colored glasses where the volatile Kostya was concerned.

"Is Drake going to be very pissed at Aisling?" I asked Jim a few minutes later, as we drove through the night, heading toward the train station, where I would drop off Cyrene.

"Yeah, but she's got him wrapped around her little finger," it answered, its hands on its neck in an attempt to rub sore muscles. It hesitated, then corrected itself. "Most of the time she does. He'll probably be all pissy for a bit, but she'll sweet-talk him around. Or she'll flash a little boob and he'll cave."

"I hope it doesn't cause trouble between them." I wondered how bad it would be if Baltic discovered I'd gone against his wishes. A few of the memories granted to me of our past several hundred years drifted across my mind. It could be bad. "Well, at least this time he won't have anything to complain about," I said under my breath as I pulled out onto a main road.

Sometimes I really would give anything not to make such statements. It just seems to tempt fate.

An hour and a half later, I looked up and asked, "Did you get her settled?"

Jim stomped down the stairs from where it had deposited Thala in one of the spare bedrooms. "If by 'settled' you mean I dumped her on the bed and slapped a pair of handcuffs on her that you found, yeah. Can I say just how kinky it is that you had a pair of handcuffs right there? Do you use them on Baltic? Or does he use them on you?"

"Neither. They're Pavel's," I said, avoiding the demon's eye as I checked my phone. There was no response to the text I had sent Baltic saying we'd successfully retrieved Thala.

"Seriously? Man, and he looks so normal. Did you ever get to watch him—?"

"No," I interrupted quickly, deciding a change of subject was in order. I frowned at the demon as it squirmed uncomfortably. "What on earth is wrong with you?"

"Big Jim and the twins don't like it in there," it answered, tugging at the crotch of the jeans I'd lent it.

"Oh, for heaven's sake—you're the same size as Baltic, and I'm sure that your genitalia aren't so massive they can't fit into a pair of jeans."

"Yeah, well, you try stuffing a human package into a pair of jeans without a pair of shorts on," it answered, still squirming. "That's a sensitive area, you know! You can't just cram them anywhere and expect them to be comfortable."

"I told you to take what you needed from Baltic's closet. You could have gotten a pair of underwear."

"I'm not wearing another guy's shorts!" it answered, looking appalled. "I don't know where they've been! Well, I do, and that doesn't reassure me any. Plus, do you think Baltic would like knowing you're handing out his clothes?"

"I think he'd prefer that to having you wandering around wearing nothing but a sarong made of two sweaters. Stop clutching at yourself and sit down. I want to talk to you."

"Uh-oh," it said, backing away. "You've got that scary-mom look on your face. Talk about what?"

"Ouroboros dragons."

Jim blinked a couple of times. "You could at least feed me before you interrogate me."

"It's two o'clock in the morning, Jim. You don't need to eat now!"

"Sure I do. I spent a lot of energy hauling Thala around. She's no lightweight, you know."

I opened my mouth to protest, but thought better of it. Jim was an endless mooch for food, and would likely be more forthcoming if it was fed. "All right, I'll make you a blue-cheese-stuffed burger, but you will tell me everything you know about outlaw dragons."

"Deal, but it ain't much, only a few things I've picked up from Ash and Drake."

By the time I made us each a burger, Jim had acclimatized itself to wearing clothing and sat docilely enough at the kitchen table.

"Baltic said that Fiat and some of his followers had been named ouroboros recently," I said, sitting down to my very belated dinner. "I know those dragons are considered outlaws now, but what about the others?"

"What others?" it asked around a mouthful of hamburger.

"Surely there are other dragons who have been kicked out of their septs at one time or another? Or are the blue dragons it?"

Jim shrugged, dribbling a bit of blue cheese as it chewed. "I don't know of any personally, but there were some at Kostya's aerie, or so Gabriel said, and I don't know why he'd lie about that unless it was ex–silver dragons holding Kostya prisoner, and I think he'd know if it was."

"Kostya," I said slowly, considering Baltic's former friend. "I'd forgotten that he was holed up in an aerie for so long. Who held him prisoner?"

"Dunno. Drake still hasn't figured it out, and although he talks about going back to the aerie to look for clues, he's too busy fawning over Aisling and the spawn to go to Nepal again."

"What does Drake have to do with it?"

"He went to rescue Kostya and got nabbed himself. Ash and I rounded up a posse and went to rescue them. I lost a couple of toes in the process, but got them back again with my fabulous new form." Jim looked down at itself with morose dissatisfaction. "My former fabulous new form. When are you going to change me back?"

"I don't know how to, or even that I could if I did know. So Drake was at the aerie, too? That means he must have seen the ouroboros dragons as well. Hmm. I think I'm going to have to talk to Kostya, since Drake is probably quite angry and not likely to tell me what I want to know."

Jim cocked an eyebrow and licked a bit of mustard off its upper lip. "And you think Kostya will tell you?"

"Yes," I said after a moment's thought. "His animosity toward Baltic aside, yes, I think I can get him to open up. If the dragons who imprisoned Kostya did so before Fiat and his followers were removed from their sept, then that means there must be two separate tribes out there. But who are the second group? And why would they want Kostya imprisoned? Why would they want to steal things from the L'au-dela?"

"You got me. You going to eat that half?" Jim asked, nodding toward the remains of my hamburger.

"Go ahead, but don't come running to me if you've got an upset stomach in the morning." I shoved the plate across the table to it and rose. "I'm going to get a few hours' sleep. Can you keep an eye on Thala until I get up?"

"Aw, man! Why do I get guard duty?"

"Because you're the only one here other than me, and you're a demon who doesn't technically need sleep, whereas I'm human. Er . . . kind of. And I do need sleep."

"Shows what you know. Demons need sleep just like any other sentient being," Jim grumbled.

"It'll just be for a few hours." I cleaned up the table quickly and started for the back stairs.

"Can I at least have a gun or a Taser like Cyrene had?"

I paused at the foot of the stairs, glancing back at the demon. There was a genuine look of distaste on its face. Insight struck me. "You truly do not want to be near Thala, do you?"

It shook its head.

"Why not?"

"She's not nice," it said with a grimace.

"Not nice as in she's mean to demons? Abuses dogs?" I asked, curious to know why a demon of its power and connections would be so uncomfortable around Thala.

"She's got a lot of power," Jim said after a few moments' pause. "She's half dragon, you know."

"I know, but I also know she's a necromancer, and

that has no influence on demons, so there's no reason for you to be worried about being around her."

Jim said nothing, but it was clear there was more it could say. I thought for a moment of invoking a demon lord's privilege to make it speak, but decided that it wasn't that important. "Take a knife if you're worried, but don't hurt her unless you have no other choice."

"What do I do if she's gotta pee?" it asked in a plaintive tone as I started up the stairs.

"Undo her handcuffs and let her use the bathroom, silly."

"But she'll whomp me!"

I bit back the urge to tell him to whomp her back. "Since she's hostile toward me, I don't want her to leave the house until Baltic gets back and can talk to her, so just do your best for a few hours, OK? Wake me at six, and I'll take over watchdog duty."

Jim's grumbles followed me up the stairs. While I got undressed, I eyed the big bed that normally dominated the room. At least it did when Baltic was around, but now it just looked cold and lonely.

I miss you, I texted to him before climbing into the empty bed. *I hope everything is going OK at Dauva. Call me when you can. Oh, and I am head over heels in love with you, and wish you were here right now so I could touch you in all sorts of wicked ways.*

Smiling to myself that the text should get a response out of him sooner rather than later, I settled down to get a little sleep, not that I expected to get much since I didn't sleep well when Baltic wasn't there to keep me warm. Exhaustion claimed me, however, and I slipped into insensibility clutching my phone.

Chapter Seven

"Then we are agreed, are we not?"

I rolled over to see who was talking in my bedroom, only to find I wasn't in a bedroom.

"Another vision," I sighed as the fog of sleep dissipated, leaving me standing next to a long, highly polished table around which five people sat. "I don't suppose anyone can hear or see me?"

"Unless Drake Vireo has anything to add," a female voice said with sultry smoothness. No one paid the slightest iota of attention to me, so I gathered I was seeing another vision of an event at which I wasn't present.

"I know that voice." I turned to consider Chuan Ren and a man at her side who I assumed was her mate. Going by her dress and elegant coiffure, I judged that this event took place around the turn of the twentieth century.

"Drake has, I believe, spoken on the subject, but perhaps he has something else he wishes to say?" The original speaker, a blond man with a lilting Italian accent, asked the question with a polite little nod down the table.

"I do not have anything more to say about the black dragons than I've already said." Drake's voice was just as urbane as it was now. I looked across the table to where he sat, his two guards behind him. "The sept is destroyed. No black dragons have been seen for almost a hundred years. Constantine Norka conducted the extermination most thoroughly."

"We had every right to take action against those who would have destroyed us," a man across the table snapped back. I looked at him, noting he was most definitely *not* Constantine. This man was dark-skinned, with close-cropped black hair and dark eyes, a tribal tattoo evident on his neck despite the high starched collar and black suit typical of an Edwardian gentleman. To my surprise, behind him stood someone else I knew: Gabriel, also clad in a black suit, but with an embroidered silver vest that almost matched his eyes. The dreadlocks were gone, and he was clean-shaven, but the look of wary caution in his eyes was all too familiar. "Which the green wyvern well knows, since he was at the *sárkány* that decreed we had the right to pursue our subjugators."

Drake bowed his head in acknowledgment, but I noticed his jaw was tight. I smiled a little smile at that, wondering how much it had cost him to keep from lashing out at the silver wyvern. Then again, perhaps he knew that Kostya was at that moment alive and well, living in the hidden aerie. I'd have to ask Aisling if she knew.

"As the requisite amount of time has passed since a member of the black sept has been seen, the weyr officially declares the sept to be extinct and, as such, stricken off the rolls."

The silver wyvern watched Drake closely, but although his eyes glittered with an emerald light, Drake's face was impassive, as were those of István and Pál, his guards whom I had briefly met some months before.

"The second order of business is the recognition of Sial Fa'amasino as official rather than acting wyvern of the silver sept." The Italian gave a pointed look at the silver dragons. "Do you have proof of the death of the wyvern Constantine Norka?"

"No. His body has not been discovered, despite our searches for it." Sial's voice was steady, but his dark eyes were watchful, as if he half expected trouble.

The Italian dragon hesitated for a moment before saying, "It is not for the weyr to interfere in sept business, but there is tradition to be considered. I don't think there is precedence for a wyvern simply disappearing with no claim of his death. Is it your contention that Constantine Norka is not dead?"

"It is not," Sial said firmly. "Were he alive, he would be here before you. We have sought him for a century, but we have come to the much-regretted conclusion that he met with harm, either from another sept or from an accident that was beyond our knowing."

Silence filled the room for the count of seven. "As I said, it is not for the weyr to interfere; thus so long as you have the consent of your sept to be named as wyvern, we will so recognize you. How say you, wyverns?"

The other wyverns murmured their assent.

"Then Sial Fa'amasino is so named as wyvern of the silver sept. Our last business concerns the silver dragons as well, specifically the attacks made upon members of the sept by ouroboros dragons."

"I thought they must be black dragons, but they are not," the new silver wyvern told the others. "I sent one of my guards to track them after the last attack, and he said their former sept was not discernible without closer contact."

"The weyr would recognize Gabriel Tauhou and question him about this," the blue dragon said politely, obviously giving Sial the opportunity to grant his permission.

"I didn't think you guys could be more formal than you are now, but I see I was wrong," I told them as Sial graciously allowed Gabriel to speak before the weyr.

"Where did the attacks originate?" the blue wyvern asked him.

"Cape Town, in the Transvaal. With my father's help." Gabriel nodded toward the small collection of people who sat along one wall. One of the men, I noticed, was dark-skinned and similar in appearance to Gabriel. He sat with two other men, all of whom watched the proceedings with grim expressions. "We tracked them northward, to Vereeniging, but lost their trail." Gabriel slid an unreadable glance toward Chuan Ren. "That's where we found two red dragons, obviously following a similar track."

Chuan Ren pursed her lips for a moment before answering with a languid wave of her hand, "The red dragons have also been attacked by these ouroboros ones, but we do not go running to the weyr to solve our problems."

Sial stiffened, but said nothing, although ire flashed for a moment in his eyes.

"And did you find where the ouroboros were based?" the blue wyvern asked.

One shoulder lifted in a delicate shrug. "No. My men lost them in the bush as well. It matters not. We have taken steps to protect ourselves from attacks by any sept."

Drake's gaze flashed to her. She smiled at him, a cat-with-a-giant-bowl-of-cream sort of smile. What on earth did that mean? I added that to my mental notes to ask Aisling.

"If you are implying that we welcome a war with the red dragons, I will assure you yet again that such an assumption is false," Drake said.

"Bah! You do everything you can to instigate a war with us!" The smile faded from Chuan Ren's face. "We are not stupid, nor are we blind to your machinations!"

"What machinations?" Drake demanded. "State just one thing that the green dragons have done to harm your sept!"

"Oh, lord, this is going to take forever," I muttered to myself, and turned to look for a chair since this vision was evidently going to take a bit.

Kaawa sat behind me, separated from Gabriel's father, dressed in a flowing robe and matching turban, her hands clasped in her lap as she watched the *sárkány*. Another woman sat on her far side, similarly dressed, and just as obviously a member of the silver sept. Next to them was a little girl of about four who sat in a stiff blue dress with a ruffled white pinafore, her black hair twisted into two stubby little braids, her bright silver eyes marking her as another silver dragon.

"I hope you don't mind if I sit next to you,' I told Kaawa, taking the chair on her free side.

"No, of course not," she murmured, causing me to freeze for a moment before looking at her in astonishment.

"What's that?" the other woman asked her, leaning toward us, speaking in a soft voice so as not to disturb the *sárkány*.

"You can hear me?" I asked Kaawa. "You can see me?"

"What was what?" Kaawa asked her friend in a whisper.

"You said 'Of course not.'"

"Don't be ridiculous. Why would I say that?"

My spirits fell. She couldn't hear me after all. Perhaps it was just a coincidence. Or was it? I leaned close to her, my mouth just a few inches from her ear. "Gabriel looks much better with his goatee."

"I told him not to shave it off. It gives him such character, but—" Kaawa froze, blinking wildly as she slowly looked around. I waved, but her gaze went right through me.

"What's wrong?" her friend asked, poking her on the arm.

"I don't quite know," Kaawa answered.

The little girl slid off her seat and said something in a language I didn't understand, tugging on the arm of the woman I assumed was her mother.

"Hush, Maata. Kaawa is not feeling well."

"Maata?" I grinned at the little girl as she, looking incredibly bored, climbed back onto her seat and, with a defiant look at her mother, stuck her thumb in her mouth. I laughed, thinking that even then Gabriel's guard showed signs of doing just as she pleased.

Kaawa shot a look to the side nearest me even as she assured her friend in whispers that she was fine.

I turned back to the dragons, momentarily distracted when Chuan Ren leaped to her feet, yelling something about Drake trying to take things that were not his. Drake, looking bored, crossed his arms and let her rant.

"Boy, that gets old fast," I said.

"Who are you?" Kaawa's voice was so soft, I almost didn't hear it.

I waved a hand in front of her face, but she obviously didn't see it, and I suspected she heard me only now and again. "It must have something to do with you being a shaman," I told her. "I'm Ysolde."

She heard that all right. She sat up very straight, her eyes wide and staring at nothing in particular. Her friend was busy trying to get Maata to remove her thumb from her mouth, and didn't hear when Kaawa, speaking without moving her lips, said, "You are a shade?"

"I'm not dead, no. Well, I was, but then I was resurrected. It's a long story."

Her expression didn't change, her gaze not moving one whit. Thinking she must not have heard that explanation, I leaned in close and added, "I know you, Kaawa. You're my friend."

"I will befriend no shade. That way lies madness," she said simply, and turned to her friend, clearly dismissing me.

I felt bereft for a moment, separated by time and space from everything going on around me, from the noise and furor of Chuan Ren in full hissy fit as she stormed around the *sárkány* table, trying to get a rise out of Drake, to the blue wyvern trying to restore order, to Sial as he chimed in when some slurs were evidently cast his way.

Gabriel turned to share a smile with his mother, immediately looking concerned when she didn't respond.

I was alone, separated from the dragons around me by centuries of time and understanding. I shivered, suddenly cold and filled with sadness. I knew I couldn't change any of the events that would unfold, but that knowledge did little to comfort me. I covered my face with my hands, wishing the vision would end, wishing the noise would stop, needing Baltic to restore order to the world.

"Why do you weep?" a disembodied voice asked me.

"All those blue dragons who will die . . . if only I could warn them. If only I could make Kaawa understand me. She could stop it. She could stop it all."

"Who is Kaawa?"

The words were whipped away on the wind almost before I could hear them. I turned toward the voice, the sting of spray making me squint. I was on a ship, strands of hair flying around me, partially obscuring my view as we plowed through the waves. "What?"

"I asked you whom you spoke of, and why you are weeping."

Baltic's large body blocked some of the wind and spray, allowing me to wipe my wet face with the edge of my damp cloak. "I wasn't weeping. I was thinking about retching, but thankfully that seems to have passed."

His arms surrounded me, pulling me into the safe haven of his chest. "Our babe is giving you grief again?"

"Not so much anymore. I thought I would have been horribly sick because of this awful sea, but it seems to make the illness better."

"Good. I dislike you feeling unwell and blaming the babe. And me, for putting him in your belly." His voice was a rumble that started deep in his chest. I turned my face into the soft linen of his tunic, smiling into his collarbone.

"I didn't really mean what I said, you know. I'm not sorry that you ever came to my father's castle, or that I didn't set you on fire while you were sleeping after the first time you bedded me."

Laughter was rich in his voice as he kissed the top of my head and pulled me tighter. "Or geld me with a blunt knife?"

"Especially not the gelding. In fact"—I wiggled against him, the scent and feel of him doing much to stir my passion—"just the opposite. I don't suppose you have time for a little dalliance?"

He pulled back to give me a wicked look. "Are you attempting to seduce me, *chérie*?"

"Oh, yes." I tipped my head back to nip his lower lip. "And to thank you for taking me to England so I may see my parents. My mother will be thrilled to know we are to have a child."

His lips thinned for a moment. "Not as thrilled as my father."

"Your father is an ass," I told him, sliding out of his embrace and giving him a come-hither look as I moved toward steps that led down to the cabins.

"Do you have any idea what would happen if he heard you say that?" Baltic asked, following with a glint of appreciation in his dark eyes. "Heads would roll at the very least."

"I prefer something else be rolled," I said with a hint of a leer as I slipped down the stairs.

"I have heard that women who are breeding often have unnatural appetites for men. I am pleased that you are experiencing this, although I will remind you that you must not be too inventive with your ways to drive me insane with lust, lest you harm the babe. I insist that you allow me to decide what is safe for you to do, and not try to coerce me into performing intricate acts of lovemaking, as you did last night. Ysolde! Cease that! I just got through telling you that you are not to do that! Or that. For the love of the saints, what are you doing with . . . oh, very well, just this once, but this is the last time, do you hear me? After this, you will do as I say!"

I giggled at the arrogance in his voice, feeling warm and loved, and pleased with the world despite the many cares that burdened me.

"You are happy, my love?"

"Oh, yes," I said on a breath, snuggling down deeper into the soft warmth of the mattress.

"As am I. I, too, missed you."

Heat started to lick up my back, spreading outward in a slow glow of passion. Warmth nuzzled my neck in a way that left me simultaneously boneless and lit by a fire from within.

"I have to say, much as I love these visions, the real thing is so much better."

"Mmm." The heat suddenly pulled away from me, leaving me feeling bereft. "Ysolde."

"Make love to me," I pleaded, moving restlessly in the warm cocoon of the bed.

"Not until you wake up."

I opened my eyes to see our bedroom, not the small, dark-paneled cabin of the ship upon which we'd sailed so many hundreds of years ago. "Baltic?"

"Yes. It is the real me, not the past version, which you seem to be obsessed with watching in moments of lovemaking. And now you demand that you participate in those past moments?" He rolled me over onto my back, all warm, and male, and infinitely desirable. The emotions of the vision lingered enough that I purred as I stroked my hand up his bare chest despite his frown and outrageous accusation.

"I did participate. We both did, so you can stop looking at me like I'm some sort of Peeping Tom pervert. And besides, I can't help it. You were extremely sexy, you know."

His frown deepened.

I licked his lower lip. "But now . . . *mrowr.*"

"I approve of your *mrowr,*" he said, letting me kiss him. I pushed him over onto his back, reaching under his pillow as I reveled in the taste and feel of him.

"Fire?" I murmured, twining my tongue around his. His fingers were busy pushing up the satin of my nightgown, stroking a path up my legs that left me squirming.

"You have your own—" he started to say, but I wouldn't let him finish.

"Fire!"

He tried to flip me over onto my back, but I held him down. "You are becoming entirely too demanding, mate. And I have been too accommodating. You forget that I am the wyvern."

"Oh, I haven't forgotten that," I cooed, nibbling along his jaw. His hands caressed my hips, then moved around to my behind when I bit his earlobe. "Before we died, did I ever tie you up and have my wanton way with you?"

"I am a wyvern. I am the one who is dominant, not my

mate." He groaned when my hand swept down his chest to his belly at the same time I gently bit the tendons of his neck. "I would not have allowed you to restrain me."

"Good. Then this should be a novel experience for you." I slid back enough for him to see the object I'd pulled out from under the pillow.

"No," he said, giving it and me a stern look.

"Oh, yes, Baltic."

"No. Where did you get them?"

"Pavel's room." I looked at the leather-and-sheep's-wool wrist restraints. "I was looking for . . . er . . . Did you get my text message about Thala?"

"Yes. I am pleased that you convinced the other mates to go against their wyverns and free her. She's here?"

"Yes. She's . . . uh . . . sleeping," I answered, thinking about the sleeping aid I'd managed to slip into the beverage she had demanded once she came out of her shock-induced stupor.

"I will see her in the morning. But first, we have been parted, and I must claim you now."

I laughed at the matter-of-fact way he said it. "That's just exactly what I'm planning, only with a little twist."

"What part of 'I am the wyvern' do you not understand?" he asked, pinching me on the behind. "I will use the cuffs on you. Perhaps someday I will allow you to reciprocate, but for now—"

"Oh, no. It's my idea, so I get to go first." I wrapped one cuff around his wrist and tried to pull his arm up toward the headboard. It didn't budge. I looked from the rounded bulge of his bicep to his face. "Please, Baltic? You're always telling me I'm obsessed with our past sex life. I just want to try something we haven't done before. I promise you will get great pleasure from it."

"I always have great pleasure making love to you," he pointed out.

I leaned down and kissed him again, swirling my tongue along his lower lip. "I'll rouse my dragon fire if you let me do this."

He narrowed his lovely dark eyes at me. "Are you trying to bribe me?"

"Yes."

He sighed, and reluctantly let me pull his arm upward, over his head. "I am growing too soft with you. I would say that you have no respect for me, but the truth is that you never did. This is the last time, though, mate. I will allow you to have your way in this because you wish to separate your memories of our past from the present, but this is the last time I will be so cooperative."

I smiled and dipped my head to swirl my tongue around one pert little nipple that seemed to be begging for just such attention. He sucked in his breath, and quickly I put the other cuff on his wrist, securing that arm, too.

He looked from one arm to the other, then to me. "I do not like this. You will hurry and satisfy yourself upon me so that I may claim you as is right and proper."

"Oh, I'm going to satisfy more than just me." I moved off the bed and padded over to a discreet stereo system.

"First you demand to restrain me, and then you leave? What is this torment?" Outrage dripped off his words as I contemplated a small collection of CDs. I picked out one and popped it on the player, turning back to face him.

"This, my darling, is Shania Twain. She and I are going to make sure that you're receptive to all the things I want to do to you."

"Music? You desire music now?"

"We never had music while making love before," I pointed out, tossing my head as my favorite song started. "It all goes along with things we haven't done in the past. Did I ever do a striptease for you?"

"No. I am not aroused by such things, and my old Ysolde would never have lowered herself to attempting to distract me suchly." His eyes widened as, moving to the bouncy music, I ran my hands down the slinky satin nightgown, mouthing "Man! I Feel Like a Woman!" to him as I started to hike the material up my legs. I accompanied the move with a few hip shakes that had his eyebrows raising.

"Perhaps I was overly hasty in my assessment of your dance," he finally said, watching with an avid light as I danced closer to him, leaning over his head so my breasts almost popped out of the thin material.

He tried to reach for me, but Pavel's cuffs stopped him. He made a noise of unhappiness, and was about to yank himself free when I stopped him by stroking my hand down his chest, from his collarbone, all the way down to where his penis was saluting. "Oh, no, you don't. You said I get to be in charge, and I say you have to lie there and take this."

"Take wha—" His eyes rolled back in his head when I bent down and took him in my mouth, letting my tongue dance along the length of him, making him moan nonstop.

"We will purchase a new pair of these restraints for Pavel," he said when I danced away, twitching the skirt of my nightgown even higher. "I wish to keep this set."

"I thought you might like them once you gave them a chance," I said, crawling onto the bed, sliding my hands along his legs until he parted them for me. I bent down and nipped at the muscle just above one knee. "You have such wonderful legs, Baltic. I love your calves. I love your knees. And your thighs make me melt."

There was hope in his eyes as I kissed my way along the sensitive inner flesh of his thighs. "I remember that about you. You used to tell me that you would never have fallen in love with me if I hadn't loved to ride."

I laughed. "Well, I won't go so far as to say that your horseman's thighs are what made me love you, but I admit"—I spread my fingers along his thighs—"they are impressive even now that you don't ride."

"I ride, just not a horse," he answered with a wicked glint to his eyes.

"I think, my adorable captive, that this time I will be the one doing the riding." I leaned across him, allowing my hair to drape across his belly. His breath hissed in as I sucked the closest nipple, gently tugging on it at the same time I teased the other.

"Do so now," he urged, his breath becoming ragged, his legs moving restlessly.

"Oh, no. Not so fast. I want to enjoy the experience of having you tied up." I licked his belly, focused for a moment on stirring my dormant dragon's fire, but gave up.

"That is my fire, not yours," he said with a tiny frown as I bathed his torso in fire. It skimmed along him, dancing as exuberantly as my fingers when they stroked and teased and touched their way down toward his groin.

"I'm sorry. I just couldn't raise mine. I'll try again another time. But now . . ." I flicked my hair so it slithered along the length of his arousal. He shivered in pleasure, his hips bucking when I whipped off my nightgown, and pressed my breasts around him.

"Mount me!" he commanded, his head thrown back, the tendons in his neck standing out with strain.

"I am the one in charge, if you remem—"

There was a snap of leather, and suddenly I was pulled upward until his penis was pressed against me. He shifted me slightly so that he rubbed against parts that suddenly became highly sensitized, causing me to moan with pleasure. I slid my knees along his hips as his hands busied themselves with my breasts, tweaking and tormenting and generally making me see stars.

"Mount me!" he commanded again, and this time I didn't bother to object; I simply positioned him and gasped with the sensation of him entering me. His hands on my hips urged me into movement, the friction of our bodies sending me on a spiraling path that I knew would end in a moment of purest ecstasy.

"Fire," I gasped, and he complied, his dragon fire sweeping down my flesh as he pulled me forward to catch his cry of completion, my muscles tightening around him in absolute pleasure.

What seemed like an aeon later, I pushed myself off his chest to give him an unhappy look.

"Why do you frown at me?" he asked, rolling us over, his leg heavy over mine as he pulled me tight against him. "I just gave you such intense pleasure I thought you might wrench off my cock."

"I'm frowning because not only did you break Pavel's nifty leather handcuffs, but you took over and wouldn't let me do all the things I had planned to do."

To my surprise he grinned as he kissed my forehead. "You were too much for me, mate. I would have spilled my seed if you hadn't mounted me when you did."

"It's very hard to be disgruntled with someone when

they tell you that you've given them pleasure," I said, sighing with happiness as I snuggled into the warmth of his body. "But now we're going to have to buy two sets of the leather cuffs, one for Pavel, one for us."

"Three sets. I shall get a smaller set for you. And perhaps a few other things. I will ask Pavel for recommendations."

I smiled, kissing his shoulder, content for the moment to leave the worries of life behind and just revel in the fact that Baltic was in my arms, safe and happy.

Chapter Eight

"Heya, Solders. Whatcha doing?"

I set down my cup of coffee and gawked at Jim as it and Pavel came in from the area that contained the garage. "Gawking. What on earth are you wearing?"

"Kilt!" Jim did a little twirl so the material spun out. Sure enough, the demon was wearing a kilt and a muscle T-shirt.

"By the rood, man! Don't do that before I've had my coffee!" I tried to expunge certain images from my brain. "Why are you wearing a kilt?"

"Pavel took me to buy it in town," Jim answered, plopping itself down on a chair at the kitchen table and helping itself to a fresh-baked scone. "Ooh, orange cranberry—my favorite. Pavel, my man, got any marmalade to go with it?"

I looked over Jim's head to where Pavel was pouring himself a cup of coffee. "Why did you buy Jim a kilt?"

He shrugged and gave me a half smile. Pavel was

dark-haired and dark-eyed like Baltic, but slightly shorter and a bit stockier. He'd been one of Baltic's elite guards for centuries before they had found me, and although I knew he had some interesting ideas of what constituted sexual fun, he was also profoundly devoted to Baltic and the best cook I knew. We spent many a long hour discussing the finer points of cuisine, much to Baltic's amusement.

"The demon said its nuts were being squashed in Baltic's jeans. It kept wanting to take off the trousers, and I figured its presence was going to go down easier if it didn't have its dick hanging out." Pavel gave me a long look. "Do I want to know why the demon is here in the first place? Baltic isn't going to be happy about it."

"Yes, but there's something else he's going to be a whole lot less happy about, so Jim's presence won't really matter. Besides, it's just temporary. We can take Jim home when we pick up Brom." I took a big sip of coffee, feeling it was better to face Baltic caffeinated than otherwise.

"Oh?" Pavel asked, looking suddenly wary.

"It's . . . uh . . . kind of complicated."

Jim snorted, its mouth full of scone. "You can say that again."

"I was just sitting here waiting for the explosion, as a matter of fact." I gave both of them a smile.

Pavel left off looking wary and went straight for worried. "What sort of a—"

Upstairs, a door slammed, followed immediately by a bellowed, "*Ysolde!*"

"That would be it," I said, quickly draining my cup before getting to my feet. The thunder of footsteps stamping down the back stairs warned of Baltic's imminent arrival.

"Enter the deranged wyvern Baltic," Jim muttered, taking another scone.

Baltic appeared in the doorway, his eyes glittering with an obsidian light, his jaw set with a firmness that boded ill for anyone who crossed his path. He started toward me, pausing when he saw Jim.

"Hiya, Balters. Like my kilt? Pavel got it for me because the ol' meat and two veg were gettin' antsy being stuffed away in your jeans."

Baltic turned his gaze to me, and I knew at that moment if he could have shot death rays from his eyes, he would have.

"I imagine you've seen Thala?" I asked, pretending for all I was worth that nothing whatsoever was the matter. "Is she awake?"

"Barely. It appears she has been drugged heavily. She is also handcuffed." He breathed loudly through his nose for a few seconds. "She demanded I remove you from the house immediately. I refused. What is that demon doing here, why is it in human form, and what the hell have you done to Thala?"

"Jim came with me to help with Thala. I couldn't carry her by myself. Would you like some breakfast? Pavel made scones earlier, but if you'd prefer something with more substance, I can whip up—"

"Mate!" Baltic bellowed again, effectively squashing my attempt at innocence.

I sighed and stood up, wrapping my arms around his waist before kissing his chin. "Jim is in human form because my magic is still wonky. Thala is drugged and handcuffed because she got nasty about us rescuing her once she found out she had to come with me—something I don't quite understand—and I lost the key to the handcuffs, so I couldn't undo them before you got up this morning. Pavel, we owe you for a pair of handcuffs, too."

Baltic glared down at me for a few moments, then hoisted me upward, and kissed the breath right out of my body, filling me with his dragon fire. By the time he set me back on my feet, I was a bit dazed with both his action and the ferocity of the kiss. "You are jealous," he said, looking very pleased. "It does not surprise me, since you were always so."

"I'm not at all—"

"You need not fear that Thala holds my affection as you do. She is the one who resurrected me, and thus I owe her a debt of gratitude. That is all."

"I didn't drug her because of—"

"She helped me reacquaint myself with the world, and find Pavel, and for both I am grateful, but not to the extent that you must keep her drugged and handcuffed to satisfy your need to separate us." Baltic gave my behind a little squeeze. "I am bound to you, mate, and no other female can change that."

"Yes, I'm aware of that, but—"

"Excellent. You will cease being jealous of her now that you understand that my affections do not waver. Pavel, do you have an extra key? Good. Let us go release Thala, and then she can tell us what the wyverns questioned her about."

Baltic marched off with Pavel in tow, the latter grinning at me as he passed.

"I am not jealous!" I yelled after the two men. "I never was! Oh, for the love of the saints, sometimes that man drives me bonkers."

"Yeah, but the makeup sex is always good, huh?"

I shot Jim a quelling look. "It was bad enough when you said things like that while in dog form. Now it's just creepy. We have to pick up Brom in three hours—that gives us a bit of time to work on changing you back. If you could call Aisling and tell her that we'll leave you with May and Gabriel, I'll go make sure that Baltic got Thala unlocked and then meet you out in the side garden."

"Why the garden?" it asked as I headed for the stairs.

"I think best around plants. And . . . er . . . there's nothing to break if my magic goes weird again."

"Nothing except me," Jim said forlornly, but it obediently rose and went to the phone.

"Hmm. I wonder . . ." I marched up the stairs puzzling over the thought that something other than the interdiction could be seriously wrong with my magic, which would explain why the summoning of the First Dragon didn't work. "It worked before, though. What's changed since the *sárkány*?"

The sight of Baltic and Pavel holding up a still muzzy-headed Thala between them drove that thought out of my brain. Despite Baltic's smug look (which I decided was more tolerable than a pissed-off look), I helped them get her downstairs and into the kitchen, and when I left them, Baltic was trying to pour milky coffee down her gullet while Pavel was likewise shoving in bite-sized bits of scone.

"Thank god she's not mortal and can't choke to death," I said to myself as Thala sputtered out bits of coffee-laden scone.

I found Jim contemplating a lovely yellow rosebush.

"Don't even think about it!" I warned.

It sighed, its shoulders slumped. "I wouldn't. There's no fun in peeing on things with a human package. It's just so ordinary."

"Moving past that, let's get this over with before Baltic gets Thala awake enough that she can talk without spewing out scone crumbs. I want to hear what she has to say about her captivity."

"Yeah, should be good, especially if Drake had her tortured." It must have seen the look on my face because it hurriedly added, "I'm sure Ash wouldn't let him do that. For a badass demon lord, she's totally wimpy when it comes to hurting people."

"I'm reassured to hear that. All right, sit down, and let me concentrate on what I need to do." I calmed my somewhat frazzled mind and tried once again to access that magical spot in my brain that gave me access to arcane powers. It remained elusive, just on the fringes of my consciousness, so close I could almost see it. Dragon fire was there, banked as usual when I wasn't physically near Baltic, but it glowed hot in my mind, and I couldn't help but wonder if it was that which had upset the balance of my magic. "I'll just have to try it regardless."

"Oh, man, that doesn't fill me to the brim with confidence," Jim said, its eyes filled with foreboding. "You'd make a horrible motivational speaker, babe. Aren't you supposed to be in charge and professional, like Aisling?"

I stared at it. "Good lord, no. Magic isn't at all orderly."

"I'm gonna die!" it wailed.

"Be quiet, I'm intoning." I turned to the east. "Air surrounds thee." I faced south. "Fire fills thee."

Jim stopped whimpering, watching me with curious eyes. "Calling the quarters, eh? Aisling does that, but she says different stuff."

"Hush." I turned north. "Earth nourishes thee." Finally, I faced west. "Water gives life to thee. Demon in birth, demon in being, by the grace within me, I release thee from thy form."

Jim's body shimmered for a moment, twisted in upon itself, and then re-formed.

"Oh, great!" it said, looking down. "Now I'm going to have to buy another kilt!"

I spun around to face the house. "*Why* are you naked again?"

"The question is more why aren't I standing here in my magnificent form? What's wrong with your magic? Why can't you change me back? Are you even trying? I don't think you're trying!"

"I am trying, and I don't know what's going on. That spell should have done the trick." I chewed on my lower lip as I thought. "It has to be Baltic's fire that's messing things up. I'll try it again without it."

Jim heaved a martyred sigh as it sat down on the grass. "Whatever. Just change me back. This grass tickles, and I don't think you want me scratching where it itches."

I cleared my mind and tried the spell again, attempting to pull energy from the living things around me, but nothing happened. "It's the dragon fire. It's interfering with my concentration," I told the demon as I mentally shooed the dragon fire away. "We'll give it another shot."

"I think something just bit my ass," Jim said, rising up on one cheek as it tried to look around at its behind. "Do bees live in the grass? Maybe it was a snake! Do they have poisonous snakes in England? Fires of Abaddon, you gotta suck the poison from my ass!"

"I am not sucking anything, and calm down. You're distracting me."

"I'm gonna die! At least it wasn't my fabulous form that has been poisoned. Things are going a bit dark, Ysolde. I see spots and stuff. I think I may ralph. Does snake poison make you want to puke?"

I ignored the demon's hysterics as I gently but persistently dampened every last bit of Baltic's dragon fire that resided within me. "Now, let's try it," I said, rolling up my sleeves as I sketched a clarity spell in the air. I spoke the words, waiting for the familiar tingle of magic to surround me.

"Farewell, cruel world. Tell Cecile I loved her!" A loud thump followed that declaration. Jim lay flat on its back, its arms stretched out dramatically.

"You're still naked. And human. And for the love of all that is good and glorious, grab some fig leaves or something! I don't want to see that."

"I *had* clothes on, until you stripped them off me," Jim grumbled, sitting upright. "Hey, the spots are gone. I guess the snake poison was no match for a demon."

"Snake poison?"

"Yeah, from the snake that bit me." It stood up and turned around. "Right here on my ass."

"That's a rock, not a snake, you idiot," I said, pulling off my T-shirt and smacking Jim on the butt with it before handing it to the demon. "Loincloth that, and don't even think of trying to give it back to me."

Jim eyed my chest as it wrapped the T-shirt around its waist. "I see you still have your sept tat on your left boobie."

I tugged up the lacy top of my camisole and glared at the demon before marching toward the house.

"Hey!" Jim called from where it stood. "You're not

going to leave me in human form, are you? I thought you were going to change me back."

"I tried. There's something going on with Baltic's fire that's messing me up, so until I get it figured out, you're just going to have to stay that way."

"What?" Jim shrieked, its voice startling the morning birds that were chattering and singing to each other from the safety of the shrubberies. "No way! I can't stay like this! I had to be human for a week, and it was a nightmare! I'll be good, I promise. I won't make you look at my snakebite. Just change me back, pretty please with dog hair on top."

I stopped at the door to the kitchen. "I would if I could, Jim, but right now, there's so much going on in my life, I think it's all affecting my magic. If I can get a few things taken care of, then I can concentrate on figuring out what's going wrong. Until then, I'm sorry, but human form won't kill you."

"That's what you think," it muttered darkly, following after me as I entered the house. "I think you can change me, but you just don't want to. Man, I'm so going to tell Baltic that you have the hots for my naked human form."

"You do and the kilt won't be the only thing missing," I warned before trotting upstairs to get a new shirt.

An hour later, after having been forced to run into town to buy Jim a replacement kilt and shirt, along with a pair of shoes and some underwear, I left the demon with a big bowl of popcorn and a stack of Pavel's DVDs. I stood outside Baltic's study for a few moments, straining my ears to hear what was going on, but there was nothing audible but a faint rumble of male voices. I tapped on the door and entered, not surprised to see Thala up and about.

She whirled around at the noise, her eyes narrowing on me. "Pavel says you are human now, and not a dragon."

I blinked at the unexpected statement. I half thought she might lambaste me for drugging and restraining her, but evidently she either didn't realize what had happened—which, given the muddled state the sleeping drugs had left her in, wasn't out of the question—or she chose to ignore it. "Yes, I am."

"No, you are not. You are my mate, and thus are a light dragon," Baltic corrected, looking up from an architect's plan.

I let that go and eyed Thala curiously. She was about my height, built a bit broader than me, with copper-colored hair and dark reddish brown eyes. There was a blackish blue aura around her that warned she had control of some sort of dark power. Baltic had told me she was a necromancer, and that her mother was his former girlfriend, the famed archimage Antonia von Endres. What was more unsettling was the fact that she was also the sister to the woman I had recently learned was the true wife of the man I had married. "Did Ruth not tell you about me?"

"Ruth?" Her lip curled in scorn. "That pretender. I haven't spoken to her since Baltic was slain."

I raised my eyebrows. "I had no idea you were present at Dauva when that happened."

"I wasn't."

"Odd, then, that you would date something to that event."

She turned her back on me, clearly dismissing my existence, addressing herself to Baltic instead. "If Kostich holds the light sword, then he must be keeping it at the vault at Suffrage House. That's the best security he can hope for in France. We will simply have to get it from there. We should go to Paris immediately and see how much protection he has added."

"That would probably be best," Baltic answered, a strange hesitancy in his manner. "Later. Now that Ysolde is here, however, we can discuss your experience at the hands of the weyr."

Thala's hands tightened around the edge of the desk. "Surely that can wait for another time? Your woman can have no concern with what was said to me."

"My *mate* is concerned in every aspect of my life," Baltic corrected, giving Thala a no-nonsense look. Love warmed my heart. I wanted to simultaneously cheer and kiss him, but that would no doubt enrage the woman who I was beginning to believe was more than a little jealous of my presence.

"Oh, to hell with it," I said, and walked over to Baltic, pulling his head down so I could kiss him. I heard a swift hiss of breath behind me as Baltic, never one to brush off a kiss, put both hands on my behind and wrapped me in dragon fire.

"What was that for?" he asked when he had retrieved his lip from where I was sucking on it.

"Nothing in particular. I just felt like kissing you."

"I approve of the sentiment," he said, a hint of laughter in his ebony eyes. "Although I suspect that situation we discussed earlier is not as resolved as you claim it is."

"I'm not the jealous one here," I whispered into his

ear as I nipped on his earlobe before turning in his arms to smile at Thala.

If looks could kill, the entire area within a ten-mile radius would have been a radioactive wasteland.

My smile grew, more to annoy her than to appear friendly. "Much as I would love to hear what the dragons did to you, I'm afraid Baltic and I have an appointment. It's time for us to pick up Brom."

"Brom?" Her fiery gaze narrowed on me again. "Who is Brom?"

"My son. He's been staying with Gabriel and May for the weekend."

"You have a son." She was silent for a few beats before a slow smile stole over her face. "How excellent. You may go retrieve your son. We have no need of your assistance in making plans."

Pavel, who had been standing behind Thala, pursed his lips and shook his head.

Behind me, Baltic stiffened, his hands under mine holding me back when I would have marched forward.

"Oh, you did *not* just say that," I said, my ire thoroughly roused.

"Am I missing something good? Who didn't say what? Hey, that chick you cuffed is up. Hiya. We met earlier, but you probably don't remember me. I'm Jim. Effrijim, really, but no one calls me that except Aisling when she's pissed about something. Don't let this human form throw you—I'm normally much more handsome. So you're Balter's old girlfriend, huh? Did I interrupt a catfight about to happen? I did, didn't I? Pavel, can I borrow your phone? It does have a camera, right? Does it do video? Man, why didn't I think to bring my digital camera?" Jim wandered into the room with the bowl of popcorn. "This might almost make being stuck in human form worthwhile."

Thala looked at Jim like it had a miniature herd of rhinoceroses dancing a ballet on its head.

"You didn't miss anything, Jim, because Thala didn't say anything. Did you?" I said in a calm, even tone.

Pavel backed away several feet.

Jim sucked in its breath and did likewise. "Uh . . . right. I can see that. Don't turn me into a banana, please. Human form is better than that."

"I haven't banana-ed anything since the *sárkány*," I said with a significant look at Thala that she totally ignored.

"Do you have any idea who I am?" She answered my threat by stepping forward, her eyes glittering with an unholy red light.

"Yes. You're the woman who is clearly bent out of shape over the fact that I'm back in Baltic's life. Get over it, Thala. I may be human, but I'm also immortal, and Baltic and I are very much together. Nothing you can do will change that, so if you don't want to force me to rain down death and destruction on your head, you'll move on."

Baltic sighed heavily. "Mate, do not threaten Thala."

"If there is any death and destruction to be done, I will be the one performing it," she snarled at me, her hands fisted as she took another step forward. Menace and fury rolled off her in palpable waves, but I knew a stand had to be made.

I tried to move forward again to accept her obvious challenge; Baltic, however, held me firmly against his body. "Thala, do not threaten my mate."

Jim moved over to where Pavel was watching the scene. "It's gonna be a catfight, and me with no camera! Lend me your phone, buddy. We could make a killing off the video, especially if they both go into dragon form. I'll go fifty-fifty in the profits with you."

"There will be no fight," Baltic said, glaring at Jim for a few seconds before transferring his attention to Thala. "Will there?"

Her jaw worked angrily before she managed another one of those bloodcurdling smiles. "I only ever have your best wishes at heart, Baltic. If you desire that I ignore your woman's insults, then I shall do so."

I tapped my fingers on Baltic's hand, where it lay over one of mine.

His sigh ruffled my hair. "There was a time when I believed that all would be peaceful once Ysolde was at my side again. I see that I was wrong."

I turned in his arms to give him a share of my scowl. "I am not the one who started this—"

"Enough." He gave me a quick, hard kiss, then turned me and gave me a gentle push toward the door. "You will no doubt wish to drive us to London, since you claim my piloting the vehicle takes years off your life. We will go to fetch our son—"

I noticed the emphasis he put on the last words, and smiled at them.

"—and Thala can fly to Paris to determine what new measures of security Kostich has put into place to guard the light sword."

Thala blinked a couple of times. "You're not coming with me?"

"No. I have business to attend to at Dauva, and Ysolde has extracted from me a promise to meet with the weyr, which she no doubt intends for me to fulfill soon. Once you have assessed the security, return here and we will make our plans."

I was about to ask Baltic why he needed to go back to Latvia when he had just returned from there, but something about the set of his jaw had me clamping down on the question. "I'll bring the car around. Jim, get your things. Pavel, are you coming with us?"

He shook his head, flickering a quick glance at Baltic that set off a number of warning bells in my head. "I have some things to attend to. You may exchange polite greetings with the silver guards on my behalf, if you like. Nothing too friendly, and I would prefer that the greetings are offered only after they have acknowledged my absence, since we are the older dragons and it is our due to be greeted before offering the same."

"You guys are downright archaic sometimes," I said, shaking my head as I herded a protesting Jim and its bowl of popcorn out the door.

Baltic claims he knows how to drive perfectly well, but experience has shown me that while he has a firm grasp on the mechanics of driving a car, he disregards all other aspects of the driving experience and thus has only a vague idea of rules of the road, laws, and even what common courtesy is with regard to other drivers. He also doesn't give a damn about any of that, which means that usually either Pavel or I drive when we go somewhere. Luckily, I enjoy driving, even on England's sometimes confusing roadways.

"Jim," I said once we had joined the throng of folks streaming toward London, "can I give you direct orders that you can't refuse?"

"Uh-oh. I don't like the sound of that," it said, looking

up from one of Pavel's risqué magazines it had filched before leaving the house. "What kind of an order?"

"I don't want you to hear what I'm going to say."

Baltic shot me a startled look.

Jim sighed. "Yeah, you can. But I'd like to point out that I can also keep my lips zipped if I have to, so you don't really have to order me not to hear something."

I thought for a moment, then shook my head, both at the driver in front of me who slammed on his brakes for no reason and at the thought of speaking my concerns in front of the demon. "Effrijim, I command you to not hear anything I say until I tell you it's OK."

Jim sighed again, and buried itself in the magazine.

"Oh, look, a hamburger place. Let's go there and have food."

It didn't even look up at my bait.

"What is it that you don't wish to say in front of the demon? Are you going to tell me some new way you wish for me to make love to you? Will it involve a phallic device such as Pavel has? I will warn you, mate, I do not approve of phallic devices for either of us. I do not care for such things to be used on me, and the only phallus I intend for you to entertain is—"

I lifted my hand to stop what showed every sign of being one of Baltic's "the old Ysolde never was into the sorts of kinky things you are into" lectures. "I don't want a vibrator, thank you. Although those little bullet job-bies look kind of . . . never mind. You're phallic enough for me, thank you."

An odd look crossed his face. "I'm not sure that is a compliment, but I assume you mean it as one."

"Yes, I do. How about this: you more than amply take care of any and all sexual desires I have. Better?"

"Much." He sat back with a smug look on his handsome face and waved a hand. "You may proceed telling me about the new fantasy you have."

"It's not a fantasy. What exactly were you doing in Dauva?"

His face went blank for a few minutes before he slid me a steamy look. "Do you have fantasies about making love in Dauva? Out in the open, perhaps? It is heavily forested now, and not visited by the locals because they believe it is haunted, so I would be willing to take you there if it would drive you to a new level of pleasure."

"If that's some sort of a crack about me having voyeuristic tendencies . . ."

He raised a hand and looked out the window. "I make no judgment, mate. I was simply offering to allow your strange new tastes some freedom; that is all. If you wish instead for me to make love to you in the lair, that is more reasonable, although we would need to bring in a blanket at the least, since the ground is quite rocky there after the centuries of disuse. Perhaps a mattress." He paused for a few seconds and thought. "I suppose we could build a bedchamber in there if you really liked, although Kostya has stolen all of my treasures, so there would be no gold to rub all over your body."

"An underground love nest doesn't appeal to me in the leas— Rub gold all over me?" My eyes went a bit glazed as I considered that thought. Although the dragon that slumbered within me must have shown the same preference for gold over all other forms of treasure, heretofore it hadn't triggered any response in me. Now, however, just the thought of draping Baltic's naked form with chains of gold had me shivering with arousal. "Maybe that would be nice. How much gold do you have now?"

His smile was filled to the rim with smugness. "Not as much as I had, thanks to Kostya, but enough to satisfy your lustful demands. It is safe in my Paris lair."

"Perhaps—" I shook myself, dissipating the erotic images that danced so tantalizingly in my head. "We got sidetracked somehow." An abbreviated gesture had me shooting him quick little glances as all sorts of warning bells went off in my head. "You did that deliberately, didn't you?"

"Brought up the subject of making love to you? I frequently discuss my desire to mate with you, Ysolde," he said, but he couldn't look me in the eye. He pretended to be interested in the passing scenery, which made a few more bells chime.

"Yes, you do, and I appreciate that fact, but I also know that you don't like saying you won't answer a question I asked you, which is why you try to distract me with thoughts of you all warm and naked with gold chains draped across your chest and belly and . . ." My voice trailed off into a little whimper as I swallowed back a sudden wave of desire and need. "What was I saying?"

He slid me another look, but sighed and slumped back into the seat, shaking his head. "You'd never let me hear the end of it," he muttered. "It would be just like in Milan, when Antonia called me to her side, but I could not tell you because you would have instantly been jealous and likely lopped off my stones with the nearest sword. I had to tell you I was away on sept business just to keep you from following me."

"I am not the sort of person who gelds other people without due cause," I started, then realized what it was he hadn't said. "Wait a minute—are you saying you went off to see your former girlfriend after we were together?"

"Not in the sense you are thinking," he said blithely.

"How do you know what I'm thinking?"

He pointed to the steering wheel. "Your fingernails have dug into the leather a good half an inch."

I loosened my death grip on the wheel, spun it when I was about to plow us into a guard rail, and got a grip on my emotions. "What did Antonia want to see you about?"

He was silent.

I glanced at him. His expression was stony.

"I see."

"I'm surprised you haven't had a vision about that episode," he said after a few more minutes of silence, during which I lovingly reviewed various forms of torture dug out from the shattered remains of my memory. "You came as close to killing an archimage as anyone ever has. It would be a worthy vision to experience."

An echo of a voice shouting in my head had me signaling and pulling over to a shoulder. Jim looked up inquiringly, but sighed and returned to its skin magazine when I turned to face Baltic.

"Mate?" Baltic asked, one eyebrow raised.

"Shush. It's there, right on the edge of my mind. I can hear an echo of it. I want to know what happened. I want to see it. I want to be able to remember things again. I want . . ."

It danced with tantalizing nearness, just beyond the range of my consciousness, where I could see it, but not grasp it. I closed my eyes in order to draw it into focus, but the echoes stayed fragmented and incoherent.

". . . shall not be! I will not . . ."

"You have no right, dragon . . ."

"Mate, you cannot . . ."

I shook my head as I tried to coax the memories forward. "I've lost them, Baltic. I can't even remember my own past."

I heard him sigh, and suddenly I was in his arms, his body warm and solid, holding me with infinite care, the scent of him seeping deep into my being. I opened my eyes to look into his, the dark, endless depths of them drawing me in and capturing me in his soul.

"Do not do this, Ysolde. You are my love, my life. You are the very breath in my lungs, and the beat of my heart. I could not exist without you."

"She tried to steal you from me," I heard myself say, and realized that he had done what I couldn't do by myself—he'd pulled the vision from my hidden memories.

"No," the past Baltic said, his face different, yet familiar nonetheless. "No one could do that. You do not need to kill her. Do not risk that which you cannot afford, my love. She isn't worth it."

I turned to look at the woman who was trapped against a stone wall, my fire surrounding her. On the edges of the shadows stood several forms, dragons and others, keeping a wary distance from the three of us. It was nighttime, the air warm and heavy with the scent of jasmine and orange blossoms, soft distant noises of the city telling me we stood some leagues from it.

The fire was silent the way dragon fire is, burning with a brightness that lit up the immediate area despite the thick darkness around us. But it was more than mere dragon fire surrounding her; a sense of power rushed through me, pouring outward to encircle Antonia. I wanted more than anything to just let the stream of power wash over her, for I knew it would end her existence, but Baltic's love wrapped me in a web that prohibited me from doing so. I could snap it with just a thought, but to do that would be to break our love, as well, and there was nothing on this earth that would compel me to such a sacrifice.

"It pleases me that I have made no error in you," a ponderous voice said from the side.

A man strolled forward through the crowd, which parted as if he were a plow on loamy soil. Soft, startled murmurs rippled around us, trailing in his wake as he stopped in front of me. His face and eyes were ageless, all-seeing, all-knowing, as if he saw all too clearly that I was on the verge of committing an act that would forever change the path of my life.

"Who are you?" I asked the man. He was a dragon, of that I was sure, but I didn't recognize him or what sept he was from.

His dark eyes were amused—at least they were until his gaze slid past me to where Baltic stood. Then they narrowed, his lips tightening. Whoever he was, he wasn't pleased.

"Baltic," he said, his gaze returning to me, "your mate is the source of much trouble, it seems."

Baltic's arm went around me, pulling me tight to his side. "She is no trouble to *me*."

The dragon's lips twitched, but he merely turned his head to consider Antonia von Endres as she was plastered to the stone wall of the villa's tower. His eyebrows rose. "You seek to destroy the mage, daughter of night?"

I hadn't intended on answering him, since my temper was riled by Antonia, but something about him compelled me to say simply, "She tried to steal my mate. I tolerate that from no one, not even an archimage."

"She is not worth your ire." His gaze rested on me a third time, the amusement back in it as he leaned toward me and said softly, "Do not fail me, little one. All my hopes rest with you."

"Hopes?" I asked stupidly, not understanding what he was saying. "What hopes?"

He said nothing, just turned and walked back the way he had come, into the deepest part of the shadows. It was at that moment that I realized that the crowd of dragons making a half circle around us had been completely and utterly silent, as if they were collectively holding their breath.

"Who was that?" I asked Baltic, touching his arm as he looked after the man, a strange expression on his face. "Why did he call me daughter? He's not my father."

"That, my love, was the father of us all," Baltic said before turning to face Antonia. "Quench your fire, and let her go. She has news that I seek regarding Constantine. That is *all* I desire from her."

Absently, I tamped down on the fire, allowing the strange stream of power that flowed around her to dissipate, just like water seeping into parched earth. "The father of us all? Not . . . by the rood, that was the First Dragon?"

The words echoed in my head as I watched Baltic confront a furious Antonia, my mind dazzled by the fact that the ancestor of all dragons who ever were and ever would be had spoken to me. Not just spoken to me . . .

"Told me his hopes rested with me," I said, blinking as the velvet night brightened into a cloudy day. I looked up at my Baltic, who gently stroked my back, his breath ruffling my hair as cars whizzed past us. "Did you see that, too?"

"Your vision? No. But I remember it." His lips twisted. "Antonia threatened to destroy you for almost a century. Only the fact that she would have had to deal with the First Dragon if she had done so stopped her. And now you will question me for weeks as to what the First Dragon meant, and I will tell you repeatedly that I do not know. It is the truth, mate; I did not know then, and I do not know now. Nor do I particularly care."

I pulled back and gave him a long look. "You don't like the First Dragon, do you?"

He made a face. "My feelings toward him do not matter."

"Uh-huh. What about Antonia? What was all that business with her?"

"As you said, it was business. She had an interest in Constantine, and I sought to find out where he was."

"Hmm. And that water?"

He looked surprised. "I do not remember water. You attempted to burn Antonia alive, not drown her—not that you could have done either, but you came close to succeeding with your dragon fire."

"There was some other form of power I was tapping into. It felt like I was standing in a stream of it, flowing around and through me."

He shrugged, and looked pointedly at his watch. "We

will be late picking up Brom if you do not continue. Would you prefer for me to drive?"

"No," I said, resuming my seat and snapping the seat belt over my chest. I gave him one last look before I pulled out into the stream of traffic. "But I do want you to tell me one thing."

"What is that?"

I gripped the steering wheel with grim determination. "If you weren't at Dauva overseeing the reconstruction for the last couple of days, just where the devil were you?"

Chapter Nine

"We'd almost given up on you," May said, smiling as she greeted us at the door of Gabriel's house. "Brom was ready to go, but then a bird hit one of the back windows, and he went outside to see if it was stunned or dead. I'm sure this is completely against the agreement Baltic made with Gabriel, but would you like to come in for a few minutes? I can promise you that no one will hold you prisoner or otherwise harm either of you."

"I do not wish to enter the silver wyvern's house, no," Baltic said somewhat stiffly. He looked at me. "Are you speaking to me yet?"

"No."

He sighed. "My mate is making a futile attempt to punish me, but she will follow my desires in this as in everything and not enter—Ysolde!"

I pushed past him into the house, glancing around the cool hallway. "I'd love to chat for a bit, May. Hello, Gabriel. We've come for a visit."

"No, we have not! For the love of the saints, woman, I just finished telling the silver mate that we did not wish to enter!" Baltic stormed in after me. "Why do I speak if you will not heed my words?"

I raised an eyebrow at him.

"No," he said, answering the unspoken question. "I am a wyvern! I do not need to explain to you, my mate, the one who says she loves me beyond all else, the one who has promised to obey me, my every move."

"Obey?" May asked, her eyes widening with mirth. "Oh, dear."

Gabriel's lips twitched in an otherwise somber expression.

I kept the pleasant smile on my face despite the desire to whomp a certain dragon upside his handsome, if annoyingly stubborn, head. "We're having a little argument. Baltic feels he can go traipsing off who-knows-where without bothering to tell me, and I feel he can shove his head up his—"

"Ysolde!"

"You are welcome to our home despite the current situation between the weyr and you," Gabriel said, clearly fighting a smile. He gestured toward the room from which he had just emerged. "Would you care to sit down?"

Baltic opened his mouth to say no, but I shot him a look that promised no little amount of retribution in the very near future, and he, no doubt sensing he'd pushed me about as far as he could without me exploding into a million bits of frustration, wisely opted to humor me.

"Where's Jim?" May asked as she had a few words with the woman I remembered as her housekeeper.

"We dropped it off at Drake's house," I said, tightening my lips at Baltic.

"Oh?" She looked from me to Baltic, who was engaged in glaring at Gabriel. "Was there some sort of trouble?"

"Not if you call the fact that Baltic barely slowed down, let alone stopped, so I could say hello to Aisling and good-bye to Jim trouble. Which, incidentally, I do."

"Demons can't be hurt by merely bouncing off the pavement," Baltic said with a sniff.

May's eyes widened even more. Gabriel seemed to have some sort of a coughing attack.

"Look," I said as I faced Baltic. "I admit that it might have been a mistake to release it from its inability to hear anything we said, especially since I was not speaking to you at that time, and it picked up on that immediately. I also admit that its innuendoes and incessant whipcrack impressions were extremely annoying, not to mention offensive, and no, it shouldn't have told you that you could wear its kilt because clearly I wore the pants in the relationship—which is totally untrue, and I have no desire to emasculate you like it hinted—but you could have let me come to an actual complete stop rather than just pushing Jim out of the car as I slowed to park. For one thing, that was rude, and for another, Jim's kilt flipped up, baring everything while it was sprawled all over the sidewalk, and if I could possibly go *just one day* without seeing its human-form genitalia, I'd really appreciate it."

May gave up the fight and whooped with laughter, Gabriel joining her.

"I knew you would not be able to resist speaking to me," was all Baltic said, smiling smugly.

"Gah!" I yelled, then marched out of the room, tossing over my shoulder, "May, can I have a few words with you?"

"About Ysolde's agreement with May regarding her help with the release of your lieutenant...," Gabriel said as we exited.

"What agreement?" Baltic asked.

I closed the door on what was sure to be an eye-opening conversation for Baltic, turning to May to ask, "I'd like to check on Brom quickly, but after that ... do you have somewhere that we can be private for a few minutes?"

"Certainly. No one goes into the study." She opened a door. "I'll wait here for you."

"Thanks, May." I hurried down the dark, narrow passage that led to the tiny back garden, pausing just outside the door to smile at Brom as he squatted on his heels, one hand gesturing as he chatted, the other stroking the head of what must have been the stunned bird. Maata was next to him, nodding her head as he expounded some point or other, looking up with a genuine smile as she noticed me.

"Sullivan! Maata found a bird that hit the window, but it's not dead. She says it's a wren, but it needs a few minutes before it can fly again. Are we going right away, or can I watch the bird?"

"We have a few minutes. Good afternoon, Maata. How's your mother?"

She looked startled for a moment, then answered politely, "Well, thank you. Have you ... er ... met her?"

"In a manner of speaking. Five minutes, OK, Brom?"

"OK." His head bent over the bird again, and a brief hope flared that he might shift his morbid interest in making mummies from deceased animals to the care of live ones. "You just never know with him," I said aloud as I entered the study.

"Baltic?"

"Brom. Is it too much to hope he'd become a vet? I would think that was a nice, normal, beneficial profession. There's not much of a call for the ability to mummify things these days."

She smiled. "We've enjoyed having him visit, mummy fascination and all. What was it you wanted to talk to me about? Something to do with Baltic?"

"Tangentially, perhaps. I'd like to try to summon the First Dragon."

She blinked at me in surprise.

"I tried doing it myself, but my magic . . . well, you know about that."

"Yes, I know." Her lips twitched.

"So I got to thinking about what was different when I summoned him before, and your suggestion about having dragons around, and discounting things like stress and unhappiness with the weyr being collective asses, I decided the difference must be you."

"Why me?" she asked, looking startled at the idea.

"You have a tie to the First Dragon."

"Yes, but so do you."

"Exactly. We both have a relationship with the First Dragon, and perhaps your presence is needed in order to make a connection with him. Are you willing to give it a try?"

"Right now?"

"If you have the time, yes."

She hesitated for a moment, then nodded. "All right, but we should probably be as fast as possible. Your wyvern isn't the most ... er ... conversational of all the dragons I've met."

"That's the understatement of the year," I said, standing up and shaking out my hands while mentally clearing my mind.

"What should I do?"

"Just stand near me, as you were during the *sárkány*," I said, my eyes closed as I concentrated. "Maybe have a mental image of the First Dragon."

"Ready," she said.

I took a deep breath, pulling hard on Baltic's fire as I spoke the words. "Light exists within me, darkness I left behind, on my left hand sits that which was made, on my right sits that which has passed. Bring forth your grace that we might—by the rood! That was quick. Er ... hello."

Before the last of my invocation had been spoken, the air in front of us began to collect itself in a shimmery sort of swirl that quickly solidified into the form of a man who despite his human appearance was quite obviously not human.

"Daughter of light," he said, a slightly puzzled look in his fathomless eyes. He glanced at May, who stared at him with delight beaming from her face. "Daughter of shadows," he said, acknowledging her. "Why have you summoned me?"

May slid a look toward me.

"I'm the one who summoned you." I squirmed a little under the regard of his eyes, his gaze seeming to strip me to the deepest parts of my soul. "I had some questions about what you said to me the last time we ... er ... met."

He waited, saying nothing, just looking at me with

those uncanny eyes. "You said I had let you down before, and to not do it again. I'm sorry if I'm unusually dense, but I don't understand what it is you want me to do. If you could just tell me, I'd be really grateful."

His eyes closed and he turned as if he was leaving, but the world seemed to slip away at that moment, the walls and furniture and the house itself seemingly melting into a white nothingness.

A cold white nothingness.

"May?" I asked, rubbing my arms as a blast of arctic wind knocked me back a few feet.

"Right here. It's another vision, isn't it? Like the one you had at the *sárkány*?"

"Yes. I think . . . yes, up there. That's me."

"Isn't this when the First Dragon resurrected you?" May asked, shivering next to me as we watched the past version of myself trundling down a hill suddenly stop and turn to look upward.

"I think so. I certainly don't look terribly with it, do I?"

"Well, I imagine being resurrected would take a lot out of you," she pointed out.

"What is it you wish of me?" the past me asked, and May and I turned to look in the direction she was calling.

The whirl of wind and snow lessened for a few seconds, revealing the figures of two men.

"Death of the innocent has stripped honor from my youngest son," one of the men said. "You must return it to him."

The past Ysolde stared at him dully for a few seconds before simply turning and continuing on her way down the snowy slope. May and I gaped at the First Dragon and the man beside him until a blast of wind and icy snow had us reeling backward.

I covered my face against the sting of it, wiping away tears triggered by the cold. When I looked up, May and I were standing in her library. I was somewhat heartened to see she had an expression of incredulity on her face, since I knew I was beyond flabbergasted.

"That was . . . that was Constantine, wasn't it?" she finally asked me.

I nodded. "I did hear the First Dragon right, didn't I? He said his youngest son?"

"Yes." She blinked a couple of times and shook her head as if to clear away mental fog. "Constantine Norka was the First Dragon's youngest son? I didn't know he had real children, since he calls other dragons by the names son and daughter." She looked up at me with speculation. "He particularly seems to like calling you daughter. I wonder if you really are?"

I shook my head. "My parents were first black dragons, then silver when they left the sept with Constantine. There's something . . ." I bit my lip, trying hard to remember something that was said to me relatively recently. "Kaawa, I think, told me that the dragon septs were originally formed by the First Dragon. His children were the first wyverns."

"I think I remember reading that in one of the weyr history books," she said, looking thoughtful. "He had one daughter and three sons, and they formed the original four septs. But I never remember seeing Constantine's name included, although it makes sense if all the other original wyverns were children of the First Dragon. I wonder why Gabriel never mentioned it?"

"That's a very good question. Another good one is what the hell I'm going to do. 'Death of the innocent stripped honor from my youngest son.' That has to be Constantine killing me. So how on earth am I supposed to return honor to my own murderer? Does it even matter since he's dead?"

She hesitated, then pointed out, "It's the First Dragon's son, Ysolde. I'm sure it matters to him."

"Good point." I thought for a moment. "How do you return honor to a dead man? I could formally forgive him for killing me, but beyond that, I'm totally at a loss."

A slam of a door nearby had us both smiling wryly.

"That sounds like the end of patience on the part of one or both of them," I said as we left the library. Baltic stood by the front door, his arms crossed and a fierce scowl on his face as Brom chatted enthusiastically with Gabriel.

"I hope he hasn't talked you guys silly," I said with a smile at my son.

"Not at all. We enjoyed having him, and I know Maata gets a kick out of taking him to the museum to see the mummies. I'm pleased Baltic let him come visit us despite all the stuff going on with the weyr. And speaking of that, I assume we'll see you tomorrow?"

"Er . . ." I eyed my volatile mate with some misgiving. He really did look at the end of his not-very-substantial patience. "I haven't told Baltic it was tomorrow, but he knows he's going to have to attend, so, yes, we'll be there. I look forward to seeing the house again, although I have to admit I'm a bit surprised that Kostya is allowing us there."

She paused as we entered the foyer. "I think he wants

some help with Cy," she said slowly, an unhappy look in her clear blue eyes.

"It seemed to me the last time I saw them together that all was not well there."

"No," she said slowly, her expression brightening when she glanced at Gabriel. "I expect Cy has done what she always does and moved on to another love interest, although I really had thought this time she'd stick it out. . . ."

Baltic transferred his frown to me. "Mate, we have been here long enough. I have stood as many insults as I will tolerate. We will leave now. Brom, take your things to the car."

"Thank you for having Brom stay with you," I told Gabriel as I moved to Baltic's side. "From the increased amount of his luggage, it looks like he was far too indulged, but I'm sure he couldn't have had a better time."

"It was our pleasure," Gabriel said, wrapping an arm around May. "I hope you will allow him to visit us again."

I looked at Baltic. His lips thinned. I elbowed him.

"No," he said.

"Yes."

He sighed. "Ysolde, one day you will go too far. Must I remind you again that I am the wyvern, and you—"

"I am only the lowly mate, yes, I know, but as a wyvern, you must have some inkling of common good manners, so let's see them."

He pinned me back with a glare for a few seconds before squaring his shoulders and making one of those elegant bows that all the dragon males seemed to know how to make. "My mate and I thank you for taking care of our son during his visit."

Gabriel, obviously fighting a smile, inclined his head politely. "We were happy to do so."

"We'll see you both tomorrow," May said, waving as Baltic escorted me from the house. "Bye, Brom!"

"Tomorrow?" Baltic's eyes were glittering with speculation as he held the car door open for me.

"What's tomorrow?" Brom asked from the backseat.

"A meeting Baltic and I have to go to."

"Oh, the weyr thing." Brom promptly lost interest and spent much of the trip back home telling us about the many wonderful mummies and mummy-related items he saw, purchased, and planned to do. I was aware the entire time of Baltic's ire regarding the meeting with the wyverns, but we both knew there was nothing he could do to get out of it.

"What did you and the silver mate discuss that was so important you had to leave me to be harangued by Gabriel?" Baltic asked when Brom ran out of steam.

"We summoned the First Dragon."

His eyebrows rose. "Why?"

"Because I was tired of trying to figure out what he wanted me to do."

"And what did he say?"

I slid him a quick glance. "He wants me to return Constantine's honor."

"He had no honor to return!" Baltic declared.

"I'm not debating his actions, simply telling you what the First Dragon said. He pulled May and me into another vision, this time of the events right after he had resurrected me. He said that death of the innocent had stripped honor from Constantine, and I was supposed to return it. But how I'm supposed to return honor to him when he is dead is beyond me. Do you have any suggestions?"

The look he gave me was unreadable. "Yes. Do not try."

"The First Dragon asked me to do it, Baltic. I don't think it's going to be a good idea if I don't at least try something."

He shrugged, and changed the subject. "Why did you not tell me the meeting with the wyverns was tomorrow?"

"Why did you not tell me that Constantine is the First Dragon's youngest son?" I countered.

"What does it matter to you who the First Dragon's children were? They were all dead by the time Dauva was destroyed," he said in typical dragon evasion.

"I give up even trying to have a conversation with you when you're in this mood," I said, irritated and yet at the same time sympathetic to his unwillingness to continue the subject. I knew the fact that he had been kicked out of his own sept and incurred the wrath of the First Dragon was a touchy subject with him, so rather than push the point, I simply told him that we would talk to the wyverns about the whole ridiculous weyr war.

"I have work I must do if I am to spend tomorrow in such folly," he told me when we arrived home. "Later, once our son has gone to bed, you will do all those erotic things you have been thinking about doing to me."

I glanced at him in utter surprise as Brom hauled his newly gotten swag to the basement, where he had a little lab. "How on earth did you know I was indulging in smutty thoughts about you?"

He smiled and pulled me against him. "I can always

tell. Your eyes go liquid with desire, and your breathing increases. And you repeatedly shoot me speculative glances, as if you were formulating and discarding several plans. I suspect you have been indulging in more inventive fantasies about me."

I bit his shoulder, reveling for a few moments in the scent and feel of him. "You love those fantasies, and I was doing no such thing."

He squeezed my behind.

"Oh, all right, just a little one, but it only involved a chase scenario, so you can hardly call it inventive."

"Chase?" His head rose from where he had been nibbling on my neck, a strange light in his velvety dark eyes.

"Kaawa said it was something dragons do."

"It is." He breathed deeply for a moment. "You used to leave me little notes, urging me to find where you had hidden. You were very good at hiding, but I could always find you. You wish to play this way again?"

"Perhaps," I said, moving the chase scenario up to the top of my mental to-do list. I gave him a long look as I strolled toward the sitting room. "We shall see, shan't we?"

A low rumble emerged from his chest, a strangely erotic sound that sent shivers down my arms. I left him standing in the hallway, making a mental note to ask Kaawa what other dragon games had been lost to my memory.

Chapter Ten

Thala returned unexpectedly from Paris that evening, seriously inhibiting my ability to tackle Baltic about the First Dragon, the upcoming meeting, or even how I was to go about finding information on the ouroboros dragons with whom Kostich's granddaughter was involved.

"I'm not jealous, I'm not jealous," I growled to myself as I stalked out of Baltic's study, where he and Thala were bent over her laptop, going over the video she'd taken of Suffrage House.

"Why would you be jealous?" Brom asked, sitting on the stairs with a grubby notebook and an even grubbier bit of shed snakeskin.

"I wouldn't. I'm not. It's just that . . . oh, never mind."

"I don't like Thala," Brom said as I sat down next to him. "She doesn't like mummies. She told me I was a weird kid and to stay out of her way. And she's always touching Baltic."

I stared at him. "Touching him how?"

"You know, touching him," he said with a shrug. "She touches his arm a lot, and earlier I saw her touch his face. If I was Baltic, I wouldn't let her do that. It's too icky."

I gave him one of the three daily hugs he allowed me. "It's not icky with the right person."

"Yeah. You can touch my face if you really want to, but I won't let anyone else do it. It's time to unwrap the mole Pavel found a week ago in the back garden. You want to watch?"

"The thought of a mummified mole is not horribly high on my wish list, but I suppose I'll survive it."

"Geez, Sullivan," he said with a roll of his eyes as he got to his feet and headed to the basement door. "You're such a girl. It's just a mole!"

"Hey, lots of girls like dead things!" I protested as I followed. "Just because I'm not one of them doesn't mean anything. I'll have you know that Baltic says he taught me how to use a sword and morning star, and that's something you don't see a lot of girls doing."

We spent a pleasant hour together as Brom showed off his various mummification projects. While he explained his technique, I mused about how a boy with such a horrible biological father could turn out so bright and charming, if a little eccentric, but when he offered to show me the mole's preserved innards, I decided enough quality time had been spent and went off to demand that Baltic do likewise for me.

"Half hour more, then bed," I told Brom as I left.

He frowned. "Sullivan, I'm not a child."

"Of course you're not. Nine is perfectly ancient, but Nico is coming in the morning, and if you want to avoid being sent to the local school, you had better show Baltic and me that you will excel with a tutor, and that means bed at a reasonable hour. Got it?"

He rolled his eyes but nodded.

"Love you. Good night." I trotted up the stairs, making yet another mental note to ask the tutor to concentrate a little more on biology, since Brom seemed to have a knack for things of that ilk.

"—not see that she is undermining your authority? Who is the one who decided that the child could visit the silver dragons? She did. Her ties to the silver sept run deep, Baltic, and it is to them she owes her true allegiance. She will betray you now as she tried to do in the—" Thala spun around when I entered Baltic's library bearing a tray.

"Sorry to interrupt your little attempt at erroneous propaganda," I said without a shred of truth. I set the tray down on Baltic's desk, and laid out a couple of espresso cups and a carafe of coffee before smiling at him. "I needn't ask if you believe that hogwash, since you know full well I would never do anything to betray you. Quite the opposite, as a matter of fact."

"I've never doubted you," he answered with a complacence that I knew would irritate Thala.

"Good. I thought you'd like a little dessert. You didn't have time after dinner for the caramel-drenched chocolate hazelnut torte I made for you."

Thala sneered as Baltic, who had an almost insatiable sweet tooth, looked with interest at the contents of the tray.

"Cake?" Thala dismissed the subject. "We have no time for cake!"

My smile grew as I held out a plate for Baltic. "There's always time for cake. Especially cake with caramel. Baltic loves caramel, don't you?"

"Ysolde enjoys cooking," Baltic said around a mouthful of torte. "It pleases her to pretend I'm starving and must be fed several times a day."

"I do nothing of the sort, and I've yet to see you turn down anything I give you."

"I don't wish to hurt your feelings," he said, a blissful look stealing into his eyes as the torte melted in his mouth. "Did you make the caramel yourself?"

"Of course. I have extra. I thought we might enjoy it . . . *later*."

"We really should make some decisions tonight," Thala spoke over the top of me, tapping on the laptop.

"Mm-hmm," he agreed, eyeing the second piece I had brought for Thala. "Do you want that?"

"Yes, I very much want to proceed—"

"No, the torte."

She shot him an outraged look before getting a grip on her emotions. "No. I do not like sweets, *as you know*."

"If Jim were here, it would give that zinger only a three-point-five. I'm sure you can do better if you really try," I told her.

She pulled herself to her full height. "Do you have any idea of the power I wield, human? I am the daughter of Antonia von Endres, the greatest of all the mages. I can raise the dead and make them walk amongst us. I can harness the powers of both the dark and the arcane, and bend them to my will!"

"But can you turn demons into men? Can you harness the power of the banana? And have you ever had a foursome with yourself? Because I can and have, and if

Baltic would just help me bring forth some appropriate memories, I will do so again!"

The man in question looked up from the two now-empty plates. "I do not understand your desire to indulge in sex with ourselves, mate. It is unnatural."

"You go too far!" Thala snarled at me. "Leave us! We have important things to discuss."

"Do *not* give my mate orders," Baltic said, frowning at her.

"Then you make her leave!"

He glanced at the laptop, hesitating, obviously not wishing to ask me to leave but at the same time wanting to finish his discussion with Thala.

"Don't worry, you don't have to," I told him with a little smile. I picked up the tray and the empty plates and headed for the door, pausing at it to sigh. "I guess if you don't want the extra caramel I made, I will just have to *enjoy* it by myself."

Baltic had leaned over the laptop to look at something, but at the obvious undertone in my voice, he shot bolt upright. I gave him a slow, wicked smile and went off to the kitchen.

By the time I had washed the plates and cups, warmed a small bowl of caramel, grabbed a new pastry brush, and made my way upstairs to our bedroom, Baltic was on the bed, naked, and anticipating my arrival.

"You will not need to see our past selves tonight," he said as I set the bowl and brush down on the nightstand. "Is that warm?"

"Yes. How pissed is Thala?"

He shrugged. "She is annoyed, but that is of little matter. She understands that to me you must come first in all things."

If I had been about to read him a lecture about his pushy lieutenant, his matter-of-fact statement melted any and all intentions.

I sat on the bed, watching him as he poked at the caramel with a finger. "It would be better cold."

"You think so?" I asked.

He grinned, his black eyes glowing with a sensual light that never failed to send shivers down my back. "It's harder to spread cold . . . and harder to lick off."

"Yes, but warmed, it can be drizzled. See?" I dipped the pastry brush into the warm caramel, then traced an artistic caramel spiral all the way up his penis.

His eyes widened as I made a little curlicue on the top. "Drizzling can be good."

"Oh, yes, drizzling can be very good," I said, leaning down to lick the caramel off him.

His eyes crossed as his hips thrust upward. "I begin to think that perhaps there is more to your fantasies than I first imagined."

"There's nothing wrong with a good sense of imagination," I mumbled, licking off the last of the caramel. "You know, this is going to make us very sticky. We're going to need baths afterward."

"We always need to bathe afterward," Baltic answered with a little grimace.

I swirled the brush in the caramel, ignoring the hopeful look in his eyes to ask, "You don't like to take a bath, do you?"

"No. Water is not our element."

"Our what?"

He nudged the bowl. "It will cool if you don't use it now."

"What element? We have an element? Why do I like

a long bath if it's not our element?" I moved the bowl out of his reach.

He looked down his body, then at me. "My cock is not happy."

"It'll survive a few questions. I can warm up the caramel if necessary," I added quickly, forestalling his next objection. "Explain to me about the element."

"Always you wish to talk during lovemaking," he said, looking aroused and disgruntled at the same time, no easy feat. "I do not understand why you cannot simply focus on me as you should, and leave the questions for another time."

"Perhaps because I know you'll brush off questions asked when I don't have you naked and lustful and willing to do whatever it takes to get me to coat you with caramel and lick off every square inch."

He pursed his lips, obviously thinking it over. "Very well. I will be magnanimous and just this once allow you to have your way, but no more, Ysolde. You have had your way too long. Our relationship will return to what is right and proper."

I smiled to myself and stirred the caramel.

"All dragon septs have an element that is sympathetic to them. Water is the element of the green dragons; thus I do not enjoy it."

"But I love to swim and take long baths, and I was a silver dragon before I met you and became a black dragon. Why do I like water?"

"You were reborn human with a dormant dragon side. Humans, I understand, like water." He looked meaningfully at the bowl in my hands. "That will change once the dragon inside you awakens fully."

"Hmm. What was the black dragon element?"

"Energy."

"Ah." I thought for a moment. "Like electricity?"

"No. It is more akin to the energy found in elemental magic."

A little tickle of a memory flitted through my mind. I closed my eyes to better focus on it.

"Are you going to use that, or should I reheat it?" Baltic asked, nudging my hands again.

"One moment. I'm thinking. There's a memory just . . . Ah, got it." I shivered as a sudden cool earthiness seeped into my pores. I opened my eyes to find that I was kneeling on a dirt floor, Baltic spread out naked next to me, an annoyed expression on his face.

"You just cannot leave the past in the past, can you?" he asked me, nodding toward something behind me.

I turned to see myself coming down a narrow stone passage, a small branch of candles in one hand, the flickering light from them casting eerie shadows on the rough-hewn stone walls.

"Here," a male voice said.

I got to my feet as the other Baltic came into view, gesturing toward the wall.

"That's stone," the past me said, holding the candles high.

"It appears that way. I have hidden the door to the lair. You must learn how to access it, and how to use your power to hide it when needed."

"What power? Dragon fire, you mean?"

"No, the power that fills all living things. It flows around us. Open yourself up to it and use it. No other dragons can do so but us. It is unique in the weyr. It is why our lairs are so hard to find—we use the power that only we can harness to hide them from other eyes."

Behind me, Baltic sighed and got to his feet, brushing off his behind, pausing to cast a look of admiration at the old Ysolde as she examined the wall. "I always loved it when you wore nothing but a chemise."

I stopped eyeing the past Baltic, clad in a pair of leather leggings and boots, to notice that the candles he now held made Ysolde's form visible through the thin material of the chemise.

"You know, it's really hard to be jealous of yourself, but if you keep ogling her, I may just manage it," I told him.

He grinned. "You wish to bed me. The other me. Where is the difference?"

"I do not! I mean, I *did* wish to, and we *did* make love, but the present me doesn't want the past you." I glanced over to where the past Baltic was showing Ysolde how to open the hidden door. "Well, all right, I wouldn't turn him down if he showed up in my bed, because he looks really sexy in those leggings."

Baltic said something rude under his breath.

"Oh, come on! Just look at yourself!" I said, gesturing toward the memory. "Those leggings and boots and bare chest . . . it's just so . . . *rawr*! I want to rip the clothes right off of him. You. Past you! And your chest . . . I've always loved your chest. . . ."

Baltic moved to block my view, his expression black as he gestured at his current self. "You will love *this* chest, mate! You will welcome *me* in your bed, not him!"

"Oh, I do love your chest," I purred, rubbing myself against his body, making sure to stroke a hand down the silky flesh that covered the steely muscles of his chest and abdomen. "I love every inch of you, Baltic. I always will."

"More than him?" he asked, jerking his thumb toward the other version of himself, one that was now, I was interested to see, pressing Ysolde up against the wall to kiss her breasts and neck.

"Good lord, we really did go at it like bunnies, didn't we?" I murmured, quickly pulling my attention back to Baltic at the outraged noise he made deep in his chest. "Of course I love you more. Present you wins every competition. You're sexier now, more handsome, and much more pleasing to me."

I thought that would assuage his ego, but his black look grew darker. "You didn't find me sexy in the past? I didn't please you then?"

"Of course you did!" I wanted to laugh, but knew he would totally misunderstand. "For the love of the saints, just look at me. Does it look like you're not pleasuring me to the tips of my toes?"

We both looked at the couple, my eyes widening a little as Baltic, murmuring something in Ysolde's ear, hoisted her upward, pressing her against the wall as he pulled her legs around his hips, quickly thrusting into her body in a way that made her cry out in rapture.

"By the rood," I said softly, my mouth going a bit dry at the sight.

Baltic moved to block my view again. "Is that what you desire? Lovemaking in the tunnel under Dauva?"

"No, of course not. Er . . . is the tunnel still there?"

He sighed and strode off. I followed, with only a quick backward glance at the lovers, but the scene melted away into that of our bedroom. "Where are you going?" I asked when I got to the door in time to see a still-naked Baltic marching down the stairs.

Brom was coming up them at the same time, casting

a curious look over his shoulder as he got to the top. He gave me a long look that was more adult than it should have been, saying simply, "Night, Sullivan."

"Good night, lovey," I answered, wondering if Baltic was truly angry or had just gone off to book a flight to Latvia. I started after him, returning quickly to the room to snatch up the caramel and brush before hurrying downstairs.

Pavel stood at the front door, an expression of surprise fading to one of amusement as I paused to consider where Baltic might have gone.

"Basement," was all Pavel said.

"Thanks. He's in one of his moods," I said.

Pavel glanced at the bowl, dipping in a finger and licking it. "Homemade caramel sauce?"

"Of course. I used fresh cream, and I think it made all the difference."

He smiled. "Have I mentioned lately how glad I am that you are not dead? Not just because you've kept Baltic from going insane with grief, but because it's nice to have someone who appreciates good food."

I laughed and pressed a kiss to his cheek before heading to the basement door.

"So if the black dragon's element is energy, what's our element?" I asked, closing the door and making my way down the narrow steps to Brom's work area. Fluorescent lights from the ceiling fixture cast a sickly hue over his worktable. Beyond it were a couple of storage rooms, one door of which was open, the pale yellow light from it pooling at the entrance.

"Arcane power," came a muffled answer.

I touched a spot over my heart, where a light tan brand of a stylized sun resided. Baltic had placed the mark there, telling me it was the symbol of our new sept and that when I had mastered my dragon fire, I would do the same for Brom. "Does Pavel have abilities to use arcane power?"

"No. But his children will. As will ours."

I wasn't prepared to talk about the possibility of other children yet. I knew Baltic wanted a child of his own blood, and I did think that we would have one together, but I didn't intend for that to happen until our lives had settled down. "You had arcane abilities before, though, didn't you? Isn't that why Antonia von Endres gave you her mage sword?"

"My grandmother was a mage," he said in an even more muffled tone, accompanied by some soft swearing in another language. "I gained some control over arcane magic from her."

"On your mother or father's side?"

"My mother's mother."

"So your grandmother was human? Huh." I sat on the tall stool before Brom's worktable. "Did I ever meet your parents? Before we were killed, I mean?"

"You do not remember?"

"No. That's part of the past that's still blank to me."

"You met my father, yes. My mother was long dead by the time you were born. She would have liked you. She would have been pleased I chose you above all others."

Wyverns, I remembered from a talk with May, all had one thing in common—one dragon parent and one human parent. "Because I was raised with mortals, you mean?"

"Because you thought like them, even after you knew what you truly were."

I digested that for a minute, about to ask another

question when Baltic emerged from the spare room. He wore a pair of dusky brown leather leggings and boots that went up to midthigh, and he bore a long, stained leather sheath. In one hand he carried a black tunic and something that looked like a small curved chest piece, one that had seen better days. He tossed the chest piece onto a chair, and as I stared in astonishment, pulled a long sword out of the sheath, balancing it in his hand for a moment before nodding. "I am glad Pavel was able to retrieve my cuirass and sword before Constantine destroyed Dauva. Now, *chérie*, you will cease thinking of the past and focus on the present."

I continued to stare for a moment, tears pricking painfully to life behind my eyes. "If I wasn't head over heels in love with you already, I would fall madly in love with you right at this moment."

He looked down at himself for a moment before cocking an eyebrow. "It is good, then, that I kept the clothing I wore when Thala resurrected me. I had no idea it would arouse you in such a manner."

"It's not the clothes," I said, setting down the caramel and taking his face in my hands, pulling him down so I could press kisses all over it.

"Then what?" he asked, placing the sword on Brom's worktable, wrapping both arms around me, and hoisting me upward. "Why do you weep?"

"It's the fact that you would go to all this trouble just to please me. Oh, Baltic, I don't need you in leggings, although they are even more sexy on you now than in the past. I don't want you to be the man you used to be—I desire you as you are, not as you were. My heart has always been yours, and always will be."

"That is as it should be," he said with a smug look that

just made me smile. "But I do not mind indulging the less strange of your fantasies. Do you have a chemise?"

I blinked at him. "I beg your pardon?"

"I cannot make love to you in the tunnel under Dauva while we are in England. This basement will have to suffice as the location for your current fantasy of the time I took you in the tunnel." He paused and thought for a moment. "The *first* time I took you in the tunnel. It was a favorite trysting place of yours."

"Was it? I don't . . . Baltic, I don't expect you to reenact this. I wasn't turned on by the idea of our past selves going at it in a secret tunnel."

He raised one eyebrow.

"All right, I was just a little, but not so much that I needed for you to dig out all your old things and the sword. Which I should point out is now a museum piece, so you should probably treat it a little better than you are. The scabbard looks like it's about to fall apart."

"Do you wish for me to make love to you here or not?" he asked impatiently.

I was about to say yes when something occurred to me. "You're always talking about my fantasies, not that I have any, or at least not like you seem to think I do. But what about you?"

His brows pulled together in a puzzled frown. "What about me?"

"What fantasies do you have?"

"I am a wyvern. I don't need fantasies," he said with a matter-of-fact finality.

I touched the tips of my fingers to his bare chest, lightly stroking them down the swells of his muscles. "Oh, surely there must be one or two little ones wyverns are allowed?"

His eyes widened just a little. "I enjoyed the caramel."

"Yes, but that wasn't your fantasy. What would make you crazy with lust, Baltic?" I breathed on a nipple, flicking it with my tongue.

He sucked in his breath.

"What would push you over the edge?" I let my fingers trailer lower, to his belly, swirling them in an intricate pattern, enjoying the way the muscles contracted there.

He stopped breathing.

I smiled, and leaned close, speaking against his lips. "What would drive you to distraction?"

"I am a dragon." His eyes glittered brightly despite the dimness of the room. His stance changed subtly, from relaxed to tense, as if his entire body was gathering itself.

My fingers brushed the front of his leather pants, caressing the growing length of him. "And what do dragons like?"

"The hunt," he said, his voice low and rough, and so filled with erotic promise, it made me shiver with anticipation. "Mates run. Dragons hunt."

I nipped his bottom lip. "Do you want me to—"

"RUN!" he snarled, smoke curling out of his nose.

I didn't wait around to tease him any more. I simply bolted up the stairs, smiling to myself that I had found a fantasy I could fulfill for him. The house held no attraction for me, so I ran straight for the garden, planning on leading him on a merry chase through the shrubs to the small, growth-protected woods that edged one side of the estate.

The night air was a bit chilly, as summer was moving toward autumn, but the cool, crisp air was pleasant on my heated skin as I wove through the long shadows of the garden, vaulting over a brick fence to the verge that led into the woods.

There wasn't a lot of light from the moon, and even less when I entered the minute forest. A sense of déjà vu struck me as I dashed from tree to tree, trying desperately to calm my breathing so Baltic wouldn't hear me.

"Always you run to the forest," a voice called out with mock dismay. "The silver dragon influences still grip you, eh, *chérie*?"

If he thought I was going to answer him and let him pinpoint my direction, he was crazy. I moved as silently as possible, clutching willow and ash trees, peering around them into the dark gloom of the woods, searching for any signs of movement.

"You do not answer me? You have learned since that first time. But I found you then, Ysolde, and I will find you now."

I wanted badly to tell him that I expected him to find me, but instead glided to a large alder tree, the base of which was at least four feet wide. With another smile, I peeled off my shirt and draped it on a branch before moving to the next tree, away from his voice.

"I can smell you, mate. Your scent betrays you." His voice resonated within me, calling to me, urging me to find him, but I simply peeled off my linen pants and left them behind on a dense clump of laurel.

Oh, he was going to have to do better if he thought I was going to rise to that puny bait.

An owl hooted directly in front of me, making me jump and glare into the shadows. Was that a real owl, or was it Baltic teasing me?

It hooted again, and with one last wary look at the silhouetted tree where the noise originated, I moved on.

"Can't be him. He's behind me," I murmured under my breath, moving silently into the deepest part of the woods, careful of where I stepped, avoiding the branches that tried to trap my hair in a tangle.

"What is this? A shirt? Are your breasts bare, Ysolde? Do you wish I was caressing them? Licking them?"

I smiled, pleased that my ploy had worked. Now I knew exactly where he was.

"Trousers, too, eh? You taunt me, mate."

Little night sounds surrounded us—the distant hum of a car, nocturnal insects announcing their availability for mating, and a small chorus of frogs from a nearby stream expounding on whatever it is frogs expound on at night, all punctuated by the occasional squeak of a night bird or a startled rodent. Beyond that, a faint sound of rustling was audible, as if a large man was brushing through the undergrowth searching for more garments.

I smashed a mosquito on my arm and headed for the far edge of the woods, planning what I would say to Baltic when he eventually found me sitting in bed.

The owl called again, this time from slightly ahead of me, near three willows that had twined around each other when they were saplings. "Must be a mating pair," I murmured as I passed the trees.

"Yes, we are."

I spun around and glared at the man who leaned casually against the entwined tree trunks, his arms crossed. "How did you do that?"

"Do what?"

"Make it sound like you were behind me. You did that before, when you first chased me into the woods. I don't like it."

He smiled a long, slow, predatory smile. "You will not escape this time with just a kiss," he warned, moving with sinuous power toward me.

For a second, I thought of running. Then sanity took over and pointed out that I very much wanted to be in his grasp. Instead I reached behind me and unhooked my bra, tossing it toward him.

"Another striptease? It's not needed to arouse me."

"No? Perhaps I need some arousing." The second the words left my lips he pounced, sending me flying, but twisting in midair so that he was the one who hit the ground.

I looked down at him, his eyes glittering with obsidian heat even in the darkness of the night, and for a moment was so overcome with love, I couldn't speak.

Luckily, Baltic wasn't waiting for me to make speeches. Before I could blink, he had rolled over, spinning me onto my front side, removing my underwear in the process. My back was bathed in fire as he dipped a finger into me, finding proof that I didn't need any foreplay.

"You are mine!" he growled as he plunged into me, making my muscles quiver with delight at the intrusion. Our brief time together had made me aware that dragons took their possessions very seriously, and that included mates, so I said nothing as he claimed me in the most fundamental way a man could. Not that I wanted to say anything, but the primitive, desperate need I felt in him to join with me was answered by my own desire, and it didn't take either of us long before I was gasping his name, clutching the soft grass as he gave himself entirely to me.

"Do you remember," I said aeons later when I could do more than just lie in a quivering pool of postorgasmic rapture, "when I used to do this for you?"

He looked down at where I knelt before him, helping him to get the thigh-high boots on. "Yes. Frequently it ended up in lovemaking because you insisted on taking me into your mouth, and that led to me reciprocating, and then I had to love you again, because you were always a demanding woman."

I bit his knee and started on the other leg. "Why do little snippets of my memories like that come through for me, but the big things, the things I really want to remember, are lost?"

"You have not yet woken your dragon self. Once you do that, your memory will return." He picked me up and carried me, naked since he hadn't bothered to collect the bits of clothing I'd strewn for him, into the house. I prayed that Brom was fast asleep.

"Why were you resurrected with your dragon fully awake, but I wasn't?"

"Questions, questions, always with you it is so many questions," he said, climbing the stairs without even the least bit of panting. I kissed his neck.

"Here's a few more: how did you get ahead of me back in the woods and make it sound like you were behind me? Do you by any chance know how to hoot like an owl? And don't tell me you can't reveal all your secrets, because then I'll lose interest in you, because we both know that's not the least bit true."

He laughed, opened our bedroom door, and set me

on my feet. "I will wash the dirt off my back," was all he said as he headed for the shower in the attached bathroom.

"That's what you get for knocking me down." I picked a few leaves from my hair. "And don't think I didn't notice you haven't answered my questions, not that I really believe you can hoot like an owl, because that's not at all your style, but still, you could tell me how you sounded like you were behind me and were really in front of me."

The sound of running water was my only answer. I climbed into bed, smoothing down the sheets, waiting until the water stopped. After a few minutes of silence, I glanced at the slightly open bathroom door. "Baltic? Are you there?"

An owl hooted.

From the bathroom.

That rat!

Chapter Eleven

"Akashic League of Great Britain. How may I direct your call?"

"I'd like to book the services of a Summoner, please. One who is familiar with dragons."

Brom, bearing a shovel and a plastic bag, marched past where I was sitting in the morning sun on the east patio, and disappeared into the shrubbery.

"Er . . ." The woman on the other end of the phone was clearly taken aback by my request. "Dragons?"

"Yes. Do you have someone who can summon a dragon spirit?"

"I . . . I don't know. I don't think anyone has ever asked for a Summoner with dragon experience. They aren't often raised as shades. In fact, I can't ever think of the time one was. Perhaps it would be best if I transferred you over to booking."

Brom headed back into the house.

I listened with impatience to the classical music

provided by the Akashic League before a male voice greeted me. "Booking."

"I'd like to engage a Summoner, one with experience with dragons," I said. "Can you hook me up with one? I'm just outside of London, but I'm willing to go anywhere in Europe to speak with her."

Brom wandered past with a large bucket, heading for the shrubs again.

"Her?" the man said, suspicion dripping from the word.

"Or him," I said quickly. "I'm good with either gender, so long as the Summoner has experience with dragon ghosts."

"Dragon ghosts?" the man repeated, his voice taking on a weary tone. "Madame, you are aware, are you not, that there are several types of spirits?"

"Well . . . not really. I mean, a ghost is a ghost is a ghost, isn't it?"

"No," he said firmly. "There are bound and unbound, released and unreleased spirits. There are alastors and alguls, as well as shades, revenants, and liches. A sentient being who is brought forth by a member of the Akashic League may take any one of those forms. How and when did the dragon you referenced die?"

Nico, the green dragon tutor whom Baltic had reluctantly engaged for Brom's education, smiled at me as he passed by carrying a large covered tray and a small hatchet.

"Oh. Um, I'm not exactly sure."

The man sighed heavily. "Your chance of success in raising the spirit or entity will depend directly on the amount of information you can give the person assisting you."

I made a rude face at the phone. "I'm sorry. I'll try

to dig up more information, but really, I think it's best that I talk directly to the person who will be doing the summoning."

Pavel, armed with a coil of rope, a small chain saw, and a plate of pastel-colored cupcakes, passed me with a determined look on his face, and disappeared into the yew shrubs.

"Well . . ." The click of keys on a keyboard followed. "As it happens, we do have a Summoner who lists dragons as an area of expertise. Would you like to book her services?"

I agreed, and provided the man with the necessary information, thanking him when he finally parted with the name and phone number I wanted.

"Her services will not be cheap," the man warned before I hung up. "Nor will she take kindly to a client who wastes her time."

"Oh, I don't think we have that to worry about," I told him, getting up to see just what was going on in the shrubs, all the while planning what I would say to Dr. Kostich.

After admiring the new archaeological dig site (Nico had devised a way to incorporate lessons in history, botany, biology, and a little physical education in a manner that kept Brom's interest), I returned to the house to call Maura Lo. She didn't answer her phone, so I left a voice mail saying I was interested in hiring her services for help with a dragon spirit.

"I don't suppose it is any good asking you to reconsider your plans."

I looked at the man standing in the doorway, hands on his hips, face set in a disgruntled expression, my stomach doing an excited flip at the sight of him. I wondered if I would ever be able to see him without that little wibble of pleasure. I sure hoped not. "I want this to end, Baltic."

He shook his head, coming into the sitting room, pulling me into a gentle embrace. "It serves no purpose, mate. The weyr believes only what they wish to believe."

"Only because they're too stubborn to see the truth, but we can help them overcome that."

His sigh ruffled my hair. "I wish that I could understand your desire to be a part of the weyr."

I snuggled against him, breathing in the wonderful Baltic scent that never failed to leave me a bit giddy. "I wish you could, too. But since you can't, you're just going to have to accept that this is important to me. To us. I don't want Brom or any of our children growing up in the middle of a war."

A wicked smile curled his lips as he pulled me tighter, grinding my hips against his. "Our time would be better spent working on those children."

"Tempting, but I think I'd rather have weyr peace first, so you can stop trying to woo me into bed. I'll just get my things and then I'll be ready to go. Where's your girlfriend?"

He stared at me with a slight frown.

"Thala."

"I cannot decide if your jealousy of her is amusing or irritating," he said thoughtfully. "Perhaps it is both."

"I'm not—oh, never mind. Is she here?"

"No." He looked away, suddenly cagey.

"Where is she?"

"She went to Italy last night after you tempted me away with caramel. My son will not come with us to the meeting with the wyverns. I will not have him put in danger."

"I didn't intend for him to come, not that I think

there's any danger. Nico is out with him digging up what Brom insists is an ancient peat bog. He's hoping for Viking treasure, so I don't think we would be able to get him away even if we wanted him to come with us."

"Good. He would not be safe."

"Don't be silly," I said, going out to change into something more suited to the dignity of a meeting with wyverns. I was upstairs, in the middle of donning a white lace jacquard coat dress, white lace stockings, and the engraved silver love token that Baltic had made me some five hundred years earlier, when I realized that once again he had adroitly distracted me from asking him a question I suspected he didn't want me to ask.

"You'd think he'd learn by now," I said to myself as I trotted down the back stairs to check on a lime-garlic marinade I'd whipped up, making sure the chicken was soaking in it before I went out to rout Baltic from wherever he had disappeared.

"There you are. Listen, I know you don't want to tell me. . . ." I stopped speaking, blinking in astonishment as the love of my life marched down the stairs. He wore a calf-length black topcoat, black pants, and a long black tunic top that shimmered with light as he moved. "By the rood, Baltic! You look absolutely wonderful. Is the shirt beaded?" I peered closely at the tunic.

"Do I look like the sort of a man who wears beaded garments?" he asked, the scorn in his voice counterbalanced by his pleased expression as I marveled over his outfit. "It's dragonweave. I had some made for you, but it's in Riga. I'll have it brought out here, if you like."

"It's gorgeous material," I said, touching the tunic. "It's like it's covered in thousands of crystals but there's nothing there but the fabric, is there?"

"You will make a dress from it to wear in front of other dragons. I hadn't thought we would have need of it, but I see I was wrong."

"Wow. It's just . . . and you look . . . I could pounce on you," I said, circling him.

"I am happy to spend the time making love to you instead of meeting with the wyverns," he offered politely.

I laughed, gave him a quick kiss, then took his hand and tugged him toward the door. "Nice try. That outfit almost did it, too, but it's more important that we take care of this. Oh, Pavel. I didn't know you were coming with us. I'm glad, though. You can help keep Baltic from losing his temper with everyone."

Pavel emerged from his room next to the kitchen, clad in black pants and a slightly different black tunic. It, too, was made of dragonweave, but it didn't appear to have quite such a glittery effect to it. I gathered that only the wyvern got to wear the really flashy version of the cloth, and I spent the next ten minutes in pleasant contemplation of just what sort of a dress I would fashion from the material that Baltic had had made for me.

My second attempt to find out what Thala was doing in Italy was met with a look that I decided I wouldn't pursue in front of Pavel. Although he might be Baltic's closest friend, I hesitated to involve him in the discussion when Baltic obviously preferred otherwise. I was content to simply give him a look that let him know the subject wasn't closed, and then I focused on driving us to the house he had built for me several hundred years before.

"We *have* to talk to Kostya about giving Dragonwood back to us," I said as I stopped just shy of the willow and lime crescent that blocked the view of the house from the long drive.

Baltic considered the redbrick Tudor mansion front, nodding at the house with approval. "Next to Dauva, it is the best of our homes."

I sighed as I gazed at it. It was utterly perfect, everything about it meant to please, from the location on the top of a gentle hill, to the center square tower, to the beautiful mullioned windows and stone quoins, all the way up to the parapets that were etched into the sky. The grounds were just as lovely, with a garden that I had designed myself, a crystal clear pond, and velvety green expanses of lawn that sang a sweet siren song to me.

"Baltic—" I stopped, my throat too tight to continue.

He took my hand and kissed my fingers. "It will be yours again, my love. I swear to you that it will."

"It wants us back," I said, my eyes swimming with tears of longing as the essence of the house seemed to wrap itself around me, an essence that was heavily imbued with happy memories of our time spent there. "It *needs* us."

Baltic was silent for a moment, then brushed away a tear that escaped my eye, saying softly, "We will get it back."

I pulled myself together, squelching the pain, reminding myself that there was a long way to go before we could negotiate with Kostya for the return of the house. "Let's tackle one thing at a time. It's more important that we end this stupid war."

"I don't see why," Pavel said as we got out of the car. "Brom visits the silver dragons and has a green dragon tutor, and you meet with the mates.... Does it really matter if the war continues?"

"Yes, it does. Just because things are amicable now doesn't mean they won't go all pear-shaped later, and I want us to be a part of the weyr so we have some protection if that happens."

Baltic sighed, but took my hand and led me up the stairs, at the top of which stood two large figures.

"Good morning, Maata. Tipene. Are you guys banished to the outside, or are May and Gabriel not here yet?" I asked.

Both of the silver guards greeted me, nodding to Baltic. "It was decided that all guards are to remain outside for your meeting." Maata looked like she wanted to smile, but she held it back. "We were going to have a stroll around the gardens that you designed. Perhaps Pavel would care to join us?"

"Oh, that sounds wonderful. I hope we'll have time to join you later. I'd love to see the flowers again. . . ."

Baltic gave me a little shove toward the big double doors.

"Gardens. How delightful," Pavel answered, looking as if he'd rather have his fingernails yanked out one by one.

"It won't hurt you," I told him, laughing as he followed the two silver dragons.

"Come. Let us have this over with," Baltic said, throwing open one of the doors. I hesitated at the threshold, since the last time I had attempted to cross it, I'd been pulled into the beyond, the shadow world that paralleled our reality, where I had seen Baltic watching a bittersweet vision of our past.

His eyes met mine. I tightened my fingers in his, smiled, and allowed him to see the love in my eyes before I crossed into the house.

"Well, I might have known this would happen," I said a moment later as a bone-freezing cold seeped into my awareness. The world shifted and lost color, resolving itself into a grey-toned scene that I realized was colorless because the building in which I stood was made of stone and metal. I rubbed my arms and looked with curiosity around what appeared to be a lobby of some sort. "Brr. Where is this, I wonder?"

"I do not know, but I dislike it."

I spun around to find Baltic directly behind me. "You're getting into more and more of my visions. I don't know if that's good or bad. I think this is the aerie."

"What aerie?" His eyes were as unreadable as his expression as he looked around and then grimaced. "Ah. The one that belongs to Kostya. End the vision, mate."

"End it? How am I supposed to do that? What dragons live in Nepal? Red?"

Noise behind me had me considering the figures of three men who emerged from the other side of the lobby.

"No," Baltic said, grabbing me and pulling me backward, as if he feared we'd be seen.

"They can't see us," I said, escaping his hold, curious now as to who the dragons were. I stepped into the lobby, pausing when a fourth man walked straight through Baltic toward the group.

"Is it done?" the fourth man asked the others.

One of the three nodded. "Aye. We have control of the aerie."

"Kostya?"

"Locked in a storage room until his cell is readied."

"Good. I'll pass that on to the chief."

"We're right—this is where Kostya went after the destruction of Dauva," I said to Baltic. "I remember Aisling saying something about him being held prisoner. But who are those dragons? What sept do they belong to?"

"None. They are ouroboros. Come, mate, we have tarried too long. The wyverns are waiting for us."

The word "ouroboros" rang in my head like a bell. "I really want to see this, Baltic. I think it's important somehow."

"It is not."

"How do you know that?" A sudden horrible thought occurred to me. "By the saints! Are these your dragons? Was it you who had Kostya imprisoned? It was, wasn't it? You couldn't kill him outright because of your past relationship, but you wanted him out of the way, so you had him locked up in his own hidey-hole?"

"I am not responsible for this, no," he said, his lips thinning.

I avoided his hold and moved closer to the group of dragons. "Then you know who did."

"—how long we'll have to stay here?" one of the men was asking the obvious leader. "It's bloody cold."

"We'll stay as long as we have to. You might as well see if there's any food. The chief will be here at any moment, and I'd like to be able to tell her that all is taken care of."

"Her? Her who?" I asked no one in particular.

Baltic looked bored and didn't answer.

"Still say it's wrong to let her call the shots," one of the three dragons said in a languid Southern U.S. drawl. "Not like she's even really one of us."

"Don't be such a snob. Her father was high up in the sept, and is said to have had the ear of the wyvern."

The man snorted. "Red dragons. All they want is to war."

"Which works to our benefit," the leader said, cocking his head as if he was listening to something.

"Who are they talking about?" I asked Baltic, a suspicion arising that I hesitated to name.

His expression was shuttered. "Do you wish to stand here all day, or do you want for us to speak with the wyverns?"

"Typical nonanswer, dragon. Who—oh!"

A man appeared out of nothing, seemingly walking through the wall straight into the gathering. I gawked at him, taking in clothing that appeared to be from the turn of the twentieth century, as well as his less than solid form.

"Is that a ghost?" I asked Baltic in a whisper as the figure drifted over to the group.

He sighed. "Mate, we must leave now."

"Is it?"

"Of a form. It is a shade. Your time is up, Ysolde. End this vision."

"My mistress comes," the ghostly man informed the others, and over the howl of the wind beating against the stone of the building, I could hear the growing sound of a helicopter approaching.

"I am leaving now," Baltic informed me, dropping my hand, which he had grabbed in a futile attempt to pull me away with him. "Either come with me or do not, but do not expect me to agree to another meeting with the wyverns."

"Just a second, I want to see—Baltic!" I started after him as he strode away into the dimness of a corridor that led off from the lobby. I glanced over my shoulder and said, "I want to see who's arriving. You know, don't you? You know who was behind Kostya's capture? And who these dragons are?"

"They are ouroboros," he repeated, pausing to let me catch up to him.

"I wonder if they're the same group as the one I'm looking for."

"You are not to look for ouroboros dragons," he informed me in a haughty tone that he had to know would just irritate me.

"Oh, I'm not? And why is that?"

"They are lawless murderers, dangerous, and without any regard for life, be it that of dragons or mortals. They are the single biggest danger to the mortals you care so much about." He opened a thick metal door and shoved me outside into a sunny but windy snowscape. Immediately the world shifted, and I found myself strolling into the dim coolness of a house that wrapped me in such a familiar embrace, I wanted to sink to my knees and cry with the injustices of life.

"There you are. I was about to go look in the shadow world for you. Is everything all right? You look like you've seen a ghost, Ysolde."

"I have." I blinked a few times to clear my still-fuzzy vision, it finally resolving itself into the sight of May's concerned face peering at me. "I'm sorry. We were sucked into a vision in . . ."

The words trailed away at the sight of Kostya emerging from a side room.

"I'll tell you later," I finished in an undertone.

May's eyebrows rose as Gabriel, who had been using his cell phone, hung up and strolled over to us. "Drake and Aisling have been detained, but they are only a few minutes away. Greetings, Ysolde." A muscle in his jaw twitched. "Baltic."

"I'm sorry, it seems this house is just vision-central for me," I said, smiling at Gabriel. "Thank you for coming. I'm sure you have better things to do with your time, but we appreciate it. Don't we, Baltic?"

"Not in the least," he said pleasantly, but I could tell his hackles were up by the way he watched Kostya.

Gabriel relaxed at that, his dimples showing as he wrapped an arm around May. "It is good to know that you are running true to form, Baltic. I wouldn't know what to think should you be anything but hostile and surly."

"You are welcome to my house, Ysolde," Kostya said, his intentions clear as he greeted me, taking my hands in his and kissing them before turning to Baltic. "I wish I could say the same for your mate."

"Sins of the saints, Kostya," I said, socking him on the arm. "Do you have to bait Baltic every time?"

"No, but it relieves my spleen if I do."

I glared at him until he snapped. "Very well. Your mate is welcome here as well."

I smiled and put a restraining hand on Baltic's arm, which was tense, as if his muscles were poised for attack. "Thank you. We appreciate it, despite the fact that this is really our house."

"Is it?" He gave a little smirk. "I believe it is held by the wyvern of the black dragons, and that is me."

"Only so long as I allow you to remain so," Baltic growled.

Kostya's eyes narrowed, a little smoke emerging from his nose. "Do you wish to challenge me for the sept?"

"I do not need to. If I wanted it, I would take it," Baltic answered.

"Oh, lord, please tell me I don't have to let you two boys break each other's noses again," I said, sighing heavily.

Both men turned identical glares on me. "Boys!" Kostya snorted. "We are wyverns!"

"That may be, but you're acting like twits dancing around each other with your hackles up."

"Twit!" Baltic repeated, outraged.

"Hackles! We do not have hackles!" Kostya said, just as outraged. "Dogs have hackles. Dragons do not!"

"Then stop acting like you do," I told him with a look that I reserve for Brom at his most fractious. I turned to Baltic, giving his arm another squeeze. "And you can cease muttering rude things under your breath. We can all hear them, and even though they're in Zilant, I can tell what it is you're saying."

He shot me another outraged look, but stopped swearing to himself.

Kostya's expression turned martyred. "You are far too outspoken for your own good, Ysolde, but it does not surprise me. It will be a cold day in Abaddon before I ever meet a mate who displays the respect proper to wyverns."

I looked at Baltic, expecting him to take offense at Kostya's speaking to me that way, but he said nothing, just glared. I threw my own good intentions to the wind. "Are you going to let him get away with that?"

"With speaking the truth?" He shrugged. "I have not seen the red wyvern's mate in centuries, but from what I remember of him, he was the only mate who knew how to behave."

"And speaking of errant mates, where's Cyrene?" May cut in as I was about to argue the point with Baltic.

Kostya, who had been matching Baltic's glare with one of his own, transferred it to May. "That is a very good question. You would have to ask her that for an answer, however, since she has apparently left."

"Left? Left for where?" May asked, not looking at all surprised.

"I am evidently not to be privy to such information. She simply hurled all sorts of insults at me, packed up her things—and several that weren't hers—and stormed out of here promising all sorts of watery vengeance if I tried, and these are her words, to follow her, woo her back to my arms in order to have my lustful way with her pristine body, or notify you that she had abandoned me for a god who evidently knows how to treat a naiad. Despite that, consider yourself duly notified."

"Oh, no, she hasn't . . . not Neptune?" May asked, groaning. "A god who knows how to treat her? He took her stream away from her until she made me help get it back. She's absolutely . . . I'm sorry, Kostya, I really am. There's no excuse for what she's done to you."

"She said she loved me! She made me name her as mate in front of the weyr!"

"I know, and I'm sorry." May put an arm around Kostya and gave him a little hug. "She swore that this time it was different, and I believed her. I thought she really was going to stay in love with you."

His martyred look returned. "I should have known she was trouble. She was always demanding I let her meddle in sept business. I told her no, that was not the bailiwick of a mate, but she would not listen. My mother said it would come to a bad end, but I didn't listen to her."

"Yes, well, Catalina isn't who I'd really go to for relationship advice," May said with a little smile as she returned to Gabriel's side. "Is she still dating Magoth?"

"No, thank god." Kostya's shoulders slumped in a manner that indicated a morose sort of pleasure. "Your former demon lord dumped her for some Hollywood starlet. Mother is currently living with a trio of body-builders in Rio, and only comes to plague us when she remembers that Drake has children."

"She sounds like a delightful person," I said dryly. Baltic looked bored, glancing at his watch. I estimated I had about ten minutes before he would demand we either get to business or leave. "Perhaps we could get started without Drake and Aisling?"

"I would prefer that we wait, but since your mate appears to be anxious to leave, I'm agreeable to begin the discussion. Kostya?"

"We might as well. No good will come of it whether we do it now or later," he said with dark foreboding, gesturing toward a door.

I looked at the door, glanced at Baltic, and spun on my heel to march in the opposite direction, throwing open the double doors that led to a room filled with tall, glass-fronted floor-to-ceiling bookcases, warmed by amber pools of sunlight that poured in through the mullioned windows. "Our library." I sighed with happiness. The furniture wasn't, of course, the same as I remembered, but the way the light streamed in through the windows, the peculiar quality of it as it filled the room, swamped me with the sweetest of memories.

"*My* library now, I believe," Kostya said with unnecessary emphasis on the pronoun. "I will allow the meeting to be held here, since you seem to desire it." His gaze shifted to Baltic. "It is a courtesy I am happy to extend to you, Ysolde, despite the fact that you and your murderous mate are at war with the weyr."

"Oh, for the love of the virgin . . . will you *please* stop trying to bait Baltic?" I snapped, tired of all the posturing the wyverns felt it necessary to adopt. "He's not so uncontrolled that he's going to fall for that."

Baltic lunged forward so fast he was just a blur. The resounding thud of the two men going down in the middle of the hardwood floor, accompanied by the tinkle of a couple of glass knickknacks sent flying as they crashed into two occasional tables, left me with the intense desire to do a little smiting, but I managed to hold on to my temper.

"You make it very difficult to convince everyone that you're not the barbarian they call you," I told Baltic as he punched Kostya in the face while trying to throttle him with his other hand.

Kostya shifted into dragon form, Baltic following suit.

Another occasional table, this one a pretty octagonal inlaid with rosewood, slammed into the wall. "No dragon form!" I yelled, looking with dismay at the remains of the table. "Human form only, and if you break anything nice, I'll have more than a few things to say to both of you."

"You're going to let them fight?" May asked, jumping aside when both men, now back in human form, rolled around beating the tar out of each other. "Is that wise? Mightn't things get out of hand?"

"I don't think so. I figure it'll clear the air a bit."

May looked like she was going to say something, but to my surprise, Gabriel spoke first. "I'm sorry, Mayling. I would like to say I'm above such things, but the opportunity is one I really don't wish to miss."

After a moment of surprise, she gave him a lopsided smile and gestured toward the combatants. "If you really must."

"I must," he said, giving her a swift kiss before flinging himself into the fray. May and I moved over to the door, out of the way of the whirlwind of three men who were accompanied by oaths, snarls, grunts of pain, and language that would make a sailor blush.

"I've never seen the dragons come to physical blows so much as when Baltic is around," May commented, wincing in sympathy when Baltic, overjoyed that Gabriel was now on his list of people to beat up, landed a solid right to Gabriel's jaw.

"He's a very primal sort of dragon," I said, watching dispassionately but cheering to myself when Kostya crashed to the floor with a fine spray of blood. "No ganging up on Baltic, now, boys," I told them sharply when it looked like Kostya and Gabriel, who had a history of animosity, had decided to forge a truce in order to tromp Baltic.

"What on earth . . . are they fighting again?"

May and I turned as the doors behind us were opened. Aisling and Drake stood staring in amazement.

"They seem to like it," I told her. "I suppose it releases pent-up emotions. Now that you're here, I'll stop them."

"Not yet," Drake said, peeling off his jacket and handing it to Aisling, his green eyes glinting like a cat's.

We all watched with utter astonishment as Drake, with a battle cry that would have done a warrior proud, leaped over the couch and launched himself onto Baltic's back.

"Oh, for Pete's sake . . . have you ever met such pig-headed men?" Aisling asked, her hands on her hips. "Ouch. That's got to sting. Oh, now there's blood on Drake's pretty shirt. Our housekeeper will have my head for that."

"You have to admit, there's something—oh, good one, Baltic!—strangely attractive about men fighting each other in this manner. Hey! I said no ganging up on Baltic! I see that, Drake and Kostya! If you boys can't fight fairly, you can just sit in the hallway!"

Aisling giggled. "You're probably the only person in the world who can get away with saying that, Ysolde. Well, ladies, it looks like the menfolk are busy with their show of masculinity. Shall we move to an atmosphere that's a little less testosterone filled?"

I cast an assessing glance at the battle. Baltic's left eye was swelling shut, and blood dripped out of his nose, but he looked in fine fettle nonetheless. The other three wyverns all seemed to fare similarly, and to my surprise, they all seemed to realize that there were limits to their fighting, and no one attempted to use weapons, makeshift or otherwise, but confined themselves to their fists.

"I don't see why not. I suppose when they get tired of beating each other up, they'll come to find us and have their injuries tended. Let us go to the solar."

I led the way up the stairs to a room that sat above the library, designed so that it, too, caught the afternoon sunlight. It was furnished now in an atrocious manner, but I did my best to ignore the hideous bloated tea roses that adorned all the furniture, imagining how beautiful the room could be given the chance.

We chatted for a few minutes about commonplace things, May explaining to Aisling what had happened to her twin.

"Oh, man. Cyrene's given him the brush-off?" Aisling shook her head. "He's going to be hell to live with."

"I'd like to say that it's just a phase, but ... well, you

know Cy. She's always been fickle when it comes to matters of the heart," May answered.

"The question is . . ." Aisling paused in thought. "What impact is that going to have on the weyr?"

"What do you mean? Why would there be an impact?" I asked.

"This was before you were awake, Ysolde—or rather, before you went into your fugue—but Kostya named Cyrene as his mate in front of the weyr."

"That's what he said. I don't see what the problem is. Can't he just *un*name her?"

"I don't think so, no. Dragons mate for life, you see. All but reeve dragons, but those are few and far between." She must have seen my look of confusion because she continued. "Reeves are special dragons. They have an unusually pure bloodline, and they are the only ones who can mate more than once. That is, if they have a mate and she or he dies, the dragon continues to live and can take another mate. Drake's grandmother was a reeve. She had two mates, one a black dragon and one a green dragon. That's why Drake is a green dragon, and Kostya is black. But we were talking about Cyrene."

"There must be some sort of policy for the unnaming of a mate," May said.

"I don't think so. Drake has never mentioned anything of the sort, and I think he would have when Kostya named Cyrene as one." She sat in a horribly overstuffed chair while May and I took an adjacent love seat. "I don't think the situation has ever come up before, which means there may be some trouble at the weyr when all the mates are present."

"Why would that be? Mates don't do much, do they?"

I asked, thinking back to the *sárkány* I'd witnessed a few months before. "Aren't you just there as support?"

"Yes, but it's vital support. Mates are excused from weyr functions for only very limited reasons—childbirth being one of them, and illness or physical inability to attend another. Mates can also attend a *sárkány* in place of the wyvern."

May's eyes widened.

"Exactly," Aisling said, nodding. "Can you imagine what would happen if something kept Kostya away from a *sárkány*, and Cyrene had the right to take his place?"

"*Agathos daimon*," May muttered, running a hand over her eyes. "I don't even want to—"

She was cut off as the door was flung open. Baltic stood in the doorway, blood dripping from his nose and eyebrow.

"Mate! You left me!"

"Of course we left," I said calmly, quickly eyeing him for signs of injuries. He seemed to be favoring his left side, in addition to his other hurts. "You were all acting like idiots. You didn't honestly expect us to stand there and watch you beat each other up, did you?"

"A proper mate knows that her place is at her wyvern's side," Drake said, pushing past Baltic into the room. He limped slightly, and appeared to be missing a tooth.

Aisling tsked and hurried over to him, wiping at the blood on his mouth.

May raised her eyebrows as Gabriel, also limping, followed Drake, a little groan escaping him when he sat in the spot I vacated. "'Physician, heal thyself' has a particularly fitting ring to it right now, but I suppose you don't want to hear that, do you?"

"No," he said, wincing as he flexed the fingers of one hand.

Kostya staggered in last, striking a pose at the door that lasted for three seconds before he crumpled and collapsed.

I looked at Baltic again. "I imagine you're proud of yourself."

"I have nothing to be ashamed of, if that is what you are implying." He nodded to where both Aisling and May (who had evidently given in to Gabriel's pathetic appearance) were murmuring softly as they tended their men. "Aren't you going to cosset me as the other mates are doing?"

"I don't think you deserve any cosseting, since it was you who started the whole thing by jumping Kostya."

A groan came from the direction of the floor. "It was completely his fault. He's wholly to blame for everything. Oh, god, I think I'm going to puke."

Baltic looked at me out of his one good eye, the sadness in it sufficient that I pulled out a tissue and dabbed gently at the blood from his nose. "Sit down," I said, pushing him into the overstuffed chair Aisling had been sitting in.

"Careful," he warned, easing himself into the seat. "A couple of my ribs are broken."

"They are?" I whirled around, suddenly furious. "All right, which one of you broke Baltic's ribs?"

Drake and Gabriel pointed to the floor.

"He dislocated my shoulder and broke my collarbone, if that makes you feel any better," Kostya said in a pained voice.

"Tough noogies. You and I are going to have a little talk later on, Konstantin Fekete," I said, glaring at him.

"If I survive, you're welcome to try," he said in between groans.

It took us a few minutes to get everyone patched up and relatively hale, although all four men had to be provided with dragon's blood, an extremely potent spicy sort of wine that only dragons and their mates could drink, before their regenerative powers kicked in and healed the worst of their hurts.

"Now perhaps we can get down to business and talk about this ridiculous war," I said after everyone was comfortably situated. "I want to discuss the death of all those blue dragons, and what actual proof you have against Baltic regarding them."

Drake's phone buzzed. With a cross between an oath and a groan, he got to his feet and moved stiffly to the far end of the room to take the call.

"The proof was laid before you at the last *sárkány*," Gabriel said wearily, sipping carefully from his glass. "Baltic was in the area at the time of the murders. He was seen by one of the survivors. He is known to have been working with Fiat, who we know also had a hand in the murders."

"Really? Then why haven't you put a death sentence on his head the way you did mine?" I asked, more than a little riled at the thought of the way the entire weyr had jumped to erroneous conclusions.

"Fiat is . . ." Gabriel glanced across the room at Drake.

"Nutso." Aisling finished the sentence. "Mad as a hatter, or so Drake and Bastian say. Jim would say he's cracked, and for once, I agree with it. Drake tried to talk to Fiat last month, but he went off about a woman plotting his downfall, and how she's arranged to have him killed after using him for her own purposes."

"Chuan Ren? I can see her wanting him dead after he stole her sept, but how has she used him? He has to be mad if he's making paranoid claims like that. But perhaps he's not so far gone that we can't reason with him. Maybe we should talk to him again," I suggested. "Maybe someone could get through to the rational part of his mind."

"That's doubtful," Drake said, returning to us with only the slightest hint of a limp.

"You think he's that mad?" I asked him.

"No." He stood before Baltic, giving him a long, cold look. "You can't question Fiat because he's gone."

His words dropped like anvils in the silence of the room.

"Dead?" Gabriel asked, his eyes watching Drake carefully.

"No. Disappeared. That was Bastian on the phone. He called to tell me that Fiat has been extricated from his prison."

"Not again." Aisling groaned. "What do you bet it was Chuan Ren who nabbed him just so she can poke him full of holes?"

"If she did, there's more to her than we knew. Chuan Ren is dead. Fiat killed her two hours ago."

A chill swept over me despite the warmth of the room. We all stared in surprise at Drake, all of us but Baltic, who looked mildly interested.

Drake's gaze was level on his. "Bastian says Baltic is the one who freed Fiat."

Chapter Twelve

"You bastard," I told Drake, taking him and most likely everyone else in the room by surprise. I know I surprised myself with the sudden blast of fury that swept through me, setting Drake's feet alight with dragon fire.

His eyebrows rose as he glanced down at his feet.

"You hate Baltic so much you would do anything to keep him from being part of the weyr, wouldn't you?" I said, my voice husky with emotion. I wanted to strike him, to call down destruction and mayhem.

"Mate—" Baltic said, getting to his feet.

"Hey, now!" Aisling interrupted, stepping between Drake and me. "Drake wouldn't do something like that."

I glared over her shoulder at him, my hands fisted. His jaw tightened, his eyes spitting green fire as I snarled, "You puling little worm. Do you think that because much of the past has been lost to me I do not know of the treachery you tried to perform on Baltic?"

The memory rushed at me, hot and fast, and I jerked it forward, wrapping it around us all.

I heard May gasp as the sunlight of the room shimmered and changed into that cast by a row of flickering torches along a stone passageway. Drake stood before us, but it was another Drake, a Drake of the past, clad in chain mail, holding a sword on a woman as she screamed at him.

"Holy cow! Are we in another vision? We are! Is that Drake? Oh, my god! What are you doing to him, Ysolde?"

We stood as shadows in the memory of that moment in the past, watching the scene that resonated deep within my soul.

"Why do you not stop him? Why do you not stop this madness?" the past Ysolde demanded of Drake. "He's your brother! Do you want to see him wyvern so badly that you would participate in Baltic's death?"

"I am not the one who is mad," Drake growled back at her. "Your mate has brought his own end upon himself."

"Your brother and your blood brother have sworn to kill Baltic, and still you claim you are not involved? Who gave the silver dragons support when they needed it? Who has lent aid and men to Kostya when he would attack Dauva? Who betrayed Baltic and me in St. Petersburg? If Baltic dies, his blood will stain your soul, Drake Fekete, for you will be as much responsible for his murder as they will be."

"Move out of the way, Lady Ysolde," Drake said in a low, mean voice. "I do not wish to do you ill, but I will if you press me."

"I will see you in hell before I let you harm Baltic!" she screamed, lunging at him, the glint of silver in her hand.

"Drake! Oh, my god!" Aisling yelled as Ysolde attacked. She did no more than graze his neck with the dagger before Drake flung her off, sending her flying backward into the wall. She connected with it with a horrible bone-cracking noise, sliding down it to lie in a crumpled heap on the floor.

"Brother! Where—Christos, is that Ysolde? What have you done to her?" Kostya emerged from the yawning black archway that led to the cellars, his armor and sword covered in blood.

Drake knelt next to the fallen Ysolde. "She is unconscious only. She tried to kill me."

"Leave, Drake. This fight is not yours," Kostya said, sheathing his sword in order to scoop my limp form into his arms. "I will take her abovestairs."

"You are my brother. I promised you support, and I will not withdraw now, when you have need of me."

"I don't need your help. Can you not hear the sounds of battle? Constantine is at the gate. I will do what must be done, but you have already risked your future for my sake. I will ask no more of you. Return to Buda and the green dragons."

Drake hesitated. "I would see this to its end, Kostya."

"That will be upon us shortly. Go, Drake. Go out with Constantine's forces, if you will, but I will not have Fodor say you participated in the death of a wyvern. Baltic is my responsibility."

"He is your curse, you mean," Drake said, his face impassive as Kostya carried me down the hallway, calling after him. "If you do not end it now, I will do so myself."

Drake's head snapped back, the sound of flesh striking flesh jerking us all out of the vision. "I . . . haven't . . . forgotten," I told him, rubbing my bruised fingers.

"OK, that's going too far," Aisling said, shoving me aside. "No one hits Drake! I know that some stuff went on in the past that no one is proud of, but that's no reason to hit him now! Are you all right, sweetie?"

Baltic shook his head as he pulled me gently into his arms. "Always you were one to think with your heart and not your head. Ysolde, Ysolde . . . and people say I am violent beyond reason."

"He had it coming," I said, nursing my fingers for a moment before sanity returned. "I apologize for punching you in the eye, Drake. I was caught up in the emotion of the moment, and that wasn't well done of me. However, I don't appreciate you making up lies about Baltic."

Drake stiffened under Aisling's ministrations, gently moving her to his side as he glared at me, one eye slightly swollen and turning dark. "I do not lie!"

"Baltic didn't let Fiat out!" I said loudly.

"His lieutenant did."

"He couldn't have, because he wasn't even in Italy. He's been in Riga, and then here," I told them all.

"It's true, mate."

"And I'm just sick and tired of you guys believing the worst of Baltic! What is it with you people that you can't, just once, believe what we're saying? Why can't you—" I stopped and turned to glance up at Baltic. "What?"

"Thala released Fiat."

I think my jaw dropped at that. I'm not absolutely certain, but I have a nasty feeling that I stood there for a good five seconds staring at him in openmouthed surprise. "She did?"

"Yes."

I prodded his arm when he said nothing more. "Why did she do that?"

"Did you ask her to free Fiat?" Aisling asked at the same time.

"If I had wanted Fiat free, I would have seen to it myself," Baltic told her with grandiose hauteur.

"Then why did Thala set him free?" I repeated.

"I don't know. She has become secretive of late. She said only that it would help achieve our goals."

"You didn't stop her," Gabriel said, his body language showing just how angry he was, despite his placid expression. "Do you expect us to believe that you will not benefit from Fiat being at your beck and call?"

Baltic sighed. "No, I do not expect you to believe that, but that is because you delight in attributing to me the most heinous of motives. And yet the truth is that Fiat threatened to kill Ysolde and Brom. I was delighted that he was in the custody of the blue dragons, and I did not want him released."

"He threatened to *kill* us?" My voice was downright squeaky with surprise. "Why?"

Baltic maintained a stony expression.

"Why?" I asked again, nudging his arm.

His brows pulled together. "I will tell you later, when we are alone."

"That sort of attitude is just going to make everyone suspicious. Why would Fiat want Brom and me dead?"

"There are times," Baltic answered, breathing heavily, "when I long for the days with my old Ysolde."

"Oh, I would have pestered you without mercy until you answered me back then, too."

He grinned, taking me by surprise. "Yes, you would have. You would have me bare my soul before other wyverns without the slightest regard for my consequence or tradition, just as you do now."

"I'm here to keep you humble," I agreed, and waited.

He flicked a glance at the other men, all of whom wore expressions of sympathy. "Fiat blamed me for his current situation. He knew the worst thing he could do to me was to take you from me, so he was plotting with a group of his followers to have you and Brom captured and killed."

My blood felt like ice in my veins. "Why didn't you tell me this?"

"What good would it have done to do so? I would never allow anyone to harm you or my son, so it was of no concern to you. He was safely held by the blue dragons, and I knew his influence would not reach to you."

I slapped my hand on his chest, drumming my fingers with more force than was absolutely necessary. "We are going to have a little talk later about sharing important information, Baltic."

A familiar martyred look crept into his eyes. "I have no doubt that you intend to do so, but we have more pressing things to discuss."

"Was that where you were instead of Riga the other day? In Italy checking up on Fiat?"

"Yes. I was uneasy when I heard that ouroboros dragons had been seen in the area."

"Why didn't you stop Thala if you were there?" I asked.

His lips tightened. "She wasn't in Italy when I was, nor did I know that she intended to free Fiat."

"For the love of . . . Do you have any idea how hard it is to make people believe you're innocent when stuff like this happens?"

He just looked at me.

I sighed. "All right, so I can't blame you if Thala is acting without your instruction, but that doesn't excuse the fact that you didn't bother to tell me about Fiat making threats against Brom."

"I am a wyvern," he said simply. "To protect you is my right and duty."

The other men nodded their agreement.

"Well, Mr. Duty, thanks to you, I have to apologize to that bast—to Drake." I turned around to face him. "It appears I was in the wrong again, Drake. I'm sorry for the rude things I said regarding your attempt to besmirch Baltic's good name. However, if you think that means he was responsible for the other blue dragon deaths, I will be tempted to punch you again."

"You do, and you'll have me to answer to," Aisling said with enough menace in her voice that we all looked at her in surprise.

"Mate, you do not need to protect me," Drake told her with an exasperated expression.

"She hit you!"

"I allowed her to strike me. Do you seriously believe I cannot keep a female from hurting me?"

"You let me hit you?" I asked. "Why?"

"Because the vision you brought forth reminded me that I had, in the past, treated you with less respect than I should have."

Aisling made a face. "That's true. All right, I forgive you for punching him, Ysolde. He did have that one coming. But no more, all right?"

I looked at Drake. "What does the weyr intend to do about Fiat, and Chuan Ren's death? You're not planning on holding Baltic responsible because Thala is a few meatballs short of a spaghetti dinner?"

"We are outside of the weyr, Ysolde," Baltic said, pulling me back against him. "They have already declared war on us. What they think does not matter to our sept."

Drake was silent for a moment, his gaze meeting those of Kostya and Gabriel before turning on us. "In this, Baltic is right. From what Bastian said, Fiat and Thala parted ways immediately after he was released. Why she sought freedom for him is unknown—perhaps your mate can determine that fact. From what Bastian has ascertained, Fiat flew immediately to Hong Kong and dispatched Chuan Ren. Although I regret the death of a fellow wyvern, that tragedy has made it clear that Fiat's madness is more profound than we imagined."

"I'm surprised he could take her down," Aisling told May, who nodded. "Chuan Ren is one tough chick."

"It surprises me as well," Drake said darkly. "I suspect he did not act alone."

"Thala?" I asked.

"I don't believe so, no," Drake said with a glance at Baltic.

"Who would help Fiat?" Aisling asked.

Drake made an elegant shrugging gesture.

I slipped my arm through Baltic's. "What about the murder of the blue dragons? You can't still think that Baltic had anything to do with that."

Drake looked weary as he sat down, pulling Aisling down next to him. "We are here to discuss that situation, and I am willing to do so. Do you have new evidence to present?"

"Not as such, no," I said, sitting on the arm of Baltic's chair as everyone resumed his or her respective seats. "But I'm sure—"

"It is still a matter of your word against that of the survivors," Gabriel interrupted. "I was there, Ysolde. I saw them myself. I heard one man name Baltic as being on the scene. If you have no fresh proof of his innocence, I do not see what more we can do."

I looked at Baltic. He looked back at me.

"Well?" I said, prodding him on the shoulder.

"Well, what?"

"Why don't you make them believe you?"

"I have said I did not kill the dragons. They chose not to believe me. There is nothing more I can do."

"Yes, there is. You can tell them what you were doing in the area if you weren't there killing off blue dragons."

He was silent for a moment, his eyes calculating. A thought occurred to me at that moment, of someone who might be able to clear up the whole thing. "Thala!"

"What did she do now?" May asked, her fingers playing in Gabriel's shoulder-length dreadlocks.

"She was there with you, wasn't she?" I asked Baltic before turning back to the others. "She's his alibi! Thala can tell you all that Baltic didn't kill anyone."

His fingers, which had been on my leg, tightened for a moment.

"I'm thinking that Thala's not horribly high in the weyr's esteem right now," Aisling said softly.

"We asked her about the night in question," Drake pointed out. "She said she knew nothing."

"Of course she did. Did she tell you *anything* you wanted to know? I just bet you that she didn't say a damned thing. She's the most stubborn, obstinate ... Well, that's neither here nor there except that if you were to say she gave you any information, I'd be surprised."

"She didn't, as a matter of fact," Gabriel admitted. "We all questioned her, but got nowhere."

"That's because you didn't let me have a shot at

her," Kostya said, cracking his knuckles in an obnoxious fashion.

"Oh, please. She'd have chewed you up and spat you out," I answered.

His expression turned black with outrage.

"I simply meant that you never could strike a woman, and I doubt if you've changed over the centuries. No, only Baltic can get Thala to talk, so that's what we'll do."

"It is, is it?" asked the love of my life with deceptive blandness.

"Yes." I glanced at him. "It's important, Baltic."

He looked as if he wanted to argue the point, but just shook his head in resignation.

"There, see? All fixed. Thala will clear Baltic, and the weyr can drop their war against us."

May avoided meeting my eye. Aisling coughed and looked at Drake, nudging him when he didn't say anything.

"What?" I asked them all. "Why are you giving me that odd look?"

"You are too honest," Baltic said, pulling me close to him. "It does not occur to you, as it does the others, that Thala's word would not be accepted as the truth."

Would Thala lie? I thought that over for a minute or two, then conceded that she might well lie if it suited her purpose. "She would tell the truth if you told her to, wouldn't she?" I asked Baltic.

He hesitated a moment, but that hesitation was all that was needed for Kostya.

"Even he cannot control his lieutenant," Kostya scoffed. "Why should we believe her word against the proof of a witness?"

My hope for peace died at that moment, and with its

death, all the frustration and anger and a strong sense of irritation that had built up over the last two months rolled around inside me, blending into something that had me spreading my arms wide and shouting, "I have had enough! By the rood, either the weyr will believe us when we say Baltic is innocent of the deaths of those dragons or I will make you all sorry you ever thought to doubt us!"

"She's casting a spell," May said, looking surprised.

"As the waning moon fades," I bellowed, determined to make them see the truth once and for all.

"Ysolde," Baltic said on a martyred sigh, "have you not learned? They will not be led."

"Grant knowledge of what has passed!" Light formed in my hands, the bluish white light of arcane power, tipped with dragon fire.

Instantly, Drake and Gabriel sprang into action, shoving their respective mates down behind various substantial pieces of furniture, despite the women's squawks of objection.

Kostya looked around for a moment, realized he had no one to protect, and with an annoyed noise, started toward me, clearly bent on stopping my spell.

Baltic leaped past me toward him, and the two of them went down.

"Bring forth wisdom in place of fear . . ."

Drake and Gabriel hurled themselves toward me, Aisling yelling something about wards, while May disappeared into thin air.

The light from my hands grew until it surrounded me, bathing me in the warmth of the dragon fire and the strength of the arcane power.

". . . tolerance where there is only hate . . ."

Drake and Gabriel struggled to reach me, but the light held them back. Baltic slammed Kostya up against one of the glass-fronted cases, shattering the glass, his furious words punctuated by the gentle tinkle of shards striking the hardwood floor. "No one touches my mate!" he snarled.

"May!" Gabriel yelled. "Do not touch her! She will destroy you!"

Behind me, a shadow flickered, but I ignored it, focusing every iota of my being on the spell.

". . . serenity where there resides anger."

"I'll slap a ward on her. Effrijim, I summon thee!"

"Oh, sure, now you summon me—hey, what's going on?" The human form of Jim popped up into the range of my vision for a moment, before being yanked aside as Drake shoved both the demon and Aisling back to a large leather couch. "Why's Ysolde lit up like a Christmas tree? Oh, man, she's casting a spell that's going to blow us all to Abaddon, isn't she? Her hair's standing all on end!"

I brought together my hands in a clap that resounded with such volume that the windows rattled. "By my grace, this I cast!"

For two seconds, everyone froze. No one so much as blinked while they all waited to see what was going to happen. I would be lying if I didn't admit that I was of that group myself, praying that my magic would have returned to me.

The light expanded to fill the room, then suddenly contracted upon itself with a whipcrack sound, forming itself into the small round shape of an extremely surprised turtle. It fell a few inches to the table next to me, blinking in surprise at everyone standing frozen in the room.

I glared at the turtle for a moment, then kicked the chair nearest me. "Well, that is just the most disappointing thing yet! A turtle? Really? I put every ounce of intention I could into that spell, and all I get for it is a turtle? I could just scream!"

May emerged from nothing behind me, reaching out to touch the turtle. "It's real," she said, glancing at me with speculation. "Might I ask what it was you were trying to do to us?"

I slumped down into the chair. "I was trying to cast a clarity spell on you all, to bring you wisdom and enlightenment, so that you would see that we were telling the truth. A turtle. I made a turtle. Hell."

"Abaddon," Jim corrected, pulling out a cell phone to snap a picture of the turtle.

"Turtles are supposed to be wise, aren't they?" Aisling asked Drake. "Maybe your spell made a wise turtle instead of bringing us wisdom."

"I thought that was owls," May said when Drake, with a quelling look at his mate, righted a few pieces of furniture that had been knocked over.

"Could be worse, Soldy," Jim told me.

"I don't see how," I said, rubbing my forehead.

"Could be an elephant. So, what's been going on? Why is Baltic holding Kostya by the scruff of his neck? Hey, Drake's missing a tooth. Man, I miss all the good meetings!"

Chapter Thirteen

"I think it's just rude of Gabriel and Drake to do this to me."

Baltic, seated opposite me, raised an eyebrow. "I am a wyvern. It is beneath me to point out that I was right and you were wrong."

My lips thinned in irritation.

"However, I was correct," he continued, just as I knew he would. No one can resist a good I-told-you-so gloat. "They believe only what they want to believe, mate. It should no longer surprise you to be treated as if you were guilty."

I looked over his head to where Maata and Tipene stood against the door. Pavel was seated by the window, while the other windows were guarded by a man who had been introduced to me as Mikhail, the son of a black dragon who had survived Constantine's slaughter. Mikhail watched me with an incredulous intensity that made me vaguely uncomfortable.

Evidently, the noise of my spell backfiring had brought all the guards on the run. "Maata, do you think I would hurt May and Gabriel? Really hurt them? No, you don't— It's ridiculous, isn't it? And yet those pig-headed wyverns insist that I have to be kept separate lest I cast another spell while they talk things over. As if I'd hurt anyone! Well, all right, at this moment I am sorely tempted to turn a couple of dragons into bananas, but I would change them back. Probably."

"Hey," Jim said, poking its head in through the door as it bumped Maata and Tipene on their backs. "Balters, Drake says you're supposed to come and talk with them."

"It's about time," I said, getting to my feet.

"Just Baltic," Jim said with a grin. "They say you're too prone to flying off the hook, Ysolde, which when you consider Baltic's tenuous grasp on sanity, is really saying a lot."

Baltic glanced at the demon, and set its shoes on fire.

"Argh! Not the shoes! They're Italian! Cost me a whole month's allowance!" Jim danced around, slapping at its shoes.

"If Drake has something to say to me, he can say it in front of Ysolde," Baltic said.

"Yes! Absolutely! We're not stupid, you know! They just want to separate us so they can do mean things to Baltic. I'm not going to allow that."

"Ash said you and her and May could talk about your little problem on the verandah," Jim added once it had stuffed its shoes under a couch cushion to extinguish the flames. "Man, and I thought demon lords had hair-trigger tempers."

"What problem do you have with the verandah?" Baltic asked me, looking mildly confused.

"I don't have a problem with any form of architectural structure, not that I know of, at least. Jim, what in the name of all that is good and glorious are you talking about?"

Jim sighed. "Next time I'll brush up on grammar, OK? Aisling wants to talk to you on the verandah. About your little problem."

Both Baltic and I looked with incomprehension at the demon.

"What, I have to draw you a picture?" It waved its hands around in the air. "Your oblempray with Ostich-kay's awnspay."

"Oh." I glanced at Baltic. "Er . . . perhaps you should talk to the dragons, Baltic. After all, we are here to clear your name."

"That is your goal, not mine." His dark, deeply mysterious eyes considered me for a minute. "What problem do you have with Kostich?"

"Nothing. Not personally. I have a little job I have to do for him, but that's all."

"What sort of job?"

I avoided the penetrating look that was attempting to bore into my head. "Just something I agreed to do in order to have him lift the interdict."

"You will tell me about this job." That was an order, not a request, and luckily, Baltic knew well that I didn't like to be ordered around, because I didn't even have a chance to get my glare really warmed up before he lifted one hand in capitulation. "Pax. I will speak with the wyverns as *you* have asked me to, but when I have done so, you will fulfill *my* request to explain what you are doing for Kostich."

"Fair enough. But no antagonizing the situation, not

that we're sitting horribly pretty at the moment, but there's no need for everyone to get riled up again."

With a noise of impatience, he rose to leave the room, standing aside when May and Aisling entered. He shot me one last penetrating glance before Pavel and he followed Jim out the door.

"We're good, if you guys want to take a little break," Aisling told the three guards. Maata and Tipene exchanged glances, hesitating.

"We promise we won't do anything but talk," May added with a smile. The two silver guards nodded and left the room, leaving us with Mikhail, who still watched me with fascinated anticipation.

"Boo!" I told him.

He jumped a good foot in the air.

"Shoo. We want to be alone," Aisling said, holding the door open for him.

He gave me a big berth, but left the room.

"Finally," Aisling said with a sigh, sitting across from me. "Before we get started, I wanted to ask you about Jim."

"I'm really sorry, Aisling. I've tried everything I can think of to change it back."

"Is it your magic gone"—she waggled her fingers in the air—"wonky?"

"I think so. Nothing seems to be coming out right."

"I thought having the Grace of the Magi put on you was going to correct that," said May.

"I thought so, too, but it hasn't. Obviously, something else is messing with my ability to draw the magic correctly. You tried to order Jim into doggy form?" I asked Aisling.

"Several times. And although it changes to its normal

form, it pops right back to the human one after a couple of minutes. It's like whatever you did is overriding its choice of form."

"That's just bizarre. I have no idea what happened with my spell to do that to it."

Jim, who had come back into the room in the middle of the discussion, gave me a pathetic look. "I'm not going to have to stay this way, am I? This form totally sucks. I can't pee on things in the yard, I can't lick my own package, I can't slobber on Cecile's adorable furry little ears. . . . It just sucks."

Aisling shot it a quelling look. "Go sit with the others."

"Why?" it asked suspiciously. "You going to talk about something racy? You going to compare techniques, or sizes, or the way—"

"Go!" Aisling ordered.

Jim went, slamming the door behind it.

"I can't believe I'm suggesting this, but it does seem to be in distress," May said, once the demon was gone. "Can't you talk to Dr. Kostich? Maybe he could help you."

"He wasn't very happy with me when I saw him last. But . . . oh, what the hell. It's not like he can do anything else to me, right?"

The room was uncomfortably silent as not one single person in it met my eyes.

I sighed. "Yeah, he could. All right, I'll talk to him tomorrow. I think it would be best if Jim came with me, though, in case Kostich can lift the spell, or whatever it is I've done."

"He'll meet you at the hotel," Aisling promised.

"Maybe if you came with us, Kostich might be more prone to fix things?" I suggested.

Aisling made a face. "There's no love lost between us, but I'll go with Jim if you think it would help. Speaking of Dr. Kostich and your job, though, May told me only the barest of information about it. What exactly is it you need help with?"

I gave them a succinct description of my meeting with Violet and her father.

"Dr. Kostich has a granddaughter who's a dragon?" Aisling's jaw sagged for a few seconds before she gave a hoot of laughter. "Oh, I can't wait to tell Drake! To think that Kostich has a dragon in the family—that's rich. That's really rich. But who are the ouroboros group this granddaughter is hanging around with?"

"I have no idea. I was hoping that perhaps you two might be able to tell me more about ouroboros dragons."

"I don't know much about them," Aisling admitted, leaning back as she thought. "We ran into some in the aerie in Nepal, but Drake wouldn't tell me anything other than they didn't belong to any sept."

"Yes," I said slowly, thinking of the vision with a sense of dread that clutched my stomach with cold, clammy fingers.

May watched me with interest. "Is something bothering you?"

The door opened before I could answer, and two pairs of arms shoved Jim inside the room before the door was slammed shut again.

Aisling raised her eyebrows.

Jim grinned. "They kicked me out of their meeting. Something about not contributing to the discussion in a manner that was helpful. Man, those dragons are a pushy lot. Literally. You guys hatchin' a plan to take down Kostich?"

"Good lord, no!" I said, startled by the idea.

"Crap. That would've been fun. So, what are we doing if not taking down Mr. Important?"

"I was about to tell May and Aisling about the vision I had."

"Did I miss another group one? I'm gonna be pissed if I did, because those are always fun. Cold, but fun. So what was this one about?"

I hesitated for a few seconds, then carefully picking my words, described the scene at the weyr.

Aisling looked confused for a few minutes. "That must have been right when Kostya was imprisoned. But who was the woman? And you said there was a ghost who was her servant? Why would a woman with a ghost be interested in capturing Kostya?"

"That's a really good question." I glanced at Jim doubtfully. "You'll keep quiet about what's said here, right, Jim?"

"Of course it will," Aisling answered for it, leaning forward toward me. "Spill."

I took a deep breath. "I can't think of any reason someone would be interested in Kostya unless that person was also a dragon. Thus it makes sense that the woman who was in charge of the ouroboros group had to be a dragon, and I can think of only one person who is a dragon and yet has the ability to raise ghosts."

"Kostich's granddaughter," May said, her eyes widening as she thought it through.

I nodded. Jim whistled.

"This Maura person is responsible for Kostya being confined in his aerie?" Aisling asked, her brow wrinkled. "Why? What would she gain from it?"

"I have no idea. That's why I hoped you two could tell me about this group of dragons."

"Tribe," May said absently. "Gabriel told me that ouroboros dragons form tribes, led by a chieftain, instead of forming septs. The question is, why would Maura's mother make it sound like the tribe is holding Maura against her will if she's really their leader?"

"Another good question. The Akashic League said she would be in touch with me, but I haven't heard anything yet. I plan on telling her that I'd like a dragon resurrected, in order to meet with her in person and assess the situation. I have no idea what I'll tell Dr. Kostich if it turns out she's leading the band of dragons that's plaguing him."

"Yes, that might do very well," Aisling said slowly, lost in thought. "Resurrecting a dragon is a good excuse, because it's such an involved act, and it takes time to prepare, which would give you some space to figure out what Maura's role is in the whole shebang."

"What dragon?" Jim asked, plopping itself down on the couch next to Aisling.

"I don't know. Does it matter?" I asked.

"Sure it does. A little itty-bitty dragon wouldn't be much trouble. What you want is a big dragon, someone important, someone who is going to give this Maura chick some trouble. Someone like Constantine."

I stared at Jim. "Constantine? Why him?"

The demon clicked its tongue at me. "Ash says the First Dragon wants you to restore Connie's honor, but you don't know how to do that, right? So you ask the man himself."

"Resurrect Constantine?" Aisling asked.

"Sainted Mary," I said, picturing what Baltic would have to say about that. "I don't think resurrecting Constantine is going to be a good thing."

"Not good at all," May said quickly, a frown between her brows. "Gabriel is wyvern of the silver dragons. If Constantine were brought back to life, he would want the sept, and Gabriel would never give it up. It wouldn't work out well at all, no matter how much Gabriel respects him."

"It's a moot point, I think," Aisling said. "Maura can't resurrect, can she?"

"Not rez, no. But she can bring Connie up as a shade," Jim answered. "That's what Summoners do."

I thought about that for a moment. "Ghosts can't challenge anyone for a sept, can they?"

Aisling looked thoughtful. "I can't imagine how they could. They're, you know, *ghosts*."

I nodded. "If a ghost couldn't try to challenge Gabriel for his sept, then that would be all right. And it would certainly help if Constantine could give me some pointers on how I go about clearing his honor of my death, but . . . but how do you go about raising a dragon's spirit? I can't imagine it's an easy thing, and Maura is bound to want some help doing it if I ask her. Where would we even start?"

Jim shrugged. "You got me. Kostich's grandkid is bound to know."

"Hmm." I mused on the best way to achieve two goals with one effort. "If I had Maura raise Constantine's spirit, I could conduct a public ceremony of forgiveness, or whatever it would take to restore his honor, and also spend enough time with Maura to figure out what's going on with her. Brilliant idea, Jim. I owe you a dinner."

The demon looked smug. "I'm there, babe."

We discussed the issue for another half hour, before Maata returned to inform us that our presences were desired.

As I entered the sitting room, my eyes went straight to where Baltic stood at a window with his back to the rest of the company. His body language read annoyance and impatience, but not the fury that would have boded ill for everyone.

"So? Have you guys worked everything out so that you can cancel the war and they can rejoin the weyr?" Aisling asked, going straight to Drake's side.

"Not as such." Drake considered me for a few seconds. "Bastian is mounting a search for Fiat. Chuan Ren's heir appears to have disappeared. Until we can talk to both of them, we are at an impasse."

"That doesn't sound good," I murmured under my breath, moving over to stand next to Baltic. He didn't take his gaze from the window, but did put his arm around me when I leaned into him. "At least Bastian didn't claim Baltic is behind it all."

"Actually, it's the opposite of that," Gabriel said, smiling at May. She smiled back, and I thought for a second he was going to kiss her in front of everyone, but he remembered in time where he was. "Evidently Fiat came back to his prison and slaughtered a half dozen of his attendants and guards before Bastian could get to him."

"Oh, those poor dragons. Bastian must be beside himself," Aisling said.

"Don't tell me that Thala was there helping him," I said, my stomach in my feet.

"No," Baltic answered before Drake could.

I eyed the man who filled my soul with so much joy. "How do you know that?"

Baltic said nothing.

I poked his arm. "You watched him, didn't you? Fiat, I mean."

"Yes," he answered, finally turning to face me. "He sent me a message telling me he would make me suffer for my part in his downfall. While he was imprisoned, his threats did not worry me overly, but the blue wyvern has been careless in the past with Fiat, and I suspected that the next time he escaped, he would come straight for you and Brom. I was wrong."

"And how," May agreed.

"I love you," I told him, standing on my toes to press a kiss to his lips regardless of the others in the room.

He wrapped his arms around me, hoisting me up so I could kiss him properly, his fire racing through us both, wrapping us in a blanket of arousal, love, need, and a sense of rightness that almost made all our troubles seem to fade into insignificance.

Almost.

"Given Fiat's madness, and the fact that he slaughtered four blue dragons who had been tasked with guarding him, as well as Chuan Ren, we are willing to readdress the question of Baltic's involvement with the slaughter of the sixty-seven blue dragons earlier this year." Drake's gaze held impersonal interest as I disengaged myself from the sweet lure of Baltic's mouth. "For that reason, I have called a *sárkány* to discuss rescinding the declaration of war between the weyr and your sept."

"Woot!" Aisling said, flinging herself on Drake. "I knew you would make it all right."

"It is far from all right," Kostya said as Drake gave Aisling a swift kiss. "The cessation of hostilities is contingent upon agreement of all the wyverns, and that will not be given until we have interviewed again the two survivors of the attack. In addition, an investigation will be launched regarding Baltic's lieutenant, specifically the reason she wanted Fiat free."

"But once that's done, then we'll be a part of the weyr?" I asked, sighing in relief.

"No."

The word burst my happy fantasy world where everything turned out all right. "Why not?"

Kostya's nostrils flared as he nodded toward Gabriel. "Evidently you have an agreement that you have not yet fulfilled."

"What sort of an . . . oh." Enlightenment dawned as Gabriel's gaze locked with that of Baltic.

"The silver dragons are willing to accept, contingent, as Kostya noted, upon a further interview with the survivors, that Baltic's involvement with the deaths of the blue dragons is circumstantial rather than actual, and for that reason I am prepared to agree to a provisional cessation of the war. However, admittance to the weyr is another subject, and we cannot condone such an act without a good-faith gesture from you."

"The curse." I slid a look up at Baltic. "It's time it ends, Baltic. I'm alive, Constantine is dead, and we're together."

I swear he just about turned to stone. "I have no reason to lift it, mate."

"We won't get into the weyr if you don't," I pointed out.

His gaze was as stony as the rest of him. "The silver

dragons were responsible for your death, and the destruction of our sept. I cannot simply forgive that."

"But—"

"No. About this I will not yield." He shook off my hand, and with a glower at Gabriel, left the room, a silent Pavel on his heels.

"I'm sorry. I'll work on him," I told Gabriel and May. "Don't give up yet."

"You are the only hope we have," Gabriel told me, taking my hand and bowing over it. "Do not fail us, Ysolde."

"I really wish people would stop telling me that," I murmured as I hurried after Baltic. "It's starting to give me a complex."

Chapter Fourteen

The drive home was conducted in silence, except for a brief interchange that began with Baltic's insistence that he would drive.

"I have done as you asked, and against my better judgment, allowed the wyverns to question me about my time in Europe when Fiat was slaying his sept. Now you will tell me about your agreement with Kostich," he said as he narrowly missed plowing us into an elm tree that grew perilously close to the edge of the country lane upon which we were driving. He shot me an irritated look when I screamed, clutching the seat belt that crossed my chest, jabbing at the window with a frantic finger. Luckily, the ditch a bicyclist flung himself into (rather than be mowed down by Baltic) was filled with tall grass. "Mate, you will cease reacting as if I am not competent to drive this car."

"Glory of god, Baltic! If you kill, maim, or otherwise injure anyone on the way home, I swear I'm never getting in a car with you again! Stop! It's not our turn to go!"

Baltic ignored both the blast of a car's horn and its occupant, who was making several rude gestures as he proceeded through an intersection toward the main highway that would take us home. "I am a wyvern. We do not take turns."

"For the love of—ack! You almost hit that cow!"

"Cows should be in fields, not on roads," Baltic said, glaring at the bovine in the rearview mirror.

I watched the cow in the side mirror, relieved to see it moving in a manner that indicated it was startled by its near-death experience but not hurt. "Agreed, but that doesn't give you the right to almost run them down. Look, you scared the cow and now it's bolted and knocked down that poor cyclist you flung into the ditch. We should stop and help him. He's just lying stunned in the middle of the road. He could get run over."

"You should stop trying to change the subject and tell me what Kostich wants you to do for him," Baltic countered.

Pavel, sitting in the backseat, had turned around to watch the drama between the cow and the cyclist, but now turned back with raised eyebrows. One look at my face had him hunkering down with a book.

"Are you willing to discuss lifting the curse on the silver dragons?"

"No."

"I can be just as stubborn as you," I told him, crossing my arms and trying not to notice how close he came to sideswiping other cars as he merged onto the main road.

"I have had ample proof of that," he muttered under his breath.

"I am sitting right next to you. I can hear everything you say." I damned his stubbornness, and wondered how on earth I was going to convince him to lift the curse.

He switched to Zilant before falling silent. Although the rest of the trip was fraught with innumerable death-defying moments, we made it home in one piece.

"Mate, you will tell me now what it is you have undertaken for the archimage," Baltic said, holding me back as Pavel headed for the house. "Is it to do with the light sword?"

"No." I stopped trying to pry his fingers from my upper arm, admitting that he had done as I had asked and it was my turn to acquiesce. "He asked for my help with his granddaughter."

His eyes narrowed. "Why would he seek *your* help for that?"

"Because she's half dragon, and I was handy. She's involved with some ouroboros dragons, and he wants her away from them. I promised to find out what's going on and to aid her as best I can."

"An ouroboros tribe?" His gaze turned contemplative. "Is that why you were asking about them? Which tribe?"

"I'm not absolutely certain, but I suspect they are the ones who imprisoned Kostya in his aerie."

He shook his head; then, taking my hand in a gentler grasp, he escorted me toward the kitchen door. "Ouroboros dragons are dangerous. I do not want you becoming involved with them."

"Dangerous how?"

"They have no respect for septs, or the weyr."

"Neither do you," I pointed out as we entered the kitchen to find Nico and Brom seated at the table, while

Pavel was obviously about to prepare some paninis. "We're technically ouroboros, too, so I doubt if we have much to fear from them."

Before Baltic could answer, Thala burst into the room. "There you are! You are late! You said you would be here two hours ago!"

Baltic looked taken aback for about three seconds, before his expression darkened. "We were detained."

She tossed an angry glance my way, then took his arm and tugged him toward the hall door. "No doubt it was intentional. Isn't Kostich friends with the green mate?"

"Not according to Aisling." I eyed the red peppers and turkey breast that Pavel was slicing.

Thala ignored my comment. "The green dragons summoned you while Kostich was moving my mother's sword to safety."

Baltic froze at her words. "He has moved the sword?"

"Yes." Her lips compressed as she shot me an unreadable look before continuing. "I told you that we needed to do more than simply establish the level of security at Suffrage House. Your woman obviously spoke to the green mate, and she told Kostich of our plans to take the sword. He has moved it from the vault there and taken it to the sepulcher."

"I would never betray Baltic in any way," I said, slamming down a quarter wheel of Swiss cheese before marching over to Thala. "And if you ever again imply I would do so, you're going to be one sorry necromancer."

She straightened her shoulders and looked down her nose at me. "Do you threaten me again, human?"

"You bet your buttons I do," I said, making a fist and gathering myself for a lunge.

"Ysolde, remember our son," Baltic said, pulling me backward against his body. "You do not wish to fight in front of him, do you?"

His words acted like a bucket of cold water tossed on my head. I sent a reassuring smile to Brom, who sat watching with wide, delighted eyes. "No, of course not. But you know full well I didn't betray you any more than Aisling did."

"I care not what the green mate did, but I know that you would never do such a thing," he agreed, patting me on the behind before releasing me and giving Thala a long look. "I have asked you to cease tormenting my mate. You will not make me repeat myself."

Her eyes were hot with anger, but after a few moments during which I thought she might just challenge Baltic's dominance, she dropped her gaze in a gesture of submission. "The fact remains that the sword has been moved to a safer location, and now it is beyond our reach."

"Not beyond it. More difficult to obtain, perhaps, but not out of the question."

"Where exactly is this—" My phone ringing had me pausing in the middle of the question. "Oh. I ... uh ... I have to take this call. It's about that business we just discussed," I added with meaning to Baltic, who simply shot me a warning look and allowed himself to be urged away by Thala.

"She and I are definitely going to have it out one of these days," I said softly as I went out to the kitchen garden. "Hello?"

"Good afternoon. I am Maura Lo, and I'm told you wish to hire me for a summoning?"

"Hello, Maura. Yes, I do. I'd love to talk to you in person about what I'd like you to do for me—are you near London, by any chance?"

"Er . . . no." Her voice had a kind of husky quality that reminded me of Lauren Bacall at her most seductive. "Actually, I'm in Estonia at the moment. Which is one of the reasons I was calling—I'm afraid my schedule is a bit hectic, so I won't be able to undertake any new projects for a while."

I just bet she was busy. Busy with things like orchestrating the theft of objects from the L'au-dela vaults and keeping dragons imprisoned in their own residences. "That will never do. I'm afraid my job is quite urgent."

"I'd be happy to recommend another Summoner since you have such a great need—"

I interrupted her offer with ruthless disregard. "I was told that you are the only Summoner in Europe who is capable of bringing back the ghost of a dragon."

"You want a dragon's spirit summoned?" she asked cautiously. "Which dragon?"

"The former wyvern of the silver dragons, Constantine Norka."

She sucked in her breath. "Why?"

I blinked at the tidy rows of fresh basil and mint that Pavel often teased me were cosseted. "I beg your pardon?"

"I asked why you want Constantine Norka's spirit summoned?"

It was on the tip of my tongue to tell her that was none of her business, but I reminded myself that a little honey went a long way. "The First Dragon has charged me with a task that involves Constantine. I've decided the best way to accomplish that task is to speak with Constantine directly."

Silence followed that statement. "I see. Well, I won't deny that the challenge is an intriguing one, but I'm very sorry, Miss ... er ... I'm afraid I didn't catch your name from the message left for me."

"It's Ysolde."

The silence that met my ears was one filled with surprise. "Ysolde de Bouchier?"

"Yes."

"Oh ... I thought you were dead."

"I was. Temporarily."

"All right. Er ... one moment, please." A hushed conversation followed. Listening carefully, I thought I could detect two other voices, both male. Just what was she doing in Estonia?

"Ysolde? I'm sorry, but I've just consulted my schedule again, and I really won't be able to take your job for at least three months."

"Are you engaged in another summoning job?"

"No, but I am terribly busy with ... er ... a little side project."

"I see." I hadn't anticipated that she'd turn me down flat. Now what? I glanced along the edge of the house, catching a quick glimpse of Baltic as he moved to his desk in the study, Thala right next to him, her hands gesturing wildly as she spoke. *Take a leaf from Baltic's book*, I thought to myself with a little smile. I straightened my shoulders and adopted a cold, imperious tone. "That is not acceptable."

"I'm sorry, but—"

"No." I cut off her excuses with determination. "Your little side projects do not interest me, Maura Lo."

I heard a small gasp as I invoked her full name, embellishing it with a little flash of arcane magic that must have been tangible even given the distance.

"I have hired you to do a job, and if you refuse to do it, you will leave me with no other alternative but to notify the Akashic League of your denial. I'm sure they will have a thing or two to say to a Summoner who refuses to honor her contract with them. I haven't had many dealings with them, but I remember someone telling me that the Akashic League takes its contracts with members very seriously, and the penalty for breaching them is very inventive . . . and quite irreversible."

"I . . . that's . . . you . . ." Anger was evident in her voice, but she bit it back. "If you can hold for a minute, I'll speak with my colleagues and see if we can't work something out."

"Of course," I agreed, absently plucking a weed from the lemon balm and noting that the dill needed to be cut back. More murmuring was audible in the background, a full three minutes' worth before Maura spoke to me. "Ysolde? I'm happy to say that my colleagues understand the importance of attending to League business over our own projects, so I will be available to summon the spirit of Constantine Norka for you after all. I will need a few particulars first, however. First and most important, where did Norka die?"

"You don't know?" I asked, somewhat surprised, since she recognized his name . . . and mine.

"No. Should I?"

"I suppose not. I just assumed that all dragons knew where Constantine died."

"Ah. I see someone told you about my father." The faint thread of humor in her voice had more than a hint of irony to it. "I'm afraid that I don't have much to do with the weyr."

"Isn't your father a red dragon?"

"He was, yes," she said cautiously. "He was thrown out of the sept when he displeased the wyvern. That was before she killed him, naturally."

"I'm sorry, I had no idea Chuan Ren would do that to her own people. Well, my memory is a bit faulty, but based on my discussions with the First Dragon, I believe Constantine died in Latvia. Outside of Riga, in fact."

"Riga? Do you mean Dauva? Of course you do; what am I saying? You were Baltic's mate, weren't you?"

"I still am."

The silence that met that statement was profound. "I see," she said slowly. "I think the best thing is to meet you at Dauva. We can search for the spirit there. Would it be possible to meet you in . . ." The muffled voices indicated a short conversation. "How about we meet in two days in that little suburb of Riga. What's the name . . . Ziema?"

"Ziema will be fine. I'll let you know if I'm unable to make it."

She murmured something polite, and gave me information about a hotel she said was on the fringe of the town, near the forest that had consumed Dauva's crumbled remains.

I hung up a few minutes later, staring blindly at the herb section of the kitchen garden, not really seeing anything but my own murky suspicions.

"Is something wrong?"

I gave a mental shake and glanced at Pavel. "Sorry?"

"I asked if something was wrong. You have the oddest look on your face."

"Ah." I thought for a moment more, then asked him, "If you were the person who captured and imprisoned Kostya in his own house, why would you be interested in me?"

He didn't even blink at the bizarre question. "The common link between the two of you is Baltic, so I assume that would be my focus."

"Yes," I said slowly, turning my gaze back to the herbs. "That's what I thought, too."

"Who is interested in you, if you don't mind me asking?"

"A half-dragon Summoner who may or may not be the leader of a notorious band of ouroboros dragons. I'm going to meet her in Riga in a couple of days. I don't think I'll tell Baltic, just in case."

He pursed his lips. "In case he would refuse to let you go?"

"No." I snapped the stalk of an amaryllis that grew in a pot next to the kitchen door, flinging away the leafy stem. "In case she tries to harm him."

It wasn't until the waxing moon was high in the night sky that Baltic finished his dealings with Thala. He found me standing in a small, seldom-used room, staring blankly at nothing.

"Did you have another vision?" He hesitated at the door before approaching me.

"No. Are you done with Thala?"

"I have been for the past hour. She went into town."

I watched him walk toward me, his movements smooth and sinuous, like a big cat on the prowl. There was something about Baltic, a sense of coiled power on the verge of being released, that heightened the general feeling of danger surrounding him. It was simultaneously frightening and very erotic. "When I first saw you, I thought you were a warrior, not the mage my sister told me about. Then I found out you were a dragon."

He stopped in front of me, not touching me, waiting for me to finish my thought.

"Of those three, I think the warrior is strongest in you."

Eyes of midnight searched my face. "I am a dragon first and foremost, Ysolde. Dragons are warriors. We always have been. Nothing has changed."

"No," I agreed. "Nothing has changed. You might wear modern clothes, and drive a car, and use a laptop, but at heart, you're still the same man you were five hundred years ago. You still make decisions for me. You still shut me out of certain aspects of your life. You're still a warrior."

"I protect you when necessary, yes. I cannot do otherwise, mate. I existed once without you, and I will not do so again. Were the events of the past to be repeated and Thala resurrected me again, I would not continue living. You *are* life to me, Ysolde. I will not live without you."

I moved into his arms, kissing the pulse point in his neck. "You make it really hard to lambaste you for doing things you know I won't like. I love you, too, you frustratingly wonderful man."

"Dragon."

"And while you may not have changed, I have. I understand that you need to protect Brom and me, and I'm grateful you do. But protecting doesn't mean keeping me utterly in the dark. You can tell me about threats or things of importance like that. I really don't like feeling as if I can't be trusted with the truth."

"There is nothing with which I don't trust you." His

breath was hot on my neck and ear as he nibbled a spot that he knew turned me to mush in his arms.

"Did Thala know about Fiat's threat to kill Brom and me?" I slid my hands under his shirt, stroking the muscles of his back, breathing in the scent of him. It was a heady experience, leaving me simmering with desire.

"Yes. Do you remember the time we were in Venice and you thought to hide behind a mask and test me?"

I stopped unbuckling his belt, prodding hard at the big black chunks of my memory. "No. A mask? Hmm."

"It was during a festival. You pretended to be a woman of no morals who desired my body, and tried to test my fidelity to you."

"Still not ringing any bells. Why don't you do whatever you did to prompt a vision before, so I can relive it?"

He unzipped my jeans, sliding his hands over my hips as he pushed them down, tossing them onto a chair along with my underwear and sandals. "I would prefer not to."

"Why not?" I shucked my shirt and bra at the same time I tackled his belt, suddenly frantic to get him out of his clothes so I could rub myself all over him.

"You did not believe me when I told you that I knew it was you from the moment you neared me."

Buttons went flying as I yanked his shirt off while he was trying to take off his pants.

"Does that mean that you let me seduce you, then told me you knew it was me?" I moaned softly as I stroked the heavy muscles of his chest, waiting impatiently for him to get his shoes off. The second he stood up, I flung myself on him, biting his shoulder as I wiggled against him, relishing the sensation of hot, satiny flesh covering steely muscles.

"Yes. You could not wait for me to take you to our bed. You demanded that I make love to you on the balcony of the villa we'd taken."

"Balcony, eh?" I stopped licking his neck long enough to look speculatively around the room.

"On a table." His voice was rich with the promise of fulfilling the intention so obvious in his beautiful onyx eyes. "Like the one behind you."

Cold wood met my behind as he picked me up and set me on the small writing desk, sweeping the accoutrements onto the floor as he took both my breasts in his hands.

"Oooh. New position. Kinky," I said, squirming as he gently tormented my breasts. I dug my fingers into his hips, sliding them around to his behind as his mouth claimed mine, his fire sweeping through me.

"You particularly enjoyed it when I did this," he said, dropping to his knees.

I swear my eyes rolled back in my head when he blew dragon fire along my thighs, following it with the even hotter sensation of his mouth as he kissed a serpentine path up toward the source of so much pleasure.

"I bet I did," I said in between pants. His mouth closed on me, licking and gently biting, and doing wonderful little swirly things with his tongue that had me grasping the edges of the desk. "By the rood, Baltic, your tongue ought to be outlawed, doing things like that. Do that again! No, the other thing!"

He chuckled at my demand, his fingers curled up inside me as his tongue did a particularly effective dance against hidden parts of me, causing me to fall back on the desk, my muscles tightening painfully around him in a spasm of purest rapture. "You were always easy to please, mate. I am glad that has not changed about you."

I lifted my head to glare at him. "You did that to me and didn't tell me you knew it was me all along? No wonder I was pissed!"

He made a face. "It was three weeks before I convinced you that I knew it was you all along."

I narrowed my eyes at him. "You don't mean to say that I didn't reciprocate?"

We both looked at his penis, clearly waiting for its turn.

"You did. But you were angry. I could tell."

I allowed him to pull me into a sitting position. "Friends don't let friends give angry oral sex, Baltic. If I made sure you were happy, I wasn't angry."

"You were." Without any further ado, he wrapped my legs around his hips and slid into my body. "You used your teeth more than was seemly."

I was in the middle of a groan of ecstasy when he spoke, making me hiccup in a few giggles, which in turn caused him to frown down at me as he stroked in and out with long, smooth moves.

"Honestly, Baltic, you're the only man I know who can frown during sex. Kiss me—my mouth misses yours."

He obliged, sharing his dragon fire with me, murmuring something in my ear about withholding it until I could access my own, but I was too busy being aroused all over again to pay much mind to his threat. The table protested his increased vigor with a rhythmic squeak that I prayed wasn't audible outside the room. By the time I flexed my muscles around him, squeezing a nonstop stream of groans from his lips as his hips moved in a way that damn near brought me to tears, I was on the edge of another orgasm, just waiting for him to push me over.

The muffled sound of the front door, situated next to the small room, as it slammed shut had me grasping Baltic's hips with desperation.

"She's back," I moaned, sucking hard on his tongue. "Hurry!"

"You must go first," he panted, his mouth hot and sweet and endlessly fascinating.

"I had my turn. You go, and that'll do it for me, too," I said, my own breath ragged and irregular.

"You . . . first . . ."

I knew that Thala would see lights on and come to investigate, so I didn't waste time arguing. I simply tightened every muscle I had around the hot invasion of his penis, gripping him with a fierceness that had his eyes opening wide for a moment before he roared his pleasure into my mouth. Like I predicted, that was all I needed, as well, as his last few convulsive thrusts sent me flying.

"Baltic, did you find someone to locate the sepulcher? If you cannot find someone with the appropriate tracking skills, we might think about hiring a blue dragon—" The door to the hallway opened, revealing Thala. Baltic spun around, screening me from sight, but I wasn't any too happy about the fact that she was getting an eyeful. I snatched up my shirt from the floor, and still behind him, held it in front of his groin, all the while peering around his shoulder to send a potent glare at the intruder.

"I might have known you would be here," she growled, seeing me. Her gaze went back to Baltic. "Did you at least accomplish what we discussed before your woman distracted you?"

"I grow weary of telling you to treat Ysolde with respect," he replied, his arms crossed. "She is my mate. You will refer to her as such."

"Did you?" she prompted, ignoring his demand.

His lips tightened, but after a moment he answered. "Not yet. I will locate one tomorrow."

"We need someone at the sepulcher as soon as possible, not whenever you get around to it." She took a deep breath. "You seem to be more concerned about your mate than you are my mother's sword!"

"Ysolde is everything to me," he said simply, which just made me melt all over his back. I licked his shoulder blade. "I will regain the sword, do not fear. But I will do it in a manner I choose. Kostich is more powerful than you credit him, and I will not risk Ysolde's well-being to regain the sword."

"He would not harm her," Thala argued. "You said she was his apprentice."

"Kostich has used her to obtain his ends before, and he may do so again," he answered. "The sword is mine, but I will claim it in a way that will not allow him to threaten her. I will find a tracker in the morning to locate the sepulcher."

"A tracker?" I asked, having managed to slip into my jeans and bra while he and Thala were arguing. I picked up his pants and moved in front of him, blocking Thala's view. "You mean someone who's good at finding hidden things?"

"Yes." Baltic donned his pants, pausing when he saw the smile I just couldn't contain. "Do you know of one?"

"Oh, yes." My smile grew as I looked at Thala. I'd

heard the tale of what happened the night May reformed the dragon heart. "I know of one who is quite good. In fact, when I was staying with May and Gabriel, he's the man I was going to hire to help me locate you."

"I will contact him in the morning," Baltic said, wrapping an arm around me. "We will go to bed now."

Thala moved aside as we left the room, her expression too placid for my peace of mind. I couldn't wait to tell Savian Bartholomew, official thief-taker for the L'au-dela and part-time rogue, that he would have the chance to work with the woman who had come very close to killing him.

Chapter Fifteen

"You know, Ysolde, Dr. Kostich and I ... well, we're not the best of friends."

Jim rolled its eyes as Aisling rose from her seat in the lobby of the hotel my former employer favored when he stayed in London. "Maybe that's 'cause you more or less told him you could take him down if he got in your face?"

"I never said that!" Aisling whapped Jim on the arm. "I just said that I bet I could give him a run for his money. And he got all bent out of shape because I zapped Caribbean Battiste that one time, which is silly because Caribbean wasn't upset with me. Well, not after I apologized and swore that I'd never again turn him into a simulacrum. And paid for a new suit, since his was ruined. And then Drake had to pony up some money for the Elderly Guardians' Home, but that's a worthy charity, so he didn't really mind. Much. Anyway, the point is that Kostich and I have a bit of a rocky history, so I'm really not sure how well he's going to take to my being there with you."

"Good morning," I told her, smiling at her protestations. "I'm well aware that Kostich has no love for you, but since he has even less for me, I figured it couldn't hurt to have a powerful wyvern's mate and Guardian there to remind him that we're no pushovers."

"No, we're not, but he's also a whole lot more powerful than most people realize," Aisling told me as we entered an elevator. "Er . . . do you know what room he's in? Shouldn't we let him know we're coming for a visit? What if he's not here?"

"He always stays in suite 1818, so I know where he is, and honestly, I've found it's better if I don't announce my visits. He usually forbids me to enter if I do."

"Oh, *that* sounds good," Jim said with ominous portent. "At least I have my cell phone and can get video footage of him when he comes unglued."

"Hush, you," Aisling said as the two other people in the elevator gave us odd looks. A few minutes later as we stood outside the suite, she said, "You sure you want me for this, Ysolde?"

"I'm sure. I'm out of ideas of what to do for Jim, and Dr. Kostich, as you pointed out, is the most powerful mage around."

"You never met Bael when he was masquerading as a mage," Aisling said with a grimace. "He was no lightweight either."

I decided I'd ask her about that later, mentally girded my loins, and hit the bell next to the door.

A familiar redheaded man opened the door.

"Jack!" I said in happy surprise.

"Tully! No, wait, it's something else . . . Isabel?"

"Ysolde, but you can call me Tully if you like. I answer to both names. I had no idea you were in London. I thought you went to Cairo."

The freckled, sunny-faced young man grinned. "Finished my training there in record time, so the master had me return. But what are you doing here? I thought you were off being the mate to that dragon mage who attacked us."

"I am, but there's a little situation that's come up, and I need Dr. Kostich's help. This is Aisling Grey and her demon, Jim."

"Hiya," Jim said. "I remember you from the day the spawn were born."

"Er . . . hi." The smile faded as Jack cast a quick glance over his shoulder. "You don't have an appointment, do you?"

"No." I touched his arm, dropping my voice. "I need to see him, Jack."

His face was filled with sympathy. "You know he doesn't see people if they don't have an appointment."

"I know, but there's really no other way. I'm doing a job for him, but if I made an appointment, he'd be sure to ask if it was related to that, and you know how impossible it is to lie to him. The man has a built-in lie detector."

The corners of his mouth went up. "I guess you get that being the most powerful archimage of this age."

"Exactly. So if you could just look the other way and let us in, I'd be eternally grateful."

An interesting parade of emotions passed over Jack's face, everything from regret to obstinacy, finally ending with a mischievous twinkle that I prayed boded well.

"It may cost me my position, but I'll do it." He stepped back, holding the door open for us.

"If it would help, I can tell him that Jim overpowered you," Aisling offered as we entered the suite.

"Rawr," Jim said, flexing his muscles.

"Er . . . no, I think I'll just take my chances with the fact that Ysolde's now an important personage," Jack said, waving a feeble hand toward the room I knew Kostich used as his office. "You won't mind if I don't announce you?"

"Not at all. Thanks, Jack. I really owe you."

He nodded, and disappeared into a side room, obviously not wanting to attract any of the wrath that I suspected would be flowing free as the wind in a few moments.

"I really hate it when I'm right," I told Aisling three minutes later as Dr. Kostich stormed around the room, ranting to no one in particular about the arrogance of people who should know better than to disturb their superiors.

"It's a curse, isn't it?" she said with sympathy, giving my arm a little pat as I took a deep breath and stepped forward to stop the tirade.

"I've already apologized twice for interrupting your work time, and I will do so again if it makes you feel better, but this is a serious matter, and although it doesn't have anything to do with the task I've undertaken on your behalf, it does have an impact on me, and as such, I am forced to seek assistance from the only one who is powerful enough to help me."

"Nice oiling of the squeaky hinge," Aisling said in an undertone.

Dr. Kostich wasn't immune to being buttered up, but neither was he overly impressed by flattery. He stopped stomping around the room and marched over to face me, his scowl almost as fierce as Baltic's. "You ask for much, dragon. First you demand the interdiction be lifted, and now you seek my aid with a bungled spell? Give me one reason why I should not have you and that troublemaker thrown out," he demanded, pointing at Aisling.

"Hey," she said, rising from the couch where she'd been sitting, and lifting her chin. "I'm a professional Guardian, thank you, recognized and duly authorized by the Guardians' Guild. I am not a troublemaker."

Kostich shot her a potent look that had her sitting back down.

"You're the only one who has the ability to figure out what's going on with my magic," I said, counting on the challenge of my situation to offset his reluctance to get involved.

He glared at me for the count of seventeen, then with an annoyed noise, sat at his desk and gestured toward Jim. "Have the demon shift."

"Effrijim, I command thee to take thy preferred form," Aisling said, sitting on the edge of her seat as Jim stood and looked to her for instruction.

The human form shimmered and compacted itself down into that of a shaggy black dog. Dr. Kostich watched with steepled fingers, narrowed eyes, and a sense of intensity that I knew meant he was focusing his full attention on the problem.

"I get to stay like this for anywhere from a few seconds to a minute or two," Jim said, and sure enough, as soon as it spoke, the form shimmered again and returned to the human version.

Kostich's eyes narrowed even further as he rubbed his chin. "Again," he commanded.

Aisling and Jim obliged.

"Do you want to know what spell I used?" I asked when Jim was once again shifted back.

"The spell is immaterial," he answered dismissively, gesturing toward a penholder on his desk. "Change that pen to a vase of flowers."

"All right." I focused my energy, recited the most basic of transmutation spells, and watched with resignation as the pen, rather than re-forming its matter to that of the requested vase of flowers, turned into a bowl of spaghetti.

"Lunch!" Jim said with a brightening of its face.

"It's like my magic is all backward. It's been that way ever since you put the interdiction on me, only now it seems to be—"

We all stared in surprise as the bowl morphed into a pigeon that blinked back at us.

"—worsening," I finished as the pigeon flicked its tail and pooped on Dr. Kostich's papers.

He closed his eyes for a moment, his gaunt face reflecting patience that had worn thin. "You are sundren."

"I beg your pardon?"

"Sundren. It is an archaic term, but it aptly describes the relationship between mages and their powers when they have ill used them."

"Me? I haven't ill used anything." The pigeon squawked and changed into a small marble statue of Hermes. "Well, not much. How did I hurt my magic?"

"You are a dragon." He held up a hand to stop my protest. "You appear human, yes, but you are not. You have yourself admitted that your current form harbors that of your previous being, and it is that which has caused the sunder between your magic and your being. This manifests itself in the misfirings that you see."

"Great. I'm a misfiring?" Jim looked pathetically at me. "Can you refire me, please?"

"But that doesn't make sense," Aisling said, looking puzzled. "We all saw the vision where the First Dragon resurrected Ysolde. She's been human ever since then, which means if she was sundren before, it would have shown up then, wouldn't it?"

"She was sundren, yes, but the division wasn't as pronounced as it is now that her dragon being has begun to awaken. Before the attack by her immense mate on the house of the green wyvern, her magic was simply ineffectual. Now the sundering has increased, causing the effects you see."

We all looked at the statue as it disappeared into nothing.

Dr. Kostich sighed. "And now I have lost a favored pen."

"OK, I changed my mind," Jim said, backing away from me. "I don't want you to try to give me back my magnificent form."

"Is there nothing I can do?" I asked Kostich, my heart heavy with sorrow at the thought of losing such an integral part of my being, not to mention leaving Jim in a form it detested. "Can't you help me?"

"With the sundering? No." His gaze shifted to Jim, his expression sour. "I can, however, act as a focal point for your magic to change the demon back to its canine form, not that I understand why it wishes to do so. But there is a cost."

"I have a credit card," Aisling said, reaching for her purse.

"No, this one's on me," I said, doing the same.

"Not that sort of a cost," Kostich interrupted, giving us both a disgusted look. "There is a cost to your attunement with arcane magic to have another act as your focal point. That is why it is forbidden in the Magister's Guild. In effect, you are allowing another mage to use your power, and arcane magic does not like being used in such a manner. So long as you are aware of the risks associated with such an act, we can proceed."

"What risks, exactly?" I asked, my stomach tight with nerves.

"Oh, man, I'm going to lose more toes. I just know it," Jim moaned. Aisling smacked it on the arm again.

Dr. Kostich shrugged. "You will not know until you try."

"You make it sound like arcane magic is . . . well . . . sentient," Aisling said.

"You were proscribed. You have felt the opposite of arcane magic. Would you say the dark power was sentient?"

"Oh, yes," she said with a shudder. "Although I didn't realize that at first. I thought someone was using it to get to me."

"Someone was," he said dismissively, getting to his feet. "Are you willing to try, Tully Sullivan?"

I flinched at the sting that accompanied my name. "Yes. I owe it to Jim. So long as you're sure that with you focusing the magic, Jim will be changed back."

"My powers have not yet begun to diminish," was all

he said as he gestured me toward him, placing his cold fingers at the base of my neck. "Proceed."

I closed my eyes and turned east, beginning the call to quarters. "Air surrounds thee."

Dr. Kostich, his fingers still on the back of my neck, turned with me as I faced south. "Fire fills thee."

"Oh, great, this is the one that left me naked before," Jim complained. "Ash, you better have a blanket handy just in case."

"Quiet, demonic one," she snapped.

Kostich and I turned north, then west. "Earth nourishes thee. Water gives life to thee."

I faced Jim again, opening my eyes and pulling as hard as I could on Baltic's fire. "Demon in birth, demon in being, by the grace within me, I release thee from thy form."

For a second, nothing happened. Jim stood with a frightened expression on its face; then the same rushing sensation of power flowed over and through and inside me, wiping out everything I had been and would ever be, before ebbing away to an abyss of emptiness.

The man looked at me with an expression of mingled annoyance and patience. "You are making a habit of this, daughter of light."

I sat up, eyeing him. He looked familiar somehow, his eyes infinitely wise, his face that of a man, and yet there was a sense of something other about him.

"Are you here to see my father?" I asked, confused about who he was. I glanced quickly around the room, startled to find other people present, a man and woman in strange clothing and a large black dog, all three of whom were staring at me with expressions of stark disbelief. "I'll fetch him for you. I think it's him you wish to see, my lord ... er ... I'm sorry, but I seem to have lost my wits this morning, and don't believe I was told a mage was coming to see my father. What is your name, sir?"

"I am not a visiting mage," the odd man said, holding out his hand to me. I took it and rose to my feet, the world spinning for a few seconds before it settled down. "You are important to me, daughter, but I cannot keep rescuing you. You must find your own path, and not rely upon me to help you again."

I put my hand to my head, my brain swimming at both his words and the strange surroundings in which I found myself.

"Fires of Abaddon," someone said. "Has she, like, reverted to her old self?"

"Hush, Jim. Um ... Mr. First Dragon?" The woman, dressed in an odd shortened tunic and leggings, gave a little wave to the man who still held my hand. "I know Ysolde has a bunch of questions about what you want her to do, and since she seems to be a little out of it, I thought perhaps you wouldn't mind if I asked them."

The man cast a glance at her, repeating, "She must make her own path."

"Yes, but—"

"A life was given for yours once, daughter. Do not repay that debt with failure."

My mouth dropped open as the man shimmered with a bright silver light, as if he was suddenly made up of a thousand raindrops shining in the sun, the drops glittering brightly before dissolving into nothingness.

"By the rood!" I gasped, waving my hand through the air that had just held the man. "I must tell Papa about that! Even he can't turn himself into light drops!"

"I would find this tedious except for my interest in elemental beings such as the dragon ancestor," the tall, thin man with washed-out blue eyes said. I didn't like him. He eyed me as if I were a bucket of slops. "Now that he is gone, however, the charm of the situation fails to engage me. Aisling Grey, please remove my former apprentice."

"You can't just throw her out like that!" the woman said, rounding on the man. Her, I liked. "She was just killed a few minutes ago! Killed because of *your* magic, I'd like to point out!"

"Someone was killed?" I asked, looking around, feeling more than a little dizzy, but if there was a body lying around, I wanted to see it. I've always had a ghoulish fascination with them, much to my mother's dismay. "Who?"

"You," a man's voice said, and my jaw dropped again when I realized it came from the big black dog.

"Me?" I squeezed my arm. It felt solid enough.

"Yup. You dropped like a sack of anvils. Then the First Dragon made his grand entrance, waved his hands around, and blammo! You were alive again."

"The First Dragon . . ." There was something about that name, some memory that tugged on the edge of my awareness.

The woman and man had been arguing while the dog talked to me. I wondered for a moment if I had gone moon-mad, but decided that if I had, it didn't matter if I talked to dogs, so I asked it, "Who are you?"

"Boy, you really are out of it, aren't you. You don't

remember anything? Baltic's going to go bonkers if you've lost your memory again."

I frowned, searching my mind. There were many fleeting shadows of memories that moved so quickly I was unable to pin them down. "No, I . . . there's something . . . a man, I think. He's . . ."

"Fine!" the woman yelled, taking me by the arms and steering me toward a door. "But if Baltic wants to know why Ysolde is all wonky from being resurrected a second time, I'm going to be sure to tell him it's your fault."

The man snarled a curse as I was hustled out of the room, down a short hallway, and out another door into a corridor filled with doors.

Something about the surroundings struck a familiar note as well. "I think I've seen this before," I said, pointing at the wall as the woman and the dog herded me into a small metal room. I touched the wall of it, lurching when the floor moved beneath me. "This is a . . . a . . ."

"Oh, man, I hope you get your memory back soon, or Baltic really *will* have a hissy fit," the woman said.

I looked at her as she pulled me backward out of the small room and into a big, bright hall.

"Not hall," I corrected myself as I looked around. "Lobby. Hotel lobby." The world seemed to resolve itself before my eyes, as if it was slowly being brought into focus.

"Thank god," Aisling said as she and Jim pushed me into a large off-white chair.

"Aisling!" I said with delight. "I know who you are! And Jim!"

She gave me a crooked smile, then gestured to a waiter and demanded coffee. "Whew. You gave us quite a fright there. I was trying to figure out how to tell Baltic that we killed you changing Jim back, and then the First Dragon was suddenly there, and . . . well, I'm just glad your brain is back, too."

I frowned as she began her sentence, but by the time she was done, I had pulled together enough of my wits to respond. "The spell killed me?"

"I don't think so. Kostich said it was the backlash of arcane magic that was suddenly released when Jim was changed back into Newfie form. You lit up like a Christmas tree for a minute, then collapsed. We'd just figured out you were dead when pop! The First Dragon was there, calling your name, and bringing you back." Aisling gazed at me with a kind of amazement. "I don't think I've ever heard of anyone being resurrected twice, especially not by the First Dragon. Drake says he hasn't made an appearance for centuries, not until May saw him when she re-formed the dragon heart. It's obvious you have some sort of a tie with him."

I took a deep breath, grateful to feel air filling my lungs. "Well, I'm not going to complain, since I'm alive. I can only imagine what Baltic—" Horror made the skin on my neck crawl as realization struck me. "Oh, dear god! Baltic! He must have felt me die!"

Frantically, I searched my pockets for my cell phone, but found nothing.

"Oh, geez. I didn't think of that. Your phone got blasted with the explosion of light. Here, take mine," Aisling said, shoving her phone at me.

My fingers shook as I punched in the phone number, remembering well the promise in Baltic's voice when he swore he would not live without me.

"Were you dead long enough to kill him?" Aisling

asked, adding a hellish nightmare tinge to an already overwhelming sense of panic.

"Please answer, please answer," I chanted as the phone rang. Tears filled my eyes as I blocked the need to examine the worst-case scenario. "Please, Baltic, please—"

A wordless snarl of anguish answered the phone.

"Baltic!" I yelled into it.

"Ysolde?" Heavy breathing was all that met my ears for a few seconds. "Christos! What are you doing to me? Where are you? Why did it feel as if my heart was ripped out anew? What have you done?"

"Oh, thank god." I covered the mouthpiece for a moment. "He's all right, Aisling."

"Thank god," she said as well, then grabbed Jim and pulled it after her to another grouping of chairs in order to give me a little privacy.

"Where are you?" Baltic demanded again. A horrible noise followed, a combination of breaking glass and screaming metal, followed by a muffled explosion. "Bloody hell!"

"What's going on? What was that?" Fear gripped my heart despite the sound of his voice.

"Pavel?" Another crash of glass sounded sharp in my ear, followed by Baltic grunting as more metal screamed. "The door is off. Are you hurt?"

Distantly, I could hear Pavel answer, "Just my arm. Air bags saved us."

"Oh, my god, you were in a car? You crashed? Are you all right?" I stood up, spinning one way and then another, needing to go to him but having no idea where he was.

"Yes. This car is defective. We will get another. Now you will tell me why I felt as I did the time Constantine killed you."

I took a couple more deep breaths, pointing out to myself that if he could talk, he was fine. "Something happened when Dr. Kostich helped me lift my borked spell off of Jim."

"Your *what* spell?"

"Borked. You know, wonky."

He sighed, and in the distance I heard a *whoomp* noise. "Mate, I know you believe you are human, but you are six hundred years old. You do not need to adopt the language of mortals to prove otherwise."

"Actually, I'm more like six minutes old, but that's neither here nor there. What was that whooshing noise I just heard?"

"The defective car has burst into flames. What happened with Kostich? Why did it feel as if you died?"

"I did die."

Stentorian breathing was all I could hear for half a minute. "Why," he finally asked in a voice that sounded strangled, "did you die?"

"I just told you. Kostich and I were lifting the spell off of Jim, and it went bad. The backlash of the release of arcane power killed me. The First Dragon resurrected me. Again."

Baltic swore profoundly. "I'll never hear the end of that," he muttered before raising his voice as sirens sounded near him. "Stay where you are. I will acquire a new vehicle and fetch you."

"Oh, no you don't. You stay where you are and I'll get a car and pick you and Pavel up. Is his arm hurt badly? Are you hurt in any way?"

"Mate, do not give me orders when you have just come close to destroying me. Stay there. We will find you."

We compromised after five minutes of argument to meet at Aisling and Drake's house.

"Are you sure Drake won't mind my showing up?" I asked Aisling as our taxi pulled to a stop at a graceful house in a exclusive neighborhood.

"Not at all," she answered, then added with a little grimace, "And if he does, tough noogies. I want you to see the babies. They're beyond adorable, even though I'm hardly impartial. Jim, stop that. Your package is exactly the way it used to be. Ysolde, I hope you don't mind being frisked. Drake's security since the twins were born has almost gone past what's tolerable, but he means well."

It took a good three minutes for me to be scanned, searched, and have an oral swab taken to determine whether I had any communicable diseases, but at last I made it into the foyer of the house, and Aisling bustled me upstairs to the nursery to see her babies.

The twins were sleeping in identical intricately carved wooden cradles, swathed with lace and filled with a number of stuffed toy dragons. I duly admired them, chatted with their nanny, a young green dragon named Grace, and reassured Aisling that I would return at a later date when the twins were awake so I could admire them as they obviously deserved.

"Drake wanted to name them both with Hungarian names, but I was adamant that I get a Celtic name in there—my family has always had Celtic names—so I picked Iarlaith, even though the pronunciation trips everyone up. Drake chose Ilona's name. It means 'beauti-

ful.' Now, while we're on the subject of children, tell me
how Brom is doing. May said he had a grand time while
visiting her and Gabriel, but I hope he hasn't been affected by this stupid war."

"Not—"

The door to the sitting room where we were having
tea was thrown open, and Baltic stood in the doorway,
bristling with indignation.

"—in the least."

"Oh, dear," Aisling said, eyeing him. "I hope Pál
wasn't overly zealous with his security precautions."

"Full cavity search?" Jim asked Baltic. "Metal detector up the ol' wazoo? X-rays and soft-tissue scans?"

Smoke swirled out of one of Baltic's nostrils. His
hair was mussed and loose around his shoulders, and he
looked like he'd been grinding his teeth. He also looked
like he was capable of tearing down the house with his
bare hands.

"Thank you for the tea," I told Aisling, forestalling
the inevitable explosion. "I think I've probably pushed
Baltic past his tenuous grip on patience, so we'll be on
our way."

"Oh, so soon?" She looked disappointed. "Maybe
Baltic would like to see the babies first?"

He rolled one eye over to her. She flinched. "No, I see
your point. Another time, then."

I took Baltic's hand and leaned in to kiss him gently.
He didn't move, but his gaze, furious and, as I suspected,
without a shred of patience, scorched me. "Come, my
darling. I will assuage your anger on the way home."

He said nothing, but a spark of interest flared in his
fathomless eyes for a moment. "It's going to take a hell
of a lot more than assuaging, mate. You asked me about

my fantasies the other day. I have one now, and it involves meting out the punishment you deserve for putting me through the last hour."

"Ooh, punishment fantasies," Jim said, cocking a furry eyebrow. "Drake has a lot of those."

"Jim!" Aisling said, pointing a finger. "Out! Don't you give me that look. I'm the demon lord here, and you just better remember that—"

We left Aisling in the middle of scolding Jim. I took one look at the dark promise in Baltic's eyes and allowed him to escort me out to the taxi he'd engaged, wondering just what form his idea of punishment would take, and whether I should make up a new batch of caramel sauce for it.

Chapter Sixteen

Riga is an odd combination of an ancient city and a modern metropolis. It was part of the Hanseatic League, which made it a valuable port for trade, one of the reasons why Baltic chose the area to locate his stronghold. It boasted beautifully preserved historic buildings, a scenic castle, and gorgeous Art Nouveau architecture that mingled with stately elegance alongside the more mundane trappings of modern life. I hadn't been to Riga in centuries, but even modernized, it had a strong sense of the familiar as we drove out of the now-sprawling city limits and through the tiny suburb of Ziema, headed for the forest preserve that protected the remains of Dauva.

"It really is amazing that no one developed this area over the centuries," I mused, as I pulled off the road serving as a boundary along one edge of the dense forest that covered about a hundred acres. "You'd think they would have needed the wood, if nothing else. But no one has touched it."

"I ensured no one would," Baltic said as we got out of the rental car.

I stopped in midstretch. "You did? How?"

Thala, who had been forced to sit in the backseat, sniffed. I half expected her to add something really nasty, but she just smiled at me. Oh, it was an unpleasant smile, but still, it took me by surprise. "You lived here and you do not remember the protections Baltic put into place?"

After eight hours of her presence while we travelled to Latvia, I was about at the end of my tether, but if she was going to suddenly switch tactics and play nice, then I would do the same. It had taken all of my persuasive powers to convince Baltic to come to Latvia when he preferred to be elsewhere. "In a way, no, I don't remember what Baltic did to Dauva. My memory was wiped, thanks to your sister and her bigamous husband."

"Bigamous?" Her eyebrows rose as her gaze flickered over me. "How do you mean?"

"Gareth married me twelve years ago in order to control my manifestations of gold. Only it wasn't a legal marriage because he already had a wife—Ruth."

She looked as if she wanted to laugh, but she managed to control the urge. "Indeed. How very . . . awkward . . . to find yourself married to a man who already had a wife. But that must mean that your child is his?"

I closed my eyes for a few seconds, wanting to do nothing more than turn her into a pineapple, or perhaps even a toe fungus. "Yes, Gareth is Brom's father."

"I am his father. The other is a usurper, nothing more," Baltic said as he gazed at the forest, his hands on his hips.

"Gareth is his biological father, but he has nothing to do with us now. In fact, I don't even know where he is. He and Ruth have gone to earth somewhere, taking all of our belongings with them. That doesn't matter, though. Baltic, how did you protect Dauva? Was it a spell of some sort?"

"Spells, wards, two banes, and several songs," he said, taking my hand and leading me down a narrow path that curved around century-old trees dripping with long streamers of moss and assorted vines of ivy.

"Songs?" I shuddered as I cast a glance behind us, where Thala walked, a small smile playing around her lips as she typed something into her cell phone. "Oh, you mean the magic kind, not the singing kind. Ugh. But . . . dragons don't do much dark magic, and you can't sing a song over a location as big as Dauva without invoking some pretty powerful dark forces, something like a dirge, and those aren't done except by experts. Who did you get to do that?"

"I did them, all three. I am a dirgesinger," Thala said with a look of obvious pride, but I heard a faint thread of warning as well.

"You're half dragon, though, aren't you? How can you be a dirgesinger? Dragons can't handle the sort of dark power needed to sing a dirge."

"They can if their mother is an archimage," she said with another of her creepy smiles.

Oy. I made a hasty readjustment of my intention to have it out with Thala about her jealousy issues. I knew she was a necromancer of some esteem, because it's not an easy task to resurrect a dragon, as she had done with Baltic. But if she was also able to cast the most profound level of dark magic spells commonly referred to as songs, it would behoove me to deal with her a bit more carefully in the future.

Baltic held back a branch, allowing Thala and me to pass. "Most of the magic has been broken by Kostya over the last few months in his attempts to access my lair, but we have begun the process of weaving new layers of protection over the ground as we reclaim Dauva. He might hold Dragonwood, but he will *never* hold Dauva."

Baltic loved Dauva beyond darned near anything, certainly more than the house in England he had built for me. I knew this, and didn't raise an objection when he had informed me two months before that reclamation and rebuilding of Dauva would take utmost precedence in his plans. I was confident that once we had straightened out the business with the weyr, I could start to work on negotiating Dragonwood back from Kostya.

"No more songs, though," I told Baltic with a little shudder. "Those are just bad juju all around. We don't need the sacrifice of innocents on our—" I stopped, the conjunction of words ringing loudly in my brain. "Sacrifice of innocents. I wonder if that's what he meant?"

Baltic waited impatiently for me while Thala proceeded ahead of us deeper into the forest. "Mate?"

"Coming. Er . . ." I held him back for a moment, allowing her to get out of earshot. "Have you ever heard of Constantine using songs on anything? He didn't try to have one sung over Dauva after we were killed, did he?"

His fingers tightened around mine. "I do not know what happened after he killed us, other than what Pavel has told me. He said that Constantine destroyed Dauva rather than let it stand as a monument to the black dragons. The spells I had woven around it while it was being built ensured that it would remain hidden from all eyes but mine, the songs and banes driving away the mortals, as well as concealing it from poaching dragons and other beings."

"Hmm."

He gave me an odd look, half curious, half annoyed, but said nothing more as we marched deeper into the forest. There was a sense of magic around us, dampening the noises from outside the woods, as if this area was isolated by time from the busy city beyond. Birds called softly to each other, leaves rustled with the passage of unseen little animals, and a slow, gentle drip of water sounded all around us as moisture slid from the leaves to the rich, loamy soil below. The air smelled of earth, green things growing unhindered by man, sunlight dappling the ground. My heart lightened as we made our way through paths long lost, flickers of memories teasing the edge of my mind just as streams of sunlight teased through the leaves. I took a deep breath, savoring the scent of the woods, happiness flowing from the living things around us through me, making me want to laugh and run through the forest.

"Dauva," I said, my eyes closed, my hands out as I reached blindly for something that was no longer there. "It's Dauva."

"It is." Baltic took my hand, and I opened my eyes to find him smiling down at me, his black eyes lit from within with pleasure. It was as if the centuries had peeled away, leaving us standing in a time that no longer existed. "Welcome to my home, mate."

I smiled, allowing him to lift me off my horse as I looked beyond him to the grey stone towers that seemed to rise to the very sky itself. The drawbridge we stood upon was not wide, but it was long, covering the broad stretch of moat surrounding two-thirds of the castle. The far side ended in a sheer cliff that dropped perilously into a gully below. It looked impregnable, as solid as the earth from which it rose, the three towers as imposing as the solid granite of their walls. "It's beautiful, Baltic."

And it was beautiful, in a stark, massive sort of way. It was the heart of the black dragon sept, its foundation, its soul, and I knew as Baltic led me across the drawbridge to the outer bailey that it would stand as a testament to black dragons for all the ages.

The light shifted, darkening to that of a cloudy sky, the wind picking up with winter chill. I shivered and rubbed my arms, glancing around. "This is like at Dragonwood—the past is imprinted on the present."

"Yes." Baltic looked with mild interest as shadowy forms of dragons long dead flitted past us. Beyond, Thala was hunched over an outcropping of rocks and ferns that was overlaid on the image of the nearest tower. "You must be envisioning it right before the fall. Not a very pleasant time, mate."

"I can't help it." I stepped aside as a small group of men charged toward the drawbridge, the hooves of their horses ringing with steely bites on the wooden planks. "Was that you?"

Baltic glanced after the horsemen. "No. I was in the tunnels, fighting Kostya and his men."

The image of Dauva wavered, and pain lanced me, regret at what could have been and sorrow at what was. I blinked away accompanying tears, knowing what pain Baltic must have felt the first time he beheld the ruins of his beloved stronghold.

"It wasn't supposed to end this way," I told him, rubbing his knuckles on my cheek. "It was supposed to stand forever."

"Only love lasts forever, *chérie. We* will last for all the ages; all else is trivial."

"For someone who is commonly held as an example of all that is bad about dragons, you certainly are the most romantic man I've ever met," I said, melting into his arms. "I love you, you know."

"I know," he said, his fire whipping around us as his lips teased mine.

I pinched his behind. He slapped mine, then wrapped an arm around me and spun me around. Visible through the partially translucent image of the castle, a small hill rose, covered in mossy rocks and giant ferns, their leaves forming great arches against the grey-brown stone. I glanced at the rocks, noticing the very faintest of images in the face nearest me, turning to the image of the tower next to us. On the lower quarter was an elaborate carved band depicting various saints. Scrambling up the far side of the mound, Thala appeared, frowning and kicking at small stones until she grunted her satisfaction and squatted, her hands drawing symbols in the air.

"The entrance to the lair?" I asked, accompanying Baltic to the top of the small hill.

"Yes. Kostya raided it a few months ago, but Thala arrived to protect it almost immediately thereafter, placing new songs and banes on it so that he could not take all that remained."

I glanced at Thala as she examined the magic she'd layered on the entrance, wondering why she and not Baltic was in charge of protecting the lair. "You didn't have guards on it once you knew Kostya was out and about?"

"It was not necessary. I knew that Thala would guard it. I had other things to take care of."

"Other things like trying to steal May?"

His lips tightened. "I did not want the silver mate. I simply wanted the dragon heart."

"Why?"

He slid me a questioning glance. "Why did I want the dragon heart?"

"Yes. From what Kaawa said about it, the only time it's re-formed is either to re-shard it into different vessels or to use it for unimaginable power, like taking over the weyr, and I can't believe you ever wanted to do that. You may be many things, Baltic, and you have committed acts that I may not have liked, but you've never been power-mad. So why did you want the dragon heart?"

"To re-form it is to summon the First Dragon," he answered.

"You wanted to talk to him?" I searched his face for answers, but as usual, there were none there. Baltic was at his most dragon, his eyes glittering with a light that wasn't human. "But . . . why?"

"Always you ask why, but the answer is ever before you," he said, shaking his head with mock exasperation. He lifted my hand and kissed my fingers.

"It was me," I said softly, reading the truth in the depths of his mysterious eyes. "You wanted to ask the First Dragon to bring me back. That's why you tried to kidnap May. And attacked the *sárkány*. You were going after the shards, one by one, systematically forcing the wyverns into situations where they would have to hand over the shards. That's why you were helping Fiat, isn't it? Aisling said he held two shards. It all makes sense now. But, oh, Baltic, no wonder everyone thought you were mad. It was a crazy plan!"

"The promise of having you back was worth any sacrifice," he said simply.

"Not that of innocent dragons. Could you have stopped Fiat from killing his own people?"

He was silent for a minute, brushing a strand of hair from my cheek. "I don't know. I didn't think he would go through with his plans. I thought . . ."

"What?" I prompted.

He hesitated. "I thought his plans too mad to be successful. I still think they were."

Thala shouted for him, asking for his help to move a heavy rock. He gave my hand a squeeze, then climbed up to heave the boulder out of the way.

I thought about what he didn't say—that Fiat's plans couldn't have been successful . . . not without help. Not unless someone else was involved, someone like the leader of a band of outlaw dragons. I looked at my watch. I had just an hour before I was supposed to meet with Maura back in Riga.

"I'm going to look around a bit," I called to Baltic, waving a hand vaguely to indicate the trees. "It's fascinating seeing Dauva as it was, even if it's not real."

"There is nothing to see out there but Constantine's army." Baltic climbed down and took my hand again, leading me past a fallen tree to where a ghostly tower thrust up out of the earth. The light shifted back and forth across the bushes and leaves, to solid stone and mortar, faint, distant noises reaching us as the castle's few remaining occupants ran about preparing for the siege that would destroy most, if not all, of them. "Thala will be busy for some time unmaking the magic. We will go into the tunnels and watch as I battle Kostya."

"I've already seen you die, thank you." I pulled my hand from his. "And I don't want to see it again."

"That was only the end. We fought the traitors for

almost a day before Kostya struck me down. You will enjoy watching me fight him. I did not wear heavy armor then, just a cuirass, but you always enjoyed seeing me wield a sword."

"I'm sure you were beyond manly with a sword, but I think I'll pass on the sight of you and Kostya hacking away at each other. I know how it ends, and honestly, I don't think I could witness that again."

"You control the vision, *chérie*, not me."

"On the contrary, I don't control it at all. It runs like a movie in front of me." A thought occurred to me. If this was, in fact, the fall of Dauva, then I might be able to see if Constantine was killed here as well. It would make summoning his spirit a hundred times easier if I knew where to find it. "I'm just going to look around for a bit, if you don't mind."

"As you like. But it will only upset you if you see Constantine strike you down again."

"I don't intend to watch that, but I wouldn't mind seeing where he died."

"That would be satisfying. You will mark the place and I will dance on it later."

I laughed at him, seeing the twitch of his lips that let me know he was teasing me.

"You think I am not serious?"

"I think you're pulling my leg, yes. You have no reason to dance on Constantine's grave, assuming I find it."

"I have many reasons, but I will not go into them now. I am more concerned as to why you are so determined to find where he fell."

"My little job for the First Dragon, remember?"

Baltic made a face. "You take that too much to heart.

Do not go beyond the confines of Dauva. You are protected here, but outside you are not."

"Protected from what?" I asked, picking my way over a fallen tree now consumed in moss and fungus.

"Kostya. He will no doubt descend upon us once he learns we are here."

I didn't think that was any too likely, but I kept my opinion to myself.

The snowy ghostly scene faded in and out of my vision, leaving me to believe it was a memory of the land I was seeing, rather than a personal vision. Those were much more immersive, whereas this was just faint images of a time long past. As I walked over the drawbridge toward the road that led up from Riga, faint snow whirled around me at the same time that birds chattered high above in the treetops warmed by the sun.

"This would be confusing as hell if it wasn't so interesting," I told a couple of snow-covered guards posted at the fringe of Constantine's camp. Men and horses milled around in the darkness of night, small fires dotting the area, their flames flickering wildly in the wind and snow. Tents cast dark shadows against the present-day trees, giving the entire place an eerie appearance.

"All right, Constantine. Let's have this out, you and I," I murmured as I started to search the ghost camp.

He wasn't in the big tent that I assumed belonged to him. As I prowled the shadowed camp, I passed a couple of men who spoke in French, pausing when one said he had two prisoners.

"Black dragons? Put them to death," one man said with a dismissive gesture.

"They aren't dragons," the other replied, shivering

and huddling into his fur-lined cape. "We caught them skulking around the north wall."

"Humans? We have no need of them."

"Human but not mortal—"

I continued on my way. Fifteen minutes later I was ready to give up. I had turned back toward the castle when I saw a flash of color from a high ridge of trees to the south. Stumbling over a snowdrift that was really a sprawling red-berried elder bush, I fought my way through the forest to the spot where, three hundred years before, I had pleaded with Constantine to leave Baltic alone, and was slain by the man who claimed he loved me.

"I really could go the rest of my life without seeing myself killed again," I grumbled as I beat back a feathery tamarisk shrub that tangled in my hair. "At least I don't have to see Baltic being—whoa!"

A brilliant flash of white light lit up the hillside for a moment, casting the figure of a man into snow-flecked silhouette. Just as the light faded, the man dropped to the ground. I stared for a moment, wondering just how many people were killed on that fateful day.

"And if it's who I think it is," I grumbled to myself as I slid down a small incline, smacking my ankle on a sharp finger of a dead tree branch, "I'd dearly love to know who was responsible for that. I have . . . Argh! Let go of me, you blasted plant!" I jerked myself free of a particularly grabby black ash tree and stumbled forward, the ground in the memory of Dauva rising, but falling in present day. I slipped down another moss-covered slope, half falling until I slammed up against a piece of manmade stone. Swearing, I got to my feet and scrambled around it, my eyes ignoring the greens and browns of the forest scene in order to focus on the past.

Ahead of me on a rise, the First Dragon stood with a newly resurrected Ysolde. He spoke to her for a moment, then faded into nothing. She nodded numbly and turned toward the castle, slowly picking her way down the drifts toward the drawbridge.

"Dammit!" I spun around and fought my way back in the direction I'd come, veering to the left in order to see if it was Constantine who had dropped in the blast of light.

"Well, this answers absolutely nothing," I said a few minutes later as I stopped, panting with the effort of fighting through the dense undergrowth. Before me, slowly being covered by snow, lay the body of the man who had killed me. A sword lay next to him, half buried, crimson staining the snow around the blade. "You killed me, and someone came along and killed you right afterward?" I asked the body of Constantine. "Why? Just because you killed me? And who had the power to do that?"

The memory of snow and wind swirled around me as I sank onto my heels, watching as the snow drifted over Constantine's body. Every now and again I heard faint voices carried by the wind, but they were worn thin by time.

"No wonder your father wants help," I told the mound of snow that once had been a dragon. "You died with my death on your soul. I don't suppose a formal statement of forgiveness right now would do the trick, would it?" I took a deep breath. "Constantine Norka, wyvern of the silver dragons, I forgive you for killing me."

Nothing happened, but I didn't honestly expect the First Dragon's demand to be so easily met. Nothing is ever easy with dragons. I sighed and got to my feet, noting my location so I could bring Maura to it later.

I stopped by the lair's entrance to check on how the progress was going. To my surprise, no one was there. A distant crack had me spinning around, but it wasn't the sound of a tree falling, as I expected.

"The outer bailey has been breached," I said sadly, watching as a stream of snow-covered men swarmed through the gate. The dragons headed straight for the inner bailey. I looked up to see the faint image of the walls, but there was no one left to defend Dauva now that its master was lying dead deep in the earth beneath the castle.

"I can't watch it," I said, my heart filled with so much sadness for what happened.

"Then don't." Thala emerged from a path leading to the north, giving me not more than the slightest glance. She nodded abruptly at the line of dragons as they rode into the inner bailey, right past where we stood. "You should go back to town if it is too distressing for you to see this."

Once again, she surprised me. "You can see them? The people from the past?"

"Of course." She bent over a smooth bit of glass laid out on a blue velvet cloth. "They do not matter. Nothing of the past matters. It is the present that should concern you."

I didn't agree with that, but I knew arguing the point with her would serve no purpose. "Baltic is off reliving his own memories, I assume?"

"So I gather." She didn't look up from her glass.

I hesitated, not wanting to destroy her good mood but needing to get something off my chest. "I know that you have quite a long history with Baltic, longer than I had with him, and that you view me as some sort of interloper in the relationship, but I assure you that I'm not trying to steal his affection. He's told me himself that he owes you a lot for resurrecting him, and although I know you're in love with him—"

Her head snapped up, a look of incredulity so stark in her eyes, I couldn't doubt its veracity. "Love? Is that the *only* thing you can think of?"

I gawked for a few seconds. "You're *not* in love with him?"

"No!" She gave me a scornful look before returning to her scrying glass.

"Then why have you been so jealous of me?"

"I am not jealous. Jealousy is a pathetic emotion borne by lesser beings."

"Well, you were sure *something*. You refused to even let me be a part of your rescue."

She made an annoyed gesture of dismissal. "I had been in a very trying situation for months. I was out of temper."

I conceded that being held captive would make me a bit testy as well, so I didn't belabor that point. "I'm sorry if I assumed you were jealous of my relationship with Baltic, but you must admit, you have been more than a little hostile during the last week."

"We were very close to seeing our plans to fruition. Baltic's attention to those plans wavered once you returned to his notice. I was rightfully annoyed that he would push aside efforts that have taken years to lay into place."

"Plans to retake Dauva?" I asked, suddenly suspicious.

"And reclaim my mother's sword," she answered without looking up from her glass.

I wondered if that was really true. Her expression

seemed benign, but I couldn't help but feel that her explanation lacked the ring of truth. I shrugged to myself, and told her I was going into Ziema for a little bit while she worked on unmaking the magic. She murmured something noncommittal in response.

It took all of five minutes to drive to the small suburb of Ziema, which I had been told was the Latvian word for winter. I spent the time worrying about meeting a woman who could well be the head of a fell group of dragons.

"If she is, she's got to be too smart to mess with me," I told myself as I waited on the train platform for Maura. "She has to know I won't let her get away with harming Baltic in any way."

Seven minutes after our appointment time, a commuter train pulled in, disgorging a handful of shoppers from Riga proper. I discounted the few men who marched past with backpacks or briefcases and eyed the women with interest. Most of them carried shopping bags, and some had small children in tow. A few lanky teens giggled at each other as they hunkered over their cell phones, texting like crazy. The last person off the train was a buxom woman a few inches taller than me, with porcelain skin and dark brown hair to her waist, streaked with warm amber lights that shone in the sun as she paused on the platform, glancing around curiously.

I stood up. "Maura?"

She turned to me with a half smile. "Yes. You must be Ysolde. It's an honor to meet you."

She didn't offer her hand, but I knew that many people in the Otherworld preferred not to be touched, given their sensitivity to things like reading thoughts.

"I don't know how much of an honor meeting me

can give, but I appreciate the sentiment." I studied her for a moment while she studied me. Her eyes were a light brown flecked with gold and black, and odd little red lights that hinted of her dragon father. She was very fair-skinned, but had a smattering of freckles across her nose and cheeks. She looked to be in her early thirties, was on the plump side, and appeared just about as far from my idea of someone who raised spirits as I could imagine.

She laughed, and for a moment I thought she'd read my mind. "I don't look anything like you imagined, do I?"

"I'm sorry." My cheeks heated. "Was I gawking? I didn't mean to be rude, but somehow I imagined someone who raised spirits to look ... well ..."

"More Goth?" she said, still laughing. "Dark and scary and mysterious? Not like Suzy Homemaker, right? It's the curse of my maternal genes. My mother's skipped me and I got my grandmother's, instead. Nanna was from Scandinavia and was as round as she was short. I assure you that despite my appearance, I'm fully trained as a Summoner. And speaking of that, I don't mean to rush you, but we'd better get started if we want to have a good chance of locating Constantine Norka before nightfall. Do you have a car?"

"Yes, I do. It's not far to the remains of Dauva."

"Oh, good. Can I drop off my bags at the hotel first?"

"Of course."

It took us another half hour to swing by the hotel and leave off her things, let her change into clothing more suited to poking around in the forest, and gather up the items she needed to draw a summoning circle. I watched the clock warily, worrying that Thala would finish opening up the lair, which would mean Baltic would come looking for me.

"So are you out here by yourself?" Maura asked when we were finally on our way to the forest, her backpack of summoning tools sitting between our seats. "Or is your mate here?"

"No," I lied, uncomfortable about doing so, but unwilling to expose Baltic to possible sources of danger. I decided to hedge my bets. "But I'm not alone. His lieutenant is here with me."

"Ah. I don't suppose he has any idea where to look for Constantine's spirit?"

"She's female, and no, I don't believe she does, but that really doesn't matter, because I think I've found the spot where he was slain."

"Great. That ought to make things much easier," she said with confidence that I found reassuring.

I pulled off the road at the entry point to the forest, deciding the time had come to do a little gentle probing on the issue of the ouroboros dragons. "So . . . how long have you been doing this?"

She followed me into the forest, pursing her lips as she thought. "About eighty years. Summoners are born, not made, so I really didn't have much of a choice, if you know what I mean. Mom discovered that was where my talents lay, and sent me off to be trained properly."

"Ah. You're not involved with your father's family at all?"

"No." She slid me a curious glance. "As I said, he was killed by the wyvern after she kicked him out of the sept, so I don't feel like I have to make overly nice to the red dragons."

A telling statement, and yet one with which I could sympathize.

"You're technically ouroboros, then. So are we. I don't particularly like being separated from the weyr. It makes me feel . . . disjointed."

"But Baltic has a new sept, doesn't he?" she asked as we skirted a minute, murky black pond.

I wondered how she'd heard that if she didn't stay in touch with dragons. "Yes, he does, but we're not part of the weyr."

"Well, it's all the same thing, really, isn't it?" She made a little gesture of dismissal. "You can't pick your family, but you can your friends—that's how I look at it. So I just make sure I pick good friends."

"Other dragons, you mean?"

She slid me another curious look. "I'm ouroboros, as you just pointed out. Red dragons won't have anything to do with me."

"But other ouroboros dragons would," I said with a complacence that I was far from feeling.

She stopped, eyeing me with a slight tinge of hostility. "I get the feeling you're skating around a subject that you don't want to come right out and say. What exactly is that, Ysolde?"

"I understand what it is to feel ostracized, and lost to everyone you love." I chose my words with care. "I know how easy it is to be overwhelmed with the isolation, and how much it means when at last you find someone or a group of people to whom you feel you belong. I also know what it's like to be in over your head, drowning with no sign of a life preserver in sight. I just want you to know that you're not alone, Maura."

She stood unmoving, her gaze searching mine, and

then she suddenly made an exclamation of irritation. "It's Emile, isn't it?"

"Emile?"

"My grandfather." She made another abrupt gesture, before hoisting her backpack higher on her shoulder and stepping out with a firm set to her jaw. "He's been pestering me for the last decade to settle down, as he calls it, and now he's obviously gotten you involved somehow. I can't believe he'd do this! Why can't he understand that I'm not going to live the life he wants me to live? I'm my own person, not an extension of him!"

I hurried to keep up with her, simultaneously alarmed and relieved that I didn't have to couch my questions in obscurity any longer. "I'm sorry if you feel it's overly invasive, but your mother and grandfather are very worried about you."

"Is that why you brought me out here?" she asked, whirling around to face me, a scowl darkening her countenance. "You tricked me to come here just so you could try to talk me into going back home?"

"No, not at all." I avoided the unpleasant thought that I had, in fact, done something very much like that. "I really do want Constantine's spirit raised. I need to talk to him about something of great importance."

She examined my face for a moment, then nodded abruptly. "All right. But the subject of my personal life is no longer open for discussion."

I watched for a moment as she strode off into the woods, musing that I wasn't so naïve as to be fooled by an obvious attempt at distraction, but feeling it would be best to let matters lie until after she'd raised Constantine's spirit.

As we wended our way along the serpentine paths,

I glanced at my watch, praying that Baltic would need the full two hours to get into the lair. "How long will the summoning take?"

"Depends on the spirit. Some are right there, ready to be summoned; others take a bit of coaxing. Let's say an hour, to be generous."

"Ah." I pulled out my cell phone. "I'll be just a second—I need to let ... er ... Thala know I'll be a little late."

Maura said nothing, just continued in the direction I indicated, making her way around the large ferns and dripping trees that isolated us from the game trail we'd followed. I walked slowly after her, allowing a bit of distance to grow between us.

"Yes?" Baltic's voice was clipped as he answered my call.

"Hi, it's me. How's the opening of the lair going?"

"I assume it's well. I am currently watching Kostya's men be cut down by silver dragons."

I stopped and frowned at an innocent baby linden tree. "That's a little gruesome, don't you think?"

"Not at all. I wish to see what it is that Constantine did to bring down Dauva, so I am remaining here, where the silver dragons are fighting Kostya's force. Thala will alert me when the lair is opened. Where are you? You said you wished to see what remains of Dauva and the lair."

"I know I did, and I do want to see it, but there's a little bit of business that I have to take care of first," I said softly. Maura showed no signs of listening to my side of the conversation, but I knew dragons had exceptionally good hearing.

"What business? That foolishness to do with Kostich?"

"Kind of. I told you that I wanted to find where Constantine died so I could have his spirit raised."

"And I told you that was folly. Even if you could find the location, he can tell you nothing of any use. You will return to me, mate."

"Yes, I will, just as soon as I'm done with this."

"Ysolde—"

"I shouldn't be longer than an hour, and then I'll come back and see what progress you guys are making. Bye."

Twenty minutes later, Maura and I arrived at the place where I'd seen Constantine fall. The snowy memory of the past still haunted the area, but it was less substantial, almost faded beyond the reach of vision. Maura squatted and pulled some items from her bag, arranging them in a tidy row before drawing a ward over her left hand and right eye. With some difficulty, she used a piece of chalk to draw a circle in the moist earth.

"Is that going to work?" I asked, watching with interest. "The chalk, I mean? You can't really draw with chalk on dirt, and there are all those rocks and things in the way."

"It won't leave a mark on earth, no, but you don't have to see the circle to know it's there. So long as I draw it, it's effective." She sprinkled grey ash over the circle, closing her eyes and murmuring to herself. After a few minutes of that, she stopped, shook her head, and looked up at me. "Nothing. Are you sure this is it?"

"Very sure."

"I can give it another shot, but I'm not getting even a little tremor."

I looked at the memory of the snowy mound that had once held Constantine's body. "I'd appreciate that."

She rubbed the circle into the dirt and leaf detritus before drawing a new one with chalk and ash, saying as she did so, "Sacred be the circle, sacred be the place, enter here you who are not founded. Here do I draw the first circle of spirit; let it cast its light into you. Here do I draw the second circle of spirit; may it bind your being. Here do I draw the third circle of spirit; may it bring forth to my hand and heart and soul those who remain."

I waited, but there was nothing.

"I'm sorry," she said, rubbing out the circle again. "There's just nothing. You know, I wonder if my ash isn't the problem. This is an old bottle, over a year old, and perhaps it's not as effective as it could be. I have a fresh batch back in the hotel room that I just made a week ago. We could pop back into town to get it and try again, if you like."

A look at my watch warned me I had limited time before Baltic would want to know where I was. "Why don't we give it another shot? Third time's a charm, and all that.'

The look she gave me told me she didn't think much of that, but all she murmured was, "You're the boss," before drawing another circle.

But this time I was watching closely, and I noticed that although the circle seemed complete, a couple of largish twigs made it difficult for her to draw correctly.

"Hang on, let me clear some of this away," I said, kneeling to brush away a layer of leaf mold, hand-sized sticks, and small rocks. "I think the ground is sufficiently clumpy to keep your circle from closing properly. Try it now."

She slid me a quick look from the corner of her eye, but obediently bent over the now cleared ground. As she had said, the dirt did not hold the chalk itself, but an outline of the circle was now visible as she drew it.

"It's not quite closed," I pointed out when she reached for the ash.

"I'm pretty sure it is," she said, sprinkling ash.

I smiled and took the chalk up from where she had set it down, making a tiny little adjustment to her circle. "There. Now it's closed."

"Please do not handle my equipment," she said sternly, snatching the chalk from my hand.

"Sorry. I just really want this to succeed."

"I assure you that I do as well, which is why I suggested going back to the hotel to get the fresher ash."

I gave her an encouraging smile. She heaved a tiny little sigh and spoke the words of summoning again.

This time there was an immediate difference. Hope rose within me as the air within the circle did an odd sort of shimmer, as if the individual atoms of light were forming together. The shimmer began to grow and elongate, coalescing into the figure of a man.

A *familiar* man.

I rose slowly, the hairs on my arms standing on end as Constantine Norka stared at me with shock and surprise chased by some emotion I couldn't identify. He opened his mouth to speak, his hands gesticulating wildly as he did so, but his voice had no sound.

"You did it!" I gasped, staring with wonder at Constantine's spirit. "That really is amazing. But why can't we hear him?"

"He's not grounded," she said with an edge that had me wondering. With a little sigh, she made a few gestures that looked like backward wards, causing the translucent ghost to slowly solidify.

"Constantine?" I asked him.

"Ysolde!" He held up his hands, still clad in leather gauntlets, looking in wonder at them. "I was dead. I know I was dead. But now I'm not? You have had me resurrected? This woman does not look like a necromancer."

"I'm not," she told him, gathering up her things. "I've summoned your shade, not your physical self."

"A shade?" He looked down at his chest, touching his stomach. "I feel real."

"That's because you're in corporeal form right now. When you grow low on energy, you will fade into an insubstantial form." Maura turned to me, her expression tight. I didn't understand why she seemed so resigned when her mission had been a success. "I can't bind him to you, I'm afraid. That's the trouble with dragon spirits—they come back as shades, which can't be bound without a whole lot of trouble. He's more or less going to be able to do as he likes. I can release him, though, if he is willing."

"I'm not dead?" He pulled out his sword, still strapped to his hip. He made a few jabs at a nearby fern. "I'm not. I'm alive."

"No, you're a shade," Maura repeated. "Why don't we go back to the hotel, and I can explain the ins and outs of shadedom to you both."

He beheaded the fern, sliding the sword back into its sheath with a look of satisfaction. Constantine was a handsome man in his own right, a little taller than me, with a muscular build, golden brown hair, and eyes just a shade darker. "You saved me, my beloved one. You truly are my mate. The Summoner is wrong—I am bound to you, Ysolde. I am bound to you until the end of time."

Chapter Seventeen

"I have to ask you some questions, Constantine. Will you please stop doing that?"

He ceased kissing my hand, but retained hold of it. "You saved me," he said again.

"Yes. About that . . ." I glanced at Maura.

"I have an idea," she said brightly. "Why don't we all go back to the hotel, and you two can sort everything out there, where it's comfortable and there are no mosquitoes to eat you alive!"

"I always knew you would save me," Constantine told me.

"You did? That's . . . uh . . . OK." I debated asking him why he killed me in the first place if he felt that way, but decided there were more important things to discuss. Baltic's patience was pushed about as far as it would go without snapping, and I had to get to the bottom of restoring Constantine's honor before I could convince him to go on to his reward. "So, about this sin against the innocent that you committed . . . What exactly do you need me to do to restore your honor?"

Constantine blinked at me. "What sin against the innocent?"

"My death. At least, I assume that was the sin. Do you need me to formally forgive you for my death in the presence of a witness? I'm sure Maura would be happy to act in that capacity."

"I'd be delighted, but if we could do it back at the hotel—"

"You're speaking in riddles, Ysolde. Why would you forgive me for your death?"

"The First Dragon told me I have to restore your honor to you."

"He did?" Constantine looked startled. "Why—"

An explosion of words sounded behind me, a flurry of oaths as a large body burst through the dense wall of shrubs that had grown between two tall elms. "I knew it! I knew I would find you here with him!"

"Oh, this is all I need," I said to myself as I grabbed Baltic's arm. He was shirtless, his arms and one side of his chest smudged with dirt. I picked off a leaf and brushed a bit of soil from his shoulder. "Where's your shirt? What on earth have you been doing?"

"Excavating my lair. Why is he alive? Why have you resurrected him? Why did you tell me you had no interest in him, and yet here you are skulking around with the man responsible for all the ills we have suffered?"

"Baltic!" Constantine's eyes narrowed as he pulled out his sword. "Long have I wished I could end the suffering of the weyr, and now I shall do so!"

Baltic reached for his sword, but he was clad in a pair of jeans, completely sans lethal weapons, airport security being what it is these days. He swore profanely, then yanked a branch off the elm tree and wielded it like a leafy staff. "There is no suffering to compare with what you have already put me through!"

"Boys, really—"

Baltic lunged just as Constantine, with a battle yell that had the birds flying from nearby trees, leaped forward . . . only to melt into nothingness.

"What trickery is this?" Baltic bellowed, flinging his branch around with abandon.

"That is what I'd like to know!" Constantine's voice answered. "What magic have you cast upon me?"

"It's no magic—I told you, you're only corporeal so long as you have the energy to maintain that state. You've obviously come to the end of that, and will have to recharge your spirit batteries, so to speak," Maura said wearily. "I don't suppose anyone would like a drink? I sure could use one. I noticed the hotel had a bar."

"You didn't resurrect him?" Baltic asked me, lowering his branch.

"Why would I do that?"

"Because you love me," the disembodied voice said.

"I do not," I told the air. "I never loved you, Constantine. I was fond of you, yes, but my heart has always belonged to Baltic."

"Bah. You were just confused," he answered, his voice now on my far side.

"This is really disconcerting. Can you make some sort of an image so we can see where you are?"

"No." He sounded surly.

"Fine. Pout if you like, but it's not going to impress me. He's not resurrected," I said, turning back Baltic.

"Maura is a Summoner. She raised his shade so I could talk to him about restoring his honor."

Baltic rolled his eyes. "I told you that was a folly, mate."

"A folly? A *folly*? Restoring my honor is not a folly, you ignorant coxcomb!"

We both ignored the unseen Constantine.

"It's not foolish if it gets the First Dragon off my back."

"Really, people, if I get any more mosquito bites, I'm going to be one giant welt," Maura interrupted, slapping at her arm. "Ysolde, can you give me a lift back to town?"

"Talking to that monstrosity will not do anything but waste your time," Baltic said, gesturing at nothing with his branch.

"You bastard!" Constantine snarled. "I am not the monstrous one here!"

"Right, if I have to separate you two, I will," I said in my best mom voice. "Constantine, just tell me, please, what I have to do to restore your honor."

"My honor has no need of your attention. That one who calls himself your mate is another matter, although he never had any honor to begin with."

Baltic growled.

"Of course your honor needs help. Your father said you lost it."

"Mate—"

"My father?" Constantine may have been invisible to our sight, but the incredulity in his voice was clearly audible. "What does my father have to do with anything?"

"He asked me to restore your honor."

"My father is dead. He has been dead for ... what century is this?"

"Twenty-first," Maura said, tugging on my sleeve. "Shall we go?"

"He's been dead for seven centuries. He could not have asked you to do anything, unless you raised his shade as well."

"Well, he's not really a shade so much as he is kind of a ... er ... I don't know quite what he is. God, maybe?"

"Mate, I insist that you leave this murdering bastard and come with me to Dauva," Baltic said, pulling me up against his side.

"I like that! You murdered far more dragons than I ever did!" Constantine exclaimed.

"Like hell I did! You wiped out the entire black sept!"

"Not alone! The red dragons helped quite a bit, so Chuan Ren has to share the body count. Besides, it was kill or be killed. We were only protecting ourselves from your madness."

"I was not mad." Baltic ground the words out through his teeth, the muscles of his arms and chest tense and tight. "I was trying to keep you from killing my mate. Which you did anyway."

"Me?" Once again Constantine's voice was filled with surprise. "I did not kill Ysolde!"

"We saw you," I said sadly, leaning into Baltic for support against the horrible memories.

"Right, that's it. Patience at an end." Maura pulled a very real-looking gun from her backpack. "We're going to the hotel. Right now."

"Don't be ridiculous. You can't kill us," I told her, startled nonetheless by the sight of the weapon. "How did you get that through customs?"

"I didn't. My chieftain had it delivered to me."

"Your chieftain? I thought *you* were the chieftain of your tribe."

"You thought wrong."

"Why is this woman holding a gun on us?" Baltic demanded to know. "Who is she?"

"Maura Lo, this is my mate, Baltic. Baltic, this is Dr. Kostich's granddaughter, the one I promised to help so that he would lift the interdict from me."

"*Enchanté*," Constantine said politely.

"I told you to leave the ouroboros dragons alone," Baltic said, bending a stern eye on me.

"Yes, and you know how much I love it when you order me around."

Constantine snorted.

"Come along, no more chitchat," Maura said, waving the gun. "I don't want to have to shoot anyone, but I will if I have to."

"Do you honestly think we're going to let you hustle us out of here? Do we look that—"

Baltic didn't wait for me to finish speaking. He simply jumped Maura, knocking her to the ground and snatching the gun from her hand.

"You are so going to regret that," she snarled as she leaped to her feet, brushing dirt and leaves from her hair.

"Yeah? You and what army?" I said, letting my inner child have the pleasure of a few words of taunting.

As the last syllable left my lips, a swarm of three men charged down the path, all brandishing large and lethal-looking firearms.

Maura smiled.

"Dammit, I hate it when my rhetorical questions go bad."

"If you would be so good as to accompany us back to the hotel, we can see about your ransoms," Maura said, gesturing toward the three guys, whom I mentally dubbed Larry, Curly, and Moe. "We hadn't anticipated taking both of you, but the more the merrier where a ransom is concerned, right?"

"I'm so going to be filing a complaint about you to the Akashic League," I told Maura.

She rolled her eyes, and started to speak, but Moe shoved her out of the way and without further ado shot Baltic in the chest.

"Interesting. I wonder if I could gather enough strength to hold a gun," Constantine's disembodied voice said with much speculation. "I wouldn't mind taking a few shots at you myself."

I stared at the small black hole on the side of Baltic's chest as it began to seep blood, then turned to glare at Moe. "Oh, that was brilliant. Now you've pissed him off."

Baltic, who had likewise been examining the bullet hole, roared with anger, shifted into dragon form, and leaped onto Moe.

The three dragons all shifted as well. Moe was a red dragon, while the other two were blue. Maura, who had stared in stunned disbelief when Moe shot Baltic, quickly hurried forward, yapping about the dragons not following the plan.

I yanked hard on Baltic's dragon fire and set the ground under them ablaze.

"We *are* following orders," the dragon I dubbed Curly snarled at her, slamming her aside with his tail. "Just not yours."

"I will protect you, my beloved one," Constantine's voice declared right next to my ear.

"You're a damned ghost," Baltic snarled as his fire lit up a circle around us.

"Yes, and you've been shot."

"Even so, I'm more of a dragon than you ever were." Baltic head-butted Moe, his claws slashing out at the same time, slicing deep into Moe's chest. The other dragon screamed and shifted back into human form, scrabbling in the dirt for his gun.

"And you're a backstabbing, lying degenerate," Constantine yelled, a slightly visible image of him forming.

Dragon fire is a particularly ferocious sort of fire, and to my horror, I saw that the damp trees and moss didn't slow it down in the least. The circle quickly spread outward, consuming several centuries-old trees as fingers of fire crept toward the forest edge.

"That's better than being a two-timing traitorous bastard," Baltic yelled back, ducking as I leaped over his head and kicked the gun out of Moe's reach. "She's my mate! I'll protect her. Ysolde, come over here and be protected."

"Resorting to name-calling isn't helping, boys," I shouted, stomping hard on Moe's hand when he tried to grab my ankle. At the same time, I began to gather up arcane magic from the surrounding living things. "Besides, it's probably not a good idea to call the First Dragon's son by derogatory terms."

"What?" both Baltic and Constantine asked at the same time.

"The First Dragon is bound to not like it, and frankly, I've had enough of being in his bad graces."

"Now you will die!" Curly said with a dramatic flourish of his gun at me.

"Hi-ya!" My best Xena, Warrior Princess shout was

the answer to that threat. I flung a huge ball of arcane power at Curly just as he was about to riddle me with bullets. He saw it coming, though, and ducked so it zoomed past him and hit Larry dead-on, causing a huge flash of light to temporarily blind everyone.

"What the—what was that?"

I shook the dazzle from my eyes and saw Maura stagger to her feet, rubbing her face.

As the dragon fire raged around us, now more or less a small forest fire, everyone stood stunned by the blast of arcane light, staring at the spot where Larry had moments before stood. In his place was a two-foot-tall rock, an odd line of runes carved in a circle around the circumference.

With synchronization that would make Olympic swimmers envious, everyone turned to look at me.

"Er . . ." I said, eyeing the rock.

Curly screamed a profanity and jumped over Baltic toward me. Constantine shouted something about saving me, but his form shivered and faded to nothing, leaving him profaning the air with a litany of oaths. I tossed out a few quick attempts to dampen the dragon fire that was consuming the forest around us, but couldn't risk losing my concentration. In a contest between Baltic and the forest, the forest was bound to lose.

Baltic grabbed Curly by the tail and with a massive effort flipped him over backward, sending him crashing into Larry the rock.

"No! Stop it, all of you!" Maura shouted, waving her hands in the air. "This isn't what we're supposed to do! We're just going to hold you for ransom, that's all. There's no shooting! I distinctly said 'no shooting' at the planning meeting."

Baltic flung himself on Curly, twisting his head with

a bone-crunching noise that left me wanting to retch. Moe jumped onto his back, but Baltic knocked him backward, toward me.

Maura limped forward, her gun raised.

"You messed with the wrong wyvern's mate, lady," I snarled, gathering up another ball of arcane magic, but before I could fling it at her, Moe lunged sideways and kicked out with one leg, sending me flying into a rock. My head connected with an audible *thunk* that was almost as painful to hear as it was to feel.

Baltic screamed my name and shifted to human form in midleap as he ran to my side, pulling me up against his chest. "Ysolde! My love, are you hurt? Do not move. I will get a healer."

"They're getting away," Constantine's voice informed us. "You go after them, Baltic. I will stay and attend to Ysolde."

"I'm sorry," Maura said, gesturing with the gun. "This isn't what was supposed to happen. We were going to kidnap you, Ysolde, that's all. I had no idea she had other plans. I really am sorry."

Baltic carefully felt my neck and the back of my head, his hands coming away red as I woozily tried to sit up. "Maura, you have to listen to me—"

"I'm sorry," she said again, then with one last distraught look, turned on her heel and fled after Moe and Curly.

Two Baltics weaved before my face, the flickering fire casting a reddish orange glow to his skin, but even woozy as I was, I could see the concern in his darkly mysterious eyes. "You're never going to let me hear the end of this, are you?" I asked him.

"Never," he swore, and kissed me.

Chapter Eighteen

It took a good half hour for Baltic and me to put out the fire that, sadly, consumed a quarter of the woods. Luckily, the firemen who arrived to assist weren't wild about entering a forest that had long been known to be cursed, so they and the curious bystanders remained on the fringes, soaking nearby buildings lest the fire jump to them.

My head ached by the time we got the last of the fire tamped down to nothing, and it was with great relief that I sank onto the rocky mound that marked the opening to Baltic's lair. "I've never known your dragon fire to get out of control like that."

"It doesn't. It was your arcane power that fed the fire into an inferno," Baltic told me, pulling out a flask from a small pack and handing it to me. I took a swig of it, relishing the fire of the dragon's blood wine as it coursed down my throat.

"Oh. I guess that was the Grace of the Magi, because

I've never seen a reaction like that before." I glanced to the side, where Baltic had tossed the runed rock. "What are we going to do with Larry?"

"Who?"

"The rock. I call him Larry."

Baltic shrugged, and pulled out his cell phone. "Leave it. It can do no harm here."

"It doesn't seem right, somehow. I mean, he was a man, even if he was trying to kill you."

"He wasn't trying to kill Baltic, my adorable one. He was trying to kill you."

I looked over to where the faintest outline of Constantine was visible as he perched on a boulder. "Me? Why would he want to kill me? Baltic, I understand—everyone wants to kill Baltic."

The love of my life shot me a look that made me bite back a giggle.

"That is because he is a reprehensible, callous beast with no morals and even less intelligence," Constantine said coolly.

"Right," I said, standing up and facing him. "That's it—do you hear? That is it! No more calling Baltic names. I know you're all pissed because I chose him over you, but I did so five hundred years ago! I loved him then, I love him now, and I will always love him. Get over it already!"

Constantine's outline straightened itself up. "Never! You gave yourself to me before he took you, and you will be mine again!"

I narrowed my glare to razor sharpness. "You just don't listen, do you? I love Baltic. You're dead. Really, those two things should say it all!"

"I am not dead," Constantine said with dignity.

I pursed my lips.

"I am simply temporarily without life. If the archimage's daughter can resurrect that one"—he waved a hand at Baltic—"she can resurrect me as well."

"Over my dead body," I muttered.

"He's already seen to that," Baltic snapped as he closed his phone and moved closer to me, glaring at the outline of Constantine. "Begone, spirit! You bother my mate."

Constantine sputtered with indignation.

"I really don't want to have to fight with you, Constantine, but until you accept a few facts, we're going to have some issues."

"Do not attempt to reason with him, *chérie*," Baltic interrupted. "It is useless. Constantine does not have the facility to do so."

"Like hell I don't," the annoyed shade said, getting to his feet. "But Ysolde has a point. I am here now, alive if not quite alive, and clearly things are different than they were in the past. Therefore, I will adapt. A good wyvern is always willing to try new things when necessary."

"You're not a wyvern anymore," I pointed out.

"Of course I am. I was a wyvern when I died, and now I am alive again. Thus I am still a wyvern."

"Are you not listening? Maura told me you may be autonomous, and you can have a corporeal presence, but you're not actually a living, breathing person."

"I'm as good as alive," he said with a haughty sniff.

"And two, you're not the wyvern of the silver dragons anymore. A very nice man by the name of Gabriel Tauhou is."

"Tauhou?" He frowned. "I do not know this name."

"From what I understand, you knew his father, although I don't know what his name is. Gabriel lives in Australia with his mate, May."

"He has a mate?"

I looked at Baltic, who was punching a number into his phone and ignoring us. "Yes, he does. She's a doppelganger."

"Ah. Created, not born. Clever, but it doesn't matter." Constantine shook his head and his form solidified about halfway. "I was wyvern before this Gabriel Tauhou. Now that I am back, he must stand down in favor of me."

"Yeah, good luck getting him to agree to that." Distracted by a glint of anger in Baltic's eyes, I watched him as he put away his phone. Despite my assumption, his anger didn't seem to be directed at Constantine. "You weren't calling Gabriel, were you? It would take him forever to get to Latvia, and I told you that my head has stopped hurting."

"I was attempting to contact Thala," Baltic said, his hands on his hips as he scanned the surrounding area. Thick wisps of heavy white smoke still tainted the air, making it a little difficult to breathe, but since we were located in the center of the forest, none of the charred trees were visible.

"Oh. I guess I must have forgotten about her. Where is she? You don't think Maura and her Three Stooges got her, do you?"

Constantine snorted.

"No," Baltic said slowly, his eyes narrowed in thought. "I begin to wonder if I haven't been misled by her."

"Misled how?"

"I will go find this wyvern and inform him of my return," Constantine said, becoming solid long enough to suddenly whisk me into an embrace and press a kiss on my lips.

Baltic spun around and started toward him.

"Adieu, my lovely. I will return to deal with your obnoxious mate another day."

A profanity shot out as Baltic lunged for Constantine, but the latter evaporated into nothing, leaving us alone.

"Dammit," I said, realizing that in all the confusion I had neglected to pin Constantine down about what I needed to do to reclaim his honor. "He left! I needed to talk to him."

"Be grateful for small mercies," Baltic said, continuing to scan the surroundings. "I am."

"Yes, but now I'll have to track him down again to find out what the First Dragon wants me to do for him."

"Bah. He is of no concern. I am more worried about why Thala has abandoned us."

"He may not be of concern to you," I said, my shoulders slumping as I made myself comfortable on my rock, "but you don't go dissing the First Dragon's son without some sort of repercussions, and I don't want to think about what those might be. He's angry enough with me already."

Baltic, who had been looking out into the distance, turned to pin me back with a look. "Why do you keep saying that?"

"Saying what? That the First Dragon is pissed enough at me, especially after he had to resurrect me a second time?"

"No, before that."

I thought a moment. "That we shouldn't go dissing Constantine? I know he irritates you, Baltic, but he's dead, and is no threat to us anymore, so really, calling him petty names—"

"You said the First Dragon's son. You think Constantine is his son?"

I looked into those fathomless eyes. "Yes. He is, isn't he?"

"No."

"But—" I shook my head. "He's got to be."

"He's not." Baltic continued to search the surrounding area for only he knew what.

"I think you're wrong. I saw the First Dragon with him myself."

"Constantine is *not* the First Dragon's son," he repeated.

"And just why are you so sure of that?" I asked, exasperated by his flat statements of denial.

"Because I know who my brothers were."

"Goody for—" I stopped, my skin crawling as realization dawned in the dusty recesses of my brain. "Your *brothers*?"

"Yes." He leaped down off his rock and held out a hand for me. "Come. I see no signs she left, which means she must be in the tunnels. We will follow her trail."

"Your brothers?" He pulled me to my feet, but I stopped him before he could help me down into the lair. "Baltic, are you trying to say . . . ? You can't be. You can't mean . . ."

"The First Dragon is my father, yes, mate." He shook his head as he wrapped an arm around me and hefted me down into a dank opening into the earth. "My old Ysolde knew that. I don't know how it is you have forgotten that fact, but you used to deal with it much better than you are now."

"Your *father*," I said, breathing heavily through my nose, ignoring the rich odor of the soil as Baltic switched on a powerful flashlight, "is the ancestor of all dragons? The most powerful being in all dragontime? On par with *a god*?"

"My old Ysolde used to call him an interfering arse," he said, doubling over and leading me down a tunnel clogged with roots, debris, and dirt. "She was not intimidated by him. She once told him to mind his own business and let us get on with ours."

"By the rood," I said, suddenly dizzy with realization. "No wonder he was disappointed in me. I used to lip off to a god!"

"It was good for him. He left us alone after that," Baltic said with satisfaction, pausing at an intersection to consider the ground. "You may do so again, if it will ease your distress."

"Sainted Mary," I gasped, my eyes glazed and unseeing as Baltic led onward, into the remainder of the tunnels that once lay beneath Dauva. "That means—that means it's you I'm supposed to help. It's *your* honor I'm supposed to reclaim. It's you who caused the death of innocents!"

"You shouldn't believe everything the First Dragon tells you," he answered, flicking his light around. The tracks he was following seemed to end in a pile of smashed wood and stone.

"That's why you don't like him! That's why he knew your name! It wasn't because of you being kicked out of your sept. It was because you were his son! His youngest son!" I put my hands to my head, wanting to scream and shout and shake Baltic, all at the same time. "Why didn't you tell me?"

"I thought you would eventually remember," he said with a shrug. "The old Ysolde—"

"Was a twit, evidently!" I interrupted. "For the love of the saints, Baltic! You could have told me! You knew I was trying to do what the First Dragon—oh, dear god, he's my father-in-law!—what he wanted me to do."

"You told me you had to do something with Constantine, not with one of his sons."

I ground my teeth. He had a point, dammit. "Are there any other family members I should know about? Your mother? Brothers?"

"They are all dead," he said, examining the wood carefully. "Look at this—it is recent. Thala must have shut down this tunnel behind her as she escaped. The lair!"

He whirled and ran back the way he had come. I followed, my mind still reeling with all that I had just found out. "What exactly happened to get you kicked out of the sept?"

Baltic swore as he touched the silver-bound door that marked his lair. It swung open with a teeth-grating noise that left me clutching the wall. He plunged into the room; I followed more slowly, trying desperately to get my brain to function. The air inside was close and dusty, as if it had been closed for centuries, which until recently it had. His light flickered around the lair, catching first a broken iron trunk, then a heap of wood that had once been a chest. Everything was covered in a thick layer of dirt and dust, disuse and abandonment just as thick in the air.

A few cracked jars remained stacked in the corner, but the rest of the lair was picked clean, no doubt by Kostya. Baltic didn't spare much of a glance for any of the remains, however; he went straight for the back corner of the room, kicking aside an elaborately carved chair that had been broken by a falling beam. He bent, pulling up a trapdoor, and jumping into the hole without a word.

"What's that? Another lair?" As blackness surrounded me in a claustrophobic grip, I hurried forward, kneeling at the edge of what seemed to be a chasm to oblivion. The air seeping out of the hole was even more dusty and mildewed, making my nose wrinkle.

The light bobbled, then returned as Baltic heaved himself up, out of the sub-lair. "It's gone."

"What's gone?" I brushed spiderwebs and dirt from his hair as he sat on the edge, his legs dangling into the hole. "What was in there?"

"My things." His eyes caught and held mine. "Our things. Our private things. Not even Kostya knew about this vault. It's where you put your love token before Dauva was destroyed."

I touched the chain that hung around my neck, the oval silver pendant that Baltic had carved for me some four hundred years before nestled safely between my breasts. "What's missing?"

"My talisman."

"Is that something I gave to you?"

"No." His expression was one of worry. I didn't often see Baltic look worried, so I took heed, and followed him as he exited the lair.

"It's important, this talisman?" I asked a few minutes later as we climbed out of the lair.

"Very."

I grabbed at his belt as he started to stride off, making him turn around and raise an eyebrow.

"I know you don't like to answer questions, but I'm going to keep at you until you tell me, so why don't you save us both some verbal dancing and just spill now?"

He sighed heavily.

"And if you dare say the old Ysolde would never have pestered you this way, I'll deck you," I threatened.

He laughed and took the fist I was waving at him in his hand, pulling me forward to kiss me. "The old Ysolde would have done just as you are doing now, questioning me endlessly until she got what she wanted. The talisman was a gift from the First Dragon. It marks me as his child. My brothers and sister all had one when they formed their septs."

"You have a sister, too?" I couldn't help but ask, pausing long enough to grab the Larry rock before allowing him to escort me down the game trail, through the still-smoking scorched area, and out to where I had left the car.

"Had. She was killed a few years after she founded the black sept."

"That must have been a long time ago." I did some mental calculating. "Over a thousand years?"

"Yes." He held the car door open for me, and it was a sign of just how bemused I was that I stuffed Larry into the backseat and didn't notice that Baltic took the driver's seat until we were already jetting down the road, coming close to plowing into a stone fence.

"Is it true that the First Dragon's children founded the four original septs?"

"My three brothers and sister, yes. You are going to ask me why I was not given a sept, aren't you?"

"Well, that and why you're driving on the wrong side of the road," I said, pointing to an oncoming car.

Baltic swore and jerked the car over to the proper side. "Mortals should standardize which side of the road they wish to drive on. I am the youngest son, Ysolde. You know when I was born—it was several centuries after my siblings."

"So you were kind of an afterthought?" I grinned at him.

He looked outraged. "Hardly. My mother was the First Dragon's descendant, a black dragon. He seduced her, and I was born. I was not given a sept because I was born into the black sept."

I gawked at him. "Your father seduced his own descendant? That's incest!"

"Every dragon is descended from him. Technically, you and I are related."

"Yes, but at a distance! Several generations and whatnot! By the rood, Baltic! That's beyond creepy. Your mom wasn't your sister, was she?"

"No." He swore as several car horns blasted him. I refused to look, deciding it was just better that I not know what he was doing. "She was the daughter of his great-granddaughter."

"Wait a minute—" I shook my head, trying to untangle his family tree. "You're a wyvern. That means you have to have a human parent, and if your mother was also your ... I don't know, your great-grandniece? Whatever the relationship, how can she be human?"

"She wasn't. She was a black dragon."

"But wyverns have to have a human parent," I argued.

"Other wyverns, yes. But not those who are sired by the First Dragon," he pointed out with complacency.

I thought about that as he parked illegally and hustled me out of the car and into the train station, growling when I insisted that he go back to retrieve the rock.

"But how—" I started to say when he slammed it down next to me, causing a little piece of it to chip off. I winced, hoping it was nothing Larry would mind losing. Assuming, that is, that I could turn him back into a dragon.

"I am done answering questions, mate. Do not glare at me—we have more important things to do than discuss ancient history."

"What important things? Track down that sneaky Maura and the two remaining Stooges?"

"More questions! My old Ysolde would have known when it was time to stop questioning me."

"Did your old Ysolde ever pop you on the nose? Because the new one is sure thinking about it. . . ."

It took us three hours to get to England, and that was only after we used a portaling service to zap us to a dirty fish-and-chips shop located on the fringes of London, the local airline not wanting to give in to Baltic's demands that it reroute airplanes to accommodate us.

"All right," I told him as I breathed in the air of London and immediately choked on the grease fumes. "I haven't asked you a single question for several hours, so you can answer a couple more without spontaneously combusting. Why do you think Thala has gone off in a huff after raiding your lair?"

He hailed a taxi, grumbling when I insisted that he put Larry into the car as well. "You saw the signs as well as I did."

"Yes, but I don't know why you're suddenly suspicious of her. I agree that it's odd that she disappeared like she did, but perhaps those ouroboros dragons made her break into the lair and then took her away with them."

One chocolate brown eyebrow rose. "Do you seriously believe that she would suffer any such thing?"

"I suppose not," I said after a moment's thought. "Anyone who calls herself a dirgesinger isn't someone who would let herself be kidnapped. You think she's betrayed you?"

"It's possible. We have never seen eye to eye on certain subjects, and it could be that she's decided to put into motion plans that she desired."

"What sort of plans?" I asked softly, so the taxi driver wouldn't overhear us.

"She wishes to restore her mother to a place of power."

I don't know what I expected him to say—perhaps something to do with Thala at Baltic's side and me long gone—but certainly not anything to do with her mother. "She wants to resurrect her, too? The famed Antonia von Endres? The archimage who was so powerful, she once bested the ruling prince of Abaddon? The one you slept with?"

He made a face. "I knew you would not forget that."

"Of course not. I also haven't forgotten that you slept with Thala."

"That was a good century before I met you, mate."

"Which is why I'm not belaboring the point, although how she has the nerve to tell me she's not in love with you . . . well, that's another subject. Surely Antonia von Endres is in the beyond?"

Baltic looked unconcerned, his fingers idly tracing patterns on my leg. "She went wherever mages go when they diminish."

"That's the beyond." I frowned, remembering something May had told me. "But you can go there, too. Have you been there to see her?"

"We are light dragons, Ysolde. We both are able to access the beyond in a limited fashion."

"Did you go to see her?"

He sighed yet another of his put-upon sighs that didn't garner any sympathy from me. "It is hard for me to compare, but I believe you are even more jealous now than you used to be, which was then of a level that made it uncomfortable to have any female around me who wasn't human or ugly enough to make you retch, and even then there were a few instances when you insisted that I lusted after leprous hags."

"Nice attempt to change the subject. Answer the question, dragon."

"I have not seen Antonia von Endres since she diminished some six hundred years ago. You may now kiss me and beg my pardon for suspecting me of an interest in any female other than you."

I couldn't help but smile at his demand, and did, in fact, kiss him, giving him just a little taste of his own dragon fire before apologizing for my dark suspicions.

He left me off at Dr. Kostich's hotel with a word of warning. "Do not do anything that will result in you dying again. I have reached the limit of the number of times I can survive your death, no matter how short that period lasts."

"I promise I won't do any magic that threatens my life," I said solemnly as he walked me to the elevators, fighting hard to keep my lips from twitching. "Did Pavel say he had any leads on Thala?"

"No, but she had an interest in a building here in London. Pavel is waiting for me there."

"All right. Baltic . . ." I bit my lip, unsure if my uneasy feeling was justified or not. "I'm grateful that you had Pavel remove Brom from the house just in case Thala went there and was out of control, but do we really need to hide out at a hotel? She seemed very reasonable the last time we talked, not at all like she used to be. I'm not saying she doesn't have something up her sleeve, because I can well believe she does, but if she's not jealous of me because she's in love with you, then she really doesn't pose a threat to Brom or me."

"I will not risk either of your lives until I speak with her," he said firmly. "It goes against my desire to have my son placed with the green dragons, but at least I know he will be safe there."

"It was nice of Nico to ask Aisling to take them in for a few hours," I said absently. "I'll pick up Brom once I'm done here. But do you really think—"

"Yes." Ignoring the stream of people entering and exiting the elevators, he pulled me to his chest. I melted against him, as I always do, the sensation of the hard lines of his body against mine never failing to send a little zing of pleasure down my spine. "Be cautious, Ysolde. You are everything to me."

I defy you to not turn to mush at a man declaring such a thing, doubly so if you know it's the literal truth. "Likewise. If she's got an axe to grind, I'd rather it not be upside your head."

His head dipped down to claim my mouth, dragon fire whipping through me. Mindful of the people around us, I tamped it down so that it wouldn't manifest itself visibly, feeling that we were drawing enough attention without setting the lobby on fire.

I watched him walk away, aware that he didn't even notice the women who stopped and stared at him with mouths agape and eyes bugged out. Still shirtless, his hair loose around his shoulders, with a determined set to his jaw, and a powerful stride that was downright feral, he was indeed a sight to behold.

And I would do anything to keep him safe.

Chapter Nineteen

Jack opened the door to Dr. Kostich's suite with only a raised eyebrow at the large runed stone I held in my arms. "Tully. Er . . . Ysolde."

"Hi, Jack. Is he here?"

"He is." Jack stepped back, waving me in.

"You didn't get in trouble for letting me in last time, did you?"

He made a wry face. "Not much. Just a little raking over the coals."

"I'm sorry—"

He stopped my apology with a smile. "It was worth it to see you again. Would you mind if I asked why you're lugging around a big rock?"

"His name is Larry. He's really a blue dragon."

Jack stared at the stone. "I thought the master placed the Grace of the Magi on you."

"He did. It doesn't really help a whole lot."

"Ah. He's in the sitting room."

Jack escorted me to the main room, murmuring my name by way of an announcement as I entered. I was relieved to see that Violet was still with her father, the pair of them looking up from small plates of cake and tiny sandwiches.

"Tully! You're just in time for tea," Violet said, waving me in and pouring a fresh cup for me.

I paused a moment, waiting to see if Dr. Kostich was going to kick up a fuss at my arriving unexpectedly again, but he simply frowned and said, "Since you offered me hospitality at your table, it is fitting I should do the same."

"Thank you." Gratefully, I took the cup Violet handed me, as well as a plate laden with teatime goodies. "Ooh, cucumber sandwiches. I do love them."

"You have news of Maura?" Dr. Kostich asked, bending his frown upon me. "You have located her?"

"Yes, and yes."

"Oh, thank the stars," Violet sighed, relief causing her to sag against the couch. "I knew you'd save her."

"I haven't quite done that. Yet."

Dr. Kostich set down his plate. "Why are you here, then?"

I took a deep breath, followed by a big swig of hot tea. "I'm here to have you change a rock back into a blue dragon, if you can, and to remove the interdiction bound on me."

His face was as solid and unmoving as Larry's stone. "We had an agreement, Tully Sullivan."

A little pinch of pain shot through me as he flexed his arcane muscles. "Yes, we did. I promised to try to help Maura, and I've done so. I met with her. I talked to her about getting away from the dragon tribe." I took another sip of tea, more for time to gather my courage than anything else. "I offered her my help. She doesn't want to leave them."

"I told you that," Violet said, sitting upright again. "But she's scared, Tully. Underneath that bravado, she's scared. I just know she is."

I sorted through my impressions, slowly shaking my head. "I hate to contradict a mother's feelings, but she didn't strike me as scared."

"How *did* she strike you?" Kostich asked, his voice level, but I could feel anger building in the air.

I met his gaze. "Not frightened or intimidated or even unhappy. She seemed very much in charge of herself ... and others."

He made an annoyed click of his tongue.

"No, that can't be right. It was an act, Tully," Violet protested.

"I don't think it was. Believe me, I wish there was an easy way to fix things, to help her escape the hold these dragons have on her, but the truth is that they have no hold. At least not the kind you mean. Far from it, I'd say. She was in command of the dragons—until they attacked us, that is." I explained briefly about the resurrection of Constantine and the subsequent assault by Larry, Curly, and Moe.

Kostich rose and went to the window, his fingers absently drawing little clarity spells on nothing in particular. "You say that one of the dragons referred to someone else, someone other than Maura?"

"Not directly, but the implication was there." An idea popped into my head, but it was so far-fetched, I couldn't give it any credence. Besides, it didn't fit. "If there is someone other than Maura calling the shots, I don't know who that could be. I had a vision a few days ago about an event that took place at an aerie in Tibet. Ouroboros dragons were there, and were led by Maura. I didn't see her explicitly, but there was a shade present, and he referred to his mistress. Who else but a Summoner would have a shade?"

Kostich made another annoyed noise, one long, thin hand waving away my question. "A necromancer or an Ilargi might. That is not what is important."

"They'd have to be dragons as well, and there are no necromancer or dragon Ilargi that I can—" I stopped, the word "necromancer" ringing a bell in my head. "Wait a minute—necromancers can summon shades?"

"Summon? No, but they are the only beings to whom shades can be bound, assuming the necromancer first gains control over the shade. What exactly did Maura say when the ouroboros dragons defied her orders?"

I repeated her words, trying to fit together the terrible idea that was growing increasingly horrible.

"She condoned a kidnapping?" Violet moaned softly to herself. "She participated in it? She *planned* it? Oh, my poor girl!"

"This is what comes of consorting with dragons," her father told her before turning back to me. "Very well. We will deal with the situation from here. You are excused."

"Huh?" I shook away my mental fog and stared at him for a moment. "Oh. Er . . . yes, I'm sorry. If there's anything more I can do to help you with Maura, I will be happy to do so. About the interdiction . . ."

"You have not freed my granddaughter from her association with the dragons. Our agreement was for you to do so," he said, returning to his seat and turning his attention to his plate of pastries.

"Our agreement was for me to try. I've done so. I want the interdiction off."

He froze at my strident tone.

"Please," I added hastily.

"Yes, Father, take it off her. She's earned it," Violet said wearily. My heart went out to her, but I was at a loss as to how I could be of further help.

Unless . . .

Kostich's face was black for a good two minutes, but finally he relented. "I will remove the interdiction, but you will remember that you are no longer a member of the Magister's Guild, and as such, may not look to us for help."

I nodded, waiting expectantly. With a sigh that rivaled Baltic's at his most exasperated, Kostich stood, drew a symbol over me, and pronounced me free of the interdiction and grace.

Tiny invisible bands that had held me tightly loosened somewhat before finally dissolving, leaving me with the feeling that I could breathe deeply for the first time in many months. "Thank you," I said with profound gratitude. "And Larry?"

Dr. Kostich's nostril's flared.

"Right. I'll take care of him myself. Shouldn't be an issue with the interdiction off, right?" I would have apologized again for my inability to bring them good news about Maura, but it was clear they both wanted me gone.

I paused at the door, looking back, unable to keep from asking Dr. Kostich, "Can mages who have diminished return to the mortal world?"

His pale blue eyes pinned me back with a look that

raised the hairs on the back of my neck. "It has not occurred, no."

"But it's possible?"

Silence greeted my question for a good minute. "Only by a mage powerful enough to overcome the forces of nature itself."

Or one whose daughter was working on her behalf, a daughter who was half dragon and who was in her own right powerful enough to sing dirges ... and raise the dead. A necromancer, in fact.

I looked at him with horror creeping along my skin. "I have to go home."

"What is in your mind, dragon?" he asked, starting toward me.

I shook my head and bolted, tossing over my shoulder, "I'll let you know if it's true."

While in the elevator on the way down to the ground floor, I made a frantic phone call to first Baltic, then Pavel, but neither of them answered.

By the time I engaged a rental car, hastily left a message with Aisling's housekeeper informing her I would be by to pick up Brom later, and tried to reach Baltic three more times, I greatly feared that the dark turn of my suspicions would turn out to be only too valid.

As I pulled up at our house to find the lights ablaze, semicircles of light from the windows piercing the night, all doubt was erased.

"Can anyone join this party, or is it by invitation only?" I asked as I set the Larry stone on a table near the door in Baltic's library.

At the sound of the door opening, two of the three occupants of the room turned to look at me.

I squatted next to where Pavel lay on the floor, feeling for his pulse. It was a little erratic, but present, and he didn't seem to be bleeding anywhere.

"Will the day never come that you will do as I ask, mate?" Baltic asked, his face filled with irritation.

I gestured toward the woman in front of him. "You're the only man I know who can be annoyed at his mate while someone else holds a sword to your neck. What exactly do you intend to do to Baltic, Thala? You can't mean to kill him; you're the one who brought him back to life."

She ground her teeth while Baltic answered in just the arrogant tone I was expecting. "Ysolde, you will leave the house. This is between Thala and me."

"I don't think it is—not anymore." I stepped over Pavel's form, skirting the two of them in their locked tableau. "Not since Thala ordered her Three Stooges to kill me in Latvia."

Baltic's gaze shifted back to Thala. His eyes glowed with ebony fury. "You tried to kill my mate? Who are these dragons you command?"

"Clever, aren't you?" Thala taunted me, her eyes nervously switching from Baltic to me. "Did that little half-dragon bitch Maura talk?"

"Half-dragon . . ." I shook my head, moving behind Baltic to the far side until I stood behind a couch, resting my hands on the back of it. "She's the same as you, Thala. You both have dragon fathers . . . red dragon fathers. Was your father killed by Chuan Ren as well? Is that why you're not a member of the sept?"

She spat out a word that I didn't recognize, but I knew it was not particularly polite. Baltic stood apparently relaxed, his hands open, but I could feel the dragon fire inside of him, demanding that he act. He was waiting to see what Thala would do. Neither of us believed she would hurt him, not after she'd gone to significant trouble to resurrect him.

"My father couldn't be bothered to recognize me, and the sept refused to allow me in because they said my mother's blood tainted the precious dragon blood, diffused it into something impure. So, yes, I formed my own tribe, just as Baltic did when I brought him back. Only we have no intention of living quietly while our usurpers reign supreme."

Baltic eyed her with speculation. "You raised your own tribe? Then it was you who acted against me."

She smiled. "You were so busy thinking of nothing but re-forming the dragon heart, I'm surprised you noticed anything else was going on."

"You gave Kostya my shard." His eyes narrowed. "You did not wish for me to re-form the heart!"

"Of course I didn't, you stupid man," she snapped, the sword waving in the air as she gesticulated. "Ysolde! Ysolde! That's all you could think of—Ysolde! 'We must re-form the heart, Thala. We must get the shards from the other wyverns so we can invoke the First Dragon, Thala. Your plans and desires must wait—it must all circle around bloody precious Ysolde!' I bit my tongue for *years* while you made your plans, because I knew that they would never come to fruition. I knew that one day you would grow tired of trying to regain that which you could never have again, and then nothing would matter to you." Her gaze shifted to me. "I didn't know that wretched sister of mine had already done the job."

"But why . . . ? I don't understand," I said, sliding my hands down behind the couch so I could start sketching a few wards and begin to gather a ball of arcane power.

"She wanted the dragon heart for herself," Baltic answered, his face impassive. The fire raged within him, however.

"Why? What could it do . . . ? Oh. I suppose if you had the most powerful relic of all dragondom, you could do pretty much anything, couldn't you? Even bringing your mother out of the beyond."

To my surprise, she dropped the sword tip from Baltic's throat and made a gesture of annoyance with her free hand. "Do you really think I'm going to stand here explaining myself to you as if I were a villain at the end of a movie? I am not so foolish, nor do I have the time to waste on your inanities."

She flung down the sword and spread wide her hands, a horrible noise coming from her mouth, part wail, part spell.

Baltic shouted and lunged toward me, knocking me down behind the couch, covering me with his body. For a moment, it seemed as if time itself stopped, the air inside the house gathering itself; then it was released in a shock wave of fury that exploded outward, taking with it everything in its path.

I opened my eyes to find a blurry face just a few inches from mine. I screamed and tried to sit up, clunking my head against something rock hard. "Ack!"

"Ow! Oh, man, you broke my head!"

I blinked rapidly, and my vision cleared enough for me to see that the face belonged to a furry black dog, who was now rubbing the top of its head along the edge of the mattress upon which I was lying. "Jim! What the devil were you trying to do?"

"See if you were still breathing. You were making

funny little grunting noises." It lifted its head and bellowed, "She's awake!"

I realized at that moment that I wasn't alone in the bed. The familiar warm, solid form who lay next to me was too still, however. I pulled myself up again as I bent over Baltic, who was lying on his stomach, and I noted signs of serious wounds in the process of healing. "Saints of the apocalypse, what happened to his back?"

Aisling bustled into the room, May on her heels. "Oh, good, you are awake. How do you feel?"

"Confused. What's happened to Baltic?"

"Dirge at point-blank range," Jim said, peering over the bed to look at the bruised and battered back. "He takes a licking but keeps on ticking, doesn't he?"

"Dirge . . ." Memory returned to me. "Thala!"

"I'm so glad you told us where you were going, or we wouldn't have arrived just as she brought the house down on you," Aisling said, fetching a soft robe from a wardrobe. Absently, I put it on over the nightgown in which I'd been dressed.

"Baltic took the brunt of it, but Gabriel and Tipene worked over him and Pavel all night." May's blue eyes considered me with a frankness that drove home the debt we owed them. "You weren't hurt badly, but the others . . . well, I'm just glad that Aisling and Drake brought you to us in time."

"I will move heaven and earth to repay all of you," I swore, tears swimming in my eyes as I gently touched the marks on Baltic's back. He moaned into the pillow, moving restlessly. I couldn't keep from bending down to kiss his cheek, whispering, "It's all right, my love. You sleep. I'm right here."

He murmured my name, his body relaxing again as I stroked his shoulder.

"If you can stand a visitor, I know of someone who's anxious to see you. Jim, stop touching Ysolde with your nose. It's unhygienic," Aisling scolded, shooing him toward the door.

"Sheesh, you yell at me for not wanting to see her when she's all bloody and gooey, and now you're yelling because I'm just checking that she's OK. Inconsistent much, Ash?"

"Sullivan?" Brom appeared in the door, his face anxious. I slipped out of the bed and met him halfway, hugging him as tightly as I could without cutting off his oxygen. "Nico said you'd be OK, but you didn't look like it when they carried you in."

"I'm absolutely OK," I said, giving him one last squeeze before he started casting glances at the others in the room. "So is Baltic. I'm sorry if we frightened you."

"I wasn't scared," he said with all the insouciance of a nine-year-old. He glanced again at Baltic, then gave a little twitch of his shoulders. "Not much. I'm glad you're back, though. Jim says Thala went postal and exploded the house. Is the basement blown up as well?"

I smiled, relieved that the strained expression had faded to one of purely mercenary interest. "I'm sure it was. We'll have to get you some new equipment for your ghastly experiments, all right?"

"OK. Nico says he'll go with us the next time Maata and I go to the British Museum. He says he knows someone who works there who will let us see behind-the-scenes stuff. He says they have mummies that they don't even let people see, but that he can talk to them and they might show them to me. He says they have mummies of cats."

"You're just a really weird kid," Jim told Brom. "Luckily, I like weird."

"And once again balance is restored to the world," I said, smiling.

Chapter Twenty

"Mate, stop fussing over me."

"Gabriel says—"

"I don't care what the silver wyvern says. You will cease trying to force me into bed, and instead give me my trousers."

"You haven't rested enough!" I stuffed the pair of pants that one of Drake's men had brought into the wardrobe and spun around with my back to the door. "Gabriel was very clear that your injuries were sufficiently serious that you needed time to finish the healing he started. That doesn't mean you can get up a few hours after you were just about blown to kingdom come!"

"I will not be ordered around by Gabriel Tauhou!" Baltic stormed, marching toward me in all of his naked glory, his scowl truly magnificent. He held out his hand. "Give me my trousers."

"If you go back to bed, I'll give you a sponge bath," I said, batting my eyelashes.

That made him pause, but after a long consideration, he shook his head. "I could not make love to you in the home of the silver wyvern. Give me the trousers!"

"How about this?" I cooed, sliding my hands up the muscled swell of his chest and stroking his neck as I nibbled on his lower lip, my body moving gently against his. "You get back into bed, and I'll give you a massage to work out the kinks in all those poor abused muscles. I bet I could get some massage oil . . . the lickable kind."

Passion kindled in his eyes, and for a minute I thought he'd go for it, but at last he shook his head, reaching behind me to yank open the wardrobe door. "I know you desire me as much as I desire you, Ysolde, but this is not the place to perform those acts in which I clearly see you wish to indulge yourself. We will return home, and then you will lick oil off me."

The faint sound of voices yelling reached my ears, followed by the thump of footsteps.

"Our home is nothing but a heap of stone and timber," I said, sighing as he pulled on the pants. "Thanks to your crazy ex-girlfriend. It sounds like we're going to have company."

He grabbed a shirt from the wardrobe, and was just buttoning it when Jim burst into the room, its eyes round with excitement. "Good, Balters is up. You're going to want to see this."

"See what?" I asked as the demon turned tail and ran back to the stairs.

"Is my son here?"

"Yes, Aisling left him here when they went off to save us, not that I expect they knew that they would be called on to do just that. She just said that she was worried because I babbled something about Thala wanting to hurt you, and she convinced Drake to make sure we were all right."

Baltic made a noncommittal noise and put on his shoes, which oddly enough hadn't been destroyed in the explosion. "Gather your things. We are leaving."

I smoothed out the dress that Aisling had lent me, May's clothing being too small for me. "Things? What things? This is pretty much it." I looked up to find him disappearing out the door. "Baltic, wait! You're not fully healed—"

Raised voices could be heard filtering up the stairwell. Baltic paused for a moment as he listened, then sighed his best martyred sigh and took my hand as we continued to the ground floor at a more decorous pace.

The hall of Gabriel and May's house was large and filled with plants. A heavy round table dominated the center, upon which an elegant vase sat filled with a beautiful flower arrangement. Now, however, the flowers and vase lay in ruins on the marble floor, the glass shattered and water creeping across toward a gorgeous old handworked rug. Brom peeked out around Pavel, who stood guarding a doorway, Nico hovering protectively behind both of them. Gabriel was being held back by Drake and Tipene, while Aisling and May stood on one side, expressions of incredulity on their respective faces. Standing on the table was a thickly built man, his voice filling the hall as he declared, "I don't care what your name is or who your father was, or what you used to be, you are no longer wyvern! I brought this sept into being, and I will not allow another to be wyvern so long as there is breath in my body!"

"Constantine," I said, sighing right along with Baltic. "I might have known he'd find his way here."

Baltic said nothing, just dropped my hand and strode forward. Constantine spun around, his eyes lighting with pleasure as he jumped off the table, obviously intent on giving Baltic yet another piece of his mind.

He didn't have the chance to, however. Baltic's fist shot out, sending Constantine flying backward a couple of feet, his body hitting the ground with a loud *whump*.

May grinned. Aisling applauded. Jim whistled as it peered into Constantine's face. "He's out like a light. Nice one, Baltic."

"Yes, nice one," Gabriel agreed, shaking off Tipene and Drake to stalk forward to us. "I take it we have you to thank for resurrecting Constantine?"

"Yes, because it's not enough I have a lieutenant who wishes to destroy my mate, and a former heir who insists on taking what is not his. I must add the treacherous bastard who slayed Ysolde into my life, as well," Baltic answered with a grim look.

Gabriel's fury dissipated somewhat, but before he could say anything, a feeble voice spoke from the floor.

"I told you that I did not slay Ysolde. How could I slay her when I gave my life for hers?" Constantine groaned as he sat up, gingerly wiggling his jaw.

"You what?" I asked, shaking my head. "No, you killed me. Baltic and I shared the vision. We saw you with the bloody sword, standing over my body."

"I found the sword," he said wearily, getting to his feet. "Lying next to your body. I knew someone had slain you, and that I could not survive your loss."

"She is not your mate!" Baltic bellowed, starting toward him. Pavel was immediately at his side, as was Drake, both of them blocking him. "She's mine! It was me who died when you killed her!"

"I didn't kill her!" Constantine yelled back. "Are you deaf as well as stupid?"

"Hey!" I said, pushing Pavel aside. "I will not tolerate any name-calling!"

Baltic shoved me right back behind him. I pinched his butt.

"I gave my life for yours," Constantine repeated. "I sacrificed myself for you. Just ask the First Dragon."

My skin prickled as I moved around to Baltic's other side, leaning into him for comfort. "You did? That was you? The First Dragon said that someone ... But I thought you killed me. If you didn't, then who did?"

"That I do not know. I found the sword next to your body, and tracks leading off, but did not see anyone." Constantine sniffed and looked haughtily down his nose at Baltic. "I did not have time to follow. I knew that I must save you. I could do nothing more than give my life for yours."

To my surprise, Baltic suddenly gave a short bark of laughter. "*You could do nothing more.* Do you think I have forgotten the past, Constantine? I know why you sacrificed yourself, and it had nothing to do with your professed love for my mate."

Constantine's gaze shifted to Gabriel. I got the feeling he was extremely uncomfortable. "The past is where it should be—long buried. It is the present that concerns me, and the welfare of my sept."

Gabriel's jaw worked, but respect for the founder of his sept clearly held his tongue silent. May moved close to him, her fingers twining through his. "Has there ever been precedence for a wyvern being resurrected?" she asked.

"No—" Drake started to say, but Baltic interrupted.

"He is not alive. He is a shade. Take my advice and call an exterminator."

Constantine's eyes widened with indignation. He spat out something in Zilant that had Jim looking shocked.

"Your opinion concerns me not," Baltic told him, wrapping an arm around me. "We will go home now."

"I told you that we don't have a home. Besides, Thala is still out there, doing who knows what."

"Thala?" Constantine asked. "Von Endres' daughter?"

"Yes. She resurrected Baltic, but evidently she's been using him to bring the dragon heart together."

"Really," Aisling said softly, nudging Drake. "I told you it had to be something like that. I told you that if it wasn't Baltic killing those blue dragons, then it had to be Thala."

We all looked at her in surprise. "You think Thala killed the blue dragons instead of Fiat?" I asked.

"Sure. It makes sense if she really wanted the dragon heart." She looked around the room at the expressions of confusion and continued. "You said she was using Baltic for her own purposes, right? What's the first thing any good plan of attack does? Divide and conquer. So she made everyone in the weyr think Baltic really is the dreadest of all wyverns."

"I am," he said with a grim look at Constantine.

"Baltic is buddies with Fiat because he gave him succor or some such thing as that, so Thala played on that fact and made it look like Baltic was working with Fiat to hurt the weyr. I bet it was Thala who was behind your kidnapping," Aisling said, turning to Tipene. "May said it was ouroboros dragons who grabbed you guys, right? I bet she was working with Fiat's ex–blue dragons."

"She didn't have to," I said slowly, my gaze meeting Baltic's. He looked thoughtful.

"Really? Why not?"

"She had her own tribe."

"Oh. Well, that works just as well. She does what she can to raise havoc and mayhem in the weyr, including either killing the blue dragons, or helping Fiat kill them, and making it seem like Baltic did it. I guess that means the weyr owes you guys an apology, right, sweetie?"

"Hardly that," Drake said, his lips tight. "It seems we have much to discuss at the *sárkány*, however."

"At the very least, you can officially call off the silly war."

Drake turned his glittering emerald eyes on Aisling. *"Silly?"*

"Sorry. *Regrettable* war."

"Better." He turned back to us, his eyes examining Constantine for a moment. "I do not know what has passed to leave your lieutenant trying to kill all three of you, but I believe there will be no problem in the weyr retracting its declaration of war. As for the issue brought to head by Constantine's shade . . ."

Constantine stopped glowering at Baltic and directed his attention at Drake. "I remember you. You're my godson's younger brother, the one claimed by the reeve for the green sept. You share her genetic traits, but you are not a reeve yourself? Interesting."

"Of course he's not a reeve," Aisling said, smiling up at Drake. "That would mean he could have more than one mate, and he'd never do that."

Drake looked startled at the thought.

"What exactly is a reeve?" Jim asked.

"One whose bloodline is particularly close to the First Dragon," Constantine answered.

Next to me, Baltic stiffened.

"Close?" I asked, my blood turning cold. "Close how? Really, really friendly? That sort of close?"

"We will leave now, Ysolde," Baltic declared, all but shooing me past them.

"Close as in close. Biologically so," Constantine said with a shrug. "Ask Baltic. He knows—as the son of the First Dragon, he also is a reeve."

Baltic swore under his breath, then took my arm.

"Baltic is the son of the First Dragon?" I heard Aisling gasp as I turned to face the man whose love was everything to me.

"You're a reeve?" I asked him.

"Whoa, he's a first-generation son. Didn't see that coming," Jim said in tones of amazement.

"Now, *chérie*—" Baltic started to say, his eyes going all warm and soft with emotion.

"You can have more than one mate? What was all that business about you dying because he killed me?" My voice rose as I jabbed my finger in Constantine's direction.

"I believe I've already established my innocence on that front—" Constantine started to answer.

I spun around and shot a fire-tinged ball of arcane light toward him.

"Er . . . my apologies for interrupting. You go ahead and continue yelling at Baltic," he said quickly, eyeing the hole in the wall where the ball hit.

I turned back to Baltic.

"Ysolde—"

"Don't!" I held up my hand to stop him. "Just answer one question, Baltic. Can you take another mate?"

"There is no other female in the world for me."

"That's not what I asked!"

He pulled me up against his chest, allowing me to search the depths of his eyes. "There is no other female but you. There never will be."

"But you could—"

His fire wrapped around us, sinking into me, merging with the slumbering fire that was buried deep within me, his mouth moving on mine. "You are my life. You are my soul. You are the beginning and end to me. It will always be so."

I stopped fighting him, accepting the love that was so evident in his eyes, in the beat of his heart, in everything he was. We were together, and there was nothing that could change that, not even death.

"That is *so* romantic," Aisling said with a little sniff.

"Serious Hallmark moment," Jim agreed.

"Why don't you ever say things like that?" May asked Gabriel.

"He's still a reeve, you know," Constantine said, marching over to us as Baltic released my lower lip. "Whereas I'm n—"

Baltic's fist shot out again. I stared into his beautiful dark eyes, basking in the glow of love and desire and need that shone in them. Behind me came the sound of wood crashing to the floor accompanied by a large, heavy object. "I love you, too."

"Come, mate." He held out his hand for me, then

cocked an eyebrow at Brom, who slipped around Pavel and obediently trotted after us, Pavel bringing up the rear with a twitch of his lips.

As Baltic passed Gabriel, who with a stunned expression stared at where Constantine lay struggling with the remains of the table, he paused. "He's your problem now."

"Like hell he is," Gabriel said, his expression changing to one of sheer horror.

"You haven't heard the last of me, Baltic," Constantine warbled from underneath the broken table. "I'm not finished wooing Ysolde. Bloody hell, I think I broke something. You, Gideon, help me up. I lost my corporeal form for a second, and now I'm merged into the wood of this table. . . ."

Read on for an excerpt from
Katie MacAlister's next Dark Ones novel,

Much Ado About Vampires

Coming from Signet in October 2011

Alec Darwin was dying, or as close to it as one could be without having that last little spark of life flitter away into nothingness.

He closed his eyes and lay back, shifting slightly when a rock dug into the small of his back. Should he go to the trouble of trying to remove it so he could lie for eternity in comfort? he wondered absently. Or was such a trivial thing worth the effort? Did he even have the strength to do it? It had been all he could do to stagger to the area, his final resting place, which the previous day he had cleared of small, pointed rocks.

He shifted his shoulder in mild irritation. The rock pressed into his kidney, the pain of it distracting him from his plan. *Dammit.* He hadn't seen a rock when he had fallen to the ground, his strength draining from him as his body squeezed the last morsel of vigor from the remaining teaspoon or two of blood that slowly was absorbed into his dying flesh.

He was supposed to be cherishing his martyrdom as he lay dying in the Akasha, not thinking about a damned rock the size of a watermelon digging into his back. He was supposed to be thinking of the pathetic tragedy of a life that he had been forced to live, unenlivened with any sort of joy or happiness or even hope. He shouldn't be wondering if he rolled over onto his side whether the damned rock would let him die in peace.

If only his Beloved hadn't died. If only he'd come to her a few minutes earlier, he could have been there when that idiot reaper had lost control. If only he'd bedded her and Joined the minute he knew she was his Beloved, rather than allowing her to give in to her mortal sensibilities, demanding he court her.

A last breath passed his lips as he tried to hold on to the image of her face—his one true love, the woman who had been put on the earth to save him, and who had died the victim of a senseless accident that was also directly responsible for his impending death.

Awareness slid away from him, the rock ceased to be an annoyance, and the last few sparks between his brain cells provided not the image of his Beloved, as he so desperately wanted, but that of a woman who had lain in a faint at his feet a few months previously.

The dream started the way it always started.

"What do you see, Corazon?"

The voice that spoke so calmly was Barbara, the hypnotherapist whom Patsy had hired for our "Girl's Night In" semiannual party.

"Mud. I see mud. Well, mud and grass and stuff like that. But mostly just mud."

"Are you sure she's under?" Patsy asked, her voice filled

with suspicion. Pats was always a doubter. "She doesn't look hypnotized to me. *Cora!* Can you hear me?"

"I'd have to be five miles away not to hear you. I'm hypnotized, you idiot, not deaf." I glared at her. She glared at me glaring at her.

"Wait just one second. . . ." Patsy stopped glaring and pointed dramatically to where I lay prone on the couch. "You're not supposed to hear me!"

"Is she supposed to know she's hypnotized?"

That was Terri, the third member of our little trio of terror, as my ex-husband used to call us.

The bastard.

"Her knowing doesn't negate the regression, does it?" Terri asked Barbara.

"Hypnotism isn't a magical state of unknowing," Barbara said calmly. "She is simply relaxed, in touch with her true inner spirit, and has opened up her mind to the many memories of lifetimes past. I assure you that she is properly hypnotized."

"Let me get a pin and poke her with it," Patsy said, bustling over to a bookcase crammed full of books and various other items. "If she reacts, we'll know she's faking it."

"No one is poking me with anything!" I sat up, prepared to sprint to safety if she so much as came near me with anything pointy.

"Please, ladies." I didn't see Barbara show any signs of rushing, but I knew she wanted to hurry us along so she could leave. "We have limited time. Corazon is in a light trance, also referred to as an alpha state. Through that, she has tapped into her higher self, her true infinite being, a state in which she is free to bypass the boundaries of time."

"Yeah. Bypassing all that stuff," I said, lying back down on the couch. Even though it was a dream, and I knew it was a dream, my stomach started to tighten at what was to come. "So sit back and watch the show. What do I do now, Barbara?"

"Look around you. Examine your surroundings. Tell us what you see, what you feel."

"I see mud. I feel mud. I *am* the mud."

"There has to be more to her past life than mud, surely," Terri said, munching on popcorn.

My stomach turned over. *It is coming. He is coming.* I felt it, felt the horror just on the edges of my consciousness.

"Are there any buildings or other structures around to give you an idea of what year you are reliving?" Barbara asked.

"Um . . . nothing on the left side other than forest. I seem to be standing on a dirt path of some sort. Let me walk to the top of this little hill—oh! Wow! There's a town down below. And it looks like there's a castle way up on a tall cliff in the distance. Lots of tiny people are running around in some fields outside of the town. Cool! It's like a medieval village or something. Think I'll go down to say hi."

"Excellent," Barbara said. "Now, tell me, how do you feel?"

Sick. Scared. Terrified.

"Well," my voice said, not reflecting any of the dream emotions, "kind of hungry. No, really hungry. Kind of an intense hunger throbbing inside me. Oh, great, I'm a peasant, aren't I? I'm a poor starving peasant who stands around in mud. Lovely."

"We are not here to make judgments on our past selves," Barbara said primly.

"Geesh, Cora," Patsy said, sitting on my feet. "Terri turned out to be Cleopatra's personal maid, and I was one of Caesar's concubines. You're letting down the team, babe. The least you could do is be a medieval princess in a big pointy hat or something."

I couldn't . . . because of him.

Loathing rippled through me as my voice continued. "I have shoes on. Peasants didn't wear shoes, did they?"

"Some did, I'm sure," Terri said, stuffing a handful of popcorn into her mouth.

"Can you walk to the town?" Barbara asked. "Perhaps we can find out who you are if we know where you are."

"Yeah. I'm going down the hill now."

A low rumble from behind me had me clutching the cushions of the couch. "Hey, watch where you're— Oh my god. Oh my god! *Omigod!*"

"What? What's happened?" Barbara asked, sounding suddenly worried.

She should.

"A woman with an ox cart just ran me over."

"What?" Patsy shrieked.

"She ran me over. Her oxen were running amok or something. They just came barreling down the hill behind me and ran right over the top of me. Holy Swiss on rye! Now the oxen are trampling me, and the lady in the cart is screaming and— Jehosophat! My head just came off! It just came right off! Ack!"

I knew in my dream state that Terri sat staring at me, her eyes huge, a handful of popcorn frozen just beyond

her mouth as she gawked at the words that came unbid-
den from my mouth.

If only she knew.

"Oh, my. I don't—I've never had anyone die during
a regression," Barbara said, sounding stressed. "I'm not
quite sure how to proceed."

"You're . . . decapitated?" Patsy asked. "Are you
sure?"

"I'm sure, Pats. My head is separated from my body,
which is covered in ox hoofprints. A wheel went over my
neck, I think. It . . . *Urgh*. That's just really gross. Why the
hell do I get the reincarnations where I'm killed by two
oxen and a cart? Why can't I be Cleopatra's concubine?"

"Personal maid, not concubine," Terri corrected, stuffing the popcorn into her mouth and chewing frantically.
"Are you absolutely certain you're dead? Maybe it
looks worse than it is."

Oh, it was going to get much, much worse, the dream
part of my mind said.

Goose bumps rose on my arms.

"My head is three feet away from my body. I think
that's a pretty good indicator of death. Good god! Now
what's she doing?"

"The ox?" Patsy asked.

"No, the driver. She's not doing what I think she's
doing, is she?"

"I don't know," Terri said, setting down the popcorn
so she could scoot closer to me.

"This is very unusual," Barbara muttered to herself.

"What's the lady doing?" Patsy said, prodding my
knee.

"She's trying to stick my head back onto my body.
Lady, that's not going to do any good. No, you can't tie

it on, either. Ha. Told you so. Oh, don't drop me in the mud! Sheesh! Like I wasn't muddy enough? What a butterfingers. Now she's chasing the oxen, who just bolted for a field. Oh, no, she's coming back. Her arms are waving around like she's yelling, only I can't hear anything. It must be the shock of having my head severed by a cart wheel."

"This is just too surreal," Terri said. "Do you think she purposely ran you down?"

"I don't think so. She seems kind of goofy. She just tripped over my leg and fell onto my head. Oh, man! I think she broke my nose! God Almighty, this is like some horrible Marx Brothers meets *Leatherface* sort of movie. Holy runaway oxen, Batman!"

"What?" Terri and Patsy asked at the same time.

"She's doing something. Something weird."

"Oh, my god—is she making love to your lifeless corpse?" Terri asked. "I saw a show on HBO about that!"

"No, she's not molesting me. She's standing above me waving her hands around and chanting or something. What the— She's like— Hoo!"

He was coming. He was just out of my sight, just beyond the curve of the hill.

He was death.

"Don't get upset," Barbara said. "You are in no personal danger. Just describe what you're seeing calmly and in detail."

"I don't know about you, but I consider a decapitation and barbecue as some sort of personal danger."

"Barbecue?" Patsy asked. "Someone's roasting a pig or something?"

"No. The ox lady waved her hands around and all of a sudden this silver light was there, all over my body, singeing it around the edges. Oh, great. Here comes someone." *No!* my mind screamed. *Not again! Please, god, not again!* "Hey, you, mister—would you stop the lady from doing the light thing? She's burnt off half of my hair."

"This is the most bizarre thing I've ever heard," Terri told Patsy. "You have the *best* parties!"

"It's all in the planning," Patsy said, prodding my knee again. "What's going on now, Cora?"

"The guy just saw me. He did a little stagger to the side. I think it's because the lady tried to hide my head behind her, and my ear flew off and landed at his feet. Now he's picking it up. He's yelling at her. She's pointing to the oxen in the field, but he looks really pissed. Yeah, you tell her, mister. She has no right driving if she can't handle her cows."

My heart wept at what was coming.

"This would make a great film," Patsy said thoughtfully. "I wonder if we could write a screenplay? We could make millions."

"Well, now the guy has my head, and he's shaking it at the lady, still yelling at her. Whoops. A chunk of hair came loose. My head is bouncing down the hill. Guy and lady are chasing it. Hee-hee-hee. OK, that's really funny in a horrible sort of way. Ah. Good for you, sir. He caught me again, and now he's taking me back to my body, hauling the ox lady with him. Whoa! Whoa, whoa, whoa!"

I struggled to get out of the dream, just as I struggled every time. It never did any good. The scene was determined to play out as it first had.

"Did he drop your head again?" Terri asked, her eyes wide.

Panic flooded me. "No, he just . . . Holy shit! I want out of here! Take me out of this dream or whatever it is! Wake me up!"

"Remain calm," Barbara said in a soothing voice. "The images you see are in the past and cannot harm you now."

"What's going on? What did the guy do?" Terri asked.

"I want to wake up! Right now!" I said, clawing the couch to sit up.

"Very well. I'm going to count backward to one, and when I reach that number, you will awaken feeling refreshed and quite serene. Five, four, three, two, one. Welcome back, Corazon."

"You OK?" Patsy asked as I gasped, my blood all but curdling at the memory of what I'd witnessed.

"Yeah. I think so."

"What happened at the end?" Terri asked. "You looked scared to death."

"You'd be scared, too, if you saw a vampire kill someone!"

I sat up in bed, torn from the dream at last, blinking as the dream memory faded and I realized I was safe in my own little apartment, alone, without the green-eyed, dark-haired monster who had killed a woman before my eyes.

I slumped back against the pillow, wondering why I kept dreaming about Patsy's party and experiencing the awful past-life scene again and again. Why were the dreams increasing in frequency? Why I was doomed to relive the experience over and over again, the sense of dread and horror so great I could taste it on my tongue?

Sleep, I knew from sad experience, would be useless. I got to my feet and headed for the bathroom. I'd brush my teeth to get rid of the taste of my own fear, and go sit with a book until I was too numb with exhaustion to stay awake any longer.

And I'd pray that the green-eyed vampire stayed out of my dreams.

New York Times bestselling author

KATIE MACALISTER

LOVE IN THE TIME OF DRAGONS

A Novel of the Light Dragons

Tully Sullivan is just like any other suburban mom—unless you count the days every year that she zones out and turns base metals into gold. Those are weird.

And now she's woken up in a strange place surrounded by strange people who keep insisting that they're dragons—and that she's one too. But not just any dragon. She's Ysolde de Bouchier, a famed figure from dragon history.

Tully can't shape-shift or breathe fire, and she's definitely not happy being sentenced to death for the misdeeds of a dragon mate she can't remember. Yet she'll have to find a way to solve the crimes of a past she has no memory of living.

Available wherever books are sold or at
penguin.com

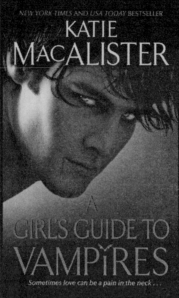

31901050549221